Also From
Maribeth Shanley & Indigo Sea Press

Crack in the World

www.indigoseapress.com

A View to the Unknown

By

Maribeth Shanley

Perseverance Books
Published by Indigo Sea Press
Winston-Salem

Deep Indigo Books
Indigo Sea Press
302 Ricks Drive
Winston-Salem, NC 27103
This book is a work of fiction. Names, characters,
locations and events are either a product of the author's
imagination, fictitious or used fictitiously. Any resemblance
to any event, locale or person, living or dead, is purely
coincidental.

First Perseverance Books edition published
January, 2016
Perseverance Books, Moon Sailor and all production design
are trademarks of Indigo Sea Press, used under license.

For information regarding bulk purchases of this book,
digital purchase and special discounts, please contact the publisher at
indigoseapress@gmail.com

Cover Concept by Maribeth Shanley
Cover design by Pan Morelli
Manufactured in the United States of America
ISBN 978-1-63066-348-3

Acknowledgements

"When facing fear, walk through it."
(Author Unknown)

As I put to bed my novel, A View to the Unknown, I am once again reminded of the poet Mary Oliver, who put words to the theme I have lived by my entire life:

Someone I once loved gave me a box full of darkness. It took me years to learn this too was a gift.

Any adult who suffered molestation knows the truth of these words, especially if they too found the will and courage to embrace their darkness while turning it into strength.

To all children and adults who still suffer the darkness that once ripped out your heart and devoured your soul, I hope I can inspire you to find the will and courage to transform your pain into power. It's the **best** revenge ever!

****

Although A View to the Unknown is the sequel to my first novel, Crack in the World, I wrote it to stand on its own. I do hope you read both. However, it's not at all necessary to read Crack in the World first.

Through my characters, I was able to view their lives, challenges, pain and grief with the eyes of an observer. The result: I feel I now have a crystal clear understanding of what I have experienced in my life and the real consequences of that experience.

I am all too familiar with the conscious torment and over time, I came to understand the deep-seated unconscious pain as well. It's taken me my entire life to comprehend what happened to me. Now, I am finally able to fold neatly that experience and all its agony and gently tuck it into the archives of my soul.

What my father willingly did to me yet failed to take responsibility for, took its toll. Through sheer grit and determination, I embraced what he did as I draped myself in its lessons. I emerged from the cave and hugged the warmth and kindness of the sunlight by making that sunlight my own.

As did Emily, I never once took my eye off that sunlight. I never wavered from seeking true happiness, so that, once I recognized that joyfulness, as did she, I pulled it close to my heart and cherished it for what it was...*Freedom to be Me.*

Molestation is a devastating experience for any child especially when the pedophile is someone that child knows and trusts, and, in my case, loved. By keeping my eye on the sunlight, I was able to grow in ways that even as I wrote the words, I marveled at my growth and my deep-seated compassion.

I wish for and hope that all children who have felt the violation in the same horrendous manner may come to know the peace I have come to know. So, I say to you...*KNOW* that what happened to you is *NOT* who you are. *NEVER* allow it to define you. You and life are much larger, and *you* are far more capable than settling for less.

Embrace the light and dance in the love and kindness of the innocence someone attempted to steal from you. In the end, if you do this, you will become the person who wins. Unlike your assailant, who threw his or her life away, you refuse to throw away yours. Stand tall and love the person you wish to become. Then...become that person you love.

****

Thanks to Indigo Sea Press and especially Mike Simpson, who continues to support my endeavors and encourages my writing. You've given me the gift of using my voice to speak my mind.

Thank you to my wonderful husband of 45 years, Bob. Thank you for sharing your love and giving me the gift of absolute love so that, when it came time for Emily and Sean to share their final Valentine cards, I was able to go to my wooden chest and pull out two of the most wonderful cards we've shared over the years. Bob, you are everything a woman desires then cherishes as she travels through life. You are my light.

To my sister, Gail, who, from the beginning, has stayed by my side. You recognized and encouraged my growth. You have been unwavering with support for my writing. You are my best fan, and I am yours. I love and cherish you with all my being.

To my sister, Colleen, who has never wavered from my side. You stood by me in the darkest hours of my pain. You walked away from our father when he wrote and mailed his last cruel letter to me. You have been by my side the entire way. I love you deeply.

To my best friend, Brenda, who cheered me on. Thank you for recognizing my talent and then encouraging me to write my novels. Thank you for being the first to call both a romantic story of love, courage and triumph. I love you like a sister, Bren.

To everyone who is reading this, I hope you enjoy reading A View to the Unknown as much as I enjoyed writing it. If it gives you inspiration, even better.

I am finally able to close the chapter on that part of my life. Now I can bask in its triumph and flourish with the continued growth it inspires. Keep up with Maribeth at www.maribethshanley.com, where you can also read several short stories she's written.

Chapter 1

It was midnight when Celia quietly opened the door to her dorm room. She had been studying at the library until about 9 p.m. On her way back to her dorm, she ran into a couple of female friends who were headed over to the Wild Colonial Tavern for a few beers. Now, she was kicking herself for having gone with them. She was tired and feeling tipsy; a physical state she didn't like experiencing during the school week.

Not very responsible, she thought.

As she entered her room, she could see her roommate, Emily, asleep in her bed, so she tiptoed across the floor, slipped out of her jeans and climbed into her bed. She was about to drift off when she thought she heard someone sobbing. She opened her eyes, propped herself up on her elbows and listened. It *was* someone crying.

"Emily, are you okay?"

Emily didn't respond. Instead, she did her best to stop crying and held her breath.

Thinking she must have imagined the sound, Celia lay back down and closed her eyes.

Several minutes went by when, thinking that Celia was now asleep, Emily wiped her eyes, turned over and tried to go to sleep. But she couldn't. She was still lost in her thoughts as she once more began to sob.

Again Celia opened her eyes and listened. Emily was clearly crying, and it made Celia feel horrible.

Celia and Emily had only been roommates for a few months and hadn't talked much. Each had her own circle of friends on the Brown campus. Yet Celia could tell that Emily was a sweet person so, as she listened, Emily's sobs tugged at her heart. She wanted to help Emily if she could, so she turned on her bedside lamp and sat up.

"Emily, I don't mean to pry, but I can hear you crying. I could tell earlier this evening that something was bothering you." She paused and then softly and caringly said, "Listen ...I know it's none of my business, but...I don't know...maybe I can help or at least listen. I'd like to help if you'd let me."

1

Emily turned over, threw off the covers and sat on the side of the bed. "I'm sorry I woke you. I was trying to be quiet."

From the look on Emily's face, Celia could tell that Emily was in a lot of pain so she took a chance as she got up and walked over to Emily's bed. She sat down next to Emily and put her arm around her. That's all Emily needed as she began to cry a river of tears. She couldn't hold them in.

Celia pulled Emily closer. Overcome by Celia's compassion, Emily buried her head against Celia's chest.

"It's okay, Emily. It's okay," she said as she caressed Emily's back with soothing strokes.

Soon Emily stopped crying and was choking on her tears, so Celia spoke, "Emily, I'm a good listener. It pains me to know you're hurting. I don't mean to pry, but I just want you to know that I'm here for you. It might do you good to talk."

Emily raised her head and stared at Celia. She then told Celia that it all began with a bad dream.

"I dreamt my father was hurting me all over again."

"What do you mean 'hurting you again'?" Celia asked as she handed Emily a box of tissues.

Choking on her words, "Celia, please promise me you won't tell anyone what I'm going to tell you. I have to know I can trust you. This is all still pretty painful, and I've only recently realized that I'm still vulnerable."

The look on Celia's face was full of compassion. "You can trust me, Emily. I've had my share of family problems and sadness. I promise I won't tell anyone. Besides, it's none of anyone else's business anyway." She still had her arm around Emily, so she squeezed her a little, hoping it would defuse Emily's fears.

Feeling comforted by and comfortable with Celia, Emily began to pour her guts out.

Celia listened to Emily describe how, beginning when she was six years old, her father had molested her.

"He always made me feel so dirty and guilty. He convinced me that it was my responsibility to keep what he always called '*our secret.*' But"—several tears trickled down Emily's cheek— "it wasn't my secret. It was his. I *never ever* wanted him to do those things to me. He did everything he could to ruin my life."

Celia still had her arm around Emily. The emotions Emily conveyed caused Celia to shiver with empathy. She reached behind her and pulled the blanket over as she wrapped both Emily and herself in its warmth.

"That's better," whispered Celia.

There was a long silence. Emily was staring at the wall opposite the two girls as she began to speak again.

"When I was about to turn twelve, we moved from Florida to Rhode Island. My dad was in the Navy, so we moved every few years. Moving and having no permanent friends only added to feelings of being all alone and isolated in the world. But that changed when we moved here."

Emily fell silent again. Celia felt Emily's pain as if it were her own. Hearing what she was telling her made Celia feel very sad for Emily, and that empathy was reflected on her face.

She hugged Emily as she also muttered, "Emily, I'm so sorry that happened to you."

Emily looked at Celia and smiled faintly. Celia's eyes were glazed over with tears which helped Emily feel safe.

There was another long silence. Celia was trying to give Emily space and time to talk more.

Finally, she quietly asked, "Emily, you said something changed when you moved here. What changed?"

Emily smiled and softly thanked Celia for listening to her. "I met a wonderful boy named Sean. He's been my boyfriend ever since. I also met my best girlfriend, Jeannie, who has been more than a sister to me. It was Jeannie's thirteenth birthday. Sean and I danced a slow dance for the first time. It was the best night I could ever remember when my dad tried to ruin it."

"What happened?"

With pain in her voice, "That night, when Jeannie's parents brought the cake down to the party, I watched how much love was exchanged between Jeannie and her parents, especially between Jeannie and her father."

Again, there was silence as Emily choked back her tears. "I always hoped and dreamed that my dad would simply love me like a daughter. As I watched Jeannie and her dad, I felt happy for Jeannie; but I felt so sad for myself. I've never known a loving father."

3

Once more there was a long silence as Emily composed herself. "Later, after the party ended, Sean and I walked home. We said goodnight and I went in my house. My father was hiding in the dining room." Emily had a look on her face as if the thought made her feel sick to her stomach. "He was spying on us from the dining room window. When I came in, he stepped out into the foyer."

Again, Emily stopped talking as a tear fell to her lap. Celia felt utter compassion for her roommate as she stroked Emily's back and asked, "What did he do, Emily?" Celia was bracing for the worst.

But Emily surprised her when she cleared her throat and said, "Everything changed that night. I don't know what came over me; but I think it was the love I felt from Sean, Jeannie and Sean's grandmother, Martha, because when he began sliding his hand up my leg, I told him I was not going to let him ruin the best night of my life. I went upstairs and told him not to follow me. I remember how angry he became, but I didn't care. I wanted to hold onto my special night. He didn't dare follow me up because he knew that Katie, my youngest sister, was asleep in my bed. Months earlier, I bribed Katie into sleeping with me so I could avoid my dad climbing into my bed, which he did a *lot*. So I knew I was safe for at least that one night."

Suddenly everything seemed to change in Emily. She sat up, blew her nose, looked Celia in the eye and said, "Everything changed again in the morning, but that was the day I took control."

"What happened?" Then Celia asked, "Say, I could use a bottle of water. Do you want one? Maybe we could sit over on the couch. I don't know about you, but I don't have a class until noon tomorrow. We're both wide awake so we might as well get comfortable. I do want to hear the rest of your story." She said this as she patted Emily's hand which she was now holding.

"Water would be good. My throat is very dry; and, yes, I'd like to sit on the couch and tell you the rest. It feels good to talk to someone about these things. It's so much to keep inside; and I feel like the more I talk about it, the more I will begin to feel better and stronger."

The two girls walked over to the small pale green sofa. "Sit down, Emily. I'll get us both water."

Emily sat down as she gave Celia a pathetic smile. She was trying hard to feel better.

A few minutes passed as the girls sat silently covered with the same blanket. Celia was trying to give Emily some latitude. Emily looked over at Celia who was staring at her. Emily smiled, knowing intuitively that Celia was waiting for her to talk more.

Emily thanked Celia again, then began describing the day after Jeannie's birthday party.

"I was all set to go to church with my mom when I came downstairs and found out that not only was my mom physically ill, but my two sisters were as well. My brother had already gone to church with a friend and his family so that left me and my dad. We're Catholic, which means we are required to go to Mass every Sunday, whether we like it or not."

Celia rolled her eyes, "I get it. I'm Catholic too. That must have freaked you out to realize your dad was going to take you to church. What happened?"

Gagging on her tears, Emily softly commented, "God, I *was* freaked out! I was so scared and didn't know what he intended to do to me. I just knew in my gut it was going to be really bad." Then, with resignation in her tone, "…and it was."

Emily described how her dad had driven right past the church parking lot and wouldn't tell her where they were going.

Again Celia was bracing for the worst. In fact, the knuckles on her left hand were red from squeezing the pillow she was holding so hard and the look on her face was full of horror.

Emily reached for Celia's hand and lightly patted it. "Don't worry, Celia. Nothing that bad happened because I wouldn't let it. He did, however, intend on raping me. I know that in my heart because, for the first time, he wanted to take off my dress; and he'd never done that before."

"God, Emily. I don't know what to say. What happened?"

Emily's tone changed again. It was now full of confidence. "As we were in the car, I began fiddling with a pencil I found in the door pocket. I had no idea what I was going to do with it and really didn't intend to do anything until he began moving his hand up my bare leg. I just knew in my heart that I wasn't going to let him do any of that stuff to me ever again, so without thinking, I raised my hand and jammed the pencil into his hand. Then I got out of the car and began screaming at him. At first, he was trying his best to get me to come

5

back in the car. He was angry, but he was also very calm at first. I know now he was trying his best to regain control of the situation and of me. But that didn't happen. I was done with all of it, so I threatened him by telling him I would not only tell my mom what he was doing to me; but I would tell his boss, Capt. James, who was the commanding officer of the base. When I mentioned Capt. James' name, I could see *everything* change on his face. I *knew* I had scared him. That's when he began to act differently. He began to stutter as he begged me to get back in the car. The name of Capt. James turned him into mush, and I could see it all over his face and hear it in his voice. It was then that I realized that, for the first time in my life, I had the upper hand so I played my hand. I got back in the car and commanded him to take me home and he did."

Celia's eyes were huge as she intently listened to Emily's story. "Damn, Emily, that was incredibly brave and, damn, smart for a thirteen-year-old kid to figure out. Wow. I'm totally blown away!" After a few seconds, Celia asked, "I'm guessing he drove you home. Am I right?"

Emily spoke with pride in her voice, "Yes ...he drove me home, and that was the last time that he tried to touch me! I was only thirteen years old, but I knew in my gut that I had completely taken control of him and my life. He told my mom a big fat lie about cutting his hand on a dirty bottle; but, hell, by that time I didn't care. I never contradicted his lie. I was just so happy to finally be free of him."

Celia asked, "Did you two ever talk about any of it? You and your dad, I mean."

"Yea, we talked briefly the following Christmas. Right before he died, we had a long conversation and actually, I did most of the talking. I basically told him I didn't love him and didn't know if I ever could or would. When I left his hospital room, he was crying; but I didn't much care at that point. Since then, I've had some remorse; but I know it's only because I regret that I never knew a dad who loved me. I'm going to counseling now; and, believe it or not, my mom is going with me."

Celia coughed and almost choked. She was completely taken off-guard by this new revelation. "What? Your mom's going with you? Did she know what your dad was doing to you?" Then Celia exclaimed, "God, I sure hope she didn't!"

"No, Mom never knew. Well, I don't think she ever knew. Most of my memories of Mom and Dad's relationship is one of complete dominance. He treated her like shit, and she felt like shit whenever he was home. Things got better after I took charge, but that only lasted a short while because he died two years later." Then Emily nervously chuckled. "As Paul Harvey says, I guess this is the rest of the story, 'cuz Mom found out all about it just before Thanksgiving when she accidently discovered my diary I had hidden in the attic."

All Celia could muster was a surprised, "Really?"

"Yea, and I guess this is the good stuff, 'cuz things have changed all over again."

"I can't wait to hear this part!"

Emily got up, "I need another water. Do you want one?"

"Yes, please. I got a little drunk earlier tonight, and the water seems to be helping me."

As Emily handed her the water, she said, "The water is rehydrating you. Alcohol dehydrates you. Jeannie is the one who told me that the day after I got completely polluted!"

"Jeannie sounds like a good friend. I'm glad she's been there for you all these years."

Emily smiled. "She's a wonderful friend. Maybe you could go out with us one night so you can get to know her. She'd like you a lot. Jeannie's a lot more gregarious than me, but she also has a huge heart!"

"I'd like to meet her. She sounds like she does, but right now I'm anxious to hear more about your mom finding your diary. I'll bet that freaked you out too!"

"Well, believe it or not, it didn't. I have these realistic dreams now and then; and one night just prior to her finding it, I dreamt my grandmother came to me and told me that Mom was going to find my diary. I forgot to bring it with me when I left for school and planned to retrieve it over Thanksgiving weekend. Mom accidently found it the Saturday night before Thanksgiving. She had been remodeling my grandma's bedroom for me when she bumped into my hiding place in the attic. Martha called Jeannie the following day because Mom was totally devastated and totally freaking out. Jeannie came to bring me home. They were all scared I would drive home and have an accident. They had no idea that I was actually expecting it."

Celia was enthralled with Emily's story, and wanted to hear the rest. First, however, she said, "Hang onto that thought, Emily. I have to pee really bad. I'll be right back, okay?"

"Go pee. I'll wait here for you. I do want to tell you the rest, 'cuz this is the good stuff!"

About ten minutes later, Celia came back into the room and plunked down on the couch. "Phew, I almost didn't make it down the hall. I was trying to hold it in so I could hear the rest. Okay, I'm ready!" Both girls laughed as Emily grabbed Celia's hand and squeezed it.

"Thanks, Celia. I really appreciate your friendship. Now where was I? Oh, yea, it was Sunday when I came home. Mom was so upset and blaming herself for what she called 'letting my dad do those things to me,' but I did my best to assure her that she hadn't and reminded her how poorly he had treated her. I felt so bad for her and she was devastated for me. Martha …God, I love that woman! She and I did everything we could to hold things together so we could have a nice Thanksgiving. My brother, Paul, is in the Navy; and he was coming home for Thanksgiving, so it was touch and go that entire week.

We were doing a good job of keeping up the appearance of normalcy until my middle sister, Lily, put Dad's picture on the table. I had set the table earlier and, thinking we'd all appreciate seeing his picture; she rearranged the place settings to make room for his. The picture sat on what would have been his plate. No one noticed until Mom asked Paul to say grace. That's when Katie innocently announced Dad's presence, and that's when all hell broke loose!"

"Wow! That's crazy. What happened?" Celia's mouth was wide open, and her eyes were bugging out of her head.

"Mom totally lost it and asked what the fuck his picture was doing on our Thanksgiving table. She got up, grabbed the picture and threw it on the floor, smashing the glass to smithereens. Then she stormed out of the room, went to her bedroom and locked the door. Poor Lily couldn't understand what she had done wrong. She was crying and so was Katie, and Paul was grilling me to tell him what the hell was wrong with Mom. Martha was freaking out too."

"Weren't you freaking out as well?" asked a very curious Celia.

"Not really. I guess over the years I just learned to deal with things best when they seemed out of control. My life was always out of control, and it turned me into a very inventive person. I've always felt like I could win an Academy Award for being the best molested daughter on this planet. Anyway, I took control and right out of the blue, I invented a perfectly believable story thinking I was stitching everything back together so none of my siblings would learn the truth. I'll tell you, this one lie I told was a whopper. *I was even surprised* by my inventiveness!"

Celia had the funniest look on her face as she anxiously waited for Emily to tell her what happened next. "Tell me, tell me ...what did you tell everyone?"

"I told them that Dad had cheated on Mom ten years prior. Who knows? I wouldn't be surprised to find out that he actually did cheat on her a lot, but it seemed to do the trick, 'cuz Paul completely bought the story. I told them that Mom had found letters from Dad's girlfriend and was having a hard time dealing with what she now knew to be true. The lie would have worked too, but Mom had had enough of all the lies and—" Emily's eyes filled with tears at the recollection— "at my having to be the one to tell all the lies so no one would find out what a hellhole I had lived in most of my life. Mom saved me from having to continue to keep the secret, and now I'm so damned relieved I no longer have to live a fake life." This caught Emily off-guard as she again began to cry.

Yet Celia was right there for Emily. She wanted nothing more than to console the person she now felt very close to. "Oh, Emily, please don't cry. God, this is one of the saddest, yet most amazing stories I've ever heard in my entire life. Your story makes all my family problems seem so small and insignificant. You've been through a hell of a lot, and honestly I have no idea how you've done it. You should be a bitch or a basket case, but you're neither. You're an amazingly nice and decent person. I'm so glad you're my roommate 'cuz I could have wound up with a bitch or a basket case. Please don't cry. It sounds like everything's going to start getting better. Am I right?"

Celia's compassion was calming Emily down as she stopped crying, grabbed several tissues and blew her nose. "Yes, everything's going to get so much better. Mom told me she would make sure that my three siblings would *never, ever* feel anything other than love for me. Mom was amazing that night. She could have easily cowered and gone along with the new lie, but she didn't. In fact, she had Martha take little Katie home with her so she could sit down with Paul, Lily and me in order to tell them the entire truth. Mom threw off all her weakness that night and declared to be the mom I always knew she could be."

Emily paused, then smiled a lovely smile. "Mom became the mom I always saw when Dad was away at sea and she was in charge. She rescued me that night, and I will always love her for what she did because it took a lot of guts to do. She's my surprise hero!"

Celia couldn't help her curiosity. "How did Lily and Paul take everything?"

"Well, Lily…and this was a shocker…already knew. She had found and read my diary several months prior to that night."

"WHAT?" Celia exclaimed.

"Yea, we were all surprised; and, even more surprisingly, she was doing okay with it. She's best friends with a girl whose stepdad had molested her. He was caught molesting a neighbor girl when Penny, that's her friend's name, told her mom what he had been doing to her. Penny's mom stepped up too by helping the neighbor prosecute her own husband. He's in jail right now. Being able to watch what Penny had been going through helped Lily cope with what she learned about Dad. She's completely amazed both Mom and me. We've never been very close, but this has drawn us closer; and I'm learning that I have a pretty nice sister in Lily.

"Paul, on the other hand, took it pretty hard. Dad was Paul's hero. But Mom and I had a long talk with him before he went back to Norfolk the Monday following Thanksgiving. When he left, he told me how much he loved me and respected me for being as brave as I was. He even took a book I'd read about molestation back with him and promised to read it. I think both Paul and Lily are forming a different opinion of our father. Paul promised me he would seek counseling when he got back, and Mom told me he was now seeing a counselor."

"And now your mom is going to go to counseling with you. Wow, that's really awesome!"

"Yes, it is pretty awesome," answered Emily. "Mom's willing to take responsibility for whatever happens. She's scared she may have known but never tried to find out, if that makes sense; but she's willing to face the truth because all she wants is for me to be happy and to stop hurting. I'll tell you, Celia, life is so full of twists and turns. I'm just so thankful that Dad died first and Mom has a chance to make things right for all of us, including herself. My life would be so different if she had died and Dad had been left to keep a lid on everything and keep me lying about my life. I feel now I have a real chance at happiness because all the lies are over and done with, and it feels like the weight of the world has been lifted from my shoulders. Oh, I know I have a long way to go, and that damned dream I had earlier is proof that I have a long way to go; but at least I'm on that journey and feel hopeful I will get through all of it. I'm determined to be happy, and now I have *everyone* I need working to ensure that happens. I am very, very fortunate!"

Celia was listening intently to Emily as she thought about her own cousin. "You know, Emily, it sounds like your life is taking a dramatic turn; and I understand about what might have happened if your dad had been the survivor. I have a cousin who was molested by her dad, my uncle!" Celia now had a look of disgust and anger on her face as she continued.

"Your dad's dead and your mom has stepped up. Margaret, my cousin, still suffers and I've always felt bad for her. She used to babysit me, and a year ago she told me about her dad. She's been physically ill for a long time and won't tell anyone what he did to her or even confront him because her dad is paying all her medical bills; and get this ...he keeps her quiet by threatening her that, if she ever tells, he'll stop paying her bills. She's thirty-five now and still scared to death of her father. It makes me sick to my stomach because Margaret is one of the sweetest persons you could ever meet. She's always been so good to me. Phew...as I was sitting here listening to you, Margaret's face just kept popping into my head. I wish she could be gutsy like you because your story makes me realize that she actually *is in charge.* He's a bigwig lawyer whose career would blow up in his face if she ever told. She actually has him by the balls and doesn't even realize how powerful she is. Your story makes me realize that she is the powerful one here."

Celia paused, then exclaimed, "Wow! My family life isn't the greatest; but, God, I've never had to suffer anything like you or my cousin. In fact, now I'm realizing my family isn't so bad after all. You're amazing, Emily. I can't even begin to tell you how much I admire you. I feel honored to be your roommate!"

Emily was smiling. "Oh, Celia. Do you realize how amazing you are as well? You've sat here for several hours listening to me pour my guts all over the floor, and not once have you complained or become bored or asked to go to bed. You're a very compassionate person, and I feel very honored and lucky to be your roommate as well. If you ever need to pour out your guts about something, please promise me you'll pour them out to me. I want to be there for you just like you've been here for me tonight. Will you promise me, Celia?"

The two girls hugged tightly. "I promise you, Emily. Thanks for trusting me. I feel as if you and this evening has changed my life. I'm so proud to be your roommate!"

"Well, I'm proud to be yours as well. I felt so sad earlier, but now I feel as if I can get back up swinging; and you did that for me, Celia. I'm thankful you're my roommate!"

Then Emily noticed the clock across the room. "God, it's almost 4 a.m. We probably should turn in. Thank God we can both sleep late. I don't have a class until 2 p.m. I think you told me yours wasn't until noon, right?"

"Yes, noon, and now I'm completely hydrated and ready to go to bed. Thanks for telling me about the water and alcohol. I'll remember that 'cuz I hate hangovers!"

As the two girls hugged, Emily said, "Boy, so do I."

The girls hugged again, turned off the light and climbed back into their beds. Emily immediately fell asleep. She felt another load had been lifted off her shoulders. It was good to tell someone else her secret. Emily even felt proud.

The more people that become educated about child molestation, the more vigilant people become, she thought as she drifted off.

It took Celia longer to fall asleep. She was totally blown away, yet amazed at the story she had just heard.

Damn, you just don't realize how good your life has been until you hear how horrible someone else's has been. I like Emily.

Chapter 2

The following day Emily called Sean between classes. She told him about her conversation with Celia. Then they began talking about Christmas.

"Sean, I miss you so much. I just can't wait until I come out there with your mom and Bill. I'm still pinching myself that they're flying me and Martha out with them. I'm so excited about the trip but most of all about seeing you again. These last few months have been torture."

"They've been torture for me too, Em, especially over Thanksgiving. I was so worried about you, but it sounds like everything will eventually work its way out. I'm so impressed with how your mom stepped up. That in-charge mother you always saw seems to be out for good! I'm happy for you, baby."

"Me too. Gosh, I was looking at the calendar this morning. Do you realize that we only have seventeen days before we see each other?"

"Seventeen, wow. That's right! I counted the days yesterday. That will go by in no time. Listen, sweetie, let me call you later tonight. Okay? I just got to my class, and the professor just walked in the door. I love you, Em."

Emily smiled, "I love you too, Sean. We'll talk later."

Since Sean had left for Berkeley, all they'd had in order to feel close to each other were emails, text messages and phone calls. Prior to his leaving and since they had first met at age eleven, the two had been apart only for short periods of time. It was one of the hardest separations Emily could have imagined; but now, in a little more than two weeks, she'd be back in his loving arms. Then she thought about how generous Beth and Bill were to pay for a plane ticket for her to fly out so she could be with Sean. Little did either she or Sean know, but Beth and Bill were also planning a much larger surprise for the couple.

****

Beth and Bill leased a one-bedroom corporate housing suite at the Steinhart Hotel in San Francisco for the couple. It was situated in one of the city's prime locations for restaurants, boutiques and must-sees close to Nob Hill and Union Square. The apartment was leased for Saturday, December 28th, Emily's eighteenth birthday, through Sunday, January 13th when Emily would fly back home, in time to register for her second semester.

Emily's mom, Sarah, and Martha had known about this surprise for over a month; but neither Sean nor Emily knew a thing about it. In fact, both Sean and Emily assumed she would return to Rhode Island with Beth, Bill and Martha on her birthday.

Beth told both Sean and Emily the three adults would take them out for Emily's birthday on the 27th. The plan was to go to the Boulevard, considered a culinary landmark, five-star restaurant.

Beth had done her homework and found out that the restaurant was considered one of the popular local hangouts in the Bay area. The couple was simply appreciative of the fact that they would be able to spend Christmas together in the magical atmosphere of San Francisco. Emily had never been west of Corpus Christi, Texas, where her dad had been stationed for three years, so this would be a real treat for her.

By the time Emily returned to her dorm room in the late afternoon, she decided to call Jeannie, a student at the University of Rhode Island. Emily wanted to catch up on what was going on with Jeannie and her new love interest, John Bertram, who Emily lovingly called "Officer Dunkin Donuts."

John was the police officer who had detained Jeannie as she sat on the interstate shoulder the day she had rushed to Emily's dorm to pick her up before Emily found out about Sarah finding and reading her diary.

Immediately after the crisis, Jeannie and John began dating. It didn't take either of them very long to fall head over heels in love with one another; and despite all their intentions of taking the relationship at a snail's pace, soon after the courtship began, they decided that Jeannie would move in with John. Emily had no idea this was their plan until she called Jeannie that day.

"Hey, Jeannie, how was your Thanksgiving? Are you still seeing Officer Dunkin Donuts?"

"God, Em, that's right. We haven't talked since before Thanksgiving. A lot's gone on. How about you?"

"'Lots has gone on' is an understatement, but I want to hear about you first. Fire away!"

"Well, let's see. John did come over for Thanksgiving, and my dad fell in love with him. You know how protective Dad is. Well, not anymore because Saturday after John's shift, I went over to fix dinner for the two of us. Oh my God, Em, John is so tender and loving when he makes love. I had no idea a man could be that tender. Anyway, we made love, ate dinner and watched a movie in that order."

"You were a busy little bee," giggled Emily.

"Well, that's not all. After the movie, I began getting ready to leave and John begged me to stay, saying he wanted to experience waking up next to me."

"Wow, so did you?"

"Well, that's the crazy part. I called and talked to Mom. I knew she was concerned about us going too quickly. I wanted her to cool Dad out and give me her blessing to stay the night. To my surprise, Dad didn't need any cooling out. In fact, he told Mom he hoped the relationship would become serious."

"I take it that it has."

"Em, I never fully grasped how you felt about Sean until now. Yes, we are both madly in love with each other. Now, don't get protective on me, but I'm going to move in with John this Saturday."

"Good grief, Jeannie. Are you sure about this? What does your mom say?"

"She's like you. She's concerned about my getting so caught up in the relationship that I drop out of school. But, like I assured her, I'm assuring you right now. That just ain't gonna happen!"

Emily was silent. Then she finally said as it sounded like a question, "Okay?"

"Listen, Em, if I haven't learned anything else from your family's situation, I've learned that I *never* want to be economically dependent on a male, no matter how wonderful he is or how in love with him I am. I *need* to maintain a sense of independence for multiple reasons, including peace of mind. I know you've thought about that aspect as well. If your mom had been economically independent, perhaps she wouldn't have felt trapped in her relationship; and maybe she would have left your dad because of how he treated her. On the other hand, due to her strong Catholicism, perhaps not. Who knows? But for John and me, believe me, neither of us are in a hurry to tie the knot. After all, living together isn't taboo like it used to be; so for now, we're content with living with each other and getting to know one another. Just like I asked Mom, I'm asking you to please trust me on this. Can you do that? Can you just enjoy watching me fall in love and quit worrying about me going off the deep end?"

Another long silence. Then Emily said with a huff, "Yes, Jeannie, I will quit worrying. I want you to be happy; and it sounds like you have actually found your own Sean, so now it's my turn to step up and just be a good friend. I'm happy for you, Jeannie, and I honestly can't wait to meet him."

"Thanks, Em. John wants to meet you too. In fact, we talked about having you over for dinner on the 14th so you two could meet before you and Martha go to California. Which, by the way, I'll bet you're getting excited about that trip."

"I am, but I only began to think about it in earnest yesterday. Guess I need to fill you in now."

****

Emily began telling Jeannie about her and her mom's first session with Dr. Wells, then about the Thanksgiving incident and everything that had happened since then. As she talked, she could hear Jeannie gasping on the other end.

"God, Em. What a Thanksgiving! Are you okay?"

"Like I told Sean a few minutes ago, I think I am. Mom and I have our second session together tomorrow. I'm really nervous about that. Mom is going through a lot of soul-searching right now, so I have no idea what to expect."

"Well, how do you feel about all of it? What if you find out she actually knew?"

"I don't know, but I'm determined not to let that get in the way. Mom was so beaten down and controlled by Dad that it probably would have been the most natural means of coping. After all, Dad did saddle her with four kids, one after another; and Grandma was an extra burden, which Dad made sure it was by being an asshole toward Grandma. Mom's had a lot on her plate all the years Dad was around, but the mom that I saw on those occasions he'd be gone is totally out in the open now. It was that mom who took charge on Thanksgiving; and instead of letting me continue to hide everything and protect everyone, she came to my rescue. I have to stay focused on that. I love Mom with all my heart, and I want to be able to get closer to her. We need each other's strength to move forward."

"Well, all I can say is that your mom is awfully lucky to have a daughter like you. That's wonderful, Emily. Good luck tomorrow. I'll be thinking about you. You're such a brave individual; that's all I can say about that."

"Thanks, Jeannie. Well, listen, I need to get off. I'm starving. I haven't eaten anything all day. Okay?"

"Okay. I've got to go over to the library for one of my classes anyway. But listen, what about coming over for dinner on the 14th?"

"That sounds great. I'm going to put it on my calendar. I'm looking forward to meeting John, and again I am truly happy for you. You deserve a true love."

"Thanks, Em. I'll call you between now and then, okay?"

"Okay. Love you, Jeannie."

"Love you too, kiddo. Bye-bye."

****

The following day as Sarah drove her car up the street to Pawtucket Avenue, Emily called her.

"Hi, sweetie, I just left the house. I should be there in about forty-five minutes."

"Hi, Mom. That's great. That gives us fifteen minutes to walk over to Dr. Wells' office. I'll wait for you in the parking lot. Okay?"

"Sounds good. See you in a bit."

The second session was intense. Instead of Emily starting the conversation, Sarah did, which surprised both Emily and Dr. Wells.

"Dr. Wells. I would like to start this session if that's okay."

"That would be great, Sarah. Go ahead."

Sarah described Thanksgiving Day and the events that had taken

17

place, beginning with her outburst and ending with her telling both Paul and Lily the truth. Dr. Wells listened the entire time without interrupting.

"That was quite a day, Sarah! How do you feel about what happened?"

"I feel good, and I feel even more determined to continue to stay in charge of everything. I know I have been absent for most of Emily's life. I've thought about how absent I have been and realize that I must take responsibility for that absence. Part of that responsibility is to *NEVER* let myself slip back into my old self. I just hope with all my heart that Emily will never resent me for my culpability."

Dr. Wells then turned to Emily. "How do you feel about all of this, Emily?"

She was very thoughtful about her response. She wanted to be sensitive toward her mother, yet she also knew she needed to be sensitive to her own needs and feelings. "It's been a lot to take in, and I don't think I've digested everything yet."

Emily then turned to Sarah and looked at her directly. "Mom, I have to get this out. I think I've known all my life that you knew something was going on. I know you didn't know what it was because you never really wanted to know, but I also know that you too suffered at the hands of Dad. I watched how he belittled you and beat you down all my life. It was why I was able to see a different mother when he was gone. I guess because I've had to watch my back all my life, I've become a pretty good observer. I don't know if I will ever feel resentment, but I want you to know that those are emotions I will do my best to not hold onto. You don't deserve that. You were fighting for your own survival while Dad was still alive. He was a cruel and insensitive person toward those he was determined to control.

I love you, Mom. I love you with all my heart; and, regardless of what happens, I need you to know that. I have a very long road ahead of me. After what happened Thursday, especially how you sprang up from your cocoon and gave me permission to stop hiding the secret …well, I can't even begin to tell you what that means to me. I just know in my heart that if it were Dad who was left behind, my future would be totally different. He would have been in control of how

Paul, Lily and Katie behaved toward me; and he would have wielded that power to the extreme. I truly believe that I would have *had to walk away* from my entire family if he were still alive and it was you who died. But that didn't happen; and, Mom, I thank my lucky stars that it was he and not you who died.

You took control of the situation the other night and helped Paul and Lily see the truth. Because of you, Mom, both Lily and Paul are able to feel love and support for me instead of hatred and resentment. That's what you and I need to concentrate on. There just can't be room for anything that could drive a wedge between us. God, Mom, Dad brainwashed me too!"

Emily was now crying. "Dad made me suspicious of you. He convinced me that if I had told you, you would have blamed me and turned on me. That day I stabbed his hand, I believe if I had told him that I would tell you and never mentioned Capt. James, he would have pulled out all the stops to manipulate the situation; and, I don't know, he may have regained control over me. But it was my ability to understand and then threaten the one true love of his life, his damned career, which turned everything around. I love you, Mom, and I never want anything else but that. I forgive you for never rescuing me before Thanksgiving. I need you to forgive yourself. Can you do that, Mom?"

Sarah was hugging Emily when Dr. Wells spoke.

"This was quite a session, Sarah and Emily. I wish we could continue, but time won't allow that right now. Sarah, I'm willing to allow a third session with Emily if you would like."

"No, Dr. Wells. I think it's time for me to begin seeing you by myself and allow Emily the safety of her own private sessions. Emily is right. It's time I begin to forgive myself so I can be there for her. I *never, ever* want to go back to the old Sarah. I like who I am becoming."

With that, the session ended. On their way out both Emily and Sarah scheduled separate sessions with Dr. Wells beginning the following week.

On their way back to Sarah's car and Emily's dorm, Sarah stopped at a bench along the path. It was nippy out, but the bench sat in full sunlight.

"Emily, let's just sit here for a few minutes and catch our breath. Okay?"

"Mom, I'd like that. I'm scared right now. I'm scared of alienating you."

Sarah took Emily's hands and squeezed them. "Oh, Emily, sweetie, that's not going to happen. I may get my feelings hurt, but I'm determined to not back down. I *meant* what I said back there. I'm determined to stand by your side with the vengeance of the mom I failed to be in the past. I promise you, Em, I will never allow any of your siblings to feel anything other than love and support for you. I love you, Emily, and I promise you I will work on forgiving myself. We have a long life ahead of us. I want to be part of your life and have you be part of mine. We need to build that future on love and support for each other."

Emily and Sarah sat on the bench holding hands and talking for an hour before they got up to leave. Emily had a class she needed to attend, and Sarah wanted to be home when Lily and Katie got home from school. They finished walking to Sarah's car where they hugged and again promised each other to hold on tightly to their love for one another.

Chapter 3

Sarah's first solo session with Dr. Wells was scheduled for Wednesday, December 11th at 11 a.m. Emily had a final exam that morning at 9 a.m. and was scheduled for her session with Dr. Wells later that same day.

The evening before, Emily called Sarah.

"Hi, Mom."

"Hi, sweetie, how's the studying going?"

"It's going okay. I have two exams left. English lit is tomorrow morning, and my physics exam is on Friday at 11 a.m. I should be able to get home by one or two p.m. on Friday; at least that's the plan. I think I told you that I'm going to have dinner with Jeannie and John on Saturday. I'm excited about meeting him. She's absolutely nuts over him."

Emily then sounded concerned. "Mom, how do you feel about your session with Dr. Wells in the morning?"

"I'm nervous, but she seems to be such an intuitive person that I feel very comfortable talking to her. I think she can help me with my guilt feelings. Say, Emily, since your exam will be over about the time I get out, why don't we plan on getting lunch before I head back home?"

"Mom, I'd love to. I was going to suggest the same thing. That way you can tell me a little bit of how it went. Why don't you park in my dorm parking lot, walk over and then come on back to my dorm when you're through? I'll meet you down at your car if you don't want to come up. Just call me as you walk back."

"That sounds good. Have a good night, sweetie, and I'll see you tomorrow. Get a good night's rest and good luck on your exam tomorrow. Love you, honey."

"I love you too, Mom. See you tomorrow."

Next Emily called Sean. "Hi, Seanie. What time's your exam in the morning?"

"Hey, baby. It's at 9. Yours is at the same time, right?"

"Yea. I'm going to meet Mom after for lunch. She has her first solo session with Dr. Wells. I just talked to her. I'm so glad I encouraged her to take the Zoloft. I think it's helping her a lot. Hey, I'm going to meet Jeannie's Officer Dunkin Donuts on Saturday evening. They've invited me for dinner. I'm really looking forward to finally meeting him. I did tell you that Jeannie's moved in with him, right?"

"Yea, you mentioned it. How's that going?"

"I think Jeannie is right that she's met her own Sean. I hope it all works out for her. She's such a wonderful person and friend. She deserves to be happy. Which reminds me, Sean, do you know how many days there are till we see each other?"

Sean chuckled at the question and decided to tease Emily a little.

"Hmm. I haven't been keeping track. Let me see. Hmm. Could it be ten?" he asked, then laughed. "Are you kidding, Em? I've been marking off the days. I just can't wait to hold my sweet Emily in my arms again. It's been way too long!"

"Oh Sean, I can't wait either. This has been so hard. It's fine when I'm in class and studying; but when I fall asleep at night, that's when I feel the ache the most. I just love you with all my heart."

They talked awhile longer then said goodnight.

Emily decided to turn in. She had studied all she could for her exam. As she lay there, she kept thinking about her mom so she decided to get back up and call Martha. It was 9:45.

"Hello."

"Hi, Martha. I hope I didn't wake you."

"No, sweetie. You didn't. I'm still up. What's going on?"

"Mom's first solo with Dr. Wells is tomorrow; and, of course, you know me, I'm worried."

"Emily, I don't think there's anything to worry about. Although I guess I need to tell you that your mom found a small booklet in the bottom of Lily's sock drawer a few days ago and has been reading it. She was a little shaken by what she read, but I think everything will be okay once she talks to Dr. Wells. The Zoloft she's been taking is helping her quite a bit. So, although I don't want you to be worried, I just think you should be prepared."

"What kind of brochure?"

"Let me think. It's called 'Incest: A Family Tragedy.' I'm pretty sure that's the title. It's put out by a survivors' group. It has Penny's name on the front so we are sure Lily got it from her."

"Oh, wow. You know, I think I recall Lily mentioning a brochure to me the other day. She did get it from Penny. What exactly shook Mom up?"

"Well, the brochure is broken up into sections. Since the booklet focuses on female victims, the first section discusses the daughter. The second discusses the mother. The third, the father and the last, the siblings."

"Oh, boy. What does it say about the mother?"

"Honey, you and I both know that your mom no doubt knew about what was going on or—let me qualify that—we know she knew *something* was going on."

"Yes. I even told her in our last session that I know she knew something was going on. So what does the book say?"

"Well, Emily, the section about the mother starts out by referring to her as the 'silent partner' but it also calls her another victim in the crime. It discusses how powerless she feels in her marriage but that she becomes an accomplice by ignoring the problem or refusing to see it. I recall at the end of that section it also suggests that the mother may have been a victim of sexual assault as well."

"You know, Martha, I've wondered about that last part. Mom has told me in the past that her mother and father allowed several of Grandma's relatives to live with them on and off. God, Mom could have been molested by any one of them! Has Mom mentioned that possibility?"

"I mentioned it, but she is way too deep in denial; however, I think it's good that she's been exposed to this pamphlet because it could open the door for her as she talks to Dr. Wells on her own."

"Wow, Martha. I thought I had a lot to deal with."

"Well, Emily...*do not* diminish what you have to deal with and place your mom above your own interest. Can you promise me that you'll work on that, Emily? You know you have a tendency to put everyone's feelings in front of your own. That's what made you the World's Best Molested Daughter, after all. It's also what gave you the ability to fabricate stories like the whopper you fabricated out of thin air on Thanksgiving."

"I know what you're saying, Martha. I'll try my best. I know that's one of my weaknesses. I put everyone in front of me in order to reduce the severity or even the importance of my own pain and problems. I've always convinced myself that I was bigger than what Dad was doing to me. I know I came to believe that myth. Thanks at least for giving me the heads-up on the brochure."

"Okay, sweetie. You hang in there, Emily. Both of you are going to get through this and be better for it. I know that in my heart." Then she changed the subject. "Have you talked to Sean today?"

"Yes. He teased me a little about not knowing how many days till we see each other."

"Well, Emily, I can tell you he's dying to see you. Let's just stay focused on that, okay?"

"Okay, Martha. I love you. Thanks so much for being such a wonderful friend."

"Anytime, Emily. I'm here for both of you. Have a good night and good luck on your exam tomorrow."

Emily hung the phone up, then turned it off. She needed a good night's sleep so she could be fresh for her exam. She needed to get an A on this exam to get an overall GPA of 4.0. In Emily's mind anything less was unacceptable. She thought about her expectations as she drifted off to sleep. She thought about the words Sean had said to her during her senior year of high school. It too was final exam week. *Emily, your expectations of yourself are set so high, you don't give yourself any slack. You've become your own worst enemy, sweetie. You need to give yourself a break now and then.*

The exam and now her new information about Sarah and the brochure gave her the second in a series of dreams she would occasionally have over the next several years. In these dreams she would suffer at the hands of her family members.

In this particular dream her mother was angry with her, wouldn't speak to her and instructed her siblings to ignore her as well. When Emily woke from the dream in the middle of the night, she was crying. She got up and went to the bathroom as she tried to shake off the dream, but instead she spent the next hour crying from the pain of feeling abandoned and alone. When she finally calmed down and returned to her bed, she promised herself she would discuss the dream with Dr. Wells. Celia was finished with her exams and had already left for home which Emily was grateful for. She didn't need a repeat performance. She needed to sleep.

The following morning Emily went to her final exam as Sarah

walked from Emily's dorm parking lot over to Dr. Wells' office. Sarah had the brochure in her purse.

Sarah didn't get much sleep the prior night. She thought about the brochure, especially the part that called the wife a silent partner. She had been thinking about her culpability ever since before Thanksgiving. The term "silent partner" shook her to the core. *I'm scared of talking to Dr. Wells about this. I'm so afraid I enabled Joe to hurt Emily, but I've got to talk about it. I can't hide anymore. I just hope Emily can continue to love me. I don't know what I'd do if Emily turned on me, and I know that could happen. If it does happen, I know I could never blame her. God, please don't let that happen. I love my Emily with all my heart, and all I want to do is make it up to her. I know this is a test, God. I'm just scared!*

At 11:20 a.m. the following day, as Sarah walked back to her car, she called Emily. Emily was sitting on the bottom step in the stairwell of her dorm waiting for her mom.

Emily immediately picked up on Sarah's tone. She sounded shaken.

"Are you okay, Mom?"

"Yes, Emily. We'll talk when I get there. Why don't you meet me at my car? I'm nearly there. We'll talk a little before we go to lunch."

Emily walked out into the parking lot and was waiting for Sarah when she saw her mom come down the walk to the car. Sarah looked as if she had been crying. They hugged and got in the car.

It was nippy out, so Sarah started the engine to warm the vehicle. "Emily, I'm really having a harder time with this than I anticipated. I'm so scared that somewhere deep inside of me I knew what was happening to you. I'm so scared of that." Then Sarah started to cry.

"Mom, don't cry. Don't be mad at me because I talked to Martha last night. She told me about the brochure you found in Lily's drawer. Do you have it on you so I can look at it?"

"Yes," Sarah sobbed as she rifled through her purse. "I need to let Lily know I found it. I feel like such a snoop, but I wasn't snooping any more than when I found your diary. They both just seemed to reveal themselves to me while I was doing something else."

"Lily will understand. I'm sure of that. She loves you a lot, Mom. I love you a lot too."

"I know, Emily. I love all you kids. I just wish I had been a better parent 'cuz if I had been, we wouldn't be sitting in this car right now talking about this."

"Mom, you don't know that. The only thing that could have happened differently would have been a result of Dad's decisions and behavior. He did this, Mom. You didn't and neither did I. We both need to remember that!"

They were silent for a few minutes as Emily scanned the four pages of the section about the mother. She had a yellow highlighter in her hand and was highlighting sections of the four pages. When she finished, she looked over at Sarah.

"Mom, please pay attention to these highlights I'm going to read to you, okay?"

"Okay, Emily."

"First, Mom, it says that the mother often feels very powerless in her marriage. We both know that was true."

"Yes, and I did feel powerless, but it also says that the mother becomes an accomplice by ignoring the problem and refusing to see it. I *did that*, Emily! I remember how your dad always told me to rely on you for extra help and that you could handle anything that was put in your path. Oh, Emily, honey, why did I allow myself to believe that? Why did I act like his robot and allow him to do those things to you?"

"Mom, listen to me. You didn't allow him to do those things to me. He manipulated you just like he manipulated me and just like he manipulated everyone in his life. He made me distrust you. He manipulated me by making me feel you were too weak to rescue me. He made me feel scared to death and so distrustful of you. But, Mom, you proved him wrong on Thanksgiving Day, and you're continuing to do that. God, Mom, you're going to a therapist where you're committed to being totally honest about everything. That's huge, Mom, and that's exactly what *we need to focus on*. What's happened has already happened, and there's not a damned thing either of us can do about that."

"Do you think, Emily, that he would have left you alone if I had just tried harder to like having sex? I don't know why I've never liked having sex."

"*No, Mom! Look here.* This is something I've known for a long time. Dr. Wells helped me to understand this the first few times I sat down with her. What Dad did to me had *nothing* to do with the act of sex, Mom. As a child, he was violated three times and never told anyone; but instead of treating it the way I've treated it, he *chose* to become the violator. *He* decided to take out *all* his hurt and anger on *me and on the two other children* and, Mom, God knows how many *other children* he hurt while he was still alive. Because it *has nothing to do with sex* but *everything* to do with *violence*, he was able to do to boys exactly what he was able to do to girls. He became a cruel human being, Mom. He allowed himself to become a cruel human being. Plus, he never, ever tried to help you like having sex. *He didn't care if you did or didn't.* As long as you did exactly what he manipulated you to do, he was satisfied. That's why when he was home, you were an entirely different person than when he was gone. When he was home, it was as if he reattached your strings so he could go back to pulling all the right ones. But when he was gone, you threw off your strings and stood on your own two feet. You were *an incredible mom* whenever he was gone. You were the mom that reared up on Thanksgiving Day, roared and took each of your children under your wings so we could feel safe and *sane*."

Emily sat quiet for a few seconds and watched Sarah's face. She then spoke. "Mom, can I ask you a very difficult question?"

"Yes."

"Do you promise that you won't get mad at me for asking?"

"I promise, Emily. I am that woman you always thought you saw. I'm just a very sad person right now that I allowed myself to live in the world your father created for all of us. Please ask me."

Emily took her mother's hands in hers, looked her in the eyes. "Mom, do you remember how you've told me that Grandma and Grandpa welcomed Grandma's relatives into their home off and on when those relatives were having a rough time?"

"Emily, I know what you're going to ask me. Dr. Wells asked me the same thing. I just honestly don't know the answer to that question. I am sure, though, that my own dad never did anything to me other than love me. I'm not sure about my uncles. I'm going to have to think about that for a while. I had one uncle, in particular, that I think deep down I never really liked for some reason; but I don't want to accuse anyone unless I'm sure."

"I know, Mom and, that's good. It would be *horrible* to accuse anyone of something as heinous as pedophilia if that person *is actually innocent.* On the other hand, I'm not sure if Dr. Wells told you this, but *one in three* girls are molested by the time they reach the age of eighteen. Plus, the violator is typically a family relative or friend. Even if you never remember *if* or *who*, it's important that you know the statistics. It could be *one of the answers* as to why Dad was able to manipulate you so skillfully."

"Well, whatever happened, I still need to own this entire situation. I don't want to make any more excuses for myself."

"That's good, Mom, and I'm so thankful and proud of what you're doing. You've single-handedly changed my life! The Sarah you've committed to being will help you get through all of this; and I promise, Mom, I am with you *all* the way! Now, I don't know about you, but I'm really hungry. Let's go get something to eat."

Sarah sat still for a few minutes. She couldn't help herself. She felt overwhelmed by everything. Now she also felt overwhelmed by the generosity and kindness of her daughter, Emily. She began to cry again.

That was all Emily needed as she too began to cry. As she did, she leaned over to her mom, put her arms around her and they cried together.

"This is such a sad time, Emily. Dr. Wells mentioned that we are both in mourning for the past. I love you so much. I'm so sorry for everything you've endured. I'm also so thankful for who you've become. You are the opposite of what your dad became. You're so generous, thoughtful and loving. I am so lucky that he died and I got to experience your love as I am now."

"Oh, Mom, I'm lucky too that you chose to step out of your old self and into the shoes of the mom I've loved and longed for all my life."

Sarah and Emily sat in the car a long time crying and holding each other. Then Sarah reached into her purse searching for a tissue. "Damn, I don't even have a Kleenex."

Emily giggled as she reached into her purse and pulled out two red bandanas. "Here, Mom. Sean pulled out a white rag the last night I saw him, and we were sitting on the slant tree reminiscing. It made me laugh when he did because he said, 'I came prepared this time.'

So, Mom, here. I came prepared this time as well."

She handed Sarah one of the bandanas and used the other for herself. They both laughed through their tears.

"Mom, please make sure you keep talking to me about all of this. It's so important now for both of us that we not keep any of our feelings and fears from each other. To keep them to ourselves could be so damaging for both of us. This is Dad's doing. We're just trying to pick up the pieces of what he tried his best to destroy!"

The two women sat in the now-warmed car for a few more minutes blowing their noses and telling each other how much they loved each other when Sarah asked, "Where do you want to go to lunch? I'm starving now too."

"Let's go to Geoff's Superlative. They've got great sandwiches and salads there. I've been there a number of times and love it."

Sarah and Emily had a wonderful lunch. When Sarah finally dropped Emily off at her dorm, Sarah looked at her with a tremendous look of love on her face. "Emily, I'm so happy you're my daughter. I love you with all my heart! You're a treasure your dad *cheated* himself out of ever knowing."

"Mom, I've been waiting for a long time for you to be the woman you're becoming. I love you with all my heart too."

They hugged very hard and Emily got out of the car. "I'll see you in two days, Mom. Drive safely and call me when you get home."

On her way home, Sarah was overwhelmed at the knowledge of how fortunate she was to not only have such a sweet, understanding daughter but also for the opportunity of having a new beginning for herself and her family. She promised herself to hold onto that thought for those times she got scared and wanted to blame herself. She was not to blame. Her husband, whom she now cursed, was to blame. He and he alone was *the culprit!*

After taking a side trip to get an oil change for her vehicle, Sarah finally arrived home. Martha was waiting for her.

In the meantimes Emily called Martha and recounted the entire conversation. Their conversation influenced Martha to arrange for Gladys to come pick up Lily and Katie for the evening. She would take Sarah to dinner in hopes of lifting her spirits.

Gladys was more than happy to do this. She told Martha that Jeannie had told Phil and her what the situation was but promised not to let Sarah know they knew. Gladys expressed delight to have the two young girls stay with her. She missed her own girl and this would give her a chance to dote on Lily and Katie. This opportunity also gave Gladys immense pleasure to know that she could have a role in helping this wonderful family heal from the hellish mess Joe had left behind for all of them to clean up.

****

Later that afternoon Emily sat down with Dr. Wells. She discussed the brochure and her conversation with her mother prior to having lunch.

"Dr. Wells, do you think my mom was molested when she was just a kid? I don't know if she told you, but several of her mother's relatives lived with them off and on while Mom was young."

"I don't know the answer to that, Emily. You know the statistics, so we both know the odds are in favor of molestation. However, whether she ever remembers or not isn't important for either of you. What is important for your mother is that *she's owning up* to all the possibilities regarding why this happened right under her nose. It's a difficult thing your mom is doing, but it's also a very brave and healthy thing; and it's one of the variables that will help your mother heal from all of this so she can move on. On the other hand, Emily, that is *not* your problem. You have your own healing to do, and that's what I want you to concentrate on. Now let's talk about you and leave your mom out of the rest of this session. Can you do that?"

"Yes, Dr. Wells, I can. Besides, there are some things I would like to discuss for myself."

She proceeded to tell Dr. Wells about her unrealistic expectations, Sean's comments about those expectations, as well as about the dream she just had and how it made her feel when she woke up.

"I've noted your harsh expectations of yourself. So, yes, Sean was very right. It's something you need to acknowledge and work on. At least you need to be aware that your self-expectations are unrealistic. The dream, well, it's not at all surprising. Emily, have you ever wondered why you became so attracted to and attached to the three members of your support group?"

"Yes, I have. Until Sean, Martha and Jeannie, I never felt as if I had a friend in the world. I felt so detached, abandoned and alone in my parent's house even though the house was full of people. It felt as if I was always sitting in my own small chair in the corner of the house watching my family behave as a family, at least my dad and siblings. He treated them so differently than how he treated me. After I met Sean and Martha and then Jeannie, for the first time in my life that I could remember I felt important. I felt like I was part of something so in a sense, they became my surrogate family, I suppose. They made me feel important and then powerful. I just know that meeting them was the thing that helped me stand up to my dad and even stab him that day in the car."

"I think you are right about all of that, Emily. One of your natural unconscious fears is that of abandonment. Your dream was trying to tell you that. But there's more to you than your fears, and you need to begin to recognize those positives. Emily, more than anyone else, *you have yourself to thank* for your bravery. You would never have been able to find your support group if you hadn't been looking for one. You certainly could have walked down the same path that your father chose for himself; and, Emily, that is actually a more likely outcome than the path *you*—and I am putting the emphasis on the word *you*—chose to walk down and create. Sean, Martha and Jeannie saw something in you that had *always* been there. They saw a warm, charming, loving and brave individual who was looking for confirmation that she was warm, charming, loving and brave. They confirmed what you already suspected of yourself. So, Emily, let's concentrate on that. Your support group was attracted to you because you were your own first support group. Those are the expectations you need to allow yourself to feel. You are a remarkable individual, Emily; and, because you are, you will not only *survive* this, but you will *flourish and grow* and touch others the way you have affected your own self."

Emily was crying at Dr. Wells' words.

"Thank you, Dr. Wells, for saying that to me."

"No, Emily, *thank you* for playing out that role for yourself and introducing yourself to me. I am richer for having gotten to know you as much as you are richer for having chosen to become who you have and are becoming." She looked at her watch. "Now unfortunately I'm guessing my next patient is probably in the waiting room pacing back and forth. You have lots of food for thought over the next several weeks. Have a wonderful Christmas, Emily. Enjoy Sean and San Francisco and I'll see you when you get back."

The two women hugged. When Dr. Wells opened the door to let Emily out, they both grinned at each other. Dr. Wells' next patient was indeed pacing back and forth in the waiting room.

Chapter 4

It was noon on Friday, December 13th. Emily had just packed her car and was headed home for Christmas and semester break. She remembered Jeannie's exam was at 10 a.m., so she called her to see how it went.

"Hey, Em, are you on your way home? I was just about to call you."

"Yea, I just left my dorm. How'd your last exam go?"

"Well, today being Friday the 13th, last night I had a horror dream. I dreamt that I hadn't been to the class all semester and didn't even remember where the hell the classroom was. So I was wandering around the campus trying to find the classroom so I could take the exam and, to boot, I was totally naked. I didn't know why I was walking around in my birthday suit; but when I finally got to the right classroom, everyone started laughing because I was naked. God, what a nightmare! I guess I was tossing and turning because John woke me up. He said I kicked him a couple of times. But I actually think I passed it, which is a big load off my mind."

Emily was laughing. "Good grief, Jeannie, that sounds like a hell of a dream, although I don't know why *you* would be embarrassed walking around naked."

"Ha, ha, ha. I'm just glad it's over with. Hey, I heard my mom took care of Lily and Katie this past Wednesday. She had a blast. She said she felt like she had two Jeannies on her hands."

"I'll bet she did. Those two, Lily especially, can be a handful; but, yea, Mom had a tough first session with Dr. Wells. It was her first by herself. She began questioning whether deep down she knew what was happening to me. Fortunately, she met me for lunch and I helped her to put all of that garbage to rest, at least for now. I'm sure she'll have a relapse down the road. I'm fully aware of my own relapses. I swear, Jeannie, my dad sure did leave a fucking snake pit behind. Martha told me that your mom and dad know."

"Yea, I hope you aren't angry with me, Em. I had to explain how I met John. I promise, though, they completely understand and want to help as much as they can. That's one of the reasons Mom was so happy she was able to take care of the girls this week."

"Good grief, Jeannie. I could never be angry with you. Everything you do that concerns me is filled with love. Besides, I figured you'd tell them sooner or later. I mean, that's something that would be hard to keep from talking about, especially given that you and I are such close friends. How did your dad and mom react?"

"Dad admitted he never liked your dad. He thought he was very conceited. Mom just cried. She felt sad for both you and your mom. I think she also felt guilty that she only sees your mom on occasion. I think my mom, Martha and your mom are going to lunch next week before you and Martha leave for San Francisco."

"Yea, they are. Martha told me they were going to have lunch. I know my mom really likes your mom, and my mom can use all the female friends she can get right now. She's been isolated for far too long. My dad liked it that way, and she never questioned that until now. She's really coming out of her shell, and to be surrounded by strong females like Martha and your mom will be good for her."

Jeannie changed the subject, "Em, you only have a few more days till you get to see Sean. I'll bet you're getting really excited about seeing him."

"Oh, my God, Jeannie! I'm dying to see him and I just can't believe I'm going to. Beth and Bill are so, so generous that I already feel like I'm part of the family."

"Well, duh, Em, you've been part of their family for over seven years; after all, you did save her little boy from drowning. You're Beth's lifetime hero, not to mention her future daughter-in-law. You looking forward to Saturday?"

"I really, really am. I can't wait to meet this hunk of a cop! Listen, Jeannie, I just got on the Washington Bridge and it's backed up like crazy. I better go 'cuz some idiot just cut in front of me, and I thought I was going to ram him in the ass."

"Okay, kiddo. Don't wreck your little red Beetle. Get off the phone and I'll see you tomorrow night. We'll have some fun!"

Emily pulled into the driveway as Katie was playing in the front yard of one of her friends a few houses down the hill and on the same side of the road. When Katie spotted Emily's red Beetle coming down the hill, she yelled to her friend that Emily was home and started running up the street to greet her sister. She reached the driveway just as Emily was putting the car into park; and when Emily opened her door and began climbing out, Katie grabbed her and hugged her.

"Emily, you're home. I've missed you so much!"

"Oh, Katie, I've missed you too. Are you getting excited that it's almost Christmas?"

"Yea, and we're going to put the tree up and decorate it tomorrow or Sunday because you're home. We didn't want to do that before you got here. You're not going to be here for Christmas, though, are you?"

"No, squirt, I'm not. But I'll be talking to you over the phone. I'm going to see Sean."

Katie hugged Emily again. "I know. You and Sean love each other. I'm glad you are going to get to see him; I just wish it were here. But that's okay, especially if I get to say 'Merry Christmas' to you over the phone."

"Well, let's go in. Can you carry this one bag in for me, Katie? Where's Lily and Mom?"

"Lily's down at Karen's house, and I think Mom and Martha went shopping. I was supposed to stay down at Tammy's house until they got home but saw your car and told Tammy you were home."

"Great, let's go in so I can settle in, okay?"

Katie picked up one of Emily's bags. "Okay."

About an hour later, Martha and Sarah pulled into the driveway. Emily looked out her bedroom window which had a direct view to the driveway. Her jaw dropped when she realized that her mom had bought a brand-new, red, Lexus convertible sports car. Emily ran out to see.

As Sarah and Martha got out, Emily yelled, "Oh my God, Mom, when on earth did you get this? I had no idea you were even thinking about getting a new car, let alone a sweet red convertible sports car. It's beautiful; but I have to ask, 'Where on earth did my real mom go?'"

Sarah laughed with delight. "It is beautiful, isn't it? And, to be honest, I wasn't even thinking about getting a new car until I went to the dealer to get the oil changed and tires rotated on the van Wednesday after I left you. I actually picked it up this morning before we went shopping."

Emily looked delightfully perplexed. "So what made you get rid of the van for something so different and out of the ordinary?"

"Well, as I sat in the customer lounge, there was a nice-looking fella sitting there as well. He kept looking at me, but I was trying to avoid his gaze because I had no idea what his intentions were. Then finally he asked if my name was Mary Clancy. I must have looked surprised because he apologized for bothering me. I told him no apology was needed but that I hadn't been known as Mary Clancy for a very long time. Then I told him that indeed my maiden name was Clancy. We began talking and discovered that he and I knew each other way back in high school. I was flabbergasted that he even recognized me since that was over twenty years ago; but he told me that I haven't really changed that much, which, of course, was flattering.

Anyway, turns out he is the general manager of the Lexus dealership in East Providence. We talked a little longer and I told him that the van was about to approach the 100,000-mile mark, and I was becoming concerned about its age. Next thing I knew I was down at the dealership; and, being the general manager, well, he allowed his salesperson to give me a deal I simply couldn't turn down."

"Wow, Mom, that's quite a story and what a coincidence running into an old classmate so far from Norfolk! Is he married?" Emily asked with a grin.

"Emily, I am not looking to get involved with anyone. But to answer your question, yes he is married to someone we both went to school with, only she was two years behind us. They have five children. He's really a nice man; but even if he were available, that's the last thing I need right now."

Martha listened while Emily and Sarah talked; then she asked with a forlorn look, "Well, what about me, Emily? What am I, chopped liver? Don't I get a hug and a big hello too?"

Emily laughed as she hugged Martha. "I'm sorry, Martha. I was just so blown away by my new mom that I wasn't even thinking. Besides," she chuckled, "You and your hot yellow Mustang are old news."

Finally, Sarah asked, "When did you get home, honey?"

"About fifteen minutes ago. Katie's home too; she saw me

pulling in and ran home to greet me. Kind of nice to have a kid sister who loves me so much!" exclaimed Emily. "Where'd you two go?"

Sarah put her finger to her lips. "We went Christmas shopping. I had a lot of stuff on layaway I needed to pick up. Martha's going to hide everything at her house. Maybe later we can all go unload the car. I can't keep anything here. Lily's too snoopy."

The three women walked inside. Katie had just come down from her bedroom. She ran to her mom and hugged her; then she hugged Martha, plopped down in the La-Z-Boy and turned on the TV as the three women walked to the kitchen.

"So, Martha, do you still like your Mustang? Sean laughed out loud when I told him you'd bought it."

"I love it. And you should see all the looks I get. It makes me feel young again. I even had a couple of young good-looking guys try to race me down the highway the other day, but I beat them!" Martha chuckled with delight.

They all laughed as Sarah told Martha and Emily she was going to quickly change.

Now standing in the kitchen alone, Emily said to Martha, "Mom seems really good. What do you think?"

"Emily, she's doing amazingly well. She talks when she needs to and seems to be moving through this whole thing. Oh, I know we're not out of the woods yet, but I'm really delighted with her progress. Your conversation with her the other day did a world of good for her. I was worried about you and me leaving for Christmas, but I'm feeling more and more comfortable about that. Besides, we're going to get Gladys closer to your mom next week. I think I told you that I've planned an outing for the three of us. Gladys really wants to be supportive. She said she tends to hide in her cocoon too much and wants to get out and have a little fun, especially now that Jeannie is starting to live her own life. I hear you're going to have dinner with Jeannie and her John tomorrow night."

"Yea, I'm really excited about finally meeting him. She talks about him non-stop and I'm just so happy for her."

Sarah walked back into the kitchen in a pair of jeans and a sweat shirt. "Well, what does everyone want to do about dinner tonight? I was thinking about picking up some Chinese from a new restaurant down on Pawtucket Avenue."

Emily looked like she just got another surprise, so Sarah said, "Close your mouth, Emily."

"Well, Mom, again I need to ask, 'What did you do with my real mom?'"

"What on earth are you talking about?" Sarah asked with a chuckle.

Emily made a sweeping gesture with her arm. "Jeans and a sweatshirt? Mom, you've never worn jeans in your entire life! I'm just so blown away but so happy at the same time. I love the new you: jeans, sweatshirt, new red car. What's next? A new haircut and color?"

"Well, I have been thinking about getting a new look. In fact, both Martha and I are going down into Providence next week to a new fancy, schmancy salon, and I think Gladys is going with us. We may all walk out looking like hot, young babes!" She chuckled. "Now back to dinner. Does Chinese sound good to the two of you?"

"Yum. That sounds wonderful, Mom. We could go pick it up after unloading your car."

"Sounds good to me," said Martha. "That would give me a chance to change while you two are gone."

****

Saturday morning Emily woke up to the wonderful smell of bacon and eggs. She got up and walked out into the kitchen.

"God, Mom, you don't know how good that smells. I get so sick of cereal or picking something up before a class."

She began setting the table just as Lily walked out into the kitchen.

"You can sit down, Emily. I'll set the table."

"Really? Gosh, thanks, Lily. It's good to see you this morning. How's everything with you?"

"Pretty good. Four more days till Christmas break! I can't wait!" said Lily. Then, "Mom, are we going to decorate the tree today or tomorrow? I need to know. Penny, Karen and I want to go see a movie whichever day we don't decorate the tree."

"Well, honey, I think we'll do that tomorrow. I just want to kind of take it easy today. What are you girls going to see?"

"I think *Cabin Fever*. It's a scary movie."

Later Lily took the bus into Providence with Karen and Penny where they went to see *Cabin Fever*. Before she left, she followed Emily into her bedroom, shut the door and told her she was meeting Kevin and that Penny and Karen were meeting their boyfriends.

"Kevin's the guy you talked about at Thanksgiving, isn't he?" Emily asked Lily.

"Yes. He finally noticed me when I was at the mall with some friends. This will be our first official date, but I can't tell Mom because she said I can't date until I'm sixteen. Mom's changing but not that fast."

"I know, Lily. It's going to take a while for Mom to un-stuff herself, if you know what I mean. Just promise me you'll be careful when you make out, okay?"

"I will. I sure don't want to get pregnant; and, besides, I don't want to get a bad reputation anyway. You and Sean spent that night over at Martha's house before he left for California. I know you didn't sleep in separate beds."

"No, we didn't. But I was and am protected because I take birth control pills."

"Where did you get them?" Lily was very inquisitive.

"Jeannie took me down to Planned Parenthood soon after we both graduated from high school. Listen, just be careful. The urge to have sex is real, and boys can be pushy about stuff like that. Just come to me first if you are ever in a place where you think you're in love and you trust a guy enough before you do something like that. Sex is great, Lily, but I really think you want it to be something you don't regret doing. Just don't treat it casually because it is wonderful with the right person. I'm not trying to be snippy. I just don't want to see you get hurt, and some boys only want what they want without considering how it will affect the girl. Know what I mean?"

"Yes, I think I do. I'm not sure I like Kevin that much anyway. I know what you're saying. I want to be in love before I even consider having sex. I've watched you and Sean and know what a special relationship you two have, but it took a long time. I want what you have, and I know from listening and talking to other girls that that type of relationship doesn't come along all the time. So I promise, Emily, I will be careful and I'll come talk to you first."

They hugged. "Thanks, Lily, for trusting me. Just know you can trust me. I will not tell Mom anything. I want you to be happy, and liking boys is part of being happy."

They hugged again, then Lily looked at her watch. "I better go. Karen will be here in about five minutes. We're meeting Penny on the way."

After Lily left with Karen, Sarah looked at Emily, "You and Lily seem to be getting along these days."

"Yea, Mom, we are and it's kind of nice. It all started when I learned she made that door plaque for me. She told me then that she'd always felt left out and thought I loved Katie more than her. She's growing up, Mom, and it's just nice to be able to play the big sister role."

Sarah smiled approvingly just as Martha walked in. The rest of the afternoon the three women watched movies, talked and had a great girls' afternoon. About 3:30 Emily began getting ready for her dinner with Jeannie and John. She decided to braid her hair. Braids made her feel close to Sean. As she braided her hair, she thought about Sean and what he would call her. *My little Irish Colleen.* She got goose bumps thinking about his pet name and could almost hear his voice in her head.

****

At 5:15 she grabbed the bottle of wine from one of the counters. Sarah had picked it up for her the day prior. At about 6:15 she rang John and Jeannie's front door.

Jeannie answered the door, grabbed the bottle Emily was carrying, handed it to John and gave Emily a huge hug, "Damn, I've missed your face, girl."

They were jabbering like two hens in a barnyard when John walked back in the living room to be introduced. He stood off to the side watching these two friends then loudly cleared his throat.

Jeannie turned and laughed. "Oops, you guys haven't met yet. Emily, this is my hot-bod cop, John."

Emily smiled broadly. "Hi, John, I've heard so much about you. It feels as if I already know you."

John shook Emily's hand. "Same here. But, Emily, you can call me DD for short if you want."

She gave John a very puzzled look, then burst with laughter. "Oh my god, DD for Dunkin Donuts …right?"

John also laughed. "Well, of course! It just wouldn't feel right if you called me plain ole John."

All three of them laughed hardily about the nickname. Then Jeannie recounted the lunch she had with her mom the first time she told her about Emily's pet name.

"She sprayed diet soda all over the kitchen table. Then later she said something about Officer Krispy Kreme."

As they all sat down, John got a very serious look on his face. "And just so you know, Emily, someday, way, way in the future, of course, I expect your kids to call me Uncle DD!"

They all laughed again as Emily thought…*What a wonderful way to start our evening.*

The three had a terrific visit. Jeannie was right about John's beef stroganoff. Emily went on and on about what a scrumptious meal it was.

John smirked. "Well, someone around here needs to know how to cook. Jeannie isn't exactly the poster child for domesticity."

Jeannie laughed and gave him an elbow in the side for that one.

Later they listened to music, and Emily and Jeannie entertained John with stories of their growing up. Every once and a while, he'd ask for definitions about what he called code words, like "slant tree," a term used for the tree that sat in back of Martha's house which had been knocked over during a storm and was growing sideways.

Later Jeannie and Emily were laughing about the week Jeannie had taken Emily to Planned Parenthood so she could get on the pill. They laughed about the crazy trip to the zoo where one of the chimps jacked off and shot his wad at a man who had been tormenting them.

Jeannie was roaring with laughter as she looked at John and said, "Dick's cum landed on top of the vanilla cone the man had been eating."

Later Jeannie kept referring to D-day as the two females laughed loudly.

Finally, looking perplexed, John asked, "Okay, you two, what the heck is D-day?"

Jeannie chuckled, then explained, "When I took Emily to

Planned Parenthood, Sean was due to spend that last summer at Martha's house. He and Emily were about to be separated. I think I told you that Sean now lives in California."

John nodded. "Yea, he's going to Berkeley."

"Well, when the nurse gave Emily the pills, she told her that to be on the safe side, she needed to wait seven days to allow the pills to kick in before having sex. You can imagine how hard it was for this one and Sean to keep their hands to themselves once she announced to Sean that she was taking the pill. So during those days before it was safe to have sex, Sean began referring to their big day as 'D-day' as in 'Do it day.'"

Jeannie and Emily were giggling like little girls when John smiled, cocked his head and simply said, "Oh, okay. Now I get it. You're a couple of nuts, and I get the impression Sean is somewhat of a nut too. But what the hell, I like nuts."

This comment made all three laugh as more stories were told and more questions were asked about code language.

By the end of the evening, they all felt as if they had known each other forever.

Around eleven p.m., Emily realized how tired she was. "Well, guys, I've had a fantastic evening, but I think it's time for me to turn into a pumpkin." Then she looked at John. "And, DD, you have been a wonderful surprise to meet. You take good care of my girl here."

"You can count on that, Emily. My life has taken a huge turn for the good since I met my smart-mouthed Jeannie. I don't know how I've survived without her," he said as he kissed Jeannie on her cheek. At the doorway he stood behind Jeannie holding her around the waist as Emily turned around on the stoop, waved goodbye and left.

As John and Jeannie closed the door, Jeannie asked, "Well, what did you think?"

"I like Emily. I can see why you two are best friends. You have two totally different personalities, but they complement each other. I can tell she thinks the world of you, and I know how much you love her."

He then sat down on the sofa. "Let's leave the cleanup for tomorrow. Come here, you."

She sat down next to him and leaned into him as he put his arm around her.

"You happy, Jeannie?"

"Oh, John, I can't tell you how happy I am. I never expected to find anyone as wonderful as you. You just fill me up."

John kissed Jeannie sweetly. "I love you, Jeannie. You're the best thing that could have ever happened to me." He then kissed her hard.

"Let's go to bed; I want to feel you in me," Jeannie whispered.

They turned off the lights and walked into the bedroom. John took off his shirt, then pulled Jeannie's T-shirt out of her jeans and lifted it above her head. He then began kissing her passionately as he unhooked her bra. She unzipped his jeans at the same time, then reached in and began caressing his dick which was getting harder by the second.

They fell back on the bed and kissed several more times before he leaned up and unzipped her jeans, slid his hand inside and began stoking her mound through her panties. Soon they both heated up and removed the rest of their clothes.

She was lying on the bed with her legs dangling off the bed as he slid down to the floor and onto his knees.

He looked up at her and smiled. "I love you, Jeannie!"

Then he buried his face in her flower, which was just one of John's terms of endearment for Jeannie's pleasure mound. He gave her the most extraordinary orgasm she had had in a while as she moaned and bucked, then cried, "Oh my God!"

He kept going until he had given her two more orgasms. She then pulled him up on the bed, slid down next to him and took his bulging penis into her mouth. She stroked his penis as she lifted her mouth in an up and down motion. He moaned loudly as he came. Once he had squirted the last drop, she reached under the bed for the towel they kept close by and gently wiped him off. She then tossed the towel and crawled back up to his side where they lay in each other's arms for several minutes.

"Did you ever think life could be this good?" he asked.

"No, never. I feel like I'm living in a wonderful dream, and I hope I never wake up."

They then pulled down the covers of the bed, climbed in and slept naked in each other's arms.

Sometime early in the morning, Jeannie woke up to John's hand stroking her vaginal area. He was positioned behind her as he slipped his penis between her legs and continued to stroke her with his manhood getting her wetter and wetter. She adjusted herself so she could experience the full effect of his penis rubbing on her clitoris. It didn't take long before she came in a half-asleep manner which was exquisitely delirious. She then adjusted herself enough for him to slip inside and they rocked back and forth with each other until he also had a delirious orgasm.

At 9 a.m. Jeannie finally woke up. John wasn't in bed, but she could smell something cooking so she got up. He had already cleaned up all the dishes from the evening before and was preparing waffles using a waffle iron one of his sisters had bought him as a Christmas present the prior year.

Jeannie sat down at the table covered only with a floral print silk bathrobe which was loosely tied, allowing her breast to peek out. She crossed her legs, allowing the silk robe to fall off her leg. The robe was so loosely tied that it was now exposing her inviting pubic area.

John looked at her and smiled. "I don't know whether I want to eat the waffle or you."

She giggled. "Well, why don't you sit down and I'll eat the waffle."

He sat. He had on a white terry cloth robe and was naked underneath. As he sat with the waffle sitting on a plate in front of him, she got up from her chair, straddled his lap facing away from him and sat down on the penis he was holding up so she could get comfortable. She was getting syrup all over her body as she moved up and down on him. He was rubbing the syrup over her breasts as he came.

He then said, "My turn."

She got up and faced him. He cleared the plate and then grabbed her by the waist and lifted her up and sat her up on the table. He then moved everything else to one side of the table and said, "Lean back so I can have my waffle."

She did as he squirted maple syrup over her breasts and onto her already sweet vulva. He began licking the syrup.

"Um," he exclaimed as he licked his way down to her mound and began licking her clitoris. "So sweet," he said as she bucked and came.

When they were finished, they looked around and realized the mess they now had to clean up. Syrup was everywhere. They just laughed, grabbed several towels and cleaned it up. Later they looked at each other and said simultaneously, "We need a shower."

That afternoon they sat quietly on the sofa watching TV as they told each other what a wonderful night and day they'd had.

Chapter 5

Sarah and her three daughters left the house early Sunday morning. Sarah hadn't been to church since discovering Emily's diary and wasn't the least bit interested in going. She had been reading and listening to the news about all the sexual abuse of children that had gone on in the Catholic Church for who knows how long and how it had devastated so many young children, especially boys who seemed to be the main target of predatory priests.

Knowing what her own husband had done to her Emily had so disgusted her that she just couldn't justify the hypocrisy that existed in the Catholic Church, especially given how it had turned its back on the crime and transferred pedophile priests from one parish to the next, thus creating more victims. Too, the memories of how every priest in each parish her family had ever belonged to had revered her husband left her feeling sick to her core.

It was hard enough for Sarah to come to terms with her own cowardly behavior while Joe was alive; but, the reality was, she *was* coming to terms with it. She was done hiding from her own spineless past. On the other hand, she just couldn't condone an entire institution that purported to be the right hand of God for routinely turning its back on the youngest of its flock.

Neither Lily nor Katie questioned why they no longer went to church. They were both content with not having to spend every Sunday morning in the church environment. Emily had quit going to church several months earlier, basically for the same reasons that Sarah had quit going.

Thus, instead of going to church that morning, Sarah and the girls had a delightful breakfast at one of their favorite breakfast cafes in East Providence. When they finished, they stopped by a Christmas tree lot run by a local Boy Scout troop and picked out the most perfect tree they could find.

Earlier Emily and Lily had measured from the floor to the ceiling in the TV room so they could have the Boy Scouts cut the end of the tree trunk for them. When they got home, Emily took a saw from the garage and sliced a small sliver off the end just to make sure the tree would soak up water.

Martha came over to watch the family put up their tree. She spent most of Saturday evening stringing popcorn and cranberries so Sarah and her girls could add a little bit of old-fashioned flavor to their tree. Katie and Lily had never heard of a popcorn and cranberry garland and were delighted and excited when Martha showed it to them. Lily even had to scold Katie for eating a couple of the popcorn kernels. In the end both Lily and Katie giggled at her antics.

All the girls were becoming closer to each other, and Martha knew full well why that was. Sarah was becoming a powerhouse of grit and iron. She was becoming the role model her three girls needed.

Once the tree sat securely in its stand, Emily brought out a pail with a mixture her roommate Celia had given her the recipe for. "It'll really keep the tree fresh, Emily. My family's used this recipe for several generations and we swear by it," Celia had said.

When Emily returned to the TV room with the pail, Lily asked her what was in it.

"Well it has a gallon of water, two cups of corn syrup, four teaspoons of chlorine bleach and four teaspoons of vinegar. I'm going to cover what's left and put it in the garage where it can stay cool. If you want the tree to stay healthy, you'll have to make sure the pan here *always* has the solution in it because if you let the pan get completely dry, the bottom of the trunk will seal itself and then the tree won't be able to drink and the needles will dry out and fall off. Do you think you girls can remember that over the next couple of weeks?"

Lily spoke with a take-charge tone of voice, "Yes, Emily, I can remember that. I'll put a sign on the refrigerator to remind us. Can you also write down the recipe so I can stick it behind the sign?"

Emily nodded as Katie exclaimed, "I'll watch the tree too, Emily!"

Then Emily expressed a concern. "Oh, one more thing, girls." She reached into her jeans pocket and pulled out a penny. "Celia's grandmother swears this is one of the most important ingredients for the tree. The copper in the penny will keep any fungus from growing in the water. So don't take it out of the pan. Remember too, this stuff is *poison* for *all creatures*, so keep it covered in the garage. We sure wouldn't want any little critter falling into it and dying. And for God's sake, make sure you two wash your hands after handling it, okay? I would hate for one of you to get sick from it."

"We promise," the two girls said in unison.

Sarah watched her three daughters as they doted over the tree and conversed about the care of their perfect tree. Martha was standing next to her; and, as if with automation, Sarah grabbed Martha's hand and squeezed it. Martha squeezed back, acknowledging her mutual delight for what they were both witnessing. Later Sarah expressed to Martha how incredibly proud she was at what seemed to be evolving under her roof.

"Sarah, it's a testament to how you have almost single-handedly raised your daughters and, more importantly, how *you* are changing. I know you don't realize how much you have changed since finding Emily's diary, but it is very evident and visible to me; and that change hasn't been lost on your girls. They are simply following your lead. It's as if all the influence Joe ever had has just dissolved into thin air, and what is left is the heart of the woman who has always put so much love into raising her family. You, Sarah. You are that woman and it's your kind, caring and loving influence you're witnessing."

Emily walked into the room as Martha expressed her sentiments. Both Martha and Sarah had their backs to the door so neither knew Emily was standing behind them.

"Thank you for saying that, Martha," Emily said through tears. "Mom, now do you believe me? Martha can see as clearly as me what a wonderful mom we have."

Startled, both Sarah and Martha turn to see the sweetest expression on Emily's face.

"Oh, Emily, watching you and your two sisters just fills my heart with so much love and pride. I think I am beginning to see a wonderful beginning to a horrible ending. I just wish this had happened a long time ago and that you had never had to suffer all you have suffered."

Emily walked over to Sarah, put her arms around her and hugged her tightly. "Oh, Mom, it is what it is. It happened and we can't wish any of that away. Besides, it's now just part of my history, and it's largely responsible for how I've turned out. The important thing here is that only good is now taking place in our family. We finally have the family I've dreamed of and hoped for but which had been sidetracked for a while, a relatively short while when put in perspective. I love you, Mom, with all my heart; and I love my two sisters and my big brother. I also love this lady too," she said as she pulled Martha into the circle. "We have only a wonderful future ahead of all of us. Now let's go put the lights on the tree. Lily and Katie are anxious to turn the finished tree on."

The three walked back into the TV room where Katie and Lily were examining the ornaments.

"Mommy, can we finish the tree? We want to turn the lights on. It'll be dark soon!" exclaimed Katie.

"That's what I came back to do. Let's get this tree finished so we can all admire the labor of our love!" Sarah hugged her three daughters. "Emily, can you help me string these lights?"

Sarah didn't want to fool around with tangled lights from the prior year so last year she threw all the lights out and bought new ones. She was glad she did. She bought the colored kind since Katie loved them more than the clear lights.

Emily stood on a ladder and put the final touch on the tree. She secured a beautiful fiber optic angel to the top of the tree. Sarah managed to get the angel at a bargain the year prior. Emily asked Lily to plug the angel in as she dropped the cord down. Lily did, then plugged in the entire tree. There was a unison "Ahh," as Emily climbed off the ladder.

Once Emily was on the floor, Lily grabbed her hand and they all stepped back as Katie ran over and flipped off the overhead light. Another unison "Ahh" was expressed.

They were all pooped from decorating. Sarah turned on some Christmas music, and Martha ran out to the garage. When she came back in, she uncovered a plate full of frosted Christmas cookies she had made a few days earlier. What a wonderful day Martha, Sarah and their three girls had.

****

That Friday evening Sarah cooked a special meal. She prepared a rib eye roast with mashed potatoes and string beans. She called it their Martha and Emily Christmas meal. As they sat down to eat, she said to the two youngest girls, "This is a special occasion so I'm going to let both of you have a small glass of wine with Martha, Emily and me."

The two girls got all excited that they were having a grown-up drink with dinner and tried to act sophisticated as they picked up their wine glass when toasts were made.

Emily wasn't yet aware, but Sarah knew she wouldn't see her daughter again until mid-January so she baked Emily her favorite, a tomato soup cake on which she placed eighteen candles. She brought the cake out once the table was cleared of the dinner dishes.

Emily expressed surprise. "But, Mom, I'm going to be back home on my birthday. You could have waited."

"Well, honey, I just wanted to make sure we got to celebrate your eighteenth birthday just in case your plane doesn't make it back till late."

Once Emily blew out her candles, Sarah exclaimed, "Now, Emily, we would like you to come on out to the Christmas tree. We want to give you your Christmas and birthday presents. You too, Martha, there's something from all of us under the tree."

All five females walked out to the TV room. Sitting around the tree was a set of five IZOD luggage pieces, red of course.

Emily's eyes got really wide. "Oh my god, Mom, I never expected this. This is wonderful!"

She and Sarah hugged. "I couldn't have my Emily take her first big trip out West with hand-me-down luggage."

Then the two girls handed Emily a big present, wrapped with birthday wrap. "This is from us, Emily, for your birthday."

Emily opened it up and found a brand-new laptop with a red skin cover.

Sarah chimed in, "Honey, it's all ready to go. I had the store load it up with all the windows software so you'd be ready to use it immediately. And one more thing."

She handed Emily another birthday present, which turned out to be a beautiful red carrying case for her laptop. Emily sat down on the sofa and cried.

"Emily, why are you crying?" Katie asked as she sat next to her sister and began rubbing her arm.

"Katie, I'm crying because I'm just so full of love and appreciation for my family. This is the family I've always dreamed of having."

Lily couldn't help herself. "What do you mean 'always dreamed of'? We're the same family you've been stuck with for years."

"Yea, I know, Lily. I just feel so thankful for what I have, that's all."

Then Lily poked Emily and said, "I know what you meant. Just kidding. This is your new and improved family you've been stuck with for years."

Sarah sat down next to Emily and hugged her daughter. "Emily, we love you so much, and I am so grateful you're my daughter and Lily and Katie's sister."

"Oh, Mom," Emily cried holding her.

Although she didn't yet understand Lily's comment, Katie chimed in, "Yea, Emily. We're new and improved," after which everyone laughed.

Martha sat over in the La-Z-Boy, crying her eyes out at this spectacle. She thought of how fragile this family had been only a few short weeks ago. She couldn't help but thank God for being given the gift of participating in such a wonderful experience as she witnessed Emily and Sarah heal and the entire family grow emotionally. "Okay, let's go cut that cake," said Martha as she blew her nose.

Sarah exclaimed, "Not yet! Girls ..."

That's all Lily and Katie needed. They grabbed a huge package and laid it in Martha's lap.

"What's this?" Martha looked surprised as she opened it to find a new pair of slacks, a yellow pullover sweater and a beautiful multi-colored scarf.

"We want you to look like the special lady you are!" Katie expressed what Sarah coached her to say.

Before she could say a word, Emily gave her a small gift. Martha opened it to find a beautiful yellow-banded watch with the time set three hours ahead to San Francisco time.

"We don't want you to be late for your plane," said Lily who was also coached.

They all hugged. "Now let's go eat some sugar!" exclaimed Martha who was very teary-eyed.

Later, just before Sarah and Emily turned in, Sarah knocked on Emily's bedroom door.

She walked in, holding a Victoria's Secret bag. "Emily, I got you a couple more items for your birthday but didn't want to show them to you in front of the girls. I certainly don't want to signal to them that they are getting the green light for anything. But this is a little something for you to wear when you see Sean."

Emily opened the bag and pulled out a really pretty red teddy with a plunging front and red lace all around the edges. She also pulled out a beautiful red with white-trimmed satin floor-length robe. One more item was in the bottom of the bag. It was a bottle of Chanel No. 5 cologne.

"Holy cow, Mom. I can't believe you bought this stuff for me. What on earth is happening to you? I love it and I know Sean will too!"

"Oh, I don't know, honey. I feel as if I've been a prude long enough. I think it's very sexy. I must confess I even bought something for myself. Who knows? Maybe one day I'll have a chance to wear it. Martha and I have joined Weight Watchers and a gym as well. I think you're going to start seeing a much different acting and looking mom in the future. I've come to realize that I have a lot of years in front of me, and I want to have some of the wonderful experiences you seem to be enjoying!"

Emily hugged her mom. "This is really strange, Mom, but I think I could get used to this for you. Thanks so much for everything. And something tells me you'll get to enjoy a lot of wonderful experiences, plus get to wear your sexy thing too."

Sarah laughed, "Who knows, sweetie? Who knows?" Then, as she stroked Emily's face, she said, "Well, I'm going to go to bed now. You have to get up early and do some packing, so I'll see you in the morning."

"Night, Mom. I love you a lot!"

"Love you too, Emily."

They hugged once more as Sarah left her room, shutting the door behind her.

Emily was in such a state of shock and surprise that she looked at her watch to see it was eleven p.m. She called Sean since it was only 8 p.m. out there.

Sean answered immediately. "Hi, baby!"

"Hey, Seanie. I hope I can sleep tonight. I'm so excited about tomorrow. I just had to tell you about my incredibly weird but wonderful day,"

They talked for about an hour when Emily began to drift off.

"Goodnight, Em," he said as he realized she was about to fall to sleep.

"See you tomorrow, Sean," she barely mumbled. She drifted off with her hand on her phone as it tumbled from her ear to her pillow.

****

The following morning the house was bustling while Sarah fixed a hot breakfast for both Martha and Sarah. Beth and Bill would pick them up around 8:30. Their flight wasn't until 1 p.m., but it was about a two-hour drive to Logan Airport.

Both Beth and Bill had been listening to how important it was to get to the airport in plenty of time since airport security had been stepped up since 9/11 the previous year.

Emily got up around 6 a.m. She showered and packed. As usual, she knew she probably packed way too much; but at least she would have choices, she told herself. She walked out into the kitchen around 7:45 a.m. However, before she did, she rolled her first bag out of her bedroom through the TV room and sat it by the door. Katie and Lily were in the TV room watching television so they both jumped up and helped Emily roll the other two pieces to the door as well. They then all went out to the kitchen when Martha walked in with her two bags. She was wearing her new outfit Sarah and the girls had given her for Christmas.

"Wow, you look amazing!" Lily exclaimed as Martha entered the kitchen.

"Why thank you, Lily. I just love my outfit and it's very comfy."

Sarah kissed Martha on the cheek and told her to sit down as she placed two plates with eggs and bacon on the table and asked Lily and Katie what they'd like to eat. They also wanted eggs and bacon so Sarah got busy preparing breakfast for the two girls plus herself.

Emily had taken a side trip to the bathroom. When she walked back into the kitchen, Sarah said, "You look pretty, Emily. Why don't you sit and eat so you'll be ready to go at 8:30?"

Martha and Emily clinked orange juice glasses as Emily exclaimed, "Martha, you look so sophisticated with the scarf and yellow sweater!"

Once the two women were seated, Sarah asked Lily to watch the stove while she ran into the TV room. Sarah found Emily's purse and slipped an envelope into it. In the envelope was $1000 worth of traveler's checks. She wanted to make sure Emily had enough money to spend while she was gone. She had been saving $100 every other week for over a year for just such an occasion. Sarah came back into the kitchen and took over for Lily. When all the other breakfasts were ready, the three sat down with Martha and Emily. They all joined hands and wished each other a very Merry Christmas and a safe trip for Emily and Martha.

There was lots of chatter when at 8:25 a.m., they heard a car pull into the driveway.

Martha smiled. "Well, looks like we're ready to go, Emily!"

Katie had already run out to let Beth and Bill in.

As Beth entered the kitchen, Sarah asked, "Can I get you two something to take with you?"

"No, thanks, Sarah," replied Beth. "We stopped by McDonalds and got something to eat and still have two big cups of coffee in the car. We probably ought to get going just in case there's traffic in Boston. With the holiday travel and the extra security at the airport, it's probably a good idea not to dillydally."

Everyone hugged as Bill and the two girls loaded up the car.

When Bill came in, he was laughing. "Emily, I had to put one of your bags in the back seat."

"I'm not surprised," Emily laughed as well. "I've always been known for packing too much, and Mom didn't help by buying me all new luggage."

As they were all saying goodbye, Sarah and Emily kissed and hugged, "Thanks, Mom for everything. I love you so much. And, Mom, please promise me if you start having a hard time over the next two weeks, you'll call me so we can talk. Do you promise me, Mom?"

"I promise, Emily. Although Gladys has offered her shoulder, if it gets too rough for me, I'll call you first. I love you, sweetie. You have a wonderful time with Sean." Sarah had tears in her eyes. "I'll miss you, Emily."

"I'll miss you too, Mom." Emily hugged her mom one last time, then headed out the door.

Bill, Beth and Martha were already in the car. Lily and Katie both hugged their sister; then the girls and Sarah waved goodbye.

Chapter 6

"How's your mom doing, Emily?" asked Beth as Bill drove up the hill to the main highway.

"She's doing really well, Beth. Don't you think, Martha?"

Martha grinned from ear-to-ear. "Yes, she is. I've been truly amazed. I honestly think in the back of her mind, Sarah has been waiting for a very long time for someone or something to come let her out of the dungeon Joe built around her. She's simply blossoming."

"Yea, and you've been one of the people who's come along and helped to destroy that dungeon!" Emily hugged Martha.

They had a pleasant ride to the airport and actually got there in plenty of time. Emily was extremely excited about flying. It was her first time on a plane, and Beth made sure she purchased a prime window seat for her.

As they boarded the big jumbo jet, they found their seats. Emily and Martha were seated together, and Beth and Bill were seated directly across the aisle from them in the first two seats of the middle section.

With delight Beth watched Emily as the plane leveled out and she got her first bird's-eye view of Boston and the surrounding area. She got tickled watching Emily's expressions as she nudged Bill a few times so he could look. He smiled approvingly and squeezed Beth's hand.

About fifteen minutes later, Beth and Bill both fell asleep. Martha also dosed off, but Emily was wide awake for the entire five-hour flight. She told everyone later how amazingly beautiful this country was from the air. She described the huge circles of green as the plane passed over the farmland before it flew over the Rockies.

The mountains. They took her breath away.

"Then just as I thought I had seen the most beautiful landscape, everything changed and became something else equally beautiful. I had no idea this country was so varied and so, so beautiful!" exclaimed Emily once the plane had landed.

Bill had the ladies wait just inside baggage claim while he went to get their rental car. Approximately a half-hour later, he picked them up. Just as Emily settled into her seat in the car, her phone rang. It was Sean. "Sean, we're here!" She sounded so excited. "Oh my god, I can't believe it either."

After they talked for a few minutes, Sean asked to speak to Beth. Beth told him approximately what time to expect them. Beth handed the phone back to Emily so she could say goodbye.

"I love you so much, Sean!" All three smiled lovingly as they listened to Emily.

"I love you too, baby. I'm waiting," said Sean.

As Emily put the phone back into her purse, she saw the white envelope for the first time. She took it out. Inside was the most loving handwritten note from Sarah which was wrapped around the traveler's checks.

Emily began to cry as Beth asked, "What's the matter, Emily?"

"I just can't believe how much my mom has done for me. She dropped $1,000 into my purse this morning. I just can't believe how much my life has changed in only a few weeks."

Martha put her arm around Emily and said, "Emily, you have no idea how proud and grateful your mom is for having you as her daughter."

Beth exclaimed, "We're all proud and grateful, Emily. I couldn't ask for a more loving partner for my precious little boy. Please don't tell Sean I called him little."

They all laughed at Beth's request.

****

As the rental car turned the corner into Sean's dorm parking lot, Emily felt as if her heart leapt out of her body.

"Oh, my god, there he is!"

Sean was pacing back and forth looking at his wrist watch every few seconds. As Bill pulled the car into the parking space, Sean had Emily's door open before Bill could put the car in park. She jumped out, and they gave each other an exquisite hug and then kissed and kissed and kissed. Beth had already gotten out and was watching with her heart full of love.

Sean momentarily let go of Emily and hugged both his mom and grandmother. He shook Bill's hand and then grabbed Emily again for more hugs and kisses.

"This is a dream come true," he whispered in Emily's ear.

Bill looked at his watch and said, "Let's see, it's 7 p.m. Eastern time. That makes it 4 p.m. here, right, Sean?"

"Yep, a little after 4."

"Okay. Why don't we take Emily's bags up to your room, and we'll go to the hotel and check in. That should put us back here around 6, just in time for dinner. How does that sound to everyone?"

"Sounds great," said Sean as he slid his hand down Emily's back and hooked his thumb in the waist band of her jeans.

Emily felt a huge rush from Sean's gesture. He looked at her and saw she was flushed which caused him to grin and wiggle his thumb.

With Emily's bags secure in Sean's room, Beth kissed Sean and hugged Emily. "See you two in a few hours."

As Sean shut the door and heard the footsteps fade down the hall, he turned around and extended his arms. "Come here, my little Irish Colleen!"

She ran over to him and leapt as she wrapped her legs around him. He carried her over to his bed and they lay down.

He brushed a strand of red hair from the corner of her mouth. "Let's just lie here a minute. I just want to fill my lungs with the smell of you. I can't believe this is actually happening and I'm not just dreaming. I've missed you so, so much, Em."

"Oh, Sean, I've missed you!" With a tear in her eye, she pointed to her heart. "I love you more than life itself."

They lay there stroking each other all over as they kissed.

"I've missed your lips, baby!"

The kissing heated up fast. "Make love to me, Sean, so I know I'm really here with you."

They both stood. He began pulling her red T-shirt with white owls on it out of her jeans as he said, "I've always loved this shirt on you." He lifted it up over her head and said, "God, I've missed this red bra!"

He then reached around and unhooked it. He looked at her beautiful breasts and cupped them. "These are the breasts I remember."

She then lifted off his shirt and pressed her body to his. "You feel so warm. I love you, Sean."

They then helped each other with their jeans and underwear. They stood naked as they soaked in each other's image. They began kissing again, and Emily could feel Sean getting hard as she reached down and caressed his manhood.

"I've missed this little guy," to which Sean said in a tiny, high-pitched voice, "Who, me?"

They laughed and fell onto the bed and became ravenous with their kisses. Then Sean looked at Emily's beautiful face. "Can I say hello to my favorite honey pot?"

She smiled, anticipating imminent delight.

He slid down and buried his face between her legs. His tongue flitted over her sweet button like a bee over a honeysuckle flower. His hand was on her stomach as he felt her first tremor. He kept going, feeling the warmth in his groin from being able to give his beloved such exquisite pleasure. She buckled two more times just as he opened his eyes and watched her toes curl under.

As Emily's body released her last convulsion, she tugged on his arm, indicating that she wanted him to come up and enter her.

He ran his tongue up her stomach and kissed her breasts as he traveled back up her perfect body. When he reached her mouth, he bit her lip ever so gently and then stuck his tongue in to meet her lovely, warm, delicious tongue.

He lifted her body and turned them over. He wanted her sitting on top of him.

She towered over him, sliding up and down as he guided her hips in a grinding motion. He opened his eyes and said, "You're so beautiful."

As he was about to come, he pulled her down to him and kissed her in a most passionate manner. He finally came in such a tremendous buck that the bed made a creaking sound. His body shuddered several times, and then she collapsed on his body.

"Oh, Emily, I know we just went to heaven!" he whispered.

They fell asleep and woke to a tapping on the door.

"Oh, my god!" Emily exclaimed.

They both jumped up and were scrambling for their cloths. She tried to fix her hair as they both went to the door and opened it. Bill and Beth were standing there.

"You two ready to go eat?" asked Bill.

"Yes," they both responded.

As they were about to walk out the door, Beth snickered, "Emily, you may want to turn your shirt right-side out before we go."

Emily looked down at her shirt and blurted, "Oh shit!"

Sean slipped out, she closed the door, turned her shirt right-side out and then reopened the door. They all giggled all the way down to the car.

As they got in, Martha asked, "What's so funny?"

Beth just laughed and said, "You would have had to have been there," as they all laughed again.

Emily was sitting next to Martha so she whispered in her ear, "My top was turned inside-out."

Martha giggled.

Chapter 7

On Christmas morning Sean and Emily woke about 6 a.m. They both promised each other they wouldn't buy a present for one another. Instead, they wanted to begin their own tradition of giving each other a special card.

Prior to Sean leaving for college, he told Emily about the same ritual his mom and dad had prior to his father's death. Sean recalled how wonderful it was to have witnessed the many special occasions during which his parents would exchange specially selected cards for each other. Consequently, Sean was keenly aware of his parents' special love for one another. As he described his parents' tradition to Emily she was so touched by the tenderness of the ceremony that she expressed she would like to start a similar tradition.

It was 7 a.m. when they finally got up. The dorm was totally empty. Naked, they walked down the hall hand in hand to the bathroom where they showered together. Once back in his room, they dried each other off, then sat on his sofa. They handed each other their card. Sean asked Emily to read hers first.

It was lovingly addressed to "My Sweet Em." As she read the card out loud, tears rolled down her cheeks. Then she read Sean's written words, "To Em, the love of my life. I was truly blessed the day I saw you sitting on the slant tree. My heart flew out to you that day, and it's never returned. It's yours forever and ever. All my love, Sean."

She put the card down, and they giggled as they kissed each other.

"Now it's your turn," she said.

Sean opened his card which was addressed to "My Seanie." He read the card, then read Emily's written words, "To my Sean. My life came alive the day I met you. I turned to see the sweetest face I'd ever seen looking up at me. I think I knew from that moment that I loved you, and my love has grown so much to where I feel as if my heart will burst right out of my chest. I will love you forever and ever, until the end of time. Love, your Em."

They sat on the sofa tucked into each other and whispered how much they've missed each other and how they would cherish each other every day of their lives.

****

At 10 a.m. Emily called home and Katie answered, "Merry Christmas, Katie!"

"Emily, I've been waiting all morning for you to call. Are you having a nice Christmas with Sean?"

"Yes, wonderful. How was your Christmas?"

"Really fun. I got lots of great stuff. Mom even got Lily and me a puppy."

"I think I can hear the puppy in the background. Is it a boy or a girl? What are you going to name it?"

"It's an all-white girl poodle. We haven't named her yet. Mom's going to help us choose a name for her, but she's so cute and tiny! Mom said she fits in a teacup!"

"Awe, Katie, that's wonderful. Is Mom there?"

"Yea, but wait a minute; Lily wants to talk to you."

Lily took the phone, laughed and said as she rolled her eyes at Katie, "Emily, she's a teacup poodle. She doesn't fit in a teacup."

Emily chuckled. "I figured that's what Katie meant."

Emily talked to Lily a little longer. She learned that Kevin had bought Lily a Christmas present which Lily was thrilled about. Then Lily wished Emily a Merry Christmas and handed the phone to her mom.

"Hi, Mom. Merry Christmas! How are you holding up?" Emily asked.

"Merry Christmas, sweetie. I'm doing fine. My last session with Dr. Wells went extremely well, and the medication is really helping. How was your Christmas morning with Sean?"

"Oh, Mom, I just can't thank Beth and Bill enough for doing this for us...and...Mom, I'm still speechless about how generous you've been with me. I found the traveler's checks. Are you sure you can afford that?"

"Well, honey, I can't think of a more deserving person than you. I love you so much Emily, and I know everything's going to work out. I really do. Dr. Wells thinks I'm making lots of progress!"

Emily and Sarah talked a little while longer before hanging up.

At 11 a.m. Sean's phone rang; it was Beth. "Hi, sweetie, Merry Christmas! Have you two had a nice morning?"

"Merry Christmas, Mom. Our morning was perfect, but I think we're getting hungry and thinking about getting something to eat."

"Well, that's why I'm calling. We thought we'd all go out for a nice Christmas morning brunch. How does that sound?"

"Yea, we'd love that," he answered as he motioned to Emily that she was asking them to go eat.

Emily vigorously nodded her head.

"Okay. Why don't we pick you two up in about half an hour? We'll meet you down in the parking lot. Okay, sweetie?"

"Perfect, Mom. We'll see you in half an hour."

Emily and Sean kissed several more times, then got ready to leave.

She was sitting at his desk putting on her eye makeup when she glanced to the right and saw the painting she had painted for Sean when she turned fifteen. It was the one with them as children sitting on the slant tree. Sean saw her looking at it, walked over, bent down, moved her hair to one side and kissed her on the back of her neck.

"God, Sean, I didn't know you still had that!" Emily exclaimed.

"Are you kidding? It's one of the possessions I have that keeps me connected to you. If I'm ever feeling like crap, I can look at that painting, crawl into it mentally and my mood will change. I love you so much, Emily," he said tenderly as he kissed her neck again.

She stood and put her arms around him. "Sean, I can't even begin to tell you how much I love you." They kissed; then she giggled. "I better get moving. I don't want a repeat of yesterday with your mom now pointing to my left eye and telling me I forgot to finish applying makeup to it."

They arrived downstairs in twenty-five minutes and were sitting on the curb when Bill, Beth and Martha pulled up. After everyone greeted each other and "Merry Christmas" was passed around, Sean asked, "Where were you thinking of going for brunch, Mom?"

Beth responded, "Well, the concierge at our hotel mentioned that the Steinhart Hotel over by Nob Hill has a wonderful brunch. How does that sound?"

"Great. I've never been there, but that's not saying very much."

They arrived and the brunch was splendid. Bill ordered a bottle of Champagne to celebrate the day. Martha was very quiet. She was just looking all around.

"Are you having fun, Martha?" asked Emily as she hugged her.

"Oh, Emily, I've never been this far west. I'm just in awe of this beautiful city. Everything is done so tastefully. I'm having a wonderful time." Martha hugged Emily back.

They all toasted the day. Then Beth gave Sean and Emily an envelope, and Beth and Bill simultaneously exclaimed, "Merry Christmas, you two!"

Sean and Emily opened the envelope, took out a piece of paper and looked at each other with their mouths wide open, "Oh my god, Mom!"

Emily got up, walked over to Beth and hugged her. "This is amazing. I never expected anything so generous. I mean, just paying to fly me out here was out of this world; but this ... Thanks so much!" Emily hugged Beth again and then hugged Bill.

Then as Sean and Emily were looking around, Martha handed them an envelope of her own. Inside was $1,000 in traveler's checks.

"Holy crap, Grandma," Sean hugged Martha; and Emily just hugged her very hard, "Martha, this is ...I can't even tell you."

"I think you two are going to live in style for nearly a month," said Martha.

They finished their brunch; and before leaving, they all looked around.

"This is so fancy, Mom. How did you come up with this?"

Bill answered, "Your mom spent a lot of time researching. She wanted you two to be in one of the hot spots of San Francisco."

The five adults had a wonderful Christmas seeing all the sights in San Francisco; and that evening they finished the day with dinner at PPQ Dungeness Island, one of the prime Dungeness crab restaurants in the Bay area.

On the way back to the dorm, Emily exclaimed, "Oh my god, I haven't eaten that much in ages."

Once back at the dorm, they all kissed and wished each other a very "Merry Christmas."

Beth said, "I think we're all going to sleep in a little bit tomorrow; but if you kids are up to it, we thought we'd take in some of the sights tomorrow and then end the evening at Fisherman's Wharf."

Both Sean and Emily agreed that sounded like a wonderful idea.

By Friday, December 27th, everyone had had such a wonderful time, seeing all the sights and eating at so many different delectable restaurants, that when it was time to go out to eat for her birthday, Emily decided to eat light all day.

****

During the day Beth, Bill and Martha helped the couple set up house at the Steinhart Hotel. Emily had saved her red teddy and bathrobe for that evening, which was another reason she decided to eat light that day. She wanted to be able to fit into the teddy without hanging out all over the place.

The room Emily and Sean were in had a beautiful view of the area. As they retired for the day, they decided to go out on the small balcony in order to enjoy the evening. The sky was clear and the city lights were beautiful.

Emily said to Sean, "I think I'm going to go put something else on. My jeans are killing me. I can't eat like this the rest of the month. I'll have to rent a wheelbarrow when I leave so I can be wheeled onto the plane."

Sean laughed. "Emily, you are way too sensitive about putting on weight. You're perfect."

"Well, I've seen what the inherited genes can do to family members, and I've just got to watch myself." She walked over to Sean and kissed him. "I'll be back in a minute."

To her amazement she hadn't put much weight on because the teddy looked pretty darned good on her. She put on her robe and a little dab of Chanel No. 5 behind each ear and walked back out to the balcony.

Sean was sitting in a chair with a drink in his hand. He made Emily's favorite drink as well, Grey Goose vodka and ruby red grapefruit juice in a tall glass.

She sat down as he looked at her. "Wow, when did you get that?"

"I've been saving it. Actually Mom got it for me. She is just blowing me away, Sean. She's like a little girl who's been kept out of the candy store for far too long. She bought something for herself too. I don't know what it is, but I think she's getting excited thinking about when she might be able to wear it."

"Come here and let me look at you," said Sean.

Emily walked over to the balcony and turned toward Sean. "You look ravishing, baby. What's under that sexy robe?"

She looked at him and asked, "Do you want to see now or later?"

Sean felt the warmth of his groin, so he said, "I want to see now. Please?"

Emily slowly untied the robe and opened it slightly. The moon was behind her and that, plus the soft glow from their room, illuminated her body.

"God, Emily, quit teasing me. Take it off. I'm dying here!" he said as he rubbed his groin.

She opened the robe all the way and dropped it to the floor.

"Fuck me. You are so beautiful. Red is your color, Em! Come sit on my lap."

She walked over to him and sat on his lap as he put his hand inside to feel her breast. "Your nipple is hard as a rock. Why's that?" he asked in a teasing manner.

"Oh I don't know. Maybe because the man I crave has his hand on my boob," she said as she wiggled on his lap. Then she said, "My boob is happy but my pussy is lonely, Seanie. It needs attention."

He kissed her as he slid his hand down to the edge of the teddy and slipped it inside. "Why, Emily, you're very wet. What's going on here?"

"I don't know. Is it normal to be so wet?"

"Hmm. I'm not sure, let me feel a little more. Oooo, you are sopping inside your hole. Do you think it needs some attention too?"

"I think it wants to sit on something big and hard." She spoke in a very sultry manner. "Do you know where I can find something like that?"

"I think I do. Lift up a minute and let me see if I can figure this out?"

She didn't lift up. Instead she turned to face away from him and leaned forward so her butt was lifted just enough to cause Sean to get even more horny.

He unzipped his jeans. "Is this what you were looking for?"

She leaned back and looked over her shoulder. "Oooo, that's exactly what I was looking for. Where did you find it?"

"It was tucked down in the chair. What are you going to do with it?"

She lifted up, moved the bottom of her teddy to one side and slid down on his pole. Then she wiggled a few times. "Oooo, that feels so naughty. How about you? Can you feel anything?"

He reached around and slid both hands inside her teddy as he caressed her breasts. "Umm. I feel a little, but you need to wiggle around a little more."

She slid up and down. "Like this?"

"Oh, yea. That's perfect." He was holding her waist as she pounded him. He guided her to slide faster. Then a guttural sound emanated from his mouth as he pulled her back and kissed her with extreme passion.

After a few minutes, he slid one arm under her rump and leg and got up.

As he carried her, she asked, "Where are you taking me, you naughty man?"

"Oh, I don't know. Where do you want me to take you?"

"Put me on the bed, p-l-e-a-s-e."

He laid her on the bed and said, "Now, you know you've been a very naughty girl tonight," to which she demurely asked, "I have? What are you going to do?"

"I think you need to be spanked."

"Oh, you wouldn't do that, would you?"

"Well, let's see."

He sat on the bed, put her across his knees, took her teddy off and started spanking her very lightly. She squealed like it hurt and laughed all at once. Then he slid his hand between her legs.

"What are you going to do now?"

"Hmm. I'm exploring this crevasse I just discovered. I need to see if there's any buried treasure here. Oooo. I think I found something sweet and hard," as his finger found her clitoris.

She started wiggling. Then he said, "It feels like a button to a secret compartment. Maybe if I roll it around a little, the compartment will open up. What do you think?"

"I think it just might, you naughty little boy. You're always playing with buttons now, aren't you?"

"Do you want me to stop?" he asked as he stopped.

She continued to wiggle. Then he asked, "Why are you wiggling?"

"It's the button. I think it's vibrating because you almost broke the code. Hurry up and see if you can unlock the code," she begged. So he began massaging again.

She was wiggling so much that he knew she was about to come. As she did, she yelled, "Oh my god!"

Just as she came, he teased, "Let me explore that button with something else. I think the combination is set for three stages."

He laid her on the bed, got on the floor and buried his head between her legs. He gave her two more orgasms, each better than the one previous. When he was done, he was hard again.

He stood up and exclaimed, "Look what happened!"

Emily giggled. "Oh, my friend is back!"

He mounted her and came again.

Later they sat on the sofa laughing at how silly they had become but also excited at how enjoyable their little game had been.

****

This is how their next two weeks progressed. They went on beautiful drives up the coastal highway one day and back down toward San Diego the next. Emily had never seen such beauty.

Once they parked along the side of the highway where they could walk down to the beach area. When down there, they found a secluded spot. No one was around; and the traffic on the highway was sparse that day, so they decided to take their clothes off and go for a swim.

When they got back to their blanket, they made love to the sound of the surf and the conversation of three lazy seals sunning themselves on one of the rocks that jutted out of the surf close to shore. They were having such a wonderful time they forgot that Sunday the 13th was only four days away.

****

On Thursday, January 10th, Emily accompanied Sean to the

campus. He wanted to register for the next semester.

He was in line for one of his classes when a young woman walked over. "Hey, Showaun!" she said with a sultry Texan drawl.

He turned to see Anne Hightower. "Oh, hey, Anne. How was your Christmas?"

She was now standing right next to him, ignoring Emily's presence and touching his arm in a familiar manner, or so Emily thought. "Oh, it was wonderful. My parents and I flew over to Paris for four days. What a beautiful city."

Then she cocked her head, "What did you do for Christmas, Showaun?"

"I stayed here. Anne, this is my girlfriend, Emily Callaway. Emily, this is Anne Hightower."

Emily wanted to choke this girl for being so blonde, so beautiful and so disgustingly familiar with her boyfriend; but she restrained herself and extended her hand. They shook hands, and Emily immediately smirked to herself at how limp Anne's handshake was. Emily felt as if she was shaking a dead fish. After all, Emily knew how to shake a hand. Firmly!

Both girls lied to each other and simultaneously spoke the obligatory, "It's nice to meet you." However, again Anne immediately treated Emily as if she were invisible. She even positioned herself between Emily and Sean with her back to Emily and asked Sean what classes he was taking that semester.

Then she blatantly and overtly flirted with Sean as she hugged him and said, "See you in a few weeks, handsome. Maybe we can have lunch one day before classes start."

Emily was livid by the time this blonde bitch with the long legs walked away. To make matters worse, Anne turned around as she walked away, put one finger in her mouth and gave Sean a little sexy wave with her other hand.

Emily was completely silent for the next hour while Sean was busy registering. When he was finished, he looked at his watch, then at Emily. "Hey, Em, do you want to go back to the hotel or go get something to eat now?"

She grumbled, "I don't care."

So Sean said, "I'm hungry. Let's go get something to eat."

Still silent they walked off campus to a sandwich shop. There

Sean spotted a few additional students he knew, two females and one guy, and introduced Emily. They were all very nice so she calmed down a little. They ate and walked back to the hotel. Sean was still innocently oblivious to Emily's changed mood.

Instead, he assumed she was tired. "Hey, sweetie, do you want to lie down for a while?"

But she acted cold, said "no," got a diet soda from the small refrigerator and went out to the balcony. Still unaware of what was taking place, Sean did the same. As he sat in the chair next to her, he asked what she wanted to do that night. She didn't even answer him. He asked again and got the same silent treatment.

He then put his soda down on the small table between their chairs, moved forward on his chair, turned and looked at her. "Are you okay?" But she wouldn't even look at him. "What's the matter? Did I do something wrong?"

Finally, she got up, walked into the room and gruffly said, "I'm fine," as she turned on the TV.

He sat on the balcony a few more minutes, going over the events of the last few hours in his head but still not able to connect *any* of the dots.

He subsequently walked into the room and squatted down next to her chair. "Em, I have a bad feeling I'm in trouble, and I don't even know what for. If I knew, maybe I could defend myself; but unless you talk to me, I can't explain or even make up for what I evidently did wrong."

Emily started crying, leaving Sean even more confused. He thought, *What the hell is going on? This is crazy!* Then he demanded, "Emily, what's wrong?"

She was silent for what seemed like an excruciatingly long time. Then she mumbled, "Do you like Anne Hightower?"

Sean was relieved as he assumed he was off the hook. He snickered. "Who? Anne Hightower? Hell no. Why would you ask that?"

Emily yelled, "Because it was pretty evident that she has the hots for you, Showaun!"

"Emily, she doesn't have the hots for me. Damn, she's way out of my league, and I wouldn't even want to be in her league. She's just a rich daddy's girl who happens to be majoring in neuroscience as well, so, yea, we have a number of classes together; but, Em, you're my girl. Anne Hightower can't hold a candle to you, and that's the God's honest truth."

Emily looked forlorn. "Are you sure? 'Cuz she's really pretty and, Sean, she acts like she really likes you. She was very blatant, and she also acted like I wasn't even there. And why did she act so familiar, touching your arm and then hugging you?"

"Touching my arm and hugging me? Emily, are you sure because I don't even remember that? God, Em. I don't know what to tell you. I don't like Anne Hightower. What can I say to convince you? She's just a rich bitch who is used to getting what she wants."

He paused for a few seconds, then scratched his head. "Now that I think of it, she touches a lot of guys' arms and hugs them as well. I've never thought about it before now, but I guess that explains why so many of our female classmates act like they hate her too."

He then gently touched Emily's hand. "God, Em, guys just aren't that perceptive or that aware of shit like that!"

He was now convinced he had made a good argument for himself.

But she startled him back to reality. "She gets what she wants and she wants you, Sean!"

Stunned, he stood up. "Emily, please stop. Just stop. Everything I say seems to dig the hole deeper for me, and I don't know how to climb out of it." He was feeling so lost that he thought, *God, she can get so out of control and totally paranoid sometimes.*

He then raised his voice and was emphatic, "I DON'T LIKE ANNE HIGHTOWER, and that's the fucking truth! I like Emily Callaway. She's the love of my life, and that's all there is to it!"

She sounded pitiful. "Are you sure?"

He sat in the chair opposite her. "God, Em, come here, please. We only have a couple of days left; and I don't want to spend them arguing about some snooty, full of herself bitch. I want to spend my time with you, all of you. Come here, *please?*"

She finally stood. He grabbed her hand and gently pulled her toward him. As she sat in his lap, she began to cry again. She finally buried her head against his chest.

He gently stroked her hair. "Emily Callaway. It's you I love. I always have and always will. We have at least three more years of school away from each other. We've got to trust each other's love that it is true and will last. I don't want to lose you, Em. I love you

71

with all my heart. Can you believe me?"

She stopped crying and choked on her words, "Yes. I believe you. Just please stay away from that skank. She's bad news, Sean. I don't want to have to come back out here and murder her!"

He began to laugh with relief. "You'd do that?"

She was also slightly laughing. "No, but I might kill you!"

"That's more like it. God, Em. I can't even imagine my life without you in it. I'd be lost!" He kissed her.

"Really?"

"Yes, really!" He kissed her again.

****

By Saturday evening Anne Hightower was a distant bad memory. Emily and Sean had a glorious last two days together. By Saturday evening they were lamenting that the next day Emily was scheduled to fly home and they wouldn't see each other again until the first part of June.

"Unless," Emily looked excited. "How much of that $1,000 do we still have from what Martha gave us?"

They counted it and found they still had a little over $500. For two weeks they ate like two college students. No fancy restaurants, but a lot of sandwiches and pizza.

"And I've got the entire $1,000 from the money Mom gave me. A round-trip plane ticket couldn't be that much more!"

Sean looked slightly lost. "What did you have in mind, Em?"

"Why don't you fly home for spring break? You could stay with your grandma, and that way it wouldn't be so painful waiting until June, which is six months from now!"

"That sounds like a great idea. Do you think your mom will mind if we spend that $1,000 on a plane ticket?"

"Shoot, no. Mom loves you, Sean. She will be thrilled we would want to spend it that way. I feel certain of that."

"Okay, I'm going to give the leftover money to you for safekeeping. I'll let you schedule my plane and; in the meantime, I'll let my mom know what we're doing."

They made beautiful love that last night and shed an ocean of tears when they had to part as Emily boarded her plane.

Chapter 8

As Emily walked down the aisle of the plane, she slipped on an ice cube and almost fell. She caught herself but caused a young blonde woman in an aisle seat in first class to spill her drink on herself. Emily was about to apologize to the woman; but the woman acted very rude and haughty, admonishing Emily for being an "ignorant klutz." She acted so poorly that Emily purposely refused to apologize. She just kept walking. The older fella behind the blonde woman gave Emily a look of empathy.

When Emily finally sat in her assigned seat, she leaned her head against the window and thought about Anne Hightower.

God, that bitch could be Anne Hightower's twin sister. I hate both of them! I am not an ignorant klutz, and I am just as good as that bitchtower!

But Emily wasn't convincing herself. So during the entire flight home, Emily allowed herself to get worked up psychologically about Anne and allowed her suspicions about Anne's intentions and Sean's vulnerability to run amuck.

Emily knew how hard she had been working through all her conscious triggers and pain. Nonetheless, she was becoming aware that there was so much more going on inside her. It was stuff she couldn't define; however, she recognized that it was causing her to think and behave irrationally. She was terribly scared of those undefined, yet hauntingly real feelings. She didn't know if she had always felt the way she had over the last several months; and, worse, she didn't know what to do about her fears and feelings.

What am I going to do? I know Sean got really impatient and angry at me about Anne. I know I was irrational, but it seemed so real. I've got to figure this thing out so I don't push him away.

But the more she thought about Anne, the more fearful and out of control she felt. She became convinced that Anne would take Sean away from her. By the time her plane landed in Providence, she was so worked up she was frantic.

Jeannie hadn't seen Emily for several weeks so she offered to pick Emily up, and Sarah gladly obliged.

Maribeth Shanley

It'll give the two girls time with each other, Sarah rationalized.

When Emily walked out on the sidewalk, Jeannie was parked close by. She waved, then ran over to help Emily with her bags. They hugged, but Jeannie immediately noticed Emily was agitated. Once in the car, Jeannie asked Emily why she seemed so off.

But Emily tried hard not to take any thunder away from Jeannie. "Oh, it can wait. Tell me about your Christmas, Jeannie. How're things going with John?"

"Em, life couldn't be better for me now. He is absolutely wonderful. Both Dad and Mom just love him. I can't wait for you to come back over because I've fixed the place up a little. It no longer looks like a man's pad. Now, Em, tell me what's going on. You did have a good time with Sean, didn't you?"

Emily told her she had a wonderful time; but then she told her about Anne Hightower and how she thought she had put her out of her mind until the incident with the blonde bitch on the plane.

"Well, what did Sean say about this Hightower bitch?"

"He said she was a spoiled daddy's girl and he wasn't at all attracted to her; but I could see what she was up to. After all, Sean is extraordinarily handsome and such a great male, any woman would want him; and I'm just afraid this one does. I feel so helpless being separated from him. Not that I want to control him because I don't. I just want to have a chance to fight for him. I'm scared I'm going to lose him to distance and time, and it's causing me to feel horrible."

"Awe, Emily, Sean loves you. He's not going to be stolen by someone like her. That's just crazy. You just need to trust him and trust yourself."

"You're probably right. I had forgotten about Anne Bitchtower until that woman in first class embarrassed me. I just can't stand arrogant people like that."

"Me neither! If I were there, I would have accidently on purpose hit her over her head with my purse or something and really given her something to cry about. 'Le'me at 'er …le'me at 'er!'" Jeannie sounded like the lion from Wizard of Oz.

They both laughed and Emily finally began to calm down.

Then Jeannie looked over at Emily, "Em, why don't you call Sean right now? That will pick your spirits way up!"

Sean immediately answered, "God, Em. I've been sitting here

74

with my phone in my hand waiting for you to call. Did you just land?"

"About a half-hour ago. Jeannie picked me up. What are you doing?"

"I just brought all my stuff back to my dorm room and am getting settled in. It's horribly lonely here. I miss my Emily. This is harder this time than it was in the fall."

"I know. God, Sean, do you think we can make it through three and a half more years?"

"We have to, Emily. You know, it seems like a long time looking forward; but it's not. It'll be over before we know it, sweetie. I love you so much and had such a wonderful time. I want my life to be filled with you and only you!"

"Me too, Sean. I can't imagine life without you."

They talked a little longer and then said goodnight.

As she hung up, Jeannie reached over and patted her hand. "See? You don't have to worry about Sean."

"You're right. God, Jeannie. I just hate being apart like this."

When Jeannie pulled into Emily's driveway, she told Emily that she would help her with her bags but needed to get back home shortly after that. John's shift was over at 6 p.m., and she wanted to be there when he got home.

"Listen, John has to work the day shift this coming Saturday. Why don't you and I get together? You can come by our place, and you and I will go have lunch and catch a movie or go shopping or do whatever we decide to do. How does that sound?"

"I'd like that. I need to register for my classes this week, and I'm going to try and get in to see Dr. Wells also. I feel I need to talk to her. I'm not scheduled to see her until the next week, so I'm hoping she can fit me in. But regarding Saturday, let's plan on it. I've missed you, and I know we have a lot of catching up to do. Plus, I'd like to see what you've done to your place."

As the two women got out of the car and went around to the trunk, Jeannie looked at Emily and hugged her. "You look like you need a hug, kiddo."

Emily began to cry a little. "I do need a hug. I think I need a lot of hugs. I don't know what's happening to me, and I'm scared."

Jeannie looked perplexed. "Of what?"

"Of me, of the world, of losing Sean, but mainly of me. I can't explain it. I just seem to fly off the handle these days, and I don't know how to control it or even why I feel this way. I've always been in absolute control."

"Gosh, Em, I'm the farthest thing from a psychologist, but maybe that's exactly what's going on with you."

Emily looked confused. "What do you mean?"

"You've spent your entire life trying to control your environment and all your emotions and have done a damned good job of it. God, Em, I didn't even know any of this stuff about your father until you were nearly eighteen, and we've been friends for almost seven of those eighteen years. Now that you don't have to control your emotions and are working on everything, your emotions are catching up with you and also getting the best of you. Kind of seems natural to me, but what do I know? Just think about everything, though. You've been through a whole hell of a lot in your life, and you haven't even slowed down long enough to take a breath. You just expect way too much from yourself. Please try your best to see Dr. Wells. I think that's a good idea. She can help you understand what's going on. In the meantime, Em, I am here and I am never going away. You can beat me with a brick, but I'll stay right here 'cuz I'm stubborn that way. I am your friend forever, whether you want that or not. Okay?"

She hugged Emily and wiped away a tear as she did. "Now let's get inside. I know your mom has missed you a lot."

Martha had been watching the two women from her living room window. Sean had told her about Emily's reaction to Anne Hightower and told Martha he wasn't sure if Emily completely believed him. He also expressed fear as well. He explained that Emily was showing signs of being quick to get angry and paranoia, and he felt helpless being so far away.

He also told her about their plans to fly him back there for spring break. "Grandma, can you talk to Emily and then help her figure out how to get me home? It'll only be for a few days, but that's better than nothing!"

"Of course, Sean. I'll do everything I can. Listen, Sean, I've been doing a lot of reading about sexual abuse. In fact, I remembered Emily mentioning a book called *The Courage to Heal*. I picked up a copy and have been reading it. I think it would be a good idea if you looked for that book and read it as well. In fact, Sean, this book would actually be right up your alley anyway. There's a section in the book called something like trauma to the brain, and it talks about how what Emily may be experiencing could be a form of PTSD. What you described to me sounds like some of the symptoms the authors describe."

"Thanks, Grandma. Thanks. Do you know who the authors are?"

Martha took a few minutes to respond. "The book's upstairs; but if you hold on a minute, I'll run up and get it."

"No, that's not necessary. I should be able to find it based on the title which I just wrote down. I'm going to pick up a copy tomorrow. I need to understand what Emily's going through so I can help her from my end."

Now as Martha watched Jeannie and Emily, she was determined to get more involved in trying to help Emily deal with her trauma.

****

Sarah was in the kitchen preparing dinner when Jeannie and Emily walked in. She peeked around the corner, dropped the spoon she had been stirring the spaghetti sauce with and ran over to Emily and hugged her. "I didn't even hear you two drive up. Did you just get here?"

"About ten minutes ago, Mom."

Sarah and Emily hugged again. "I've missed you so much, Emily. Jeannie, we're going to have spaghetti tonight; why don't you stay and eat with us?"

"I'd love to, Sarah, but I'm anxious to get home. John will be home around 6:30, and I still need to pick something up for dinner. Maybe some other time. Thanks for asking, though." Then she said, "Wow, Sarah, your hair looks spectacular! I think Mom mentioned the two of you got your hair done together last week. She looks fantastic, but you look stunning!"

Sarah smiled and just said, "Thanks, Jeannie. I was way overdue for a change. I kind of like it myself, and it was fun spending the afternoon with your mom."

Emily touched her mom's hair. "You look great, Mom. I'm not kidding. I think it won't be long now till you get a chance to wear that Victoria's Secret thing you bought. Oops, guess that's a secret. Oh well, Jeannie's the last person to hide something like that from."

Jeannie patted Sarah on the back and said, "Oooo, Sarah, a little naughty behavior does everyone good!"

Sarah just blushed. Jeannie pinched Sarah's cheek and then helped Emily put her bags in her room and hugged her.

"Call me in a few days to let me know if you are able to see Dr. Wells. If you don't call me, I'll call you."

"Thanks, Jeannie. I don't know what I'd do without you."

Jeannie caressed Emily's face. "Gotta scoot, kiddo, but call. And don't forget about next Saturday!"

Just as Jeannie was leaving, Katie came down the stairs. Sarah was back in the kitchen finishing the spaghetti sauce when she turned around to see Katie. "Did you know Emily's home?"

"She is? Where?" Katie sounded excited.

"She's in her room. Go say 'hi' then come on back out and set the table, okay?"

"Okay, Mom. I'll be back in a minute."

Katie ran back upstairs to get the new puppy. She was carrying the puppy in her arms when she knocked on Emily's door. Emily opened the door as Katie held the puppy in front of her face.

Emily was excited to see Katie. "Katie! Is this the new puppy?"

"Yes, Muffin is so happy to meet you, Emily, and I'm just so glad to see you. I've missed you a bunch!" Katie put Muffin on the bed and hugged Emily.

"So you and Lily named her Muffin?"

"Yea, we had a couple of names and decided on Muffin. I need to take her out back to pee. Do you want to go with me? Then I need to set the table."

"Okay, then you and I can set the table together. How about that?"

"Okay. I'll just run and get her leash."

When she came back, Lily was with her.

The two sisters hugged, then Lily said, "Hey, Em. We sure have missed you around here!"

"Really?" Emily looked surprised.

"Well, yea. You know when you're away at school, we all know you're not too far away. But with you being all the way out in

California, well, it's been lonely without you. Besides, it gets boring when the only person I can bug is Katie." Lily laughed.

Katie looked disappointed. "Hey!"

Lily laughed again. "Just kidding, Katie. I love bugging you and you know it!"

The three girls took Muffin outside. Sarah heard them chattering as they walked out the back door. She put down the spoon, walked out to the TV room and watched them from the window. It filled her heart to see the three of them together again. They were having fun with the dog and laughing as Muffin ran from one to the other jumping up excitedly.

She was back in the kitchen when they came back in. "Hey, girls!" she yelled. "We need to set the table and feed Muffin."

The three walked to the kitchen; and while Emily and Katie set the table, Lily fed Muffin.

"You'll need to take Muffin right back out as soon as she's finished eating so she can poop," commanded Sarah.

"Okay, Mom," answered Lily.

They had a really nice dinner that evening as Katie and Lily asked Emily what San Francisco was like. When they were finished, Emily got up and automatically started clearing the table.

But Lily jumped up. "Em, you and Mom go on in the TV room. Katie and I will take care of this."

When Sarah and Emily sat down, Emily asked, "What's gotten into Lily?"

"Well, honey, I think Lily realized just how much you mean to her while you were gone. You've never been more than a stone's throw away, you know. She commented several times while you were gone how much she missed you. I guess too she's just growing up and is realizing what's important and what's not. Plus, I don't know if you've noticed, but I'm that in-charge mom you always talked about."

"Yea, Mom, I began to notice you were the captain of this ship before I left for San Francisco and I love it. It's nice too about Lily. I was hoping we were getting closer before I left. Have you and she talked about that brochure?"

"Yes we did. She wasn't surprised that I found it. In fact, I think she was glad I did. She's amazed me at how mature she is about all of this. She confessed that it's taken her a long time to accept that the dad she knew wasn't real. She told me she was angry and hurt at first and didn't know who to blame. She's evidently confided not only in Penny but also in Penny's mom as well. Penny's situation seems to be helping her put everything into perspective. Plus, she told me that my attitude and behavior about all of this has really helped her too. She even told me what a wonderful role model I've become, which made me feel pretty good."

"Well, Mom, Lily is very right. You have become a hell of a role model for all of us. I'm so grateful and proud of you. If only Dad had had the guts you do, things may have been different. How've your sessions with Dr. Wells been going?"

"It's been touch and go, Emily. This is still all so new for me. I can get so angry out of the blue at times. Your father is damned lucky he's not around anymore. I just ache for you and all you've been through. A lot of your past behavior has just clicked in my mind. Dr. Wells tells me that my conscious mind is connecting dots that have been buried in my subconscious mind. It just pains me that I didn't even ask when I could see you were clearly sad. I'm so sorry, Emily."

"I know you are, Mom." Emily walked over and sat on the ottoman in front of Sarah and took her hand. "Everything's okay, Mom."

But Sarah sat back, looked at Emily and emphatically said, "No, it's not okay, Emily! That's one of the things Dr. Wells and I have discussed. You've always been the one to try and smooth things over and take all the burden on yourself, and I just can't let that happen anymore. Like right now. I can sense that there's something gnawing at you, and you're trying your best to push it away. What's making you feel so sad, Emily? I want to be here for you, honey, but you need to let me be," Sarah begged.

Emily told Sarah about the Anne Hightower incident and about the woman on the airplane who reminded her of haughty Anne. She told Sarah about how scared she was because she was having fears she didn't recall ever experiencing in her past. She was also losing her patience easily and getting angry and sad over small things and having a hard time controlling those emotions.

"I'm going to call Dr. Wells in the morning to see if I can get in to see her this week. I'm also going to ask her if she thinks I might need to start taking medication."

Emily looked terrified. "I'm afraid of losing Sean, and now I'm also afraid I could push him away."

"Oh, Emily, honey, do you remember I told you that the distance will test your love to the limits?"

Emily nodded as she wiped a tear from her cheek. "It's so, so hard, Mom. Even Sean said today that this time it seems even harder than it did in the fall."

"Emily, it's natural to be concerned, especially since you were witness to another female overtly demonstrating her interest in Sean. He's a very good-looking young man, and his sweetness makes him even more desirable. I'm sure if he witnessed another male coming on to you like that, he would experience the same emotions. You're both vulnerable so much more than normal only because you are physically distant from each other. It takes a ton more effort to keep a relationship going while doing it long-distance than when you are in the same vicinity. I know. Do you recall my telling you the story about Mattie?"

Emily nodded.

Sarah was referring to a romance she began with a young man named Mattie Lynch. She was head over heels in love with Mattie as he was with her when Mattie enlisted in the Army and was deployed to Vietnam during that war. It was during their three-year separation that Sarah met and married Joe, never to see Mattie again.

Sarah's recollection of Mattie and her feelings for him reflected on her face as she continued, "It was distance and time that took a toll on what, I now know, could have become a wonderful romance. Three years was too long to be apart." Sarah frowned. "You and Sean have an additional year to contend with. Unlike Mattie and me, you two will get to see each other over the semester breaks and summers, but *still* it's going to be tough on both of you. You'll both just have to do your best realizing that your best might not be enough. On the other hand, if you are meant to be together, you'll somehow find a way to hang in there. I know that doesn't sound very encouraging; but, as you well know, life is a bitch sometimes."

Emily empathized with her mother as she did originally when Sarah told her about Mattie; but, then Emily thought about how her mother just expressed herself. That made Emily laugh a little.

"Sorry, Mom, but I just realized you used the word bitch. I've never heard you swear in the past. Well, I take that back." She chuckled again, "You did say 'fuck' on Thanksgiving Day when you saw Dad's picture."

Sarah chuckled as she also blushed. "Yes, I did, didn't I? Well, Emily, you haven't heard or seen me do a lot of things. I'm changing too. I'm realizing how much of life I've missed out on with your father. He was smothering in a very devious way. He kept me in check, which I know you saw; but now I have no one trying to keep me in check, and I'm *looking* for change!"

Mother and daughter talked for a couple more hours; and by the time they both expressed being too tired to talk anymore, they hugged and said goodnight.

Just as Emily climbed into bed, her cell phone rang. She was half-asleep when she answered it.

On the other end was a sweet, concerned voice. "Emily, sweetie, were you asleep?"

Emily sat straight up. "I was, but not anymore. Oh, Sean, it's so good to hear your voice. I can't tell you how good."

"I've been worried about you all day long, Em. Listen, I have been thinking about a lot of things. I bumped into one of my professors today and had a long talk with him. We talked about the best schools for neuroscience, and he mentioned that Berkeley and Harvard are considered to be in the top ten universities for neuroscience; and, even better, Harvard is ahead of Berkeley in the area I want to specialize in—neuroplasticity. He also mentioned that Harvard is a bit more expensive; but when you factor in the non-residency portion of tuition and the lack of dormitory expenses, Harvard may be less expensive. Do you see where I'm going with this?"

"I'm not sure," she replied.

"Well, what if I stayed out here for one more year and was able to transfer to Harvard for my junior and senior years, then do my graduate work there? My grades for my first semester here are 3.8, and I know I can keep that up for another year. What do you think?"

"But, Sean, you had your heart set on Berkeley."

"Yea, I did but I'm just not willing to pay the price of staying out here. I want to be with you all the time. I am aching in my heart for you, Emily."

"Oh, Sean," she was now sobbing, "I've been so sad since leaving this morning. I even caused a woman, who I swear looked like Anne Hightower, to spill her drink on herself. She was seated in first class; and when I slipped on something in the aisle, she was very nasty and loud, calling me an ignorant klutz."

"Emily, sweetie, please put that stupid stuck-up bitch out of your mind. Okay? I actually can't stand Anne Hightower, even more now that I know how she's affecting you. I've seen her interact with a few people she feels superior to. I don't like people like that anymore than you do. Sweetie, you're my girl, and I want nothing more than to be with you and not away from you. I'm in agony tonight, Emily. Last night you were asleep in my arms, and tonight I'm back in my impersonal dorm room with only your painting to keep me company. I don't want to live like this. I want to be with you!"

"Sean, we are meant to be together, aren't we? Mom told me tonight that if we are meant to be together, we'd find a way. I want to find a way, Sean. I know we are meant for each other. I just know it in my heart. Life without you would be half a life. I love you so much."

"Sweetie, do you remember what my mom called us? She called us soul mates. I know that sounds corny, but I believe in that shit. I believe with all my heart my dad and mom were soul mates. She believes it. She loves Bill, but I know it's a different love than what she had with Dad.

When I was in that coma, I felt things and saw things that no one gets to see or feel when they're wide awake. I can't explain it, but I came away from that coma with an awareness that I know I didn't have before I fell into the pond. Emily, I can still close my eyes and feel the intense love you had for me during those five weeks. We were connected. We've always been connected. In fact, I think our souls have been together for a long, long time; and I feel like half a person without you with me. I want to feel whole again; and, if that means transferring to Harvard, then that's the answer."

Emily began to cry. "Oh, Sean. You make me so happy. I've been so sad and scared all day long. We can make this work; and, when I think back on August, just before you left and now, it doesn't

83

seem that long. We can make it one more year."

They talked a little bit longer and then said goodnight. "Call me tomorrow, sweetie. Let me know if you can get in to see Dr. Wells, 'cuz that's another reason I want to be with you. I want to be there while you go through all this. I want to be able to support you and help you. Go to sleep now, Em, and don't worry anymore about being away from me. We'll be together permanently before we both know it."

"I can't wait, Sean. I love you too." She put her phone on her night stand, laid down and drifted off to sleep.

****

That night she had the strangest dream. She dreamt her grandmother Bertie came to talk to her, and standing next to her was a man she didn't recognize. It wasn't Walter, her grandfather. The man was talking to her grandmother as if coaching her on what to say. Bertie finally introduced the young man as Sean's father, Davie. Then Davie began to speak.

He told Emily that Sean really wanted to stay at Berkeley but was willing to give all that up in order to be with her. He then told her that she needed to encourage Sean to stay at Berkeley.

"His future in his field depends on it."

Davie told her she needed to be willing to make the same hard sacrifice Sean was willing to make. He further told her that both she and Sean were about to have some rough times ahead of them. She needed to look for help for all her internal pain because it was all caused by fear. She needed to look for and find a way to release her fear. Then both he and Bertie assured her that after a period of separation, she and Sean would once again join each other, but that this time it *would be forever*. They told her the separation would be painful but necessary and that she needed to trust in both herself and Sean that they were meant to be with each other.

They finished by telling her that in the end, it would seem like a miracle; but Sean would come looking for her and because he would be determined to find her, he would.

"You are soul mates," Davie told Emily. "Nothing can or will keep you apart. But you _must_ be willing to let events take their course so that you will both know when it's time to commit to each other forever."

Bertie was in the middle of saying something when Emily woke up. She sat up in the bed feeling very delirious but remembered the entire dream. She didn't want to lose the dream to the night so she got up, found her diary and wrote everything down. She determined she would show it to Sean when he came out for spring break. She thought that might be what her grandma was saying to her when she woke up.

The next morning when she got up, she wondered if the dream had happened or if she had dreamt about a dream. She didn't have to doubt for long, because there on the floor and lying next to her bed was her diary. She picked it up and realized it was opened to the page on which she began recording the dream.

That very same night Sean also had a strange dream. He dreamed Davie came to talk to him. He told Sean that he needed to follow his dream and stay at Berkeley.

"You can't take a chance on ever feeling you made a mistake. It would be a mistake for you to leave Berkeley and go to Harvard."

Davie then told Sean that he had a very bright future in neuroscience, especially with the breakthrough discipline of neuroplasticity; but it all hinged on his staying at Berkeley and finishing his education all the way through his doctorate. He told Sean the same thing about Emily and him being separated but that the separation was a necessary part of Emily's healing.

"Emily needs to do this on her own. She needs to discover how to heal internally. You could slow her down if you were there babysitting her. You need to trust me, son, because I know what I'm talking about."

Davie was there for a few additional minutes; but by the time Sean woke up, he couldn't remember most of his dream. He just felt certain that his dad had talked to him that night.

Chapter 9

Emily walked out of her bedroom carrying her diary. Sarah was in the kitchen making coffee when Emily walked in.

"Mom, I need to talk to you about a lot of stuff this morning; but I know you're trying to get the girls ready for school. So…why don't I drive them to school and stop by McDonald's? That way there will be no dirty dishes in the sink, and the girls will feel like they're getting a special treat with McDonalds. Then we can talk. How does that sound?"

"That sounds like a great plan! I must admit, I wasn't looking forward to preparing breakfast for the girls. Instead, I was going through the motions. I sure could use the morning off for a change. Thanks, sweetie."

"Then that's what we'll do," Emily said just as the girls both walked out into the kitchen.

Muffin was waddling behind them as Sarah said, "Lily, why don't you quickly feed Muffin, then take her out? Once she's used the bathroom, Emily is going to take you both to school and get you breakfast at McDonald's."

Sarah didn't have to say another word. Both girls had huge grins on their faces.

Lily looked at Katie. "Katie, take Muffin out to pee, and I'll fix her breakfast for her; then we can both take her out to poop."

Katie was out the door with Muffin on the leash before Lily said "poop." Within a matter of minutes, Muffin was fed and taken out one last time. As Katie and Lily came back in with Muffin, Sarah was handing Emily a twenty-dollar bill.

"Okay, girls, are you ready?" Emily asked enthusiastically.

"We sure are!" Both girls said simultaneously as they kissed their mom goodbye.

They were out the door, and soon Emily was driving them up the hill in her red Beetle.

Martha was standing at her back door when she saw the Beetle drive up the street. She finished doing the dishes, wiped her hands, walked across the street, and knocked on Sarah's door.

"Martha, why on earth are you knocking on the door? My goodness, you should know by now to simply walk in," Sarah admonished.

"Well, I saw Emily and the two girls drive up the hill. I didn't want to startle you."

"You're probably right," Sarah chuckled. "I may have reacted like Gladys did when Jeannie came home for Thanksgiving; except I don't have a safe room to hide in, do I?"

They both laughed. Then they sat down as Sarah fixed two cups of coffee. Sarah told Martha that Emily wanted to talk to her about several things when she got back. She then told Martha about the Hightower situation which Sean had already told her about.

"Sarah, I don't want to jump ahead of everything, but you need to know that Emily and Sean are planning on using the rest of the money you and I gave them to fly him home for spring break. Now, I think that's a great idea. However, I also know from talking to Sean a little while ago that he's now thinking of transferring to Harvard when he finishes his second year at Berkeley. *That* I'm not so sure is a good idea. I absolutely know how set on Berkeley Sean was and how much he loves the curriculum and the faculty."

Sarah was listening intently to Martha. "I wasn't aware of either plan, but I agree with you that spring break would be a nice treat for them." She paused, then said, "Hmm ...you're right! Sean's leaving Berkeley could be a negative thing for their future relationship. The *last* thing either of them needs is to feel as if they were forced into a change."

The two women cut off their conversation when they heard Emily's Beetle.

Emily came in, grabbed her diary and walked out into the kitchen. She was surprised to see Martha, but delighted as well.

"Martha! I'm so glad to see you. I've missed you."

Emily and Martha hugged. "I've missed you too, Em! I heard you and Sean had a wonderful time. Well, I need to get back over to the house, so I'll leave you and your mom alone."

Emily put her hand on Martha's and said, "I'd really like you to stay, Martha. I have some things to discuss with Mom, but I think you should be part of this conversation."

Martha agreed while Sarah made another pot of coffee for the three of them. Emily began filling Martha in on the Hightower situation which of course she already knew about. However, Martha looked very concerned.

"He's worried, Emily. He's worried you don't completely believe him, and he's terrified of losing you."

Then Martha confessed that she had already filled Sarah in on Emily and Sean's plans to bring him home for spring break.

Sarah spoke up. "Honey, both Martha and I think that's a great plan. The money we gave both of you was for you two to spend any way you wanted to. I think it's wonderful that you want to spend it so that the two of you are together before summer break. But, honey, I think we need to talk about Sean's decision to transfer from Berkeley to Harvard."

Before either Sarah or Martha said another word, Emily opened up her diary and said, "Mom, I've changed my mind about Sean doing that. Let me read both of you something."

She then told them about her strange, yet vivid dream and read the recap of that dream to them. Both women were stunned and sat with their mouths opened as she read.

Emily smiled. "I know I sound like a kook right now, but I swear the dream seemed like it was more than a dream. Sean told me the other day of some of the strange things that had happened to him while he was in his coma. When Sean comes home for spring break, I'm going to talk him into staying at Berkeley. I think that's where he needs to get his education. He had his heart set on that. It breaks my heart that he and I will be completely separated for some years, but that's why I took the time to recap my dream. I think I am probably going to be the cause of our separation, but I'm also going to hold onto my faith that we will come back together; and whenever I am in doubt, I have my diary to remind me that it will seem permanent but will only be temporary. I've got to get myself healed; and if that means doing it without Sean, then that's just how it's going to have to be. I'm sure I'll probably waver back and forth on that, but I don't want to ruin any part of Sean's life because I can't handle this without him. Does any of that make sense?"

Neither Martha nor Sarah knew what to say. What they both agreed on with Emily was that she should get in to see Dr. Wells as soon as she could. Martha promised and insisted she would keep her promise that she wouldn't talk to Sean about the transfer.

"It isn't my place to tell him, Em. That's your job. So, rest assured, my lips are sealed. That's a decision the two of you need to make together and without outside influence." She chuckled, "At least outside living influence."

Emily laughed, "So you believe me about my dream?"

Martha smiled broadly. "Emily, I believe you had a dream, but I don't know if Bertie and Davie were really there or if it was your own mind telling you what you need to do. But that doesn't matter, does it? What matters is that the two of you take care of each other. He is willing to make that sacrifice for you, but you're willing to make an equally difficult sacrifice for him. That is true love; and when true love is involved, I guess the best thing to do is to trust that love and let the chips fall where they fall. What do you think, Sarah?"

"I agree with Martha, honey. I know I've had some very vivid dreams like that and who knows where they come from? They may be real, and they may just be our own minds helping us solve problems. I'll just go back to my original thinking and say that if you two are meant to be together, you'll find a way. I just wish with all my heart that Mattie and I had the strength to have weathered his being gone, but I guess that wasn't meant to be. We'll all just have to wait and see. Nevertheless, whatever happens, it will be the right thing for both of you individually and together."

Emily got up. "Well, I guess there's not much more to talk about. I need to go call Dr. Wells."

She left and Sarah and Martha sat at the table both amazed and befuddled by the entire conversation. Emily wasn't gone very long when she came back in to the kitchen and told Sarah she was going to go see Dr. Wells that day.

"She told me that with the break she wasn't very busy and invited me to come up today. I'm going to get ready and leave. My appointment is at 2 p.m. and it's nearly 11 a.m. now."

****

Later that day Emily sat down with Dr. Wells and told her

89

everything. She told her about the wonderful time she and Sean had had but also about the Hightower incident. She expressed fear and concern about some of the strange emotions she was experiencing. She also told her about her dream and even read from her diary.

Dr. Wells had no reaction to the dream but did talk at length about Emily's new emotions which were causing her to behave erratically. She then pulled out a book called THRESHOLDS OF THE MIND, and told Emily about The Centerpointe Institute located in Oregon which was doing some unusual but seemingly breakthrough research on what they called dysfunctional behavior resulting from childhood trauma.

"Last week I attended a conference at which the institute founder, Bill Harris, spoke. I found his discussion to be quite captivating. Everything they do at Centerpointe involves meditation, which is becoming more and more a topic within the community of psychology. You know, Emily, I believe I recall that Bill Harris is going to be in Boston next month to talk at a Harvard function. You ought to see if you can attend. Oh, and by the way, Dr. Williams happens to be a very good friend of Mr. Harris. I recall you took a course of his last semester. When you come back from break next week, you ought to set up an appointment with Dr. Williams and ask him if he'll introduce you to Bill. I'm willing to bet that Dr. Williams plans to attend the discussion at Harvard."

"Wow," said Emily. "I'll do that. I've never thought about meditating, but I'm very intrigued. Do you mind if I borrow this book and read it?"

"Not at all. I intended to suggest that, but I'm glad you are open-minded about this. I think you're doing a splendid job of dealing with all of this on a conscious level; but, Emily, the subconscious, which now many call the 'old brain,' can be a powerful instrument. It's where all our memories exist; and because it's hidden from the conscious realm, time doesn't exist for the old brain. Instead, it continues to function just as it did when, as in your case, you were in danger from your father. It could very well be the source of your new and unusual emotions and behavior.

Plus, just as Jeannie intuitively pointed out, you've spent your entire life until just a month ago controlling your world so that the secret remained a secret. Now, the secret is out leaving **no** more reason to protect it. With the secret no longer a secret, all the energy you spent **controlling** the secret is no longer necessary. Keeping that secret gave you a false sense of control. Without that sense, new situations feel more out of control than you are consciously used to. You know, and this is just a suggestion, I think you ought to invite your mom to go with you when you listen to Bill Harris. She could benefit from meditation as well."

Emily felt so much better after her session with Dr. Wells that, instead of going home right away, she took a side trip over to Dr. Williams' office to see if he was there. As she walked down the path to the physics building, she saw Dr. Williams getting out of his car in the parking lot. As she approached him, she waved.

He walked over to her and said, "Why, Emily, what a pleasant surprise. How has your semester break been? Oh, and how is your family situation coming along?" Then with a pensive expression, he asked, "Is it better than it was around...if I recall...Thanksgiving?"

"Yes, my family situation is coming along better than I expected, and I had a wonderful break. Thanks for asking. Do you have a few minutes, Dr. Williams?"

"Well, as a matter of fact, I have about an hour before I need to be in attendance at a faculty meeting. I was going to do a little preparation; but, in reality, that's not at all necessary. Why don't we walk over to the student cafeteria and grab a cup of coffee?"

She was delighted, so they walked over to the cafeteria. He bought a cup of coffee for himself and a diet cola for her; then they found a table away from all the other people and sat down. She told him about her session with Dr. Wells.

"Professor Williams, I hope you don't mind; but I'm going to tell you about my family situation so you understand why I wanted to talk to you. Is that alright?"

"Why, yes, Emily."

Emily took a very deep breath and began telling Dr. Williams about her childhood and about her mom finding her diary and all the other stuff that had been going on.

Dr. Williams listened intently, shaking his head occasionally and facially expressing empathy and sadness for all that Emily talked about. He finally spoke, "You poor girl! You've been through a lot. Your poor mother...but it's wonderful that she's so supportive of you."

Then without even thinking, he picked up Bill Harris' book and turned it over. "I thought I recognized the back cover. Yes, this is my friend Bill. He's going to be here next month. Did Dr. Wells tell you that?"

She nodded. "That's one of the reasons I wanted to talk privately with you. Do you think you could help my mom and me get an invitation to come listen to Mr. Harris? It would mean so much to both of us. Dr. Williams, I want to get through this before any of my strange behaviors get out of hand because I think I'm headed in that direction and it scares me to death."

Dr. Williams put the book back down on the table. "Yes, I will be more than happy to get both of you an invitation. In fact, why don't we plan on the two of you going with me? I could personally introduce you to Bill. Have you read any of his book yet?"

"No. Dr. Wells just gave this to me to read."

"Well, once you begin reading it, you'll discover why Bill became so interested in meditation and about the audio meditation inducement he and his institute have been working on. Bill had a *lot* of emotional problems when he was much younger, and those problems did indeed wreak havoc on his life. He began meditating and found it to be quite helpful in releasing a lot of the internal, unconscious fear triggers which were causing his behavior. 'Unconscious' and 'subconscious' are basically the same, just different terms; but this could be something that both you and your mom could benefit from. So, why don't we do this? You get registered for classes and next week make an appointment to come see me. In the meantime, I'll look into what I need to do to get you and your mother an invitation to come with me to listen to Bill. Will that work?"

"Oh, yes, Dr. Williams. Thank you so much. And, by the way, if I can get into it, I think I'm going to take another course of yours this semester. I think it's called the 'Physics of Environmental Change.'"

"Well, Emily, if for any reason they tell you at registration that the class is closed, because it is a popular one, you just immediately call me up; and I'll make sure an exception is made so you are able to take the course. Here (he wrote down his cell phone number on a napkin), this is my cell phone number. You just call me from the registration line and we'll get that handled immediately." Then he looked at his watch, "I don't want to be rude, but I do need to go. My meeting is in fifteen minutes."

They both got up and Emily hugged him. "Thank you so much, Dr. Williams, for everything."

Dr. Williams blushed and said, "You're quite welcome, Emily. Good day and I'll see you in class next week."

They parted and Emily headed back to her car. Before she left, she called Sean. He answered after the third ring.

"Hey, baby. I was just thinking about you. How do you feel today?"

"Oh, Sean, I feel incredible."

She told him she had just finished seeing Dr. Wells and about her discussion with Dr. Williams. When she mentioned *THRESHOLDS OF THE MIND*, Sean said he knew about the book and Bill Harris and also about the Centerpointe Institute and the meditation audio called Holosync.

"That's wonderful, Em! I'm excited for you. From everything I know, this could be a real breakthrough! I do think you need the extra help because I have noticed that your behavior has changed over the past several months. Please don't be mad at me for saying that."

"Sean, I'm not mad at you. I hate feeling like this, and I hate all the paranoia I've been experiencing and my out of control feelings as well. I want to try and nip this in the bud."

"Well, Em, just be aware this won't be an overnight thing. It's going to take some time and some real dedication on your part to stick with the meditation; but once you begin to experience how it's helping you, you'll automatically become more dedicated. At least that's my assumption from everything I know."

Emily purposely didn't tell Sean about her dream. She wanted to discuss that with him when he came home for spring break, but she did tell him that Sarah was very much in favor of their spending the rest of the money on a plane ticket.

"See, Sean, I told you she would understand. Mom loves you a lot, and she wants nothing more for us than to give us every chance we can get to make this work and last. I want you to know, Sean, that I will always, always love you. You're the only male in this entire world for me, and that's just the way it is."

"Oh, sweetie, you're my girl. I neither want nor can even imagine ever wanting another female. I think, whether we like it or not, we're stuck with each other."

She laughed, then told him she was going to drive home. They said goodbye.

"I'll call you tonight, Em, to say goodnight to my precious sweetie! I love you, baby."

"I love you too, Sean."

Chapter 10

Emily pulled into her driveway a little after 5 p.m. She walked into the house and found Katie and Lily watching TV.

Emily said "Hi." She walked through the rest of the downstairs, then back into the TV room. "Where's Mom, girls?"

Lily waved her hand. "She went over to see Martha for a few minutes."

"Okay. I need to go talk to her so I'll be back when she comes back."

Neither girl paid attention to Emily. They simply continued watching TV.

Emily walked across the street and knocked on Martha's back door. She could see Martha and her mom at the kitchen table. Martha waved her in.

"How did it go, sweetie?"

"Well, I'm glad you two are together because now I only have to tell this story once. It's all good, Mom. Dr. Wells even gave me this book." She laid it on the table. Martha picked it up as Sarah listened intently.

"She suggested I try doing meditation since it helps get at a lot of the subconscious triggers that cause what she called dysfunctional emotions and behavior. The guy who wrote this book is going to be at a conference next month at Harvard. Dr. Wells mentioned that my physics professor, Dr. Williams, is a good friend of the author and that I should talk to Dr. Williams to see if he could get both you and me invitations to the conference. Isn't that great, Mom?"

Sarah looked skeptical. "Meditation? Wow, that's way out there, isn't it?"

Martha had been reading the forward to the book. "I don't know, Sarah, this sounds very fascinating. It sure wouldn't hurt to at least go and listen. Maybe too you could read the book when Emily is finished with it."

Sarah relaxed a little. "Well, I'm not going to close my mind to anything. Who would have even thought I'd be seeing a psychologist a few months ago? Sure, honey, I'll read the book and go with you."

"That's great, Mom. Dr. Williams invited us to ride up there with him. He's really nice."

"Okay. I'm open for anything." Sarah made a gesture with both her hands as if to say, "Why not?"

****

The following Saturday, Emily and Jeannie got together just as they had planned. When Emily walked into the townhouse, her jaw dropped.

"Wow, Jeannie, this is amazing! You weren't kidding that this no longer looks like a man's place. I love the abstract art and the new furniture. How does John like it?"

Jeannie frowned. "Well, he's more of a traditionalist, but he's getting used to it. When he came home the first night, he just said, 'Well, I guess I'm outnumbered by Jeannie anyway.' He really doesn't care one way or another how it's decorated. Even if he did, he was right about being outnumbered or outvoted."

The two girls laughed. "What do you want to do today, Jeannie?"

"I fixed us a little lunch, so why don't we eat and then we'll decide? How does that sound?"

Emily told Jeannie about her session with Dr. Wells and how Dr. Wells said Jeannie had hit the nail on the head with regard to a few things like Emily losing control over the secret and how now that control had become replaced by other needs to control, most of which were subconscious.

Emily smiled. "So, see, Ms. Smarty Pants, you do intuitively know a thing or two about how people's minds work."

"Wow, I deserve a big pat on the back for that one," Jeannie laughed.

Then Emily told her about her dream and about Sean's thinking about coming back here to attend Harvard. Jeannie was frowning when Emily opened her diary and began reading the recap of her dream.

"Gosh, Em, what a strange dream! But it seemed to resolve a lot of issues. I think that's a good idea about not letting Sean leave Berkeley. The last thing you two need is to have any suggestion of disappointment due to expectations hanging around. I'm proud of you for making that decision. Have you said anything to Sean?"

"No. I don't want to mention any of this until we can sit down and talk face-to-face, and it looks like that's going to happen over spring break. We have about $1,500 left from Christmas so I'm going to book a flight for him to come back here. It will only be for a few days, but at least it will break up the six months until summer break."

Jeannie smiled as she patted Emily's hand, "That's great, Em. Have you two talked anymore about the nasty bitchtower?"

"Yea, just long enough for him to assure me that I don't have anything to worry about. I can't help but worry about the part of the dream that told me we would be separated for a while, but that was one of the reasons I wrote the dream down. I wanted to have something I could look at when I feel scared that it's going to be permanent. Oh, Jeannie, I love Sean so much, I just can't and don't even want to think about a future without him."

"Well, Em, just keep believing and I will as well. I can't imagine not having the two of you together in my future. Tell me more about this meditation thing."

Emily did. She also told her about Dr. Williams and how nice and concerned he was the other day. "You know, when I went through registration, I asked a few people if he was married and found out he's divorced and has been for a long time."

Jeannie scrunched her face. "What on earth did you ask that for?"

"Jeannie, you sound like your mom. I didn't ask for me, silly. I just got this strange feeling while I was talking to him that he would be someone I would like Mom to meet. I can't explain it because it was a truly uncanny feeling, but what a coincidence that she's going with me to this conference and with Dr. Williams. Say, Jeannie, I just thought of something. Mom and Martha are planning to come up to Brown the weekend after next to go to dinner. If John's working, why don't you plan to come along or bring him along if he's not working? I'm going to try and find out where Dr. Williams hangs out. I know he lives close by the campus. Maybe we could just happen to run into him."

Jeannie was smiling her Cheshire cat grin, "Very devious, Emily Callaway, but I like the plan. It's about time your mom got to experience what real sex is like. Oooo, you are such a naughty little daughter. Now, what do you want to do this afternoon?"

****

The girls went shopping and had a ton of fun. When they got back to the apartment, John was sound asleep on the new sofa. Jeannie put her finger to her lips as she walked over to the sofa and sat on it next to John.

As she leaned over to kiss him, he woke up, said "Hi," and began rubbing her crotch. "I was just dreaming about my favorite flower."

Jeannie giggled. "You might want to stop, John. We have company."

John jumped up, turned around and got redder than the red on the accent chair opposite the couch. "Oh, my god. Emily. I'm sorry."

Emily laughed joyously. "Don't be, DD. I'm just going to go home jealous that it was your hand on Jeannie's crotch and not Sean's on mine. So with that, I'm going home so you can continue to explore her flower more."

They all laughed as Jeannie and Emily hugged. On her way out the door, Emily exclaimed, "Don't you two do anything I wouldn't do!"

When Emily shut the door, John said, "God, Jeannie, I'm so embarrassed!"

"Well, don't be. Now where were we?" She unzipped her jeans and slid them down, then sat down next to him and said, "My flower is screaming for more."

Before Emily had her key in the ignition, John had his face buried in Jeannie's flower. They had glorious sex and then got dressed and ran out for dinner. Jeannie filled him in on everything and asked him to try and arrange his shift so that he could go out with all of them in two Saturdays.

****

Both girls started classes the following Monday. When the Saturday of Martha and Sarah's visit rolled around, Emily called Jeannie.

"Hey, Jeannie. Mom and Martha will be here around 6:30 p.m. Is John coming?"

"Yes. He gets home around noon and will sleep for a few hours so we'll be ready to meet you all around 7. He doesn't have to work Sunday until the late shift. Did you find out where Dr. Williams hangs out?"

"Yea. He hangs out at a few places. I hope this works. I just have a feeling about this, and I would love for Mom to start dating someone who would treat her like she deserves to be treated."

It was about 5 p.m. that Saturday when Sarah called Emily, "Hi, sweetie. Listen, Martha and I decided to spend the night here. The girls are spending the night at Gladys' so we won't have to worry about driving home later."

"That's great, Mom. That way we can go have fun after dinner. Listen, I hope you don't mind, but Jeannie and John are going to join us. Is that okay?"

"Sure. The more the merrier. I'm dying to meet John anyway. Gladys adores him. Well, listen, we're going to finish checking in and then we'll come by at 6:30. Have you decided where to eat?"

"Yes, we'll meet John and Jeannie at Camille's. A couple of classmates recommended it. Then I thought we could swing over to a pub called the English Cellar Alehouse which should be fun."

"That sounds great, Emily! We'll pick you up at 6:30, okay?"

"Okay, Mom. I'll be outside so you don't have to come up."

****

Emily was hoping to run into Dr. Williams at the English Cellar Alehouse, only a short walk from Camille's. Jeannie and John were standing outside when the three ladies walked up.

Jeannie was shivering. "Oooo, it's chilly out here! Let's go in to make introductions."

They went inside. Emily walked up to the receptionist's stand and put their name in for a table and was told the wait would be about fifty minutes. When she got back to the group, everyone knew John.

Emily couldn't help herself. "Any flowers on the menu tonight, DD?"

John blushed and Jeannie burst out laughing. Sarah and Martha looked lost so Emily said, "I'll fill you in later."

That made John blush even more.

As they walked into the bar area, there were five seats that had just become available at the bar so they all sat down. Jeannie and Emily ordered a beer while the others ordered cocktails. Sarah ordered a glass of Merlot. They were sitting and chatting when Emily looked across the bar at a man who was looking their way. It was Dr. Williams. He waved at Emily and she waved back.

"Who's that, honey?" asked Sarah.

"It's Dr. Williams, my physics professor. He's the person who invited us to go listen to Bill Harris in a few weeks." As she finished, Jeannie poked her in the side and giggled.

Then the two stools next to them became available, and the next thing they knew Dr. Williams and an older gentleman were headed their way.

"Why, Emily, it's so nice to see you. Do you mind if we sit down?" Dr. Williams asked.

"No, not at all. Dr. Williams, this is my mom, Sarah, and our next-door neighbor, Martha; and this is my best friend, Jeannie and her boyfriend, John."

Sarah blushed at his British accent as she shook his hand, then asked, "Are you from Britain?"

"No. I'm actually from Australia, but my accent is similar to a British one. Everyone, this is my big brother George."

They all shook hands. Emily invited Dr. Williams and George to eat with them. Everyone was in agreement so Emily walked over to the host stand and asked to add two more people to her table. An hour later they were all seated.

Jeannie and Emily managed to sit next to each other as Jeannie whispered, "Did you expect him to be here?"

"No, not at all. Isn't this a wonderful coincidence?"

Jeannie smiled, "Might be more than that."

They ate; and by the end of the meal, Dr. Williams, whose first name was Zachery or Zach for short, was asking them to go to another venue where they could have some drinks and listen to a little music. Emily could tell that Zach liked her mom; and what was even more of a surprise, Martha and George seemed to hit it off as well. George was eight years older than Zach, which caused Jeannie and Emily both to giggle at what they considered to be a wonderful surprise given Martha was ten years Sarah's senior which made George about the same age as Martha.

They excused themselves to go to the lady's room. "God, Em, I feel like I'm on an adventure. What if this works out for both your mom and Martha? Wouldn't that just be the cat's meow? Oooo, I hope!" Both Emily and Jeannie crossed their fingers, then smacked each other's hand in the air.

By the time they all got to the next venue, Sarah, who didn't drink often, was a little tipsy and laughing like a school girl. She kept telling Zach that she just loved his Aussie accent. There were a few couples who were dancing on a small dance floor so Zach asked Sarah to dance. At first she declined; but between Zach's pleas and Emily's prodding, she finally gave in. Emily watched her mom with delight as Sarah seemed to really take to Zach. They all had an absolutely wonderful evening. Zach even kissed Sarah on the hand as he and George said goodnight.

On the way back to Emily's dorm, Sarah said, "What a wonderful man your professor is, Emily, and he sure can dance."

Martha giggled.

Emily asked, "Martha, George seemed to take a shine to you. Does he live around here?"

"He said he lives in Quincy. He asked for my phone number, so who knows?"

Emily laughed. "Well, did you like him?"

"As a matter of fact, I did. And, if you must know, I hope he calls me. I could use a little male excitement in my life."

The three women talked a little longer outside the dorm, then Emily said goodnight. "I'll meet you two down here in the morning around 10. We'll go get some brunch."

When Emily arrived at her dorm room, her phone rang.

"Okay, spill the beans." It was Jeannie.

"Wasn't that weird, Jeannie? Mom really likes him; and believe it or not, George took Martha's phone number. He lives in Quincy where Beth and Bill live. I told you I had an uncanny feeling about Zach. Martha and George are a big bonus. Won't this be fun?" Then she said, "Oh, I hope I didn't embarrass John too much with the flower crack."

"No, you didn't. We were just talking about that. He said I was rubbing off on you. Talk about rubbing ..." to which Emily could hear John say, "Jeannie!"

Jeannie and Emily both laughed. "Have a nice evening with Officer Krispy Kreme, if you get my meaning."

"Oh, I get your meaning, Emily. I love donuts. Talk to you next week." Jeannie hung up.

****

As Jeannie hung up, John said, "Take your panties off so I can get my hand warm."

"Roger that, Officer Krispy Kreme." He looked at her, smirked and rolled his eyes.

She slid her panties off, and he began stroking her with his hand. They were only fifteen minutes from home. By the time they arrived, she was sopping wet. "Let's be naughty and climb in the back seat," Jeannie said as she buried her tongue in John's mouth.

They climbed in the back seat and began tearing at each other's clothes. They had such steamy sex that the windows were completely fogged over when they were done. It was past midnight when they stuck their heads out the door. No one was around so they ran the short distance from the parking space to their front door buck naked. Once they got in, they began rolling around on the floor and had another steamy session.

****

While Jeannie and John were driving home, Emily got ready for bed. Just as she was about to turn off the light, Celia walked in. She had been out with a male friend.

"Hey, Celia! Did you have a nice time tonight?"

"Hey, Em!" She knew about Emily's short cut name which Sean had given her shortly after they met. "Yea, I did. Kurt is really nice. We're going to meet for lunch tomorrow. So, how did it go with your mom and Martha? Did you run into Dr. Williams?"

Emily giggled. "We sure did and he and Mom hit it off. They even danced when we went to a place where they had a band. What's more, Dr. William's brother George was with him, and George and Martha hit it off. This is going to be fun, I think. Mom was hilarious. She got a little schnokured and was laughing about Zach's, err, Dr. William's Aussie accent."

The girls talked a little longer before turning in.

Chapter 11

The following Wednesday evening, Sarah was sitting on her bed. It was 8 p.m. She had just finished changing and was headed out to the TV room to watch TV with the girls when her phone rang.

"Hello."

"Well, good evening, Sarah. This is Zach. I hope it isn't too late to call you."

"Hi, Zach. Not at all, and I would have known who you were by your accent. What a pleasant surprise. How are you?"

"Well, Sarah, I'm extremely well. Thanks for asking. Listen, I had such a wonderful time the other night." He nervously cleared his throat. "I have tickets to the ballet in Boston and would be very honored if you would accompany me this Friday."

"Goodness, Zach. I'd love to. I need to make sure I can find someone to stay with my two daughters. But I should know something tomorrow night if that's not too late."

"Not at all. I'll call you about the same time tomorrow. I do hope you say 'yes,' and in hopes that you do, the dress is cocktail. Good night, Sarah, and I'll talk to you tomorrow."

Sarah hung the phone up and sat on her bed for several minutes. She was totally dumfounded. Then she called Martha.

"Oh my god, Martha, you'll never guess who just called me."

"Did he have an Aussie accent?"

"Yes, how did you know?"

"Well, George called me to ask if I would have dinner with him on Saturday and mentioned that Zach wanted to call you to invite you to a ballet in Boston Friday evening but was a little hesitant, so I assured George that Zach shouldn't be hesitant at all. I will take the girls to dinner that evening, and they can sleep over here in Sean's room. You make sure you say 'yes' to him and have a wonderful evening. Hmm ...sounds too like you and I need to do some shopping tomorrow."

"Oh my god. It's been so long since I've worn anything fancy. I'll have to buy a whole new outfit. Besides, with the fifty pounds

I've lost, nothing in my closet would fit me anyway, which is a good thing. I'm nervous as all get-out but excited beyond belief."

"You should be excited. George said Zach was really taken by you. Oh, Sarah, I'm so happy for you. This is what you deserve."

"Well, what about you going to dinner with George? Are you excited?"

"You bet I am but like you, a little nervous as well. It's been so long since I've been to dinner with a male. I'm very nervous, yet excited. What time did you want to go shopping? I think I'll buy myself something new as well."

"Let's leave around 10 a.m. That will give us plenty of time to find something nice for both of us."

The following day Sarah got the girls off to school and ate something light. She was about to call Martha when she popped in.

"I thought I'd drive the Mustang today. Are you ready to go?"

"Yes. Oh, Martha, my head is swimming. I don't know what to make of any of this."

"Sarah, dear, you're a very good-looking woman with a winning personality. You need to get used to that and accept that you're on your way to a brand-new existence. Now let's go."

The ladies left and headed into Providence. Sarah bought a beautiful champagne-colored dress with spaghetti straps, a plunging back, and a cinched waist. She bought some jewelry to go with the dress. They were headed to the shoe department in Nordstrom's when she spotted a light chiffon evening coat. It was a hot pink color.

As Sarah tried the coat on, Martha smiled broadly. "That looks stunning, Sarah. You should buy it."

Sarah did buy the coat. "I was going to look for beige shoes, but I think I'll look for hot pink to match the coat."

As she tried on several pairs, she told Martha she'd forgotten how to walk in heels to which they both laughed. Martha bought a simple but pretty yellow dress and flats.

"I'm just not too comfortable even thinking of wearing heels. Besides, heels would make me taller than George."

That evening almost right on the hour, Zach called Sarah. She told him the girls would spend the night at Martha's and that she was looking forward to Friday evening.

****

Friday night came around in a flash. Sarah had her hair done that day and walked out into the TV room just as the girls came downstairs to go over to Martha's. Martha knocked on the door and came in.

"Mom, you look like a princess!" Katie exclaimed.

Lily looked thrilled to death. "You look beautiful, Mom. I hope you have a wonderful evening, and I can't wait to meet him."

Martha said, "Your girls are right, Sarah. You look like a beautiful princess. Okay, girls, are you ready to go get some dinner?"

The three left as Sarah looked at her watch. It was 6:45. Zach was due to pick her up in fifteen minutes. She was so nervous she was almost shaking. *Oh, I hope I'm doing the right thing,* she thought.

Before she knew it, she heard a car pull into the driveway. When Zach rang the front door bell, Sarah opened it and invited him in.

He smiled with delight. "You look ravishing, Sarah. Are you ready to go?"

"Yes, let me just get my coat and purse."

She walked back into the living room where Zach helped her with her coat. Sarah wasn't used to such chivalry.

As he helped, he commented, "Sarah, you smell delicious."

She blushed. "Thank you, Zach. It's Chanel No. 5."

"Well, it smells wonderful on you."

What a night Sarah and Zach had! She felt like the princess Katie had called her, and the ballet was wonderful. It was *Sleeping Beauty* which, as a child, she had loved. She told Zach about her father and how he used to read fairy tales to her when she was just a small girl. *Sleeping Beauty* was one of their favorites.

Zach was swept off his feet by Sarah but did his level best to contain himself. Something told him she was fragile, and he needed to go slow in order not to scare her away. His mind was telling him she was a keeper.

"Sarah, do you like sports?" he asked on their way home.

"What did you have in mind, Zach?"

"The Celtics are playing at the arena in Boston on Sunday, and I was hoping you would go with me. We could go back to my apartment later; and, if you would like, I'd like to prepare dinner for you. I'm an excellent gourmet cook, even if I sound like I'm bragging. What do you think, Sarah?"

"I do like basketball. When Joe was alive, we went to watch Providence College play a number of times and it was fun. Yes, I would like to do that and then have you prepare dinner for me. That would be a treat." She looked over at him, and he was grinning from ear-to-ear.

When they arrived home that evening, he got out and walked around to her side. She was about to automatically get out when he opened the door for her and reached for her hand. He walked her to her door and she opened it. Then she turned.

"I don't have much to drink, but I do think I have a bottle of Cabernet in the cabinet. Would you like to come in for a glass?"

"I'd love to, Sarah."

Martha was across the street watching in the dark from her window. She got very excited when she saw him walk in and crossed her fingers.

Once in, Zach helped Sarah with her coat. Then they went into the kitchen and got the bottle of Cabernet and two wine glasses. He poured and handed the glass to Sarah. She took a sip and then he put his down.

"Sarah, I don't want to seem presumptuous, but would you be offended if I kissed you?"

"No, but I am nervous."

"That's okay, Sarah. To tell you the truth, I'm a little nervous as well. It's been a long time since I've kissed a woman."

He leaned over, held her face with his one hand and kissed her sweetly. Then he picked her glass back up. She was blushing.

When it was time for him to leave, Sarah said, "Zach, I don't know what's gotten into me, but would you kiss me again?"

He turned around, looked surprised but put his arms around her and kissed her deeply several times. He then kissed her neck, and she made a tiny squeal noise.

"I better go before I make a complete fool of myself, Sarah. I had an absolutely wonderful evening and look forward to Sunday."

As he was about to pull away, Sarah put her hand around his head and kissed him again and again.

"Oh, Zach, I'm terrified of asking this, but would you stay tonight, please?"

"Are you sure, Sarah?"

"I've never been so sure of anything in a long, long time. I want you to stay."

He removed the coat he had just put on, and they walked into her bedroom as she turned off the front stoop light. Martha was almost jumping up and down in her living room. She was ecstatic for Sarah.

Once in the bedroom, Zach picked Sarah up off the floor and kissed her with such passion that she nearly fainted.

He then unzipped the back of her dress, and it fell to the floor. He sat on the side of the bed as he pulled her close. He kissed her stomach as he cupped her behind and pulled her toward him.

He then stood and unhooked her bra and pulled it off her. "Sarah, you're beautiful."

She was surprising herself every second as she pulled his shirt out of his slacks, unbuttoned the buttons and pushed it off his body. She buried her face in his chest and began unbuckling his trousers. They fell to the floor, as he slid his hands down the back of her panties and pulled her close so she could feel his bulge. Then holding each other, they collapsed on the bed.

He began kissing her ravenously as he tugged at her panties and she pushed his boxers off him. He rolled her over so that she was lying on the bed. He then kissed her again and began working down her body. Her legs were dangling on the floor as he looked up at her, smiled, then buried his face. Sarah didn't know what to do so she just lay there feeling physical sensations she'd never felt before. He was gentle yet passionate as his tongue gave her clitoris such joy that Sarah moaned when she came. He kept going, giving her three more orgasms. Then he lifted his head and smiled. She pulled him up to her, and he mounted her as she wrapped her legs tightly around his beautiful body. When he came, he groaned loudly as he buried his face against her neck and took a deep breath of her perfume. He then stopped and rolled over next to her.

"Do you want me to go, Sarah? I will if you do."

"No, no. I want you to stay and sleep with me."

"I was hoping you'd say that. I don't think I'm fit to drive right now anyway."

They both sat up and he kissed her breasts.

"Oh, Zach, I don't know what to say. I've never had anything like that happen to me."

"Well, the important question is, 'Did you like it?'"

She began to cry. "You'll probably think I'm stupid, but I've never had an orgasm before. That was the first time and you gave me four." She then began to giggle.

"Oh, Sarah. I don't know what kind of man your husband was, but he didn't do you justice. But if you allow me, you'll never miss out ever again. I feel honored to have given you those orgasms. Mine was quite spectacular as well. And, Sarah, for the record, I would *never,* nor could I *ever* think you were stupid. You're a very delightful woman, whom I'm very happy I've met."

They kissed a few more times and then climbed into bed and were both asleep in a matter of minutes.

The following morning Sarah woke to Zach serving her breakfast in bed.

"For you, mi' lady."

"Oh, goodness. I can't recall the last time anyone served me breakfast in bed. Have you eaten?"

"Not yet. I wanted to make sure you ate first."

Sarah smiled. "Would you be insulted if we took this out to the kitchen so we could eat together?"

"Of course not. I'll carry this back out to the table while you put on a robe."

He lingered at the door so he could watch her naked body walk across the floor. She turned and smiled as he stroked his groin and said, "You make me horny, Sarah."

Once in the kitchen they had a delightful breakfast. Sarah called Martha, and she told Sarah that the girls were in her bedroom watching cartoons.

"Don't worry, Sarah. I'll keep them here for a couple more hours. You and Zach just enjoy the morning. This is our secret."

When Sarah walked out, Zach was preparing his own meal. She walked over to him; he turned, put his arms around her and kissed her.

"Sarah, I can't remember the last time I've had such a wonderful evening and morning. This has been...trying to find the right word...fun!"

They ate breakfast; then he said, "It's 10 a.m. I better get going. I don't want your daughters coming back and asking questions."

Before he left, he even did the dishes.

He went out the TV room door as he kissed her again. "The game on Sunday is at 3 p.m. I'll pick you up around 1, okay?"

"One it is, Zach. Thank you so much for a delightful time."

They kissed once more and he left.

Sarah called Martha and told her the coast was clear. She was soon walking in the side door with the girls.

"Mom, did you have a wonderful evening?" asked Lily as she hugged Sarah.

"Sweetie, I felt like Cinderella; and he called me a princess, Katie."

"I told you, Mom. When can we meet him?" asked Katie.

"Well, Sunday; that is, if we can find you two a sitter."

Martha spoke up, "That's me. I should be back from my fantasy adventure well before noon. Will that work, Sarah?"

Sarah was blushing. "That would be perfect. He's picking me up at 1 p.m. We're going to a Celtics game, and then he's going to prepare dinner for me. Imagine that?"

"Goodie, Mom." Lily was smiling from ear-to-ear. She was so happy to see her mom this happy.

"Are you girls okay with me dating?"

"Are you kidding?" Lily poked Katie. "We want you to be happy!"

"Yes, Mommy. We want you to have your own prince." Katie looked so innocent.

"Thank you, Lily and Katie. That makes me feel very relieved. Now, if you don't mind watching TV for a while, Martha and I are going to the kitchen."

Once in the kitchen, Sarah held up a can of diet Pepsi to which Martha nodded. They both sat down and Sarah began to whisper.

"Oh, Martha. He is such a gentleman and a very sexy one at that. I had my first orgasm last night. In fact, I had four. I thought I was going to faint. He gave them to me with his tongue if you can imagine."

"Sarah. This is a long time coming. Just go with this and see where it takes you both. Sunday you need to put that teddy you bought yourself in your purse. And don't even think of coming home until Monday after the girls are off to school."

"What about you, Martha? You need to make sure you indulge yourself as well."

"Trust me, I plan to. I'm not planning on coming home until Sunday morning. I'm going to jump George's bones tonight if he doesn't make the first move."

Both ladies were giggling when Emily called.

"Hi, Mom. How are you doing?"

"I'm doing fantastic, honey."

Just as she said that, Martha grabbed Sarah's phone and told Emily that her mom went to the ballet with Zach the previous night and he spent the night. Then she whispered, "He gave her four orgasms."

Sarah grabbed the phone back and was about to apologize, but Emily was crying. "What's wrong, sweetie?"

"Oh, Mom, I'm so happy for you. It's a wish come true. I have a confession to make. The other night I was purposely looking for Zach. I knew where he hung out, but he surprised me because he was at the restaurant. He's such a wonderful professor, and he seems like an equally wonderful man. When are you seeing him again?"

"Sunday afternoon. We're going to a Celtics game, and he's going to cook for me later. What should I wear to the game, Emily?"

"Mom, those jeans and that red sweatshirt you had on the other day would be perfect. You need to look very dressed down. Oh, and bring that sexy thing you bought from Victoria's Secret so you can christen it that night. I'm so happy for you, Mommy!"

Sarah smiled warmly at how young and sincere her daughter sounded. She then reflected on her good fortune.

I'm happy Joe died first, and I was given a second chance in life to prove I do have a backbone. I'm so proud to have Emily as my daughter. Thank you, God, for giving me this opportunity to be proud and happy.

****

Sunday Sarah dressed in the jeans and sweatshirt. She slipped on a pair of flat boots and tucked her jeans in just as she had seen Emily do. She admired herself in the mirror and then began fiddling with her hair. She pulled it into a pony tail, then changed to two pig tails, took two pictures with her phone and sent them to Emily, then called her.

"Mom, you look so youthful. Wear the pigtails. Do you have a little red ribbon to tie around them?"

"I think I do. Are you sure?"

"Yes. I'm positive. He'll think he's dating a young girl. It will make him very hot."

"Emily, I'm blushing."

"Good. Guys like it when females blush; so blush away, Mom, and have a delightful day and night."

A little after 1 p.m. Sarah heard Zach's car pull up. The girls were in the TV room. Sarah wanted them to meet him.

He knocked on the back door and Lily opened it. She introduced herself and Katie and asked Zach to have a seat while she got her mom.

When Lily and Sarah came out, Zach was playing a game of Operation with Katie; and Katie was winning.

As Sarah walked in, Katie exclaimed, "Mommy, you look like a little girl and Zach is fun!"

Martha walked in the door just as they were about to leave.

"Well hello, Martha! George called me on my way over and told me what a delightful day and evening the two of you had." He shook Martha's hand as she blushed.

Then Zach took both Katie's and Lily's hands and kissed them.

"Just like in the fairy tales, Mommy." Katie giggled and Lily rolled her eyes, then laughed.

Once in the car, Zach looked at Sarah. "You look like a young girl, Sarah. I'm afraid I must be blushing. And your daughters are delightful."

"Do you have any children, Zach?"

"Yes, I have a son who is in his early 20s. He's in college and plans to go to medical school. He'll be here visiting next Saturday. Perhaps you could meet him. I'd like that."

"I would too. Emily thinks the world of you, Zach. She tells me you're her favorite professor."

"Well, Emily is a very bright young woman. I believe she has a promising future ahead of her."

They had a delightful day and the meal he prepared was heavenly. After eating and cleaning up, they settled in to sitting on his sofa with a glass of wine and classical music playing in the background. They talked for about two hours about both their backgrounds and experiences. At 9 p.m. Zach asked, "Sarah, would you like to go home now? We better go before I have any more wine."

She looked over at him, feeling embarrassed and unsure of herself. She didn't know if he had changed his mind about her, so she answered reflecting her thoughts, "If that's what you want."

He put his glass down on the end table, moved closer and began caressing her face. "I don't want you to leave, but I also don't want to seem aggressive or presumptuous. I just don't want to scare you off, Sarah. I like you quite a bit."

She was immediately relieved. Then she giggled, reached into the bottom of her purse and pulled out her turquoise blue teddy. She was a bit tipsy as she slightly slurred, "Good, because I was hoping to wear this tonight. I've had it for a couple of months now and nowhere to wear it."

He blushed and gleefully pled, "Please go put it on. Oh, Sarah, hurry. I'm afraid I'm getting very flush just thinking about you in that."

He kissed her, she got up and he patted her on her behind as she giggled like a little girl.

When she came back out, her hair was down, and he began to swoon. The best he could do was gesture with his hand for her to come to him. She did.

He pulled her to his lap so she was straddling him as she faced him. "I feel utterly honored that I am the lucky man to get to see you in this utterly sensual piece."

He began to kiss her passionately. She could feel his hardness under her. He then pulled her shoulder straps down and kissed her breasts. Then he unzipped his pants.

She looked at his manhood and asked, "May I sit on it?"

"Please, Sarah!"

She lifted up and he pushed the crotch of her teddy to one side as she slid down. She was looking at his face as he became overwhelmed with passion. She was smiling when he was about to come. He grabbed her face and said, "Kiss me hard, Sarah!" He moaned loudly as he came.

They quietly sat still as he caught his breath. Then he softly spoke. "Stand up, Sarah, so I can take your teddy off."

She did. He kissed her breasts and her stomach, then patted the sofa as he tossed a pillow to the other end. She lay down and he began to kiss her thighs as he stroked her clitoris. "Does this feel good?"

The best she could do was close her eyes and nod enthusiastically. So he kept rubbing. Soon she bucked and immediately bucked again. He kept going until she had two more orgasms.

She opened her eyes and said, "Oh my god, Zach. You know so much about the female body. I can't believe I've missed out on this all my life."

He said, "Stay the night and we'll do this again later."

They did. They had glorious sex two more times before they left to go have brunch and then home to her house.

When they pulled into Sarah's driveway, Zach looked across the street and said, "Looks like George is with Martha. Shall we go over?"

Sarah put her hand on his. "Not just yet. Do you think we could have sex one more time today?"

"Why, Sarah! You naughty girl. You read my mind."

As they got out of the car and she unlocked the side door, he scooped her up and carried her inside. They never made it past the floor of the TV room. They fell asleep on the carpet as he lay behind her and continued to stroke her clitoris. This time he gave her four orgasms, fucked her again and gave her two more.

"I feel like I've died and gone straight to heaven." Sarah kissed him.

Zach replied, "Sarah, you've stolen my heart."

Chapter 12

A few weeks passed. Sarah saw Zach at least three times each week and had sex numerous times. He called her one evening and reminded her that Bill Harris would be in town the following week. Later they talked at length about the family's past and Emily's problems.

"I've known Bill for fifteen years. His work is groundbreaking. I think Emily will benefit tremendously from meditating. I think it could help you as well, Sarah. Please don't be upset with me when I say this, but Joe did a number on your self-confidence. The meditation could release the triggers that cause you to be fearful and unsure of yourself. Joe was a fool to have not encouraged you to blossom. I, on the other hand, want to enjoy watching you blossom and grow. It would be our adventure together."

"Zach, I'm not upset. I know now what he did to me. Emily told me numerous times how I would almost physically shrink when he would come home from duty abroad. He was so intent on keeping me dumb or at least feeling that way. I never noticed that until Emily first mentioned it when I think, believe it or not, she was only eleven.

"What her dad did to her made her grow up emotionally so fast. I do want her to get through all of this. I don't want her father to hold her back from his grave. And, believe me, I was beginning to change before I met you, but knowing you has accelerated those changes. In fact, Martha and I went to dinner the other night at a restaurant with a piano bar. We had a delightful evening. By the way, you and I need to go there. But, anyway, I used to play the piano. I think I got a little tipsy, and the piano player took a break and asked me to take over. Do you know that the restaurant owner came over to me later and asked me if I could work on the evenings his regular player was off? I was totally flattered. I haven't played for years, and it just seemed to come back to me. I'm actually thinking about getting a piano for the living room and getting rid of some of my furniture to make room for it."

They were lying in bed during this conversation. Later Sarah would tell both Emily and Martha that she had no idea how they got on the subject of Zach leasing his condo and moving in with Sarah and the girls. He told Sarah he was head over heels in love with her and wanted to be with her on a permanent basis. She said, "Yes, of course" because she was totally in love with him as well.

That Saturday evening Zach took Sarah and her three daughters to dinner at McCormick & Schmicks Seafood Restaurant in Providence. He told the girls he wanted it to be a special evening for all of them.

Emily thought for sure he had something up his sleeve. In fact, she was waiting for him outside class that Thursday. He told her that he planned to ask her mom to marry him and showed her a huge diamond solitaire he planned to give her that Saturday. Emily was so overwhelmed she hugged him and told him what wonderful things he was doing for her mom.

"Emily, your mom is doing wonderful things for me as well. I haven't felt this alive for years. I love your mother with all my heart and promise you all the years of her first marriage will be scrubbed away only to become a very distant memory."

He and Emily went over to the student cafeteria and talked about the conference he was taking her and Sarah to the following Thursday evening to listen to Bill Harris.

"Emily, I've arranged for the four of us to have dinner after at Anthony's Pier 4 Cafe in Boston. I've talked to Bill about your situation and he's anxious to meet you. He's even offered to personally work with you as you move through his Holosync program. He is going to offer you the program as a complementary offer if you allow him to write about you and your progress."

"Gosh, Zach, that sounds scary. But I'll talk to him about that. I'm open, but I don't want it to interfere with my life. Let's get through Saturday first. I'm so excited for both you and Mom."

"Well, don't tell her this either, but I've also arranged for a baby grand piano to be delivered to the house on Monday of next week. I intend on treating your mom like the royalty she is."

****

Later Emily filled Sean in on all the excitement. He was blown away by all that had happened but very happy for Sarah and for her daughters. She also told him she had purchased his plane ticket to fly into Providence in five weeks.

"Sean, I can't wait to see you. I miss you so much."

"Em, I think about you every minute of the day. I can't wait to hold you in my arms again. I can't wait to give you a little of what it sounds like your mom has been enjoying. I want to taste you again and cup your sweet breasts. So get that red teddy prepared because you're going to take me to heaven when I see you, red Emily heaven."

They laughed together and talked more about how wonderful it was going to be to see each other again.

Before she hung up, Emily told him that she couldn't wait for him to meet George. "Sean, I think George is going to move in with your grandma. Isn't that just wild?"

"Yea, Mom and Bill have been thrilled with Grandma's new love. They can't wait for me to meet him. Guess we're going to have to find somewhere else to spend time together."

"Oh, we'll figure it out. We don't need much. Just each other."

****

That Saturday Zach did indeed take the four ladies to dinner. He had partially moved in that Friday night, and the girls were thrilled to have a handsome man living in their house again; only this time their mom seemed to be utterly happy. Even Lily and Katie were getting wise to how Joe had stifled her while he was alive.

Saturday rolled around. Emily was home for the weekend, and the two girls were up in their bedroom putting their best dresses on. When Lily and Katie walked downstairs, Emily was in the TV room talking to Sean. As the girls walked by Sarah's room, they heard a lot of commotion and heard their mom giggling. Zach had been teasing Sarah by not letting her get dressed until he gave her what he called a good pussy lathering. When they emerged from the bedroom, Sarah was blushing but grinning from ear-to-ear, and Zach looked filled with satisfaction. Lily and Katie were too young to understand, but Emily knew exactly what they had been doing.

Zach summoned the girls to go get in the car while he helped Sarah with her coat. As Sarah and Zach emerged from the side door,

Lily exclaimed, "God, Em, I don't remember the last time Mom was so happy. I'm just so thrilled to have Zach around."

Katie concurred and Emily said, "Well, just wait till you see what's going to happen tonight."

"What? Tell us, Emily!" Lily excitedly begged.

"Just wait." Emily grinned widely and winked at both of them as Sarah climbed in the car.

Both Lily and Katie were very quiet that evening. They didn't want to miss out on what they both expected to be a huge surprise.

They ate dinner and were about to have dessert.

Zach had arranged with the pastry chef to dress up a slice of cheesecake for Sarah with the diamond in the middle of a red tulip flower on top. When the waiter put the slice down on the table in front of Sarah, Zach looked over at Emily and winked.

Emily leaned over to Lily and said, "This is it, Lily. Watch. Tell Katie." Katie was sitting on the other side of Lily.

The three girls were totally silent and staring at Sarah as she was about to take a bite of cheesecake when she looked at the girls, put her fork down and laughed.

"What are you girls staring at?"

"Not a thing, Mom." Emily was grinning as she then said, "Look, Mom, the chef put a red tulip on your slice."

Sarah looked down, lifted the plate up and said, "He or she certainly did. Zach, did you tell them to do this?" She then put the plate down and saw something glimmer inside the tulip. She looked closer and gasped.

Zach reached over and pulled the ring out of the flower. He then slid his chair back and knelt on one knee. "Sarah, will you do me the honor of marrying me? I would be happy for the rest of my life if you would say 'yes.'"

Both Lily's and Katie's mouths were wide open, and Emily just sat smiling while a tear rolled down her cheek. She grabbed her phone and started taking pictures as Sarah had the biggest surprise smile Emily had ever seen on her mom.

Then Zach said, "Hurry up and answer me, Sarah; my knee is killing me."

They all began to laugh as Sarah kissed him and said, "Yes, yes, yes, a thousand times yes!" Then she looked at the girls and said,

"Someone pinch me so I know this is real."

Katie jumped up, walked over to her mom and pinched her arm.

Lily looked at Katie and said, "You knucklehead. Mom was just using a figure of speech."

But now they were all laughing and hugging each other.

Several tables around them had all hushed, and the occupants were turned toward the five as they began applauding. The pastry chef came out of the kitchen to see what the applause was all about only to realize what had just happened. The waiter was taking pictures of the five with Emily's phone as the chef got in the act holding up her tulip creation.

Emily spent the entire ride home sending the pictures out to Sean, Martha and Jeannie. Her phone was ringing off the hook.

"Mommy, Mommy, when will you and Zach get married? Can I be in the wedding?" Katie begged.

"Oh, honey, I think you all will be in the wedding." Zach looked over at Sarah and grabbed her hand. When they stopped at the red light, he lifted it up and said, "Look, girls, how it sparkles on your mom's hand."

The girls clapped joyously.

Then Zach urged, "You know, girls. I've always wanted a daughter, and now I'm going to have three!"

The girls clapped again.

That evening when the girls were in bed and Zach and Sarah were behind closed doors, she told him how happy he made her.

"You have no idea, Sarah, how you've changed my life. I was so bored and convinced I would never find joy again. I was even resigned, thinking I was going to grow old all alone, and then you came into my life. My god, you just don't know what you've done for me!"

He kissed her ever so gently, then grinned widely. "We need to set a date and then decide where to go for a honeymoon. The world is your oyster, Sarah. I have enough invested that we can go anywhere you desire to go. I want to make you happy for the rest of your life. Now please put a cherry on this wonderful evening and go put on that naughty turquoise teddy so I can rip it off. My penis is throbbing for you, Sarah!"

She did and when it came time to take it off her, she said things she never thought she would hear herself say.

"Hurry up, Zach. Devour my pussy and then fuck me to heaven."

"Sarah, I've never known a woman who enjoyed sex as much as you!"

She was breathless. "I never knew how wonderful sex with the right man could be. I'm making up for lost time! You make my body scream for more!"

He laughed joyously and obliged with gusto.

Chapter 13

Monday afternoon Sarah was totally surprised when someone rang her front door bell. She peeked out the living room window on the way to the door and saw what appeared to be a delivery truck from a music store. Martha saw the truck from her car as she pulled into her driveway after running an errand. She jumped out and ran across the street just as Sarah opened the door.

"Ma'am, we're here to deliver your piano."

Sarah looked totally confused? "My piano? You must be at the wrong house. I didn't order a piano."

The driver scratched his head, unfolded the invoice and asked, "Do you know Zachery Williams?"

"Well, yes, I do."

Martha was standing behind the driver on the front walk. "Sarah, Zach wanted to surprise you!"

"I don't believe this. I have nowhere to put a piano."

The driver smiled. "He paid us extra to have us move some of your furniture into your garage temporarily."

Sarah had her hand on her head and a look of total disbelief on her face. "Okay, maybe we should move some of the furniture first."

Martha walked in and laughed. "What do you want them to move, Sarah?"

"Wow …well, I guess the sofa, two chairs and tables. We can move stuff back in after, I guess. I just can't believe this."

The driver called over his helper, and they began moving furniture. Left on the floor was a large oriental rug.

"How big is the piano?" Sarah still couldn't believe what was happening.

"It's a grand piano," replied the driver. "This rug, if pulled to the center of the room, would work perfectly. We could put the piano in the middle of the room."

"Okay, okay." Sarah went over on the stairs and sat as she watched the men move the rug, then walk back to the truck.

Soon she had a beautiful ebony Steinway grand piano sitting

smack dab in the middle of her former living room.

When she finished signing for the piano and closed the door, she dialed Zach. He didn't answer so she looked at her watch and realized he was in class. She left a message.

"What on earth were you thinking, Zach? I just don't know what to say about this piano; and, my god, it's a Steinway. You must have spent a fortune. All I can say is you are a crazy man. I'm just so happy you're my crazy man!"

He felt his phone vibrate in the pouch on his belt. He was in the middle of a lecture when he took it out. He smiled broadly, put it back in the pouch and asked his graduate student assistant, "Now where was I, Cheryl?"

That evening there was a lot of commotion in the house as Lily and Katie played "Chopsticks" on the piano, and Zach and Sarah were in what was now *their* bedroom. Later they all went out for Chinese food.

"What do you think of your mom's new toy, girls?"

Lily exclaimed, "Zach, it's beautiful. I hardly remember the last time I heard Mom play."

Katie tugged at Sarah's sleeve, "Mommy, will you play for us when we get home?"

She did and she played magnificently. Of course, all three members of her audience had to sit on the floor since all the furniture was sitting in the garage, but they didn't mind; and they were mesmerized by her playing.

Before playing, Zach spread a blanket on the floor. "Girls, it will seem as if we're at an outdoor concert."

The girls clapped and plunked down on the blanket. Zach asked Sarah to wait till he came back.

He came back with three small juice glasses of wine. "Girls, a little wine is in order."

Sarah was still suffering from provincialism. "Zach, the girls are too young to get used to that!"

He simply laughed and waved his hand.

"Sarah, you Americans are overly concerned about wine. It's the tradition in most of the world for children to have a little wine on special occasions. Relax, sweetie."

"Yea, Mom," smiled Katie. "We're just being Aussie!"

121

Sarah laughed and began playing.

When it was time for the girls to go to bed, Lily said, "Mom, Zach has brought so much love and fun to our house."

Katie exclaimed, "Mom, can we keep him?"

They all laughed as Zach kissed both girls and said goodnight as the girls climbed the stairs.

As Sarah and Zach sat on the bench of the piano, Sarah broke down. "What's the matter, Sarah? You should be happy."

"I am, Zach. I'm happier than I ever imagined I could be. That's why I'm crying. Like you, I never, ever expected my life to turn out like this. I was so unhappy for so long that I just accepted it. You make me so very happy."

He kissed her, stood up and extended his hand. When they went into the bedroom, they didn't make love, at least not in the sexual way. They lay in the bed and tenderly cuddled, simply enjoying being physically close to one another. They fell asleep wrapped in each other's arms.

****

That following Thursday in early evening, Sarah drove up to Brown and parked in the lot of Emily's dorm building. She was about to call Emily when Zach pulled up next to her. She got out of her car and went over to Zach, kissed him and hugged him and told him she would rather run up and knock on Emily's room vs. call her on the phone. He said he'd just listen to music while he waited.

Emily opened her door. "Mom, I've been waiting for you to call me. I would have walked down."

"I know, sweetie, but I thought I'd come up and get you, rather than do the impersonal thing of calling."

"Okay, is Zach out there?"

"Yes, he is, Emily. He's waiting."

Emily threw her coat on.

As she did, Sarah sat on her small bed.

"Is everything okay Mom?"

"Honey, everything is more than okay. Everything's perfect. I just want you to know that I treasure you for who you've become. My life has turned from being a life of sadness, self-doubt and resignation into one of optimism, love and sheer joy; and I know I have you to thank for most of that. I just wanted to tell you that, Emily."

Emily sat down, took her mom's hand in hers and smiled. "Oh, Mommy, I've longed for this day for so long; I can't even remember when I wasn't wishing for this. You're such a good person who deserves to know and enjoy all the happiness I've found with Sean. This is just such a joyous time for me as well, and now we're both going to put the rest of the damage Dad did behind us."

They hugged, stood up and walked hand in hand down to Zach's waiting car.

Emily climbed in back.

Zach turned as Emily closed the door. "Hello, Emily. Are you ready to go listen to Bill Harris?"

"Yes, Zach, I am. I also want to tell you how much I appreciate you and how happy you're making my mom. She told me about the piano and how much fun you and the girls had listening to her play."

Zach was smiling as he backed out of the parking space. "It's not at all hard making your mom happy. It fills me with joy to do that because she's brought so much joy into my life, and we have you to thank for that."

"What do you mean, Zach?"

He chuckled. "Your mom told me you had planned on going to some of my hangouts that evening we ran into all of you. You weren't expecting me to be at the restaurant, though."

Emily laughed. "I confess. I wanted you and Mom to meet, but what a surprise it was to see you at Camille's. Makes me feel you two were meant to meet."

She watched Zach look over at Sarah and smile. She sensed that he also squeezed her mom's hand by the way her mom responded.

Zach looked in the rearview mirror and said, "I hear Sean is coming home the week after next. I'm looking forward to meeting him. Your mom tells me you've been sweethearts since the age of eleven."

"Yes, he is and I'm so looking forward to that. It's only been a few months since we've seen each other, but it seems like an eternity. Sean has been through a lot with me. I wish he could be here for this evening. He's studying neuroscience at Berkeley and is interested in neuroplasticity, into which the Holosync falls. So it's kind of cool that I have the opportunity to go listen to Bill Harris and even get to meet him. I'm looking forward to tonight. Thanks for doing this for us."

"My pleasure, Emily, my pleasure. I hope this is something that can help you gain a little inner peace. I'm also hoping it will help your mom believe in herself more. I just want to say to both of you that I'm so sorry for what Joe did to you, Emily, and to both of you. It's sad that there are people like that in the world, let alone have one of those individuals become your dad and your mom's husband. But all that is changing, and I see a bright future for both of you; and, even more, I'm going to be part of that future!"

"Well, I can see a bright future for Mom for sure. You make Mom so happy, Zach. By the way, have you two decided on a wedding date?"

Sarah turned. "I'm waiting for Paul to get back to me. I want to make sure he's able to attend. I'd like him to give me away."

"Oh, Mom, that would be beautiful. How did he take all of this?"

"I think at first he wasn't sure; but after talking to him several times, he can tell I'm happy, so he's happy."

****

Listening to Bill Harris talk was spellbinding. Both Emily and Sarah had read his book, so everything Bill talked about made perfect sense. Later at dinner Bill repeated what Zach had talked about.

He did indeed want to monitor Emily's success and asked if, in the future, she'd be willing to give testimony and even attend some of his discussion conferences. She agreed. Bill was so delighted that he handed Emily all the material and the CD for the first stage of what he called *Awakening*. He also handed Sarah the same and told her it was compliments of Zach.

When Emily got back to her dorm room that night, she listened to the first thirty minutes of the CD. She had promised Bill she would follow the protocol by not moving into the second thirty minutes until after her first week in order to allow her unconscious to become acclimated.

When Zach left for the university the following morning, Sarah popped the CD into her new CD player and listened to the first thirty minutes.

Once Emily was through the first week and was now listening to the full hour, she realized she was feeling very sad and was crying constantly. She immediately called Bill who had given her his personal cell number.

"Emily, do you recall what we talked about? This is normal. Your brain is resisting letting go of something. Just step back mentally, acknowledge something is happening, then step out of the way, giving your unconscious the green light to let it go. Don't try to analyze the situation because you'll never be able to. In reality, however, the *whys* of your situation don't matter. It simply matters that you allow your unconscious to clean out all the cobwebs of your past. Emily, you're going to be experiencing a lot of this type of thing. You have a lot of excess baggage to let go of. But this is a good thing that you're having results immediately. Call me if you feel anything else or question anything. I'm happy for you, Emily."

Chapter 14

Two weeks rolled around fast. Emily was on her way to the airport to pick up Sean.

She was beside herself with excitement, and she couldn't wait to tell Sean about the surprise George and Martha had popped on her that afternoon.

Sean texted Emily as soon as he landed, "Where's my sweet Emily? I just landed!"

She texted back, "I'm out here watching the doors for your beautiful face. Hurry up!"

He had only a carry-on so he ran through the terminal almost falling once and slamming into someone who stopped dead in his tracks just in front of him; then he was out the door. Her heart flew over to him when she saw him.

She jumped out of her car and waved like a fool until he spotted her. He ran over to the car, dropped his bag on the ground and picked her up. They were kissing when a patrolman strolled by and told them they needed to move the car.

Sean picked up his bag and threw it in the small trunk of her red Beetle. "Do you want me to drive, baby?"

Without a word she handed him the keys and hopped into the passenger side. She sat sideways jabbering like a magpie. Then she remembered her surprise.

"Sean, you'll never guess! First your mom and Bill are coming down to your grandmother's for dinner. Second, George decided to postpone moving in with your grandma until after you leave to go back, so your grandma's house is ours. We don't have to find somewhere else to be alone."

"You're kidding. Where's Grandma going?"

"George's youngest daughter lives with him at his house, so Martha is going to stay up there while you're here. Isn't that just perfect?"

He grabbed her hand and squeezed it. "Em, it is perfect. God, we're so lucky to have such caring and understanding families. I'm

126

still in awe of what your mom did for us my last night before heading out to Berkeley!"

He was referring to Sarah's painful decision to go against her staunch Catholic upbringing and side with Martha, who had offered that she stay with Sarah and the girls that night while Emily spent hers and Sean's last evening together at Martha's home.

Emily laughed joyfully.

"God, I know. That was just the first of my being blown away by my mom's changes and look at her now: engaged to be married to my professor and acting like a little girl in a sex candy store. Isn't it wonderful?"

He snickered, "Yes, it is, Em. It's wonderful for all of us."

They were holding hands when she said, "Wait a minute."

She unbuttoned her blouse and pulled her blouse back so as to expose her chest.

"Do you remember this?"

"My god, my little red bra. How could I forget? I've masturbated to that mental image."

She looked down at his lap and giggled, "My, my, Sean. Did I just make you horny?"

He smiled as she moved closer, reached over, unzipped his pants and reached in. She then said, "Pull over into that parking lot for a minute."

It was a Stop & Shop lot he pulled into. "What are you going to do?"

She just smiled, squirmed down on the seat and took his penis into her mouth.

"Holy shit, Em. Where'd you learn that?"

"Jeannie told me guys like this, so I thought I'd see how you like it. If you like it half as much as I like your giving me an orgasm with your tongue, then I'll be happy as can be. Now just sit there and look natural so no one knows what I'm doing."

He was rubbing her head and back while she moved her mouth up and down. She had a small towel in her purse which she managed to pull out. When he came, he exclaimed, "God damn, Emily!"

She spit his cum into the towel, sat up and smiled. "Did you like that?"

"All I can say is I can't wait till we're alone and I can reciprocate.

Your pussy is going to ache when I'm done with it."

"I can't wait. Now let's go home."

He was smiling from ear-to-ear as she leaned against the window, buttoned her blouse and put her seat belt back on.

When they pulled into Emily's driveway, Martha came running out of her house waving them over.

Beth and Bill were already there. Zach, Sarah and the two girls were also, as well as Jeannie, John and George. Martha had prepared a feast.

Sean told Sarah how thrilled he was for her and Zach. He and Emily then sat down on the sofa and began talking to John who began by saying, "So you're the person responsible for Jeannie and me running into each other."

"I don't know. Why's that?"

Jeannie, who was sitting on John's lap, laughed. "Remember? I pulled over to the shoulder to call you. It was the day after Sarah found Emily's diary. I met John when I was pulling back onto the highway. He stopped to arrest me for sitting on the side of the road."

All four laughed. "God. I forgot all about that. I guess I am the culprit, John. Guilty as charged. But I hear it all worked out anyway. In fact—" He squeezed Emily. " — look how well everything's turned out since then. Grandma's getting some. Emily's mom is getting some. I got some. Err ...whoops, I wasn't supposed to say that, was I?"

Jeannie began laughing again, then whispered, "Emily Callaway, did you go down on Sean today on the way home from the airport?"

Emily just giggled and wiped her mouth with her sleeve.

They all had a wonderful evening. When it was time to clean up, everyone pitched in; but they wouldn't let Sean and Emily participate. "You two go do whatever you want," Martha and Beth both said.

Emily whispered, "Let's go sit on the slant tree, Sean."

Once seated, Sean put his arm around her, "I've missed you, Em. I can't wait till everyone leaves."

"Why? What are you going to do to me?"

"I'm going to ravish you!" He moved his hand off her shoulder and around her back, pulling her close as he reached around the front and touched her breast.

Emily was giggling when they heard a voice from behind, "I can see what you two are doing."

They jumped and turned to see Lily who was laughing.

Emily waved for her to come up. The three of them sat on the tree talking and laughing till Martha called them in for dessert.

They all, including the two young girls, had a small sliver of cheesecake and a small glass of Grand Marnier.

Bill began by toasting Sean's welcome. Then came a toast for Sarah and Zach and lastly, Sean toasted Martha and George for being so thoughtful and giving up the house for Emily and him.

When the dining room and kitchen were cleaned, everyone began to leave. Martha ran to her bedroom and returned with a suitcase.

"Thanks, Grandma, for doing this for us. You too, George."

"Seanie, we want you and Emily to have your privacy. You two only have a few days so we all wanted you to be able to enjoy every minute without worrying about that."

George and Martha were the last to leave as Emily came back into the kitchen. She had been saying goodnight to her mom and Zach.

Sean was sitting at the kitchen table. She sat down and they clutched each other's hands. He looked at her and kissed her fingertips. "Let's go upstairs, Em. I'm getting really tired."

They turned off all the downstairs lights and made sure the two doors were locked; then they walked up to Sean's bedroom. Martha had set it up again with a scarf over the small night stand lamp. The two fell to the bed in each other's arms. They made exquisite love, then climbed under the covers and fell asleep.

The following morning Emily woke to Sean sitting next to her on the bed. She smiled. "I thought I was dreaming you were here."

"Em, I'm here. I just wanted to watch your sweet face as you slept. Are you hungry?"

"Umm." She stretched. "Yes; I'm starving."

"Grandma left a refrigerator full of food. Let's go downstairs. I made some coffee." He laughed. "She left me a pad full of instructions on how to make coffee, bacon and eggs and all sorts of things. I think she wanted me to take care of you this week vs. you taking care of me. Grandma's full of surprises."

"Sean, I know you know this, but I just want to express how

special your grandma truly is. She's done so much for both Mom and me to help make us feel safe and hopeful. I don't know what I would have done without her in our lives. She's also done a great job of filling in for you while you've been away…in most departments."

He snickered, "Most departments?"

"Well, no one can make me feel sexy except you." She lowered the covers to expose her bare breasts.

He smiled and bent down and kissed both. "Well, I was going to suggest we go downstairs to eat, but now I think we're going to have to wait awhile."

"Why's that?" Emily sounded very demure.

He stood up and removed all his clothes and climbed in next to her.

He leaned over her and sweetly whispered, "I love you, Emily Callaway. I'll love you forever. I know we need to talk about some things this week, but for now I want to feel your warmth close to me."

She didn't say a word. There was plenty of time to talk about what she intuited he was referring to. She just wanted to feel him close to all of her as well.

As they lay in each other's arms a half hour later, both exhausted and covered with sweat, they kissed one last time. Sean then got up and extended his hand to her. As she got up, he wrapped her in the red with white trim silk bathrobe. They went downstairs and Sean asked Emily to sit while he fumbled through making them breakfast. She began to giggle joyfully as she watched him try his best to cook and read the instructions at the same time.

"I can't stand this. I don't like hard fried eggs; and if I don't jump in and help, that's what I'll get, I'm afraid."

They both laughed between kisses and made breakfast together. When they were finished, he commanded her to sit. "I do know how to clean up and don't need written or verbal instructions for that part."

She lovingly watched him clean up the dishes, shelf and stove and remarked to herself how different in *all* ways Sean was, compared to her father. She thanked her lucky stars for Sean and also for Zach for her mom.

She was fearful of the future because she had an uncanny feeling that she and Sean would be apart for some years, but she tried hard to hold onto the belief that it would be short-lived in perspective to how long they'd already been together and would be together again.

A few days later Emily told Sean she would like to have that discussion.

They talked about her behavior over the last few months; and although they both knew where the behavior came from, she told him she didn't know what would happen in the future.

"I'll try my best not to let my fears get in the way; but, Sean, sometimes I don't seem to be able to control them. I don't even know they're about to rear their head until I'm in the midst of fear; then it takes all of me to try and push the fear away, only to realize that my efforts are fruitless. Yet I feel confident that over time and with the help of meditation, my unconscious will become a healthy one."

She then told him about the dream she had that night and read him the recap of that dream from her diary.

He remembered that night. It was the night he told her he was thinking of transferring to Harvard. He then looked off into the distance as if something were trying to make him remember.

"What's going through your head, Sean?"

"I don't know. Somehow I remember that night I also had a dream, and it was my dad who talked to me. I remembered he had come to me that night but couldn't remember what it was he told me. Your recap of your dream is making me think he told me some of the same things. You know, Em, maybe I am supposed to stay at Berkeley. I want to work with vets who suffer from PTSD. Between your decision to begin meditating and a psychiatrist I've read about who has been working with patients who suffer from obsessive compulsion disorder, I'm thinking that I want to begin formulating my work toward working with these vets in order to do my doctorate thesis on how meditation could help soldiers suffering from PTSD. Berkeley isn't far from the Centerpointe Institute. Dr. Schwartz, the psychiatrist, is at UCLA. I was thinking maybe you could put me in touch with Bill Harris to see if he'd be interested in working with me on a project where I could amass enough data to get a huge jump on my thesis. Unfortunately, if I'm here at Harvard, it would be more difficult to do that. But Berkeley gives me access to everything, including Fort Irwin which is a major training facility for the Army."

"Sean, just promise me you won't marry anyone else until you find me, and we learn what our future is supposed to hold."

"Oh, baby, I don't think we're going to be apart. I think you're just overreacting to your dream. But, just in case it's true, I promise you with all my heart I'll come find you before I do anything as stupid as to marry someone else. You're my future, Em. You're my life, sweetie. I don't think there's another human being in this world that could hold a candle to what you mean to me."

"Oh, Sean, I love you for saying that. I know there's no one in the world for me but you. I just believe that with all my heart!"

Then she pondered. "Well, now that that's settled and we both agree that you need to ditch the Harvard plan, let's just put all this aside and enjoy all the time we have together. I love you, Seanie."

They kissed sweetly and passionately, then discussed what they were going to do that day and for the rest of the time they were together during the break.

Chapter 15

The summer of 2002 and the next four years were years of lots of changes for everyone. During that summer there were two weddings. By then Sarah had completely abandoned the Catholic Church, and Zach leaned more toward atheism than any religion. Thus they chose to marry in a lavish Unitarian Church ceremony while Martha and George were married in a far simpler fashion.

The day prior to Sarah's wedding, she and Zach accompanied Martha and George to the Providence marriage license bureau where they not only got their marriage license but also were married in a very simple ceremony conducted by a Justice of the Peace. As a surprise for Martha and George, the reception for Sarah and Zach also turned out to be a reception for Martha and George. Sarah and Zach's wedding ceremony was beautiful as was the reception for both couples.

Sean was home from school. He, Emily, the two girls and Zach's son Dylan were at the courthouse for Martha's wedding as were Beth and Bill.

During and after the ceremony, Sean noticed that Dylan was conspicuously sweet on Emily. That realization gave Sean a dose of what he had experienced during semester break with Emily's reaction to Anne Hightower. He didn't at all like what he saw. But, as he dissuaded Emily's fears, she did the same. She liked Dylan, but Sean was her love.

Besides, she told Sean, he was now her half-brother. "Good grief, Sean, it would be like you driving an automatic in your Mustang. If driving an automatic vs. a stick shift in a Mustang is like kissing your sister, then, being sweet on Dylan would be like kissing my brother!" Then she exclaimed with a shudder, "Yuk!"

Satisfied by the joke, Sean felt much less threatened. However, Emily admitted to Jeannie later that she was glad it happened because it helped Sean understand her reaction far better than he did prior. It was a reality check for Sean which she felt he sorely needed.

****

Emily and the girls had a wonderful time helping their mom prepare for her wedding. All three girls insisted that Sarah wear white.

Lily was the most vocal. "Mom, that stuff about white and virginity is old school. Do you know how many weddings there are nowadays with the brides being anything but virgins?"

Of course, Lily's comment led to an interrogation about her sexual activity which, as Emily knew, was non-existent.

Once she admitted to Emily she did let a boy feel her breasts, but that was as far as Lily had ever gone. She wanted to save herself because she believed Emily was right about making sex very special. It took a lot of convincing, however, to get Sarah off her case; but with Emily's help, Sarah finally believed Lily that she was still a virgin and had no desire or plans to change that in the near future.

With encouragement from her girls, Martha and Zach, Sarah did indeed wear white. She added a little blue, however, by wearing her birthstone, sapphire.

Zach had given her a beautiful sapphire pendant necklace, the girls gave her sapphire earrings and George and Martha gave her a sapphire bracelet as wedding presents.

Sarah clung to some of her traditionalism. "I feel better by adding the color to the white. I don't want anyone gossiping about my choice to wear white. Besides, if I recall, a little blue is appropriate for the bride."

Of course, no one even hinted at being dismayed she was wearing white. The wedding attendees were just pleased as punch that Sarah had found such a delightful husband and step-father for her son and daughters.

Emily was thrilled when Sarah asked her to be her maid of honor. She assumed Sarah would ask Martha, but Sarah wouldn't have it any other way. She was so proud of her daughter and couldn't think of anyone else she wanted to stand up for her other than Emily. Martha and the two younger girls were her bridesmaids. George, of course, was Zach's best man. His son Dylan and two of Dylan's cousins were part of his wedding party as well.

Paul came home for the wedding and did indeed proudly give his mom away. He brought home a surprise as well.

****

In Italy on his last cruise, he had met a young woman whom he married. Her maiden name was Alessa Giovanni. She was three months pregnant when they arrived for the wedding. While home, Paul told Sarah that he and Alessa had made the decision that he would stay in the Navy and make it his career. He was so highly thought of by ranking officers that he moved through the grades rapidly and was soon to be promoted to Petty Officer 2nd Class.

"Mom, as you are aware, it's steady work, good pay, excellent benefits, and when I retire, I'll retire at 80% of my pay grade. I'm happy in the Navy, Mom; and now I'm happy in the other part of my life. Alessa is a wonderful partner and will make a wonderful mother, just like my mom."

Sarah loved Alessa as did Paul's sisters. Katie even told the couple it was fun having another person in their family with a strange accent.

"Zach's Aussie and Alessa is Italian. How fun is that?"

****

Prior to the wedding ceremony, Sarah began filling in at the piano bar. She was asked a month later to become their prime piano player when the person for whom she substituted left for another venue. She tried it out for about three months but found the time away from her two younger daughters, who were growing up fast, was more than she wanted to handle so she went back to playing on off days for the full-time person the bar hired. On those evenings, Zach was one of the bar's regular customers. He hardly missed a night when Sarah played and was a great help in getting bar patrons to sing along.

There was more good news that summer. A few weeks prior to Martha's civil ceremony and Sarah's lavish one, Beth, who was pregnant, found out she was going to have a little girl. They had already chosen her name. Sean's baby sister would be named Abigail Patricia.

That summer of 2002 was a great summer for Sean and Emily. They were together non-stop. Martha and George would often leave for the weekend in order to take weekend trips or just go back and camp out at his home in Quincy. The young couple also spent a lot of time with Jeannie and DD whom Sean really liked and Emily adored.

****

2002 was a good year for everyone as was 2003 and 2004. 2005, on the other hand, was a sad year and a tumultuous one with a sprinkle of joy mixed in.

Joyous events included Emily's, Sean's and Jeannie's graduations. Emily and Sean had both graduated Cum Laude and were looking forward to beginning their graduate work the following fall. Jeannie, not so obsessed with grades, also graduated and was scheduled to begin teaching junior English Literature at East Providence High School in the fall.

There were other joyous events as well.

That previous December John proposed to Jeannie, and their wedding was set for Saturday, July 16th. Jeannie and her parents were busy making plans for a large wedding.

John was now a detective and had recently transferred to the Providence Police Department's Special Victim's Unit (SVU) which is what he had been working toward for several years.

Phil Chandler was thrilled that he and Jeannie were marrying and was looking forward to becoming a grandfather. He was relentless with his suggestions that the couple anoint him Granddad. Jeannie and John, on the other hand, wanted to wait a few years. They wanted to buy a house first before starting a family, and Gladys was very supportive of that plan.

Jeannie also entertained the thought that she would get her master's degree in order to give her the opportunity to move up to a principal's position. She was determined to remain economically independent, and John loved her for that.

He had watched too many of his fellow officers struggle with financial matters, and he knew the temptations for earning additional cash illegally were all around him. He didn't want that temptation, and Jeannie loved him for that.

****

Lily had just finished her junior year of college. She was working toward a bachelor's degree in nursing. She attended Jeannie's Alma Mater, URI. She was dating a pre-med student who would begin his senior year the following fall. Sarah liked Lily's beau, Peter Statler.

Lily managed to remain a virgin all through high school; but when she met Peter, she told Emily it was time for that trip to Planned Parenthood. Emily was thrilled to be the person to help her little sister become protected.

****

Paul and Alessa had purchased a modest home in the Norfolk area where he was still stationed when he wasn't out to sea. They were expecting their second child. Their first, a boy now three years old, was named Walter Paul after Sarah's father.

****

Sarah and Zach were still madly in love. He was scheduled to spend most of the summer in the Himalayas where he had managed to put a team of scientists together to study the environmental effects of global warming which were taking place at an alarmingly accelerated pace.

Scientists were learning that the melting of the glaciers in the Himalayas foretold dire consequences for the entire world. He leased a flat in Katmandu, Nepal. He was scheduled to leave at the end of June. Sarah would follow immediately after Jeannie's wedding. She had become very close to Gladys and wanted to help her with the wedding plans. Her plane was scheduled to leave on Monday, July 18th. Her absence would leave the three girls to manage the household by themselves.

****

Katie was no longer the baby of the family. She was fifteen, beautiful and full of energy. She loved sports and was captain of the high school soccer team. She also had lots of boys chasing after her.

Emily had the same discussion with her that she did with Lily about sex and Planned Parenthood. Emily had a feeling, however, that they would make that trip before she finished her senior year.

That same year, Sarah sat down with Katie, Lily and Emily. It was time to tell Katie about her father. Katie cried for several days after she was told. It would have been harder on her, however, if she didn't love her sister Emily as much as she did. Too, the fact that Zach was filling a void left by Joe helped. Nevertheless, she took it so hard that Sarah arranged for her to see a female counselor Dr. Wells recommended. Over time, Katie came to accept the terrible truth about her father. She still had fond memories of him and with Emily's encouragement was able to hold onto those memories while accepting the reality of her childhood.

One evening when Katie was feeling especially sad, Emily offered these comforting words, "Katie, I know how much you loved Dad, and it was also evident to me how much he loved you. Hold onto your loving memories."

Emily paused momentarily before speaking again. "You know, Katie, I once heard a friend say this about his mother."

Then, Emily held her two hands at chest level. Her palms were positioned upward, and they were cupped as if she were holding something. "Katie, my friend held up his two hands just as I am doing now. As he did, he said, 'Emily, I hold my mother in both hands. In my right hand, my mom is the loving mother whom I came to know. In my left hand, she's the mother my sister came to know. The two moms are different; but if I accept the difference with courage, I will always be able to support my sister in her emotional journey, and that makes me happy.'"

Katie was moved to tears by Emily's generous words. "Em, thank you for saying that. This is so hard for me. I will do just that. I will hold Dad in both my hands. I can't even imagine the pain, both physical and emotional, he caused you; but I know in my heart it had to be great. I just want you to know that I've always loved and admired my big sister, Emily. You've been and are still, even more so, my hero. So, I will hold a different father in my left hand and the weight of *that* hand will be great because the weight in my heart for you is great. I love you, Emily. I love you with all my heart."

The two sisters felt especially close that evening. They hugged tightly and, prior to turning in, talked for over an hour more.

That evening Emily wrote in her diary, "Dear Diary. Katie and I had the most wonderful conversation tonight, and I am so grateful for the love she expressed for me. That love reminds me of one of my favorite quotes by one of my favorite poets, Mary Oliver. 'Someone I loved once gave me a box full of darkness. It's taken me years to understand this too was a gift.' I am so grateful the future has turned out as it has. Mom has become the mother I always imagined her to be. Lily's courage and acceptance has been so much more than I ever expected. Paul has remained my loving big brother.

Then there's Katie. We've had a special relationship for most of my life. I was just so afraid she wouldn't be able to handle the truth. She was Dad's favorite. He doted on her. I think that relationship made me scared. I worried that our relationship would be changed forever as a result. But she surprised me tonight. She's been tormented by her new knowledge, and the torment hasn't just been for Dad. It's also been for me; and, diary, I can't tell you what that means to me. I always thought I was the big sister she worshiped. Tonight I learned I still am; and, that, in and of itself, fills my heart and soul with such hope for my future.

I thank the lucky stars that I have the family I have. I thank the stars for who I am, who I have become and who I will aim to be. I am happy for the first time in my life, I think…because, diary, I simply don't remember my life before my earthquake. I don't remember if I was ever happy beforehand. Those memories are all gone, erased by Dad's inability to turn toward goodness instead of the rotten path he chose. He lost everything in the end. He lost himself, his family and the three children whom he fooled. Most of all, he lost me. He had no idea who I was and what love I was capable of. He didn't care. He only cared about himself. I don't know where he is right now; but wherever he is, if he can think and feel, I hope he feels the burden of sadness for all he threw away. I hope he feels the pain of all the pain he caused. I hope he sees all he missed out on because he only cared for himself. With all my heart, I wish life with Dad could have been different; but it wasn't. I will learn to accept that and I'll work toward putting that knowledge into the perspective of my life as a whole. He *will not* ruin me, because surely he tried to. I am stronger than that. I am stronger because I **know** the true meaning of life, which is love; and now, despite him, I'm being rewarded with the love of each member of my family, all of whom I love completely. Thank you, diary, for listening to me tonight. I needed to talk to someone, and you were there just as you always have been there for me. One more thing. Please kiss my Sean for me. Give him wonderful dreams tonight. As I drift off to sleep, he will be close to my heart. Love, Em."

****

That same year there were also sad events. The saddest occurrence that took place was Martha's passing.

She and George were having a wonderful life. They purchased an RV and traveled frequently. It was on a June evening that she suffered a heart attack and was rushed to the hospital. Sean was home for the summer.

As the ambulance pulled into the emergency entrance and she was rushed into doctor's care, everyone was present in the waiting room. Sean had been staying with his grandma, and Emily was staying across the street in Zach and Sarah's home. They rode to the hospital together. Emily cried the entire way.

By 2005 Sean and Emily's relationship had become strained. They seemed to argue much of the time; but when they would finally make up, they both realized how trivial the bases for their arguments were. Nonetheless, being away from each other for such extended periods of time was taking a toll on the relationship.

The periodic misunderstandings and arguments were putting a lot of strain on them individually and on the relationship as well. Their lives, after all, were evolving separately, making the physical distance an emotional chasm. That night, however, the couple was solidly united as they comforted one another.

Everyone, including Emily and Sean, fell asleep in the waiting room. Emily buried her head in Sean's lap as he caressed it.

The following early afternoon Martha had been stabilized, and the doctors allowed everyone to individually sit with Martha, who was wide awake. When it came time for her to talk with Sean and

Emily, she talked to them together.

She told them that she was proud of how they had hung in together over the past several years. Then she said that these next three to four years would be their most difficult. They were both about to begin their graduate work, and that would take up all their time and give them very little time to be together physically.

"You need to let what will happen, happen. Your first priority should be your careers, only because they will become the bases of your relationship if there is to be one in the future."

At one point Martha crossed her arms and became very serious. "Sean, Emily, you need to be realistic about the future without being bitter. That's very important for both of you individually. Life is not always a guarantee."

Then she unfolded her arms and her face softened. "On the other hand, if you are to be together in the future, it will happen naturally. By allowing that to take place, your bond will become even stronger than it has ever been. Of this I am certain."

At one point Sean left the room for a few minutes, and Martha said things that Sean simply wasn't spiritually prepared for.

"Emily, I know you are more open-minded than Sean. I will not leave the two of you forever. I was very skeptical about the dream you had several years ago. You know the one I'm talking about?"

Through tears, Emily nodded.

"I'm not skeptical anymore. I am finding that when people are close to the end of their life, they become less attached to this world and are able to see things beyond it, which I think you've referred to as the other realm. I have knowledge now that I haven't had in the past.

"I've had discussions with Davie, and that's why I'm able to feel confident about your dream. He did talk to you that night as he also talked to Sean that same night. He advised both of you that Sean should stay at Berkeley. I'm so proud of you for listening to Davie.

"Emily, dear, I want you to know and believe that you and Sean *will* come back together, and you will have a wonderful life; but it will have its trials.

"You are going to have three children; and, like most individuals, they will be reincarnations of souls that have lived in this conscious realm. The most important thing for you to remember is that love is the answer to everything. If you keep that knowledge and understanding of that knowledge close to you, everything will be good.

"Never doubt who you are, Emily. You are one of the strongest, most loving individuals I have ever known in this lifetime. With all your might, hold onto that. It's the basis of your strength."

It was such a strange conversation with Martha, yet Emily felt certain that in time she would understand the meaning of it all.

When Sean came back into the room, the conversation became less spiritually charged. She told Sean that she was leaving him her house and that she had already purchased the land the slant tree sat on.

"I wanted you to own that land so it would be protected. It's now sacred land because of all that's happened there. Guard it with your life, Sean, and take good care of it."

"But, Grandma, why aren't you leaving the house to George?"

"Honey, George and I discussed this, and it's the main reason he never relinquished ownership of his house in Quincy. We both want you to have my house and the land the slant tree sits on. One day it will belong to you, Emily, and your children. There's still a lot of living and loving to be done in that house and on that land. Stay close to George, Sean. He's a wonderful man and can become a wonderful great-grandfather one day. He'll teach your children many valuable lessons."

Later Jeannie was allowed to come in and say goodbye to Martha. She cried profusely. "We've experienced so many wonderful things together, Martha. I've loved you as if you were my own grandmother."

"And I you, Jeannie. You're a wonderful woman, and you have a wonderful man in John. I believe you two are going to have a very rewarding life together and produce much happiness for your children and everyone else who is in or comes into your life. Take care of Emily, Jeannie, she's going to need your friendship in the next several years as much or even more than she has in the past or even now."

Jeannie told Martha she didn't have to worry about her and Emily's relationship.

Through tears, Jeannie said, "I told her once she could even smack me with a brick, and I wouldn't go away. She's stuck with me forever."

It was a sad three days for everyone except Martha. She was ready to leave because she felt certain it wasn't the end. Even George felt more comfortable with her passing when she finally did on the fourth evening. She died in her sleep after suffering massive heart failure. George was lying by her side holding her. He told Emily later that he actually felt her soul pass right through his body.

"It was such a strange, yet utterly loving feeling, Em. I feel comfortable telling you this because I know you believe me."

She hugged George tightly.

"I do, George. I've had so much happen to me that I just know what you experienced is true and real. Martha was a very strong soul when she left, and she loved you so very much. You gave her tremendous joy these last few years. I'm sure it was her final way of professing her love for you."

The funeral was bittersweet. Martha had asked to be cremated and to have her ashes spread around the slant tree where her heart had become attached.

One Sunday, everyone gathered at what was now Sean's home. They had a huge feast that day. Oddly, no one could explain the sense of joy they all felt. *No one* felt sad.

When it came time to spread the ashes, a light breeze had picked up; and the ashes were spread wide on the land she had purchased around the slant tree.

Beth, Emily and Sean decided to keep a little bit of the ashes in Martha's antique sewing box which they dug a hole for and buried at the base of the tree. That late fall Emily planted yellow tulips at the base of the tree and asked Martha to fertilize them with her ashes.

The evening after sowing Martha's ashes, Sean and Emily spent the night together. They sat on the slant tree before retiring. It was a bit chilly for a summer evening, but at midnight they both felt a very warm breeze pass between them; and it felt as if it circled around them for several minutes before dissipating. Emily was convinced it was Martha's spirit comforting them. Sean was indeed more of a skeptic, but his own experiences allowed him to open his mind to the possibility of that explanation. They made love that night and felt closer to each other than they had felt for a long time.

The following day Emily told him about her conversation with Martha when he had stepped out of the hospital room. He told Emily he loved her deeply and that he would keep his promise of finding her if he were ever tempted to marry someone else. He asked her to do the same thing which she promised with all her heart.

They discussed how Emily was changing as a result of her meditation. She felt the changes internally and remarked that she was no longer reacting to the triggers she used to react to. Sean acknowledged that he could see the dramatic changes in her, and it made him even more excited about working with PTSD-diagnosed soldiers returning from Iraq and Afghanistan.

One evening at a local restaurant, they ran into Henry. Henry was the young boy who lived on their street and had been a good friend of Emily's brother, Paul.

Henry had joined the Army. He was a Ranger and had just returned from his second tour in Afghanistan.

When Henry told Emily and Sean he had been diagnosed with PTSD, Sean asked him if he would agree to be one of his subjects. Henry wanted nothing more than to get better. Once he heard about Emily's background and progress, he agreed.

One evening Sean told Emily that he had an uncanny feeling that regardless of what happened over the next several years, he felt deep in his heart and soul that they were meant to be together. When the end of summer break was upon them, they felt very close and very much in love.

They knew and discussed that in the next three to four years, the chasm they felt prior to the beginning of that summer, would no doubt return and grow resulting in a great silence for a few years. Yet, they promised each other to cling to their hope and faith in one another. They then recalled Martha's words. They were the same words Bertie and Davie spoke to Emily in her dream, and Davie spoke to Sean in his dream. Sean acknowledged that he was remembering that dream more as time passed.

During that summer when they were together and not agitating each other, they felt very close and secure in that closeness.

****

There was one last happy event during the summer of 2005 and that was Jeannie's and John's wedding. Emily, of course, was Jeannie's maid of honor. Sam Hendricks, John's old patrol partner, was John's best man. It was a spectacular wedding befitting an only child. They were sent on a honeymoon out west by both sets of parents where they traveled by car across the country in a brand new Jeep Grand Cherokee.

After the wedding, Sarah left to join Zach in Nepal. She told Emily that Zach was going to have Emily come to Nepal the following summer especially since Emily and Zach had discussed his becoming her thesis chairman. He wanted Emily to get a good dose of field work and later told her that there were privileges of his being her stepdad that she should simply accept and not feel bad about because she was sure to feel resentment from some of the other graduate students.

"Emily, you're a bright girl and are going to make a wonderful environmentalist. Regardless that you are my stepdaughter, as your chairman, I would have asked you to come to Nepal beginning next summer. You'll just have to accept and weather any resentment you may experience from fellow grad students. On the other hand, your abilities will stand on their own; and most of your fellow students will know you're deserving of this opportunity."

****

When Emily took Sean to the airport at the end of the summer, they both cried. They felt as if both their hearts were broken. They told each other to study hard over the next three to four years, and they promised to stay in touch as much as possible. Sean already knew that beginning with the following summer, Emily would spend her summers in Nepal. Likewise, he knew he was going to be very busy with his research with little time to come home. They kissed profusely just prior to his boarding. He was, in fact, the last to board.

As he walked down the first stretch of the ramp to the plane, he walked backward, never taking his eyes off Emily. When he rounded the corner, he tried to make light of what was happening by disappearing around the corner, then jumping back out to wave one last time. They both cried and laughed together as they yelled "I love

145

you!" to each other one last time. The flight attendants who witnessed this exhibition were so touched that Sean was given special attention during his entire flight.

****

The following four years the couple tried their best to stay in touch. That final year, 2009, they were so busy and immersed in their disciplines that they lost all contact with each other. Both of them were published during that year, and Emily watched Sean's career take off via the internet as he began to receive recognition for his work with PTSD soldiers.

****

During those four years, Sarah put her house on the market. She and Zach bought a house closer to the campus. By September of 2009, Katie was scheduled to begin classes at Brown, and Lily was finishing up her education and was ready to start a nursing career at St. Joseph's Hospital in Providence. Lily decided she wanted to work as a surgical nurse. She and Peter Statler were still together and very much in love. During the summer of 2008, they moved in with each other. He had decided he wanted to become a heart surgeon and was embarking on another grueling ten to twelve years toward that goal.

Chapter 16

In 2009 both Emily and Sean received their doctorates. Emily decided to continue with the field work she had begun during the summers. With Zach's teaching obligations, he and Sarah both returned from Nepal every August. In 2009 Katie spent the summer in Nepal. Too, both Lily and Peter were flown over during that same summer for three weeks.

As a congratulations gift to Emily, Zach arranged for her to spend her first post graduate summer with two scientist friends who were traveling to the Galapagos Islands to study the process of evolution. Emily had minored in Biology, and Zach knew it would be a thrill for her but would also give her some invaluable real-world experience. When that project ended, instead of returning home, she returned to Nepal to rejoin the group she and Zach had been working with.

After receiving his doctorate, Sean did additional work with PTSD subjects and continued to publish results. Emily persistently continued to watch his career unfold via the internet. He had made quite a name for himself in the field of neuroscience and was highly regarded.

It had been such a long time since she had had any dreams or inclinations about the future that she had given up hope of ever reuniting with Sean as anything more than old friends.

At the same time Sean kept up with Emily via Jeannie and internet searches he would occasionally do. However, he too had given up. He felt small in the world Emily was now traveling. His heart was broken, but he was determined to mend and move on.

Emily was becoming a significant member of the Himalayan group of scientists and was not only well-published; in 2010, she had a major appearance in a segment of the PBS series, *Nature,* on which Zach was the featured scientist. Sean recorded the show and played it numerous times just to see her face.

During that time of complete separation, Sean and Jeannie talked often; and she was relentless in trying to influence Sean to contact Emily. By mid-2010, however, his broken heart was on the mend;

and he was now seeing a young woman who was also a colleague. Also, Sean had been offered a teaching/research position at Harvard which he accepted.

He never planned for it, however, before he knew what was happening, he became engaged to Angela Hawthorne. The two planned to wed in August of 2010. When Sean spilled the beans to Jeannie, she was livid.

"What is wrong with you, Sean Mahoney? Have you completely forgotten the promise you made to Emily? You owe it to both of you to follow through on that promise."

"But, Jeannie, she's obviously moved on from where we were. I haven't heard from her in a several years. By now, she's probably involved with someone else."

"Sean, I would know if she were involved with anyone else. She's not. She's poured herself into her work so, I guess you could say she's married to what she's doing."

"Well, there you have it, Jeannie. I don't want to create any problems for her or make her feel in the least bit obligated because of some silly promise we made to each other several years ago."

"I swear, Sean, between you and Emily, I don't know who is the most-stubborn or bull-headed? She still loves you, Sean. I'm sure of it."

"How do you know? Have you asked her lately? Does she even mention me to you?"

"We've talked about you, and I can hear the pain in her voice; but, like you, she's resigned to believe that you have moved on. Ugh…I just don't know what to do with either of you; but I will say this. If you marry this woman, when you do see Emily again, which *you will*, you'll regret it and then what will you do? Think about it, Sean. Just think about it a little?"

He promised her he would, but it was too painful to think about Emily. It was also too easy to accept what he called his new fate. So he stayed out of the way of Angela and her mom's wedding plans.

In June of 2010, he and Angela were scheduled to fly into Boston. They were going to stay with Beth, Bill and his sister Abbey. In April he packed up all his belongings, gave away what little furniture he had and drove his car back to Quincy. He intended to fly back to San Francisco for Angela.

Beth was heartbroken that he and Emily had split up and that he was going to marry someone else. Sarah wasn't thrilled about the situation either, but she accepted it as the way it was meant to be. She was hesitant to tell Emily and decided to wait until she and Zach were back in Nepal. It wasn't something Emily needed to hear over the phone or via Skype, which had become their main means of communication.

One day in May of 2010, Sean did a search to see if he could find any recent news about Emily. After his last conversation with Jeannie, as hard as he tried to avoid thinking about her, he thought of her often and wondered if they would or could feel the same for each other. She was on his mind that evening when he fell asleep.

He woke in the middle of the night after having a dream in which his grandma came to talk to him. He noted how good and happy Martha looked as she spoke.

"Sean, I know you realize that your involvement with Angela isn't genuine. You've been very lazy about this one since you've allowed the relationship to evolve without any real basis. Think hard about Angela, Sean. She's a very nice woman who deserves to be loved…truly loved. Your heart belongs to Emily. To deny that or run away from that would be a huge loss in your life. In addition, Sean, you'd forfeit experiencing one of the greatest adventures of a lifetime. You *know* who your true love is. It's time to keep your promise and *go find her.*"

When he woke, he was amazed at the detail he remembered, so he wrote down his dream just as Emily had done years earlier. The following day he called Jeannie.

"Jeannie, this is Sean. Do you have a minute?"

"Well, I don't mind telling you that I'm still upset with you; but yes, I have *exactly* **one** *minute*, and counting."

He told her about his dream and his strong desire to go find Emily. He asked if she was still in Nepal; and Jeannie told him that as far as she knew, she was.

"She has an apartment in a place called Katmandu. I recall she said it's close to the center of the town, and I also recall she sent me a picture of her next to a fountain in what looked like a town square."

"Do you still have that picture?"

Jeannie said she had it in her phone so he asked if she would send it to him. "I'm going to book a flight today. You're right. I owe it to both of us to see her one last time before I commit permanently to someone else. I haven't been able to get her out of my head since the last time you and I talked."

"Well, it's about time one of you began making sense. Do you want me to get her schedule for you?"

"No. Just get an idea when she comes home each day, but don't tell her I'm coming. I don't want to upset her or scare her away."

"Okay. I'll find out and this will be our secret. Oh, Sean, I haven't been this excited for a long time. You better call me the minute you two get back together."

Jeannie did find out that she walked right past the fountain every day around 5 p.m. She begged Sean to tell her what his plan was, but all he would tell her was that he was bringing his guitar.

That was enough information for Jeannie to dream about and imagine the couple coming back together. She told John that evening that she wished she were a bird so she could fly over there and watch from a rooftop.

****

That day Sean booked a flight for Friday. He'd be in Katmandu by the following Sunday afternoon. He managed to reserve a room at a hotel close to the center of the city. When he arrived at the hotel, he showed several locals the picture Jeannie sent him. They told him where the Durbar Square was and how to get there. It was about ten blocks from where the hotel was located.

Once he settled into his room, he took his guitar out of its case, put on some comfortable shoes and began walking in the direction of the square. When he arrived, it took him several minutes to become acclimated. The photo Jeannie had sent him was a small segment of the *huge* square. Jeannie texted him that her balcony faced the square, but she wasn't sure where. So he found his small piece of the square, sat down facing a building that had balconies and began playing his guitar. He played for three hours while the sun set in the sky. He drew a small crowd, but Emily was nowhere to be found.

He returned to the square every day for a week between 4 and 5 p.m. and played, looking up every once and awhile to see if he could spot a beautiful redhead. On the fifth day a few young males recognized him so they came over to watch him and listen to him play.

One of the young men wore a Neil Young T-shirt which made Sean smile. He sat down next to Sean and began to keep beat with a drum he called a Madal. The young man could speak fluent English and told Sean he wanted to meet Neil Young. Sean told him that he once played with Neil which left the boy awestruck.

It was approximately 5:30 p.m. when Sean looked up to see Emily standing across the street from the square. He was playing "We Never Danced" when she heard the music.

****

She couldn't believe her ears and thought she surely was imagining that she could hear someone who sounded like Sean playing what they used to consider their song, so as she approached the square, she stopped to see a man sitting on a small concrete wall with several other people around him, including the young man playing the drum.

He was in the middle of the song when he sensed something, looked up and saw her. His heart leapt out of his body.

He was amazed at his reaction as he stood. She began walking toward him. He soon put down his guitar and walked over to her.

The boy with the drum immediately grabbed Sean's guitar and pulled it close to him so as to guard it from being taken. Then he watched as Emily and Sean stood face-to-face.

"Sean, what are you doing here?"

"I came to see you. I've been coming to the square ever since Sunday, hoping that one evening you would stroll by."

He then pulled out his phone and showed her the picture Jeannie sent him so he could locate the area where Emily lived.

She was dressed in jeans and a khaki shirt with a very dusty khaki hat on, and her hair was covered in dust.

"I'm just returning from work. Would you like to come up to my apartment while I get cleaned up?"

She wanted so much to throw her arms around him, but she practiced restraint. For all she knew, he was there to tell her that he was marrying someone else.

He walked back to where he had been playing, got his guitar and thanked the young man for playing with him and for guarding his guitar. He then gave the young man his guitar pick and told him it was the same pick he had used when he played with Neil Young. The young man literally threw his arms around Sean and hugged him.

On the short walk to her flat, he couldn't believe how nervous he felt. He also wanted to just pick her up and hold her, but he didn't want to scare her. It had been far too long.

They walked up a short flight of stairs and into a beautifully-appointed yet humble apartment. She got a bottle of water for herself and offered him one as well. He took it and she excused herself.

"I need to get cleaned up. I must look a mess."

"Emily, you could never look a mess. You look as beautiful as you always have."

Those words resonated in her head as she walked from the living room area to her bedroom, closed the door, sat on the bed and quietly cried. As she did, she texted Jeannie that Sean was there.

Jeannie was sound asleep when she heard her phone beep under her pillow. She was keeping her phone close until one of them got word to her that they were together.

John was working the night shift, so she sat up and looked at her phone and began laughing and crying all at once. She was so happy for both of them. They texted back and forth for a few minutes.

"Are you happy to see him?"

"You have no idea. I'm sitting here on my bed crying. I can't believe he's here."

"Well, what are you waiting for? Go dry your eyes and get out there. He loves you!!!! Don't make me come over there and smack you."

Emily laughed at Jeannie's text so she wrote back and said, "I don't need to be smacked, just pinched."

"Consider this your pinch. Now get back out there and tell me all about your first sex."

Emily got up and jumped in the shower. She was towel drying her hair when she walked back out to the living room. She was barefoot but looked fresh in a paisley print maxi dress.

Sean was bent down next to a painting. He was trying to read the artist's name. He didn't realize she was back in the room until she walked over to him with a glass of Merlot.

She handed him the glass as he jumped back from the painting. "Emily, this is your painting! Holy crap. This is good. I didn't know you were still painting. Have you sold any of your work?"

She tried to act as humble as possible. "Yes. I guess I never stopped sketching and painting. My favorite style is abstract, although I've done some sketches of some of the exotic animals I've seen in the Himalayas which one day I'll probably put on canvas."

"This is really good. Have you sold any of your paintings?" he repeated.

She turned crimson and quietly responded, "Well, yes, I have. I once sold a piece for $2,000. I don't know if it was worth that much, but the person who bought it was foolish enough to pay it. When the buyer asked me what I would take for it, I facetiously said $2,000 and was quite shocked when he pulled out his checkbook and wrote me a check. I had a few friends over that day.

"After graduating, I kept a small apartment near the campus, and this fella was with one of my friends. He literally took it off my wall and carried it home with him. I couldn't believe it until I looked at the check, but I wasn't going to tell the fruitcake I was only joking about the price."

"Joke my ass, Em. If that piece was anything like this, I'd say he got it for a bargain. You're that good. And don't play modest. You need to know how good you are. This is remarkable! Tell me about this painting. I'm really intrigued. What does it represent?"

They sat on her sofa, which was directly across from the painting. "I call it 'crack in the world' and for me I guess it represents how fragile life is, whether it's individual life or that of our precious planet."

She paused as she sipped her wine. Then she looked at Sean who was waiting for her to continue.

"Okay." She breathed deeply. "When I was seeing a therapist, whom I saw for nearly four years, I kept returning to the first day my dad molested me. I don't remember much of what he actually did to me all those years. I have random memories with some of them quite incomplete. In fact, when I try to remember my childhood I can only see snippets. It's as if I am looking at my childhood through a pin hole. Yet, for some reason I remember the first time as if it were yesterday. I also remember smells. I can still sense the air outside, the smell in the car and the smell of his cologne which still gags me whenever I encounter a male with that same cologne. He wore Old Spice, and just the thought of that smell makes me want to vomit. But probably most of all, I remember the thunderous sound the car door made when he slammed it to go into the liquor store.

"When I described the sound to the therapist, she said she wasn't surprised at how impactful it was for me. We decided that the sound represented the crack in my world that had just happened because it was at that very moment in the car that my childhood came to a violent end."

She had to pause and catch her breath as a tear ran down her cheek. She took another sip of wine, breathed deeply, then continued.

"Since then, I've thought about that sound and have equated cracks in the world with events such as the day you fell through the ice. I thought I lost you that day. You were my entire world then, Sean. It was you and how you felt for me that gave me the courage to get up every day. It was you and your sweet, innocent love that gave me the courage to fight back when I just knew my father intended to rape me. I have no doubt that was his intention when he said he wanted to take my dress off.

"Can you imagine the deafening crack I would have heard that day if he had been able to do what he intended? I don't want to even think of it. But it didn't happen because I stabbed him in the hand with that pencil."

As she then stared off into space, she said, "I remember too the last time he and I had a conversation while he was in the hospital. He admitted that he had only molested two other children besides me. I wanted to believe him; but several years later when I began reading all the new studies being done on child molestation, I realized that he most likely molested who knows how many children. He's just damned lucky he died when he did because he probably would have finally been caught and thrown in prison. That would have killed my mom."

She then swallowed hard, trying not to let her emotions overwhelm her. "When I began reading about child molestation, I had to briefly go back for therapy because I began feeling responsible for all the other children; but I know now that I couldn't have known because no one knew how prevalent molestation was or how pedophiles operate."

Looking very disturbed, she again spoke, "You know, I sometimes think about the access Dad had when he would go overseas on his cruises. It's appalling how men with money can get access to small children via these prostitution rings. Finding all of that out was a huge crack for me. Then there are other cracks."

She stopped talking and stared at her painting.

"Tell me about the other cracks, Em."

"Oh, Sean, I don't know." She paused before speaking again. "I guess I decided to study the environment for a reason. I minored in biology and got to travel to the Great Rift Valley in East Africa where geologists anticipate a cataclysmic event will soon devastate that area, killing millions and maybe even causing the continent to split at the rift. Then there are the climate changes that are causing the snow in the Himalayas to melt at such an unnatural pace. That's why I'm here. I'm with a group of scientists studying the melt and the effects on local fauna and flora. It's really fascinating but terrifying at the same time.

"And, of course, there's the constant warfare that continues to erupt in so many parts of the world. I just hope humans are able to prevent the complete annihilation of everything. It never ceases to amaze me how people refuse to believe the consequences of human action and reaction."

She looked exhausted when she stopped talking.

"I'll get off my soap box now. Phew!" She said this as she took a big gulp of wine. Then she asked, "How about you, Sean?" She blushed to herself as she said his name. "Tell me all about what you've been doing."

Sean looked at Emily for a few minutes. "I don't know how I can top that, Em. That was pretty profound."

She smiled broadly and waved her hand. "Well, Sean, I wouldn't call neuroscience trivial. Besides, I've kept track of your career. You're pretty accomplished and well-known wherever neuroplasticity is mentioned. Your work, especially with PTSD victims, is all over the internet. So don't act humble with me. I want to hear all about what you've been doing."

Sean took a huge gulp of wine, put the glass down and began. She was fascinated to watch how animated he had become with hand gestures. She felt so warm inside just to have him there with her. She secretly hoped with all her heart that Jeannie was right and that he still loved her.

God, help me. I don't know what I'll do if he doesn't, she thought as she also thought of how very much she still loved him.

Sean continued, "I guess falling through the ice and being in that coma for five weeks was a huge game changer for me in so many ways. It's what inspired me to study neuroscience.

"While I lay in the coma, Dad came to talk to me often. Toward the end I could hear everyone in the room and everything that was being said. Dad told me it wasn't my time and that I had to fight hard to go back in order to live my life.

"Most of all, I remember you and Grandma. The two of you hardly ever left my side. I remember how you kept wiping my face with a wet cloth. It felt so soothing physically, but so loving emotionally. I was just bursting with love for both you and Grandma and my mom. Mom wasn't able to come to see me as often, but I know it was because she was busy with her new practice. Plus, it was a heck of a trek for her to drive from Quincy all the way over to East Providence.

"I recall her saying over and over that she knew I was in the best of hands with the doctors at the hospital and with my two guardian angels…you and Grandma. I know she felt guilty about not being there every day, but eventually I think I convinced her that she was there in spirit because I could feel her aura in the room whenever you and Grandma were there. Then, Em, do you remember when I finally woke up and could play the guitar?"

"I remember how blown away I felt and how dumfounded your mom was."

"Jose told me later that he was convinced I could hear him; and because he wanted to surround me with positive sounds and energy, he made it his mission to help bring me back. I recall how some of the other staff thought he was strange because he was a very spiritual person, but he impacted my life tremendously with his energy.

"It was then that I became fascinated with the human brain. I couldn't figure out how I knew how to play, yet I did. That's why when I learned about neuroplasticity, I knew I had to make it my life's work. By the way, are you still meditating? Because I can sense a tremendous calm in you that was only beginning to emerge the last time we saw each other," he said as he smiled sweetly.

Emily smiled and nodded. "Yes, I do. I finished the Holosync program several years ago, but I just love the state it puts me in. It's very relaxing so yes, I still use my CDs for meditation and you're right. I feel I've overcome most of the unconscious stuff that was wreaking havoc on my life back then. It all just seemed to dissolve little by little.

"I'll never forget sitting in a chair one day and not even feeling affected by something that would have caused me to go ballistic previously. It was an amazing realization to know how much the Holosync helped me. Did you see the same results with your soldiers?"

He gulped his wine as he vigorously nodded. "Yes, at least with the ones that were religious about meditating. Henry was one of those success stories. He still emails and calls me. He went on to use his GI Bill. He's now a pharmacist, is married and has two children and is very happy. He is always thanking me; but, as I tell him, he did all the work. I just watched him and encouraged him.

"I'm really excited about this new field and fascinated with what I've seen. Neuroscientists traditionally considered the brain to be ridged and thus unable to change. For example, it used to be thought that the part of the brain that controls motor movement —if severely damaged—could not recover completely. But what we're finding is that when that happens, it *is* possible for other parts of the brain to become more active and actually rewire so that motor abilities become possible again.

"Last year I watched a young man who was severely injured in the Middle East, who the doctors said would never walk again, get up and walk. Have you ever heard of Temple Grandin?"

Emily nodded.

"She's a perfect example of how the brain is *not* ridged but malleable. And, my god, Em, look at you! Look what a vibrant, beautiful, well-adjusted woman you've become. Look how far you've come in your life. A lot of other victims of molestation become emotional basket cases, but not you. You're proof that the human brain is capable of remarkable recovery regardless of whether injuries are physical or emotional.

"'Phew' is right. I guess we've both been very busy for the last several years. Say, are you hungry? I'm starving."

Emily cocked her head as if she hadn't thought about her stomach, then said, "Yea. Now that you mention it, I could eat a bear!"

They both laughed, then Sean turned to her. "God, Em, it's so good to see you again. I've thought of you so many times and wondered where you were and what you were doing. It's incredible to be here with you!"

"I'm still pinching myself that you're sitting in my living room." She blushed, then quickly changed the subject. "Say, I know a really quaint little restaurant where several of my colleagues hang out. In fact, Zach is here. He arrived just yesterday and would be thrilled to see you again. Plus, I'd love to introduce you to my other colleagues. What do you think?"

"Sure. That sounds great, but I hope it's within walking distance. Those three glasses of wine really hit me."

"It is. Listen, you sit here a few minutes and I'll finish dressing. Just make yourself comfortable."

Emily went back to her room where she slightly rewet her hair and blew it dry, slipped on a pair of sandals and grabbed a red shawl with yellow tulips printed on it. She remembered to put her locket on. It was the same locket Sean had given her on the first Christmas of their friendship when they were both twelve. Sean's photo was inside and on one side. Her photo was on the opposite side. It had added sentimental meaning for Emily because the locket originally belonged to Martha.

Over the last several years, Emily often took the locket from her jewelry box. She would then lay on her bed, clutch it to her heart and remember all her most wonderful memories of the love she and Sean had cultivated over the years. Often, Emily would fall asleep as she softly cried.

Now…at last…here she was…standing in front of her mirror admiring how her precious locket rested just below her middle collar bones. She couldn't believe that the love of her life was sitting right outside her door. As she mentally pinched herself, with her right hand, she picked the locket up, brought it to her lips and kissed it. She then laid it back down on her skin, gently patted it and mouthed, "Sean, I still love you with all my heart" to her reflection, flung her hair back and walked down the hall to her small living room.

Sean was still sitting on her sofa. His empty glass sat between his legs as he loosely held it. He was sound asleep.

She smiled as she bent down and gently pried his hands from the glass stem. Just as she was about to lift the glass, he woke up.

He jumped a foot off the sofa and Emily jumped back, holding the glass but nearly dropping it on the floor.

"My god. I didn't know where I was for a minute."

"That's okay." She felt out of breath from the scare. "What were you dreaming about? Your eyelids were fluttering like the wings on a hummingbird."

"Now, I'm a little embarrassed. But, if you must know, I was dreaming about you. We were sitting on the slant tree together. We were just kids. I was talking to you about how the sun was literally creating what looked like laser beams popping up from your red hair. Then just before you woke me up, we were standing at the entrance of my uncle's cabin. You remember, the cabin...."

He paused as she said, "Sean, how could I ever forget? It was our beautiful D-Day."

Sean smiled. "Yes, but you never let me finish the dream because you woke me up."

"I know how it ended. It was one of the most beautiful days of my life. Now, before I say anything more, I need to ask you the million-dollar question."

"What's that, Em?"

"I don't see a wedding band on your finger; but I've learned that some men don't wear them. Are you ..." Emily was hoping with all of her heart that the answer would be "no."

Sean smiled as he touched her hand. "No, I'm not married. I came very close in this last year. I wasn't very enthused about getting married; but I was so unsure of the future that I was, I guess you could say, very lazy by letting it take place."

"So, are you getting married?"

"I was about to be married to a colleague; but, thanks to our friend Jeannie who has been relentless about my keeping my promise to find you, the answer is, 'no, I'm not getting married.'"

"Do you regret that decision?"

"No, Emily, I don't. It's a marriage that would have eventually ended in divorce because, although she's a wonderful woman, she's not ..."

Emily sat on the coffee table facing Sean, waiting for him to finish his sentence; but he didn't.

"You never finished your sentence."

"What do you mean?"

"Well, Sean, you said she's a nice woman, but she's not ... Not what?"

"Okay, okay. I hope I'm not saying anything premature, but I was going to say, 'She's not you.' Now I guess I need to ask if you're seeing someone because if you are, then I just made a monumental fool of myself."

Emily laughed. "No. I could never quite get past the fact that I'd already experienced the greatest love affair I would know in my life, so I guess you could call me an old maid."

He laughed as he brushed a strand of red hair from the corner of her mouth.

She blushed, then immediately changed the subject, "Zach would really like to see you again; and I'm getting quite hungry so, let's go. There's plenty of time to embarrass ourselves later."

She stood and extended her hand. He took her hand in his and beamed such an incredible smile, it sent chills of splendor down her spine.

As they arrived at the quaint, yet elegant, restaurant, Emily spotted Zach and three of her colleagues sitting and laughing in the bar area, a small room just off the main dining room.

Emily greeted the maître d' Bhadra in his native language, Nepali. As she gestured to the bar, she told Bhadra they were going to join her friends. Bhadra smiled and shook Emily's hand and, using heavily accented English, told her the group was waiting for a table but that he would make sure it was one which would accommodate two additional people. He then escorted Emily and Sean over to the bar doorway.

"Wow, Em, you're still full of surprises, talking to him in his native language. I'm impressed."

She waved to Zach, "Well, don't be. I try and Bhadra is one of the gentle locals who allows me to practice on him."

Zach walked over to them. "Are my eyes playing tricks on me?"

Sean laughed. "No, Zach. It's really me."

They hugged as Zach whispered, "Good for you, Sean. Good for you."

Then he kissed Emily on the cheek as the three walked over to the bar. "We were about to send Chandra over to your place to drag you out. We weren't about to let you out of celebrating this evening, especially after the news today!"

As Emily and Sean pulled two stools closer to the group, Emily began introducing Sean. "Sean, this is my lovely friend and colleague, Dr. Chandra Darji, and—" She took the woman's hand in hers. " —Chandra's beautiful bride-to-be, Dr. Amshula Gadal. And this is Dr. John Patrick. Dr. Sean Mahoney, everyone." They all shook hands and hugged.

Once Emily and Sean had drinks in hand, Zach proposed a toast.

Sean asked, "What success are we toasting?"

Zach beamed with pride. "I guess Emily hasn't told you. As a result of our studies here, we've all been invited to participate and speak at the 2010 World Congress of Environmental and Resource Economists in Montreal in July."

John Patrick chimed in, "It's actually pretty good stuff, Sean. Glaciers are one of the most sensitive indicators of climate changes, and we've been monitoring the melt of the Himalayan glaciers and also monitoring the action from satellites to predict how fast they're melting and the consequences. Don't know if you're aware, but there are several major rivers that originate in the mountains here; and we've been able to map out some pretty dire scenarios that we consider will begin to take place within the next ten to twenty years, especially since the consequences will affect several countries and their people."

Sean raised his glass. "Well, congratulations to all of you. That's great news, err ... the conference, that is."

"Okay, everyone," said Amshula. She spoke perfect English with a slight British accent. "Sean didn't come out with us tonight to hear about our initiatives. Let's find out if our table's ready."

"Good idea." Chandra hopped off his stool and walked over to discuss the table with Bhadra. Chandra waved to all his colleagues and Sean that they were ready to sit down.

Once they were seated, the conversation became more relaxed and personal. They were all dying to hear more about Emily and Sean's childhood. Emily alluded to the day Sean had fallen through the ice and how Sean was able to play the guitar. Amshula and Chandra especially wanted to hear, particularly given their long courtship and impending marriage.

The evening became an extremely pleasant one with lots of good food, good wine and great conversation. By the time they were all ready to leave, none of them was able to walk a straight line. Amshula and Chandra called a cab while John Patrick, who lived close by, decided to walk. Zach, who also lived close by but was even more inebriated than the rest of them, invited himself to stay in his stepdaughter's spare bedroom.

****

As Emily, Sean and Zach began walking, it became pretty apparent why Zach didn't want to walk the eight blocks to his apartment; he could barely stand up, let alone walk a straight line. Emily took one of Zach's arms while Sean took the other, and they laughed all the way home as Zach stumbled.

Halfway home, Zach said, "Oh, dear. I'll just pop over here behind the bushes."

Emily exclaimed, "No-o-o, Zach. We only have a few more blocks to go."

"Okay, okay. I'll try my best." Zach grossly slurred his words.

Zach began snoring a few seconds after his head hit the pillow. Sean snickered as he and Emily tiptoed out of the guest room.

"Em, I better get going. It's late and I'm sure you want to get some sleep yourself."

Emily reached for Sean's arm. "Oh, Sean, don't leave just yet. It's Saturday, and I don't have to get up until I feel like it."

"Are you sure?"

She vigorously nodded.

"Well, if I stay, I don't want anything more to drink. Man ...I'm going to have a monster of a headache as it is. I rarely drink that much wine."

He fell into the sofa as Emily slipped off her sandals, "We aren't going to drink any more wine. I'll get us a few bottles of cold water. Besides, it's the best thing to drink to counter a hangover. Jeannie once told me hangovers were a result of dehydration."

He got back up and followed her to the kitchen. He didn't want to chance falling asleep again.

She handed him a bottle. "Let's go out on the balcony and talk until the sun comes up."

****

There was a pleasant breeze blowing. They each sat in one of her deep-cushioned wicker chairs and talked about the past, bringing each other up to speed to the present.

Soon they both became quiet. "I'm going to get more water; do you want another?"

Sean stood. "No, but I'll walk in with you."

They walked into the house; and, as she bent over to get the bottle of water from the bottom shelf of the refrigerator, Sean felt a warmth in his groin. Her dress clung to her rear end. She wasn't wearing panties, and her behind looked delicious.

When she turned around, he had the strangest look on his face, "Em, I need to get out of here before I do something I'm going to regret."

She put the bottle on the counter, walked over to him and pressed up against him. "If you don't do something pretty quickly, *I'm* going to be the one with *tons* of regrets."

He took her face in his hands and kissed her with such a long, delicious kiss that she swooned and nearly keeled over.

He caught her. "Are you okay?"

"More than okay."

She looked at him, took his hand in hers and led him to her bedroom. Once in the bedroom, she reached behind, unzipped her dress and let it fall to the floor. She was standing with her back to him. She was absolutely naked.

Sean walked over to her, pressed up against her and reached around front and began caressing her breasts. "Umm, I remember these breasts."

She turned to him and they began kissing passionately. Emily reached down, pulled his shirt out from his pants and pulled it up over his head. They began kissing again as she unbuckled his jeans, bent low and pulled them along with his briefs to the floor. He reached for her, pulling her back up.

They stood naked as the full moon's light shown through her double window illuminating their bodies.

She whispered, "Come to bed. I want you inside me so bad."

They walked backward, locked in an embrace as they kissed. Emily managed to grab the covers and began to pull them down as they fell onto the bed. They were half-lying on the bed. Emily's legs were straddled on the floor. Sean was on top of her with one leg between hers. They were kissing as he began rubbing his leg on her clitoris, and she was becoming moister by the second. Then she bucked and moaned in absolute pleasure.

She bucked a second time. "Oh Sean! That's how you gave me my first orgasm." Her body vibrated with pleasure a third time as she buried her tongue in his warm, sweet mouth.

Then she reached down and put his penis in her vagina as she opened her legs very wide. They wiggled themselves up onto the bed into a more comfortable position, and a rhythm took over both of them as they were swept away. Several minutes later Sean held his breath and moaned loudly.

Emily stroked his back. "I love you, Sean. I love you so much."

Sean lifted up so he could see her face in the moonlit room. "My sweet, sweet Emily. I've missed you for such a long, long time. I've been lost in this world without you."

She began to sob. "You asked me about the painting. Oh, Sean, the biggest crack in my world were all these years of being separated from you, then believing I would never see you again. The cracked world is my heart. It's been so broken for such a long time."

"Don't cry, Em. I'm *never* going to leave you ever again."

They lay in each other's arms for several minutes when Sean asked, "Em, do you still have that shirt?"

She lifted her head and smiled. "Well, of course, I still do. I told you earlier that it was the most wonderful love affair I've ever had. I kept everything and especially that shirt." Then she got a far-off look in her eye. "I guess this is chapter two of the greatest love affair."

She smiled and lowered her head again to his chest as Sean kissed the top of her head and began stroking her hair. They fell asleep in each other's' arms and didn't awake till nearly noon that day.

When Sean woke, Emily was already up and showered. She was wrapped in a huge pink bath sheet.

He propped himself up on his elbow, patted the bed and said, "Come here, gorgeous."

She dropped the towel and began walking toward the bed when they heard a huge crash outside the bedroom. Emily looked at Sean, grabbed the bath sheet, flung back her hair and ran out of the room. Sean grabbed the sheet from the bed and was right behind her.

Emily ran to the kitchen. "Oh my god, Zach, I forgot you stayed over."

Zach, who had dropped a quart of milk on the floor, was bent down picking up pieces of glass and trying to mop up the milk when he turned to see Emily and Sean standing behind her.

"Oops," Zach was smiling from ear-to-ear. "I was trying to be quiet before I left. I went out and got us some biscuits from the deli down the street. I'll just clean this up and get out of here."

"No, no, Zach. Leave it. Sean and I will clean it up as soon as we're dressed. Now go sit down. We'll be right back."

Zach got up off the floor. "Alright. I'll make another fresh pot of coffee and put out the biscuits. Would you care for anything else to eat, Mi' lady?"

"There are a few melons in the fridge. Why don't you cut those up? We'll be right back."

She then went back to the bedroom where Sean was already dressing. She walked over and kissed him. Then they both laughed at the whole incident.

"That was embarrassing!" laughed Sean.

Emily got dressed and they walked back out to the kitchen. The milk and glass were cleaned up; but as Emily turned her head toward the balcony, she saw what she was certain was a soaking wet pile of towels.

Men, she thought. *You've gotta love 'em.*

She opened the balcony door. Zach was sitting at the table with three small plates, a bowl of cut melon and a plate of her favorite biscuits, as well as three cups and a carafe of what she guessed was coffee, along with a small pitcher of cream and a bowl with blue packages of sweetener. She motioned to Sean to follow her.

Sean and Emily sat down as she exclaimed, "You got enough biscuits for several people. Who were you expecting, Zach?"

Zach was smiling and had a twinkle in his eye. "Well, I somewhat expected that Sean was still here because there's a guitar and a pair of men's shoes in the living room; and I know you don't play an instrument...well, not that kind of instrument anyway." He finished with a wink. "Now let's have a nice brunch so I can go home. I'm going to pick your mom up from the airport this afternoon if you remember."

"Oh, yes. My god, I almost forgot what day it was." Emily brushed her hair back and twirled it into a ponytail.

Zach dunked a biscuit in his coffee and popped it in his mouth. "So, I'm curious. How did you two bump into each other? I'm guessing that's what happened, or was this planned?"

Emily shook her head. "No. I would have told you."

Sean looked guilty. "I confess. It wasn't an accident. I came looking for Emily. Jeannie sent me a photo of Durbar Square. I arrived Sunday and walked down to the square, only I had no idea it was a monster square. It was hard to tell from the picture because the picture showed only a small section, but Jeannie told me to look for a building with balconies. So I returned to the square every day this week around the time she said Emily usually returned home. I was beginning to lose hope when yesterday I looked up and saw this goddess of a red head dressed in a pair of jeans with a hat on her head, dusty from head to foot."

"Well, that's quite a romantic story. Wait till I tell your mom. She'll be absolutely delighted! Now I better get going. I need to shower and change. I'll leave you two to whatever you were going to do when I dropped that bottle." He grinned hugely as he kissed Emily on the cheek.

When they heard the door to the apartment close, they smiled at each other.

Sean reached over and touched Emily's hand. "You heard the man. What were we about to do?"

They laughed, got up and went back into the bedroom where they made splendid, brawny love for more than an hour.

Later they went back out to the balcony with two glasses and a bottle of wine. It was a pleasant day. The sun was high in the sky, and there was a slight breeze that tousled their hair. They melted into the oversized wicker chairs, and reminisced for over an hour, laughing and simply enjoying each other's company. Then everything became quiet as they both stared at each other. It was Sean who broke the silence.

"So, Em, tell me more about your work."

"Are you sure? It's all really boring."

"I sincerely doubt that it's anything but boring. Please tell me. I want to know."

She began.

At first she didn't sound at all excited; then something inside of her sparked and she exclaimed, "Oh, Sean, the things I've seen have been mind-blowing. The experiences I've had, including observing the observers like John McCosker who studies shallow-water species and Bruce Robison who studies deep-water species.

"I was fortunate to spend a few short weeks with these two men, as well as other scientists on sacred ground in the Galapagos Islands. They were there to continue their study of documenting and discovering evolution as it *is happening*, in living color and motion. I felt as if I were standing at the event horizon of all living beings waiting to be sucked into its cauldron of knowledge. It was orgasmic in the most profound sense."

Then as if coming down from an extreme altitude, she looked at Sean. "It was like learning to play a guitar while lost in a deep slumber."

She finally sat and breathed a heady breath. He was sitting there smiling at her with a look of amazement on his face.

"What …what …what are you staring at?"

"You, Emily …you. You take my breath away. It's mind-blowing to realize I'm talking to the same girl I met so many years ago. The little girl who apologized for trespassing on my land. You've transformed into this beautiful, articulate and absolutely intriguing person who just takes my breath away."

She smiled broadly. "It is amazing, isn't it? But it's the same as you. I've been keeping up with you over the years. I search the internet to see what you've been doing, and you've been involved in some groundbreaking findings. Tell me, please tell me, Sean, of your most wonderful experiences. It's been far too long."

As did Emily, he began talking in an unenthused manner; but the more he talked, the more excited he became until he looked almost intoxicated.

"God, Emily. It's just thrilling to be in the middle of observing the collision of one school of thought with another during this period of time. That's what it's been like: like watching the evolution in a sense of neuroscience as it collides with an old, worn-out view of how the brain works. During these last four years, I've studied with some of the most progressive minds in the field. I can fully comprehend and mentally sense the orgasmic pleasures you describe. It's like standing at the edge of a vast universe, knowing that you may just get to experience life on another planet, for instance, because that's what neuroscience is like right now. It's as if we're learning the workings of an alien intelligence once thought to be ridged and fixed. An alien intelligence that exists right here —" He tapped the side of his head. "—within the boundaries we call a cranium. Our own personal universe and like the vast universe, we're learning there *are no boundaries.*

I knew when I woke up from my sleep, never questioning that I could play a guitar, that there was something extraordinary going on in my brain; and I just had to find out what it was. It was torture those eight years while I anxiously waited to go to college where I could surround myself with other minds seeking the same discoveries. I was just more fortunate than most of my colleagues because I had you to distract my attention and keep me tethered to the present. But once I got to what you passionately describe as that event horizon, I didn't want to wait to be sucked in. I ran toward it and jumped in, and it too has been a mind-blowing experience."

Emily was now the person with glossy eyes as Sean's passionate story washed over her mind.

"Wow!" is all she could muster because right then, there were no other words she could think of for what she had just encountered; and now it was Sean who was wondering what she was so captivated with.

"My god, Sean, you're the boy with the goofy smile and hilarious antics who stole my heart so long ago. Why have we waited so long to rediscover each other? It's as if the vast universe has been orchestrating two bubbles that have been carrying each of us separately and yet floating them toward each other so they could become one."

This type of conversation excited both of them in such a like manner that they stood and, without speaking another word, began removing their clothes. The urge was far too intense for either to resist. Just as their individual bubbles attached to one another, they were driven by the most powerful of all desires.

They collapsed, arms locked around one another, kissing more deeply than ever before as they walked backward into the apartment where they sank to the floor.

Soon his hand was between her legs bathing in her succulent juices, and she was mentally and physically reeling with ecstasy.

Within seconds she experienced an orgasm that shattered her mind and caused her body to bend and sway in a demonstration of utter rapture. Her nipples were so hard; he couldn't help himself as he slid down her body and took one of her buds into his mouth as his tongue flitted wildly over the flower.

He continued to stroke her clitoris as she continued to exude the juices of their passion; and she came not twice more but four more times, each one more intense than the previous. She then wiggled herself free, and they rolled on the floor until she was seated high above him with the fullness of his pulsating phallus soaked in her nectar. She was gyrating up and down as if she were riding the most beautiful, exquisitely-chiseled carousel horse the world had ever encountered. Behold the pale horse as it carried her through the gates of heaven and beyond.

She orgasmed again as her clitoris rubbed on his wonderfully sweat-soaked body; and as she did, he grabbed her hips and guided them to a motion that gave him the most extraordinary orgasm he had ever had in his entire manhood.

They both buckled and rotated like two tops perfectly balanced on each other's tip, fueled by the other's spin, knowing that gravity couldn't break the spell.

Then it wasn't at all gravity that ended their rotation but exhaustion of the most wonderful kind, and Emily collapsed on his beautiful body.

Within seconds they were both asleep, locked in yet another unconscious ballet of memories, recent and past, as they danced together in such a motion that neither memory could distinguish time nor space. They had found perfect nirvana in each other's arms, and it was profound.

Chapter 17

Emily woke to a distant ringing. As she opened her eyes and emerged from the most exquisite sleep she had ever had, she realized it was her phone.

She couldn't remember where it was but as she sat up, she saw it. It was still ringing and twirling on the coffee table. She reached for it and moaned, "Hello."

It was Sarah. "Honey, did I wake you?"

"Yes, Mom, but that's okay. We just fell asleep…well…if I must tell you, in the middle of the living room on the floor. You'll never guess who is here on the floor with me."

"Honey, that's what I'm calling about. I just got in and Zach couldn't wait to tell me that Sean is here. Oh, Emily, sweetie, I'm so happy for you." She was talking through tears.

"Mom, it's better than wonderful. It's a miracle; and he's still as beautiful as he ever was, only more so. I can't wait till you see him."

As Emily said those words, Sean opened his eyes, rubbed them, smiled and sat up. He leaned over and kissed her on the cheek.

"Have you two eaten yet? Zach and I were going to stop and get something to eat. If you haven't eaten…well…you have to, so you might as well get dressed and come out to see us. How does that sound?"

Emily was motioning to Sean to go eat. He rubbed his eyes again and stretched as he vigorously nodded.

"Yes, Mom, we're starving. We haven't eaten since this morning."

"Great, will forty-five minutes be long enough to get ready? Zach and I can stop by, and then we can all walk to whatever restaurant you two want to go to."

"Okay, that sounds good. Forty-five minutes will work."

They said goodbye, and she put the phone on the coffee table again. She and Sean sat on the floor with their legs crossed, just looking at each other and smiling.

"Em, Grandma was right. If I had remained lazy about my future, I would have missed out on the adventure of a lifetime, not to mention utterly to-die-for sex. Thank God for Jeannie!"

He told her about the conversation he had had with Jeannie and how angry she had become. He expressed how he couldn't get her off his mind after that conversation and how the day before he booked his flight, he had done another search on the internet and then the dream he had where Martha came to him and told him he was making the mistake of his lifetime. They both told me to find you, and that's what I knew I had to do."

He sighed then frowned. "I was terrified, Emily. I was so afraid of being hurt again. Our separation hurt tremendously, and it took me several years to accept that our separation was permanent. That's when I began to get lazy about my personal life. I just decided to let events play themselves out; but it wasn't as if I knew I'd be pointed in the right direction. It was because I just didn't care. The love of my life was gone, and I was just resigned to that. And—" He beamed and made an elaborate gesture with his hands. " —here we are."

He took her hands as their fingers entwined. She smiled and looked down between his legs. He was as hard as a rock.

"I told Mom we could be ready in forty-five minutes. I just need to throw something on. Let's fuck quickly."

He laughed loudly. "I can't believe you just said that, but let's fucking fuck!"

They did and then they got up, got dressed and went out to the kitchen where she got a bottle of wine and directed him to the wine glasses. They walked back out to the living room where they heard a knock at the door.

Emily sang, "It's open!"

She put the bottle down and said, "Hurry. Put your arm around me. I want Mom to see us."

He put the glasses down, and one tipped over but didn't break. Then he stood up and gladly put his arm around his girl.

Sarah walked in and just broke down crying as she walked over and threw her arms around the couple, "Miracles do happen."

Zack stood back with his hand on his chin. He was totally amazed. Sarah stopped crying, looked back at Zack and said, "Get over here, you. This is your family!"

He came over and they had a wonderful group hug as they laughed loudly.

When they all finally sat down, Emily poured a little wine in each glass; and they proposed a toast to the future of all of them. Then Emily looked at her mom and said, "To our miracles!"

Both women toasted their men as Sean and Zack both said, "To our miracles!"

Then, always the pragmatist, Zack stood up. "Let's go eat. I'm starving." He then peppered. "Besides, I haven't seen my beautiful wife naked for far too long, and I don't want to wait past this evening."

Sarah scolded him while both Emily and Sean looked at each other, raised their eyebrows and laughed uproariously.

All Zack would say to his scolding was, "What? What did I say wrong? I'm only stating a fact!"

They left, walked a few blocks and had a wonderful meal. Around 10 p.m. they stood outside the restaurant. Zack was slightly inebriated and was rubbing Sarah's back.

She looked at Emily and Sean. "I need to get this naughty boy home before he embarrasses all of us."

They all kissed and walked in opposite directions. At one point Emily turned around, then nudged Sean to turn around. Zack had his hand on Sarah's ass, and she kept trying to brush it off as she giggled the entire way. They looked at each other and smiled approvingly as Sean put his hand on Emily's ass.

When they got back to Emily's flat, she said, "I have to text Jeannie. She's been waiting. Do you want another glass of wine, before …hmm?" She pointed to his penis.

He just snickered and said, "Sure, why not? I'll go get it."

Emily texted Jeannie, "Lost track of how many times we've made love but one billion times better than ever, which used to be pretty amazing!"

Jeannie texted her back that DD was home and he had his hand between her legs. Emily's text made them both horny.

Then Jeannie texted, "I'm so happy for both of you, girlfriend. Now go fuck his brains out!"

Emily was laughing when Sean came back in with two glasses of wine. He asked her what she was laughing about so she showed him Jeannie's last text.

"I can accommodate that!" He handed Emily her glass, sat down next to her and put his hand between her legs.

The following morning Sean woke to a commotion in the room. Emily was up and dressed for work.

He leaned up on his elbow. "Do you have to go?"

She frowned. "Yes, unfortunately. We have a major test we're doing today, and I need to be there."

He got out of bed and kissed her, then patted her behind. "Okay. I need to go check out of the hotel anyway. Can I stay with you the rest of my time here?"

"Of course, silly. But we've never discussed this. When *do* you go back?"

"Three Sundays from now. I'm flying into San Francisco. I have something I need to take care of, then I'll fly into Providence and head to Grandma's house."

"Is that where you're going to stay?"

"I originally hadn't planned on it; but now with everything changed, I can't wait to get back to the house."

"Why's that?"

"Grandma left me a fairly decent insurance policy I've never cashed in. I honestly wasn't sure what I was going to do with the house. I figured I'd eventually sell it because…well…without you, I didn't want it. I knew it would become too painful. But everything's changed, and I want to use the policy to renovate it. What do you think?"

Emily played coy. "Why are you asking me?"

"Now who's being silly? It's our house, Em. I want to cash in that policy and begin getting it ready for our future." Then he looked down at the floor. "Besides, I have a confession to make; and I hope this doesn't get me into trouble or change anything."

"You didn't tell Angela the truth about where you were going, did you?"

He looked extremely guilty as he peeked back up at Emily. "No. I was supposed to fly back to San Francisco for her, but I flew here instead. All she knows is that something very important came up and I needed to…well…deal with it.

"Em, I never had the chance to tell her I can't marry her. I'm really sorry. I wanted to make sure you still wanted me before I purposely broke her heart. Although I fully intended to break it off anyway, just because marrying her was never the right thing to do. But I figured if this didn't work out, I could let her down more easily."

Then he looked directly at Emily. He appeared puzzled. "How did you know her name? Oh, wait a minute. Jeannie told you her name. Am I right?"

"Yes. So we have basically three weeks before you go back?"

"Yes. Then I don't know if you know this; but I've taken a position at Harvard, so I need to have time to get that all squared away. That's why she and I were going back to the Boston area. We were going to look for somewhere to live. But now I don't need to do that. I know where I'm going to live and with whom. That is, if you'll still have me."

"Harvard and live in East Providence? God, Sean, that's a long way to drive to work every day. Do you think it's wise to set up housekeeping in Martha's house?"

"Em, I don't know but I want to give it a shot. I love that house; and now that you're going to be back home in it, I love it even more. Maybe you could think about at least spending the majority of the year around that area just as Zack does. I'm sure any of the universities would jump at hiring you."

"Hmm ...something to think about. Well, we'll talk more later. Right now I really do have to go."

"We will talk later, right, Em? We don't need to be apart any longer. We have a life to live together ...right?"

They kissed; then she told him not to worry and left.

She wanted the day to digest everything. She knew, if it were up to her, she'd never leave him regardless of how annoyed she felt at the moment. She loved him and there was nothing that could change that. She would fight off an army of Angelas before she would ever let that change again.

He sat in the flat for over an hour after she left. He felt like such an ass for how he left Angela hanging and now how he imagined he made Emily feel. When she kissed him goodbye, her kiss lacked the warmth he'd felt the last few days. Then he threw caution to the wind, cleaned up and left the flat to go check out of the hotel room and pay the bill. On the way back to the flat, he threw more caution to the wind and picked up some groceries. He also called Angela and

175

told her he would be back in three weeks and that they needed to talk.

Of course, by that time Angela had already figured out that the wedding was off; but she wanted to cause him some pain by giving her the real explanation face-to-face. She felt more resentment toward him than she felt hurt for herself.

When Emily arrived home that evening, Sean had prepared a meal. He set the table on the balcony and bought a couple of candlesticks and candles. He was waiting for her in the living room when she got home.

"I didn't know what time you'd get back. I have dinner on the stove. Are you hungry?"

"I'm starving. Did you move out of the hotel?"

"Yes. Is that still okay? Are you mad at me about Angela?"

She sat down, frowned and then looked at him with a soft, reassuring smile. "No, Sean. Of course I'm not. I felt hurt and a bit angry and confused this morning, but now I only feel bad for Angela because I know you never told her where you really were."

"No, I didn't. I called her today and told her we need to talk when I get back. I'm sure I detected resignation in her voice that she knew what the topic will be. I hate this. I hate that I let it get that far with her. Grandma was right. I was being a lazy prick when I allowed her to get her head filled with marriage plans. But I had no idea what to expect when I got over here." He looked forlorn and genuinely sorry for everything.

She gently put her hand on his. "I know, Sean. If the tables were turned, I probably would have done the same thing. We just need to work through this. We put ourselves and each other in this predicament. In the end, though, it will all work out; and Angela will thank you for not ruining her life."

She then looked excited. "Listen, I talked to Zack today about my trying to get on with one of the universities and spending just my summers here. He told me he remembered there was a position at URI, and he knows the chairman there. He's going to contact him and recommend they take a look at me for that position. I'm ready to go home. I'm ready to be where I belong."

"Emily, I've been so worried all day long. We've had such an incredible few days. I was so scared I'd ruined it."

He put his arms around her. "Do you want to get cleaned up before we eat?"

"Yes. But only if you wash my back. This is the beginning of our future, Sean. You'd have to do something far worse than lie to your fiancé to lose me. I'm here forever. In your arms is the only place I've ever wanted to be."

He was unbuttoning her blouse as they walked into the bedroom, then the bathroom. They were both naked as he reached in and turned on the shower, then turned to her, lifted her up and walked into the shower stall. They stood under the shower as it rained on them. They were devouring each other as he guided her into his manhood. She wrapped her body around him and rode him hard. He came hard as well. When he was finished, he gently put her down, stood behind her and lathered her with soap. When his hand reached her vulva, he lathered her and began stroking her clitoris. He sensed she was about to come when she leaned back, grabbed his head and kissed him deeply.

"I love you, Sean. I'm never going anywhere. We belong together. I'm sorry I ever doubted that."

"Emily, I was so scared that I'd lost you forever. I love you with all my heart."

****

On the Thursday morning before his plane was scheduled to leave, Sean had a remarkable dream.

He dreamed Martha came to visit him. She told him that everything would work out for Angela. She had run into a former boyfriend who was head over heels for her. She never lost her feelings for him but was going to go slow because she knew what you and she were going to discuss, and she didn't want to get involved as a rebound. Sean asked where Davie was, and Martha told him he would see him soon. He asked her what she meant; and she simply asked him to trust her, that it wouldn't be long before he and Davie would be together again. She then produced two rings, a simple yet elegant engagement ring and a wedding band. She told him the rings were hers and that she wanted Emily to have them.

"You need to propose to Emily before you leave, Sean. You need to reassure her that this is real and it will last forever. Take these rings and give her the diamond. She will cherish it, knowing where it came from."

Before he could ask his grandmother anything else, he woke to a noise that sounded like someone was gagging.

He sat up in the bed. Emily was not there so he called her name.

She came out of the bathroom clutching her hair. She had been throwing up.

"Are you sick, baby?"

"Sean. I've been very, very stupid. God ...I can't believe this." She looked bewildered and terribly distraught.

"Sean, I quit taking the pill over a year ago. I made up my mind to never sleep with another man again. I think when I quit taking them, it was my way of convincing myself of that pledge. I don't know."

She paused. "But now...I think I'm pregnant. My period is over a week late, and now I'm throwing up. I'm so sorry, Sean. I didn't mean for this to happen. This is the last thing I ever expected. I just got so swept away with you being here that I just never thought about it. I know that sounds stupid and careless, but..."

Before she could say another word, he laughed and patted the bed for her to sit. "Come here, Em, you don't have to apologize. Everything's okay." Then he looked off into space. "No! Everything's good, and now I understand what Grandma was telling me."

She sat down and looked perplexed. "You're not angry?"

"No, of course not. I think this was meant to happen."

Emily looked confused, yet relieved all at once. Tears began rolling down her cheeks.

Sean gently kissed her tears. "Sweetie, what if I told you that Grandma just visited me?"

She looked even more confused. "I don't know, Sean. It's been so long since I've believed in stuff like that. And now I've made a mess of things."

He reached over and began wiping the tears from her face when something fell from his hand onto the bed. It was the diamond ring and wedding band. They both looked stunned.

"Jesus, Sean, where did they come from?"

He picked them up and looked at them with his mouth wide open and a look of utter amazement on his face. Then he looked down at Emily's stomach and put his hand on her stomach.

"What's the matter, Sean? You look like you've seen a ghost."

"I ...I ...I think I have, Emily. Grandma gave me her engagement ring and wedding band in my dream and told me to give you the engagement ring. She also told me that my dad and I would be together soon. Jesus, Mary and Joseph, you don't think, do you?"

Emily stood up. "God, I just don't know about this stuff. I've always thought I was crazy when I would have dreams like that, but..." She was clutching the ring as she opened her palm to look at it.

He stood and took the ring and looked at it. They both began to tremble, laugh and cry all at once.

"Em, I think this is real. Will you marry me? God, Em, who cares if it's real or not? Marry me. I love you. I've always loved you and always will. So what difference does it make? Besides," he touched her stomach again, "I'm going to be a daddy."

He put the ring on her finger, picked her up and they twirled around the room in a state of delirium.

As they did, a warm breeze blew hard through the open bedroom window, and it swirled around them.

Emily whispered, "Martha!" as Sean put her down next to the window.

Just as he put her down, one of the sheer curtain panels brushed her stomach area, clinging to her stomach as if it were something or someone touching her place where their baby was growing. The curtain clung to her stomach for several seconds as Emily put her hand over the curtain and her stomach and Sean put his hand over Emily's hand. They just looked at each other with tears rolling down their cheeks. Then as suddenly as the breeze picked up, it was gone. When they moved their hands, the curtain dropped down to its still position and the room became totally void of sound.

Emily whispered, "I'm pregnant."

Sean whispered, "I'm going to be a daddy; and you're going to be my wife and the mother of my child. This is a wonderful miracle, Em."

They both fell back on the bed laughing as she held her hand up and admired her ring. "No one's going to believe us, you know."

"I know, but who cares? We believe it; and if it turns out this baby is a boy, then what's not to believe? Oh, Em, this is such a miracle."

"Kiss me, you fool. We have nothing to lose anymore. We're already pregnant. I love you so much, Sean. God, how I love you! Thank you for finding me. Thank you for being you."

"Awe, Em. I can't believe how stupid I was to think you wouldn't want me back. I just love you so much. When I saw you looking over at me in the square, I swear it felt as if my heart leapt out of my chest. I was totally amazed at how, after all this time, nothing had changed except that my love for you had become stronger than ever."

He turned toward her and kissed her completely as he laid his hand on her belly. "Our miracle baby."

"Let's show him how much he's loved."

She still had her nightshirt on and pulled it up over her head as he kissed her bare breasts and slid his hand down to her vagina.

"Go inside."

He did as he slid down and began to massage her clitoris with his tongue and put two fingers in her vagina. He gave her such a magnificent orgasm that she shuddered. When she stopped, he looked up at her and smiled.

"I want you all, Sean."

He gladly mounted her, and she wrapped her legs tightly around his body as they kissed ever so deeply. He exploded with a deep, dramatic moan; and she whispered, "Oh, Sean, I love you with all my heart!"

He rolled off and lay next to her as their legs dangled off the bed. They laughed and cried with extreme joy and satisfaction.

Sean turned and looked at his sweet Emily. "Em, are you ready to jump into the future?"

She kissed his sweet lips. "As long as I'm with you, Sean, I'm ready for anything. *You are my future and I am yours.*"

Chapter 18

Friday evening Sean and Emily would have dinner with Zach and Sarah one last time before Sean flew out on Sunday. Emily decided the night prior that she would not go to work that day so they slept in late.

It was approximately 9 a.m. when they both began to dream. Martha was talking to each of them individually when she said, "Before I say anything more, look around at everything slowly. Don't focus on any one object but look with your heart."

In their individual dreams they did what Martha told them to do, when all of a sudden they saw each other.

"That's right. This isn't a dream. It's a vision just as many of your other dreams have been visions. Now, however, it's time you both knew what they truly were. Tonight when you have dinner with Zach and Sarah, tell them your good news about getting married and having a child. However, do not tell them anything about what you already know about your son.

Sean, Davie wanted so much to give you the pleasure of loving him as he so loved you. He will teach you both more than you ever knew you could learn. If those who knew Davie, one-day suspect who he is, it will be their own intuitiveness that will guide them to that conclusion."

Then she told them she needed to leave but that they would see her again. As she faded from view, she smiled at both of them and said, "Be happy. You've stayed true to love and never questioned that love. You both deserve your happiness and will have an abundance of it."

Then she was gone.

Emily woke first, sat up on the side of the bed facing away from Sean. She felt intoxicated and was trying to shake it off when she heard Sean.

He was sitting up in the bed, also trying to shake off the emotional high he was feeling. "Baby?"

She turned around and knew immediately. "Did that really happen?"

He was nodding his head. "I think so, Emily. Tell me what happened so we both know we experienced the same thing."

She climbed back in the bed and moved close to him as he put his arm around her. She began telling him what she had just experienced. All he could say was, "Yes," as he vigorously nodded his head.

"God, Em. This is totally freaky. I always knew there was something else going on. I mean, ever since my coma, I've never been able to shake the feeling I have at this moment. It's always been there inside me!"

They sat in each other's arms for the longest time, discussing the vision and acknowledging that they should keep all of this to themselves. They swore they would let others make the same conclusions but on their own and with no coaxing from either of them.

"Sean, I think we're being blessed with this. I think our life together is going to be very special. But I also think we're being tested in a sense too. We must stay true to our love. We both know from our entire lives that love is the answer to everything. We need to fill our lives and our home with nothing *but* love."

He told her he believed the same thing. "This is a gift, Em. We need to remember that and treat it like a gift...with absolute reverence."

They sat still for a long time, over an hour, when Emily's phone rang. It was Sarah. She wanted to confirm that they were still having dinner that night.

Sarah detected something in Emily's voice. "Sweetie, are you alright? You sound very strange. In fact, Zach just mentioned that you seemed to be in another world yesterday. What's going on?"

"Yes, Mom. I'm actually perfect. Sean and I have something to tell you tonight. I think it will make you very happy."

Sarah tried her best to coax Emily to tell her now but after a while said, "Okay. I'll be patient. I can wait!"

Emily looked at Sean. "Well, we may have visited another realm together, but we're still humans and I'm starving. Let's get dressed and go eat, then have a glorious day to ourselves, all three of us. We have a lot of planning to do."

They got dressed and went to a small café and ate brunch. Emily asked Sean to take his guitar with him. She wanted to go back to the square and have him play for her.

The young man with his Madal was at the square; and when he saw Sean and Emily, he stopped playing and ran over to them. Around his neck was a chain, and the pick Sean had given him was encased in gold. The young man whose name was Darsh told Sean his uncle was a jeweler.

Sean and Darsh played for over an hour when Darsh told them he needed to go home. He asked if he would see Sean and Emily again. Sean told him he was going home on Sunday but that he knew he would be back occasionally because Emily would come back to work. Then Emily and Sean showed Darsh her ring as they told him they were to be married.

When Darsh got up to leave, he told them that he had a strong feeling that they would be happy and that the little boy growing in Emily's belly would give them much joy.

When Darsh was gone, Emily and Sean just looked at each other. Neither of them had mentioned the baby. Simultaneously they both commented that the day had been a truly bizarre one. They soon got up and went back to the flat so they could get ready for dinner with Zack and Sarah.

It was 7 when Sarah and Zack knocked on the door. Emily was still dressing so Sean let them in. The three were sitting in the living room talking when Emily walked in. They all had a glass of wine in their hands.

Zack got up and kissed Emily on the cheek. "Let me pour you a glass, Emily."

"No, thank you, Zack. I think I'll just get a bottle of water."

Sean literally jumped to his feet. "I'll get it for you, Em. Just sit down and relax."

She did and when Sean returned with the bottle, he asked her if she needed anything else. She smiled and said "no."

Then she smirked to herself, *Oooo, this is going to be fun. I think I'm going to enjoy Sean's attention these next nine months. I promise, though, I won't take advantage.*

When Sean finally sat, Sarah said, "Okay. I have waited all day long to hear the news. Spill the beans, you two."

Emily held up her left hand and Sarah gasped. "Oh, Emily. It's beautiful!"

183

Then she asked Sean when and where he bought the ring. "It looks special," was her way of saying it didn't look brand-new.

"It was Grandma's. She gave it to me a long time ago and told me to give it to Emily when the time was right."

Zack held up his glass. "Sounds like the time is right. Congratulations, you two." Then he chuckled. "I guess men are out to lunch because I never saw your ring yesterday. Now I know why you were acting so out of it and—" He grinned. " —why you were so late getting to work." He chuckled again.

Emily smiled, yet looking a little embarrassed, confessed, "That's not all, Mom and Zach. We're expecting."

Sarah nearly spit her wine out. "You're what? So that's why you're not drinking wine. Well, I should have guessed that one. How do you know?"

"My period is very late and I threw up this morning. We stopped to buy a pregnancy test kit and it tested positive. Guess the bunny doesn't lie."

Sarah looked at Sean. "How do you feel about this, Sean?"

"Are you kidding, Sarah? I'm going to be a daddy. I'm thrilled beyond belief. I came over to find Emily; and not only did I find her and discover that she still wants me, but I'm getting a huge bonus."

Then he told Zack and Sarah about renovating Martha's house. "I want to get that started immediately. I'd like it to be finished by the time the baby arrives."

"Well, Emily, honey"—Sarah smiled as she looked at Zack— "You ought to think about going back with Sean so you can help get things ready. I'm sure he could use a female's opinion about the renovation."

Zack chimed in, "Emily, you should think about that. We're nearly finished here for the summer, and all that's really left is the conference in Montreal. We can finish up without you. What do you think?"

"Well, I would like to go back. We still need to get married; and, although neither of us wants an elaborate wedding, we'd like to plan that, as well as get the house ready."

"Oh, honey, I'm so happy for both of you. And, just think, I'm going to be a grandma! We have a lot to celebrate this evening."

They had a wonderful evening. Sarah was beaming from ear-to-ear, and Zack was enjoying Sarah's bliss.

When Emily and Sean got back to the flat, they discussed her flying into Providence once he was back in that area.

Emily asked him, "When will you fly back to Providence?"

"I'm going to see Angela Monday evening. Then I thought I would immediately fly back to Providence, so next Tuesday if I can get a flight."

"Does your mom know yet?"

"No, I was going to call her in the morning, then work on my flights. Let's work on yours too. I want you back as soon as possible. Okay?"

"Okay. If you get back by Tuesday evening, why don't we plan on my flying back the following Friday? That should get me back into Providence by Saturday sometime, which means basically we'll be apart only one week."

"That sounds great, Em. By that Saturday, we can start our future with a clean slate."

It was settled. The next afternoon she did book a flight for the following Friday which, after changing flights, would put her into Providence around 3 p.m. that Saturday.

They were so excited about everything that they stayed in bed that last Saturday until noon, then spent the rest of the day lounging on the balcony. The temperature was perfect and there was a light breeze blowing. That evening they made exquisite love and feel asleep in each other's arms.

When Sunday morning rolled around, they were both sad; and Sean was a little preoccupied with the dread of seeing Angela again. When the cab arrived at noon to take him to the airport, they both cried, regardless of knowing that they would be together again in a few short days. They both lamented that now *any time* away from each other would be unbearable.

****

That Tuesday evening Sean met Angela. She didn't want him to pick her up. She simply wanted to meet with him, have a drink and hear him out.

She wished to be in control of leaving when *she* wanted to leave.

He was waiting for her in the cocktail lounge of a restaurant they frequented.

When he spotted Angela, he ordered a drink for her. She walked over to the table, sat down and stared at him.

He nervously and apologetically explained everything, beginning with the history. He expressed sincere regret and sorrow for leading her on and letting it go as far as it did. It was apparent from her facial gestures that she was more angry than hurt. She simply listened.

When he told her that Emily was pregnant, she got so angry that she picked up her glass and threw her drink in his face and left. As she walked away, she told him she hoped she would never see him again.

He sat at the table a while longer. He felt like shit, but he also felt light-headed and excited about his and Emily's future. He called Emily but she didn't answer. He was staying at a hotel near the airport that evening so he left the bar and jumped in a cab. When he got back to his room, he tried Emily again. This time she answered but sounded half-asleep.

"Em, are you awake? God, I forgot about the time difference."

"That's okay. Is it over? Did you see Angela?"

"Yes, sweetie, I did. It's over."

"Oh, Sean, I miss you terribly. I've been a terrible grouch ever since you left here on Sunday. I've snapped at Mom a couple of times, but she doesn't seem to be fazed. She told me my hormones were totally out of kilter with the pregnancy, and I've been throwing up every morning. I'm miserable."

"Sweetie, I wish I were there. I've been miserable as well. I've had a hard time sleeping; and then when I'm awake, I have a hard time staying awake. I'm sure it's the time difference, which …go back to sleep, sweetie. I'll call you tomorrow when I get home to Providence. I love you, Em. Go back to sleep, baby."

She was asleep before he hung up the phone.

****

The following day Beth picked Sean up at the airport. She was anxious to hear all his news since he was very vague about what all had gone on the last several weeks. All she knew was that he flew over to Nepal to look for Emily.

He told her that he did find Emily and gave her all the details. "She's flying in this coming Saturday, Mom, and we're moving into Grandma's house. We're going to renovate it and also begin making plans for our wedding. We've decided that we want to be married on Sunday, September 5th, in a small but nice ceremony. Emily wants to wear a white wedding dress. She wants to see me in a tux." He chuckled at the thought.

Beth was listening intently when she said, "Is there something else?"

"Why do you ask?"

"I don't know, Sean. I've had an uncanny feeling the last several days and can't explain it."

"There is something else, Mom. Emily's pregnant. I'm going to be a daddy, and you're going to be a grandma."

"Oooo. I just knew in my gut that she was pregnant. That's weird, but I somehow knew. Oh, honey, I'm so excited for both of you. I've been so disappointed ever since you told me you were marrying Angela. I'm sure she is a fine woman, but I've always felt you and Emily were soul mates just like your dad and me. I'm so proud of you for going to find her. It will make everything so much more significant. And to think, I'm going to be a grandma. You make me so happy and proud, Sean. I wish your dad were alive so he could see what a wonderful man you've turned out to be."

"Mom, somehow I think he knows."

Beth smiled and patted his hand. "I think you're right, sweetie. Poor Angela. How did she take it?"

"She was angry, especially after I told her Emily was pregnant. I knew immediately I should never have told her that part. It must have been like rubbing salt in a wound. I so regret having led her on although at the time, I didn't realize I was. I had just resigned myself and would have done everything I could have to make it work."

"Sean, honey. I know you would have, but it wouldn't have been fair to either of you. She'll mend, and you need to put all that out of your mind. After all, you're only human and humans are imperfect beings."

"That's basically what Emily said. She was very understanding about everything. God, Mom, I'm still pinching myself over all of this.

It's like I've been asleep for so many years, and now I feel so alive. I just can't wait until Saturday. She's supposed to be in around 3 p.m."

"Have either of you talked to Jeannie? She called me yesterday."

"I don't know if Emily has. She talked via text several times while I was there. I think I'll give her a call tomorrow, but I want Emily to tell her about the baby. I don't want to steal the thunder away from the two of them. Jeannie will be beside herself with joy."

"What are you going to do for dinner tonight, honey? Bill and I would love for you to come eat with us."

"Gosh Mom, I'm wiped out. Between the time change in Nepal and the stress of having to talk to Angela and now the three-hour difference between California and here, if you don't mind, I just want to go to sleep. I'll probably just call for a pizza."

"Okay, sweetie. I didn't think you'd be up to it but felt I should ask anyway."

Beth pulled into the driveway of what was now Sean and Emily's house. "Everything should be working, Sean. George came down last weekend and made sure of that. He's been taking good care of the house ever since your grandma died. I think he even stocked the refrigerator so you may not even have to call for a pizza."

She helped Sean carry his other bag into the house. It was as clean as a whistle, and the temperature inside felt perfect. Indeed, George had stocked the refrigerator and the pantry.

"Wow, Mom. This is amazing. Grandma told me to stay close to George. She really loved him."

"Yes, she did, Sean. He loved her a lot as well. I think they gave each other something special during the last of her years with us. Well, I'm going to scoot. Bill is home alone with Abbey and she can be a handful. She has him wrapped around her little finger."

"Okay, Mom. I can't wait to see her. Tell Abbey her big brother will see her soon."

He kissed Beth and she left. He took his bags up to his old room, lay down on the bed for what was intended to be a few minutes. He didn't wake again until 10 a.m. the following day.

When he woke, his phone was ringing. He had plugged it in and laid it on his old dresser. It was Emily.

"Sean, where are you? I was terrified. I've called numerous times since yesterday."

"I'm fine, Em. I evidently was tired because I lay down on my bed for a couple of minutes after Mom dropped me off." He looked at his watch.

"Shit, that was yesterday. Wow. I guess I was tired. Wait a minute, Em. Someone's at the front door. I just heard the doorbell and now they're banging."

She laughed. "It's probably Jeannie. I texted her when I couldn't get you to answer."

He was opening the door as Emily told him that.

"It is Jeannie and DD is with her."

He motioned for them to come in.

"Okay. Listen, call me when they leave, okay, Sean?"

"Yes. I'll call after a while. Love you, baby."

"Hey guys, sorry about that. I fell asleep just after Mom dropped me off yesterday. Damn, Jeannie, you didn't have to bring the police force."

Jeannie grabbed Sean and hugged him.

"Come on out to the kitchen. George left a ton of groceries for me, and I'm actually starving. I don't even remember the last thing I ate. I could use some coffee. How about you two?"

DD sat down. "That would be great, Sean." Then, looking at Jeannie, he urged, "Jeannie, relax. He's fine."

"God, Sean. You gave us all a scare. Emily was beside herself worried about you. I was going to have Mom run up here but remembered she and Dad aren't even home. They're up in Maine for a few weeks. Then I couldn't get in touch with Beth and left her three messages."

Sean began making sandwiches. "I remember Mom said she would be in court all day. That's probably why she never answered. She dropped me off yesterday about 5:30 p.m. I lay down for a minute or two and just got up. Guess I was tired. You two want a sandwich or something?"

DD shook his head "no" as did Jeannie.

"I guess you were tired, you rascal. You've had a busy four weeks, haven't you?" Jeannie was laughing.

"Yea, you could say that. How much has Emily told you?"

"Everything. You guys are getting married, and—" She snickered. "—there's a bun in the oven. Good job, Sean. That was fast work!"

189

DD was laughing at Jeannie because she was making huge gestures with her hands as she talked.

Jeannie was still laughing. "Yea, I guess we're going to be aunt and uncle in about nine months. You ready for that, Sean?"

"It's not what I expected, but none of this was actually. I'm thrilled about everything. You were right, Jeannie. Thanks for giving me that swift kick in my ass. Emily's coming home in a couple of days. What day is today, anyway?" He looked genuinely confused.

"It's Thursday. She comes in on Saturday. She'll probably be very tired, but why don't you ask her if she's up to stopping at our place before coming home?"

"I'll do that. Don't expect it though because that's a hell of a time change and with her being pregnant, even more so for her right now."

"Well, let's just play it by ear, okay? If you do stop, it won't be anything elaborate."

DD nudged Jeannie. "Well, buddy, we need to go now that we know you're alive and kickin'. I have to be at work in about three hours."

Jeannie hugged Sean as she left. "Sean, I'm beside myself happy for you two. You have no idea."

Chapter 19

When Emily arrived on Saturday, Sean had parked the car and was waiting for her at the gate. She wasn't expecting to see his beautiful face as she walked through the gate. She was exhausted. She laughed when she saw him standing behind an empty wheelchair.

"You're kidding, but I'll take it. I'm worn out." She kissed him and collapsed into the chair.

He bent down as he stood in front of her. "I need a proper hug and kiss."

She leaned forward and they hugged and kissed. "I'm sorry Sean, I'm not feeling very romantic. I just want to get out of here."

She looked like she really felt bad. He wheeled her out to the car. "Em, how many bags do you have?"

"Five. Here's my ticket stub with the baggage numbers. I tried to make it easy. They're red bags, and I tied green ribbon around the handles. I'm sorry, Sean, I just don't feel well. So far, pregnancy isn't fun."

"Don't worry, Em, I can see how bad you feel. Just relax and I'll be out as quick as I can. Okay, sweetie?"

"Yes. Thanks for understanding."

A half-hour later he came back out with a cart and the five bags, loaded them in the back of his red Land Rover and came around to the driver's side.

"Do you need anything, Em?"

"Can we stop for something to drink? Maybe a water would be best. I'm afraid to drink or eat anything else right now. I threw up several times on the plane."

He pulled into a convenience store; and just as he was about to get out, she reached over and put her hand on his. "I'm sorry, Sean. I was hoping to feel better by the time we landed. I've missed you."

"Em, sweetie, don't sweat it. Mom filled me in on what to expect and not expect. She had a rough pregnancy when she was carrying me. She said the first few months for her were hell. I just want to get you home so I can take care of you. I love you, Em. So don't worry about me. I'm not pregnant. I'm just so happy you're sitting here in the car with me."

When he came back out, she had put the seat back and was sound asleep. He had a small blanket in the back seat, so he put it over her.

Once home, he quietly got out, unlocked and opened the side door of the house, then went around to her side of the car and opened the door. She woke up and began to get out, but he wouldn't let her. Instead, he picked her up and carried her inside. Once in, he walked to what used to be Martha's bedroom on the first floor and laid her on the bed. He had the bottle of water and gave it to her.

"I'll go get your bags."

As he was about to get up, she reached for him. "Kiss me again, Sean."

He leaned over and kissed her gently. "Why don't you lie down, sweetie? I'll be back in a few minutes."

He brought all five bags in and lined them up in the bedroom. He then sat on the bed next to her, and she laid her head in his lap. He began to stroke her head as she fell asleep. She felt like crap, but she was so happy to be home with her love.

She slept for three hours. When she woke, she caught the delightful aroma of something cooking. She got up and walked down the hallway to the kitchen. Sean was busy at the stove.

"Umm. Something smells wonderful."

Sean was so engrossed in preparing stir-fry that he didn't hear her walk into the kitchen. Startled, he dropped the wooden spatula on the floor.

"My god. You scared me to death!"

She walked over and put her arms around him.

"I'm sorry, Seanie. I finally feel like a human being again. What are you cooking?"

"Sesame chicken stir-fry. I thought I'd make something not too spicy or heavy for you to easily digest."

He pulled the wok off the burner, turned around and hugged her.

"It's so good to have you home, Em. I've missed you so much."

"I'm so sorry I wasn't much company when I got in. I felt just horrible. I don't know if it was the cabin pressure or what, but I felt like I was going to die. I filled three of those damned barf bags. The guy who sat next to me finally excused himself and found another seat. Kind of embarrassing, but one of the attendants was so kind. She recently gave birth and knew exactly how I felt."

"I'm just so glad you feel better. I was really worried and didn't know what to do to help."

"Oh, Sean, you're doing it."

"Well, you just sit over here and I'll finish up. The stir-fry is almost done. All I have to fix now is the rice. Do you want a water? I also got some ginger ale. Mom said it helped her both times when she was pregnant."

"Ginger ale sounds wonderful." She sat down and watched him.

He finished cooking, put everything on two plates and turned around. She had her head resting on her hands.

"What are you looking at?"

"You," she giggled. "The last time I watched you cook was that spring break of our first year of college. I recall how you were having a hard time making eggs and reading directions at the same time. This is wonderful!"

"Well, these last few years I got so sick of pizza and fast food that I decided to learn how to really take care of myself. I'm not a bad cook; and, believe it or not, I really enjoy cooking. It's relaxing," he said as he put her plate down.

She waited for Sean to sit. He sat and began eating with a fork, then looked at her. "Is it okay?"

She laughed as she picked up her fork. "Yes. I'm just glad you're not going to make me eat with chopsticks. I've never been a big fan. Guess I'm all American."

"Well, you don't need to worry. I'm a klutz with those things. Guess I'm all American too," he said as he held up his fork. Then they clinked each other's fork and laughed.

When they were done, she sat back and held her stomach. "That was really fantastic! It hit the spot." Then she looked around and said, "Someone pinch me so I know I'm not dreaming. I am here, right?"

He leaned over, took her hands and kissed her fingertips. "You're really here, and I couldn't be happier than I am at this moment. Em, I'm still pinching myself that this is happening too. It was only a few weeks ago that I thought my life was going to be filled with…well…settling for things I didn't necessarily want."

She got up and he asked her where she was going.

"I'm going to do the dishes."

"No you're not! There's plenty of time for that. Tonight you are going to take it easy and let me be your genie." He then kissed her hand. "Your every wish is my command."

He then smiled and exclaimed, "Listen, when I'm done cleaning up, how about going out to Friendly's for a coffee cabinet (a type of coffee ice-cream milkshake)? Could you handle that?"

"Oh, my god, I can't remember the last coffee cabinet I had. Yes, that would be fun!"

****

As they were about to pull out of the driveway, Sean's phone rang. It was Jeannie.

"Hey, Jeannie. Yea, she got in on time but was so sick we rushed home and I got her into bed. No. It's the pregnancy. Here, wait a minute."

He handed the phone to Emily.

"Hi, Jeannie! God, it's good to be home. Yea. Pregnancy isn't a piece of cake, at least not so far. Hopefully it'll get better. Tomorrow? Sure, wait a minute."

She put the phone down and asked Sean if he wanted to have dinner with Jeannie and DD? He told her he was game, but it was up to her.

"Yea, that would be fun. Maybe we can talk a little bit about the wedding too. Oooo, I'm looking forward to seeing you guys too. No. Sean's taking me out for a coffee cabinet. No, not the wooden kind."

She was laughing as she got off the phone.

"What was that about the wooden kind?"

Emily told Sean about the first time her father took all the kids to get their first coffee cabinet and how she sat in the booth at Friendly's waiting for them to bring out big wooden cabinets to all of them. He snickered as he got an image of that.

They had a wonderful evening. They drove around downtown Providence before going back home. When they got home, he helped her unpack.

When they finally climbed into bed, he felt clumsy and didn't know what to do. She was kissing him passionately, but he was afraid of hurting her.

Finally, she looked at him and said, "Are you too tired to fool around?"

"God, no. I just don't want to hurt you. Is it okay to have sex?"

She giggled like a little girl. "Sean, I'm pregnant. I'm not dead and I won't break. I'm horny for you. I just want my man to fuck me."

He laughed and said, "I'm going to have to get used to hearing you swear like that, but I kind of like it. It's sexy!"

She was brawny with her lovemaking, and that made him relax. All he wanted to do was devour her and he did. He had a glorious climax; and when he was done, he smiled at her and went down to work, giving her four magnificent orgasms. They both had big smiles on their faces when they were finished. But they weren't tired so they got up, threw on some sweats and went out to the slant tree.

"Oh, my god, Sean. The moon is gorgeous! I didn't know there'd be a full moon out. It feels as if the moon is welcoming us home. This is our tree now, isn't it?"

"This is all ours, baby. Grandma bought two acres so, if we want to create a garden out here, we can."

"I think I'd like that! A flower garden with red and yellow tulips in the spring."

Chapter 20

The next several months were a whirlwind for Emily and Sean and everyone else involved with helping them get ready for their wedding, the baby and life in general.

The wedding was top priority for Emily. She and Sean were adamant about wanting a small, simple ceremony with all their closest friends and relatives. Sarah came home from Nepal in June so she and Beth could help the couple pull that list together. They wound up with about 100 guests, and it was pretty much split down the middle for each side.

The year prior, Beth and Bill had bought a beautiful Victorian-style home in Quincy, and it had a huge, relatively flat backyard which would be perfect for an outdoor wedding. With the partnership of Sarah, Beth took over planning that side of the wedding.

Jeannie went to work with Lily and Katie to help Emily find the perfect dress. She had her perfect dress in mind, one which would have an empire waist just in case she was showing by then. They looked at dresses on the Internet; and she found what she wanted, which was a very simple, yet feminine design.

It had a wide satin bodice band just under the bust and a neckline cloth which crisscrossed, creating a soft V-neck which stretched up over the shoulders with four-inch wide shoulder straps. The back of the dress had the same crisscross, giving the back the same gentle V shape. It was long and just barely touched the floor. Emily described it as a Greek goddess look. The fall of the dress was elegantly simple yet extremely fluid and feminine.

She decided she wanted to wear flowers in her hair and found the perfect style on the Internet when Katie typed in "Greek goddess hairstyles." There were lots of ringlets with tiny white flowers sprinkled throughout the hair. When combined, she did indeed look like a Greek goddess.

Jewelry was a no-brainer for Emily. She would wear her precious locket as the joining of she, and her beloved was made official. She chose a simple pair of blue topaz drop earrings that Sean had given her for her birthday years prior. Her bouquet would be a combination of white roses and baby's-breath with trails of white satin ribbon.

When Emily couldn't find the dress in any of the stores, Jeannie and Gladys got together, pooled their money and hired a professional seamstress to create the perfect dress. The dress became their wedding gift to Emily and Sean.

Zack and Sarah commissioned the same seamstress to make the bridesmaids' dresses with empire waists and cap sleeves, giving the necklines a squared look. Emily wanted Jeannie, her maid of honor, to wear a red dress while, in honor of Martha, her two sisters would wear a yellow version of the same dress. They would all be floor length. Abbey was asked to be the flower girl. She had just turned eight so they dressed her in a yellow dress with hints of red. She was cute as a button as she sprinkled white, yellow and red rose pedals in front of Emily as she walked down the aisle.

Sean decided to ask his Uncle Peter to be his best man and two close childhood friends to be in the wedding party as well.

Emily wasn't sure if Paul would be home for the wedding but wrote to him and asked anyway. She wanted both Sarah and Paul to give her away.

The aircraft carrier Paul was currently stationed on wasn't due back until October, but he was able to hitch a ride from the ship in order to get back to Norfolk in time to collect his family and drive up to Quincy for the wedding.

****

During all the planning, Emily and Zack went to Montreal and met their three colleagues for the July conference. In addition, Sean began teaching at Harvard.

Emily helped Sean investigate the best means of transportation to and from work every day. They discovered that Amtrak had a commuter rail system from Providence into Boston which could drop Sean off only blocks from the campus. It meant getting up early every day, but the commute wasn't at all bad; and the time on the train allowed him to do last-minute class preparations. He taught three classes that first year and became heavily involved in several research projects.

As August came around, Emily was becoming more excited

about their wedding. By then the morning sickness had disappeared and she was feeling excellent. She managed to keep her weight under control and was barely showing by the end of August.

The week before the wedding, the temperatures turned unseasonably cold; but by the following week, a warm front came through, making for a beautiful, sunny, warmish September 5th outdoor wedding.

Beth and Sarah had done a remarkable job of coordinating everything as Beth's backyard was transformed into a wedding scene, complete with a dance floor for the reception. Although tradition called for the bride's family to foot the bill, Beth and Bill insisted on splitting the cost down the middle. Beth wanted to cater in food for the wedding so Sarah happily agreed.

Weeks earlier Sean contacted East Providence Hospital. His intention was to find Jose, the nurse who taught him how to play the guitar. He discovered that Jose had stayed in the Rhode Island area and was currently Chief of Nurses at the same hospital.

Once Sean and Emily found that out, they decided to go to the hospital to meet with Jose. Emily arranged for Jose's administrative assistant to schedule the meeting but not tell Jose who they were. They wanted to surprise him.

He was indeed surprised. He was now married and had four children. He was totally thrilled when he realized who Emily and Sean were. He was sitting behind a desk when Sean jogged his memory. He came out from behind the desk and hugged Sean and Emily. He was such a sensitive man that tears rolled down his cheeks as they hugged.

Sean told Jose what a tremendous impact he had made on his life; and that, because of Jose, he was now teaching and doing research at Harvard in the Neurological Science Department. Seeing Sean was enough of a thrill for Jose; but when Sean and Emily asked Jose to come play and sing at their wedding, he was beside himself with delight.

When September 5th was upon them, it was a glorious day indeed. The wedding was scheduled for 3 p.m. that Sunday. Sarah brought in a crew of hair designers to do everyone's hair, including her own. Beth had blocked off one portion of the house where no males were allowed to trespass, including and especially Sean.

Everyone wanted him to see his goddess for the first time when she walked down the aisle. Sean coordinated the music selection with Jose, who brought his family along.

Jose would sit up front and to the side. Sean asked Jose to play Neil Young's "Such a Woman" as Emily walked down the aisle and then "We Never Danced" when they kissed and the ceremony ended. He was asked to repeat the songs during the reception as Emily and he danced. He wanted the day to be as romantic as possible. He wanted his undying love for his Emily fully expressed. He wanted her to know how much his heart burst with love for her. He was so happy that day.

Jose practiced for several weeks. He wanted to be perfect for Sean and Emily.

The day was full of surprises as well.

****

Jose and his wife were sitting in a restaurant in downtown Providence one Saturday afternoon when he spotted a tall, red-headed woman walking into the restaurant. She and the two people who accompanied her sat at a table right next to him but behind his wife. He kept staring at the redhead when his wife, Maria, asked him who he was looking at.

He told her, "I could swear that's Melody Rogers who interviewed me years ago when Sean came out of his coma."

"Go say 'hi' to her. Even if it's not her, at least you won't have to wonder."

He got up, walked over to the table and asked. It was Melody Rogers. She was in town visiting her parents who were sitting with her. When Melody learned who Jose was, she jumped up and hugged him. She told him that it was that story that had launched her career. She invited Jose and his wife to join them.

Sean and Emily's wedding was the following weekend; and, although she was not scheduled to be in town, she gave Jose her card and took his phone number. She was headed to New York City where she was scheduled to become co-anchor for one of the local channels. She told Jose she would try and postpone her trip. This story and this couple were near and dear to her heart. She wanted to cover it so she called her producer and told him what she wanted to do.

Her producer was familiar with the coma story which, at the time, had been picked up by AP. He was excited and asked her to cover it for the station. They would contact the local CBS affiliate to ask for a camera crew; but Melody requested that her fiancé, Tony Russo, who was a cameraman and photojournalist in his own right, film the wedding and interview.

Emily and Sean had an old friend of Beth's who was a Methodist minister perform the ceremony during which they, of course, read their own vows they had each written.

****

At 3 p.m. all the guests were seated, and Sean was standing up front. He was so nervous that he kept asking his Uncle Peter if he was sure he had the ring. He finally settled down when he saw Emily walk out flanked by Paul and Sarah. His heart stopped when he saw her. He couldn't take his eyes off her as she seemed to float down the aisle. Then Jose began playing "Such a Woman."

Emily couldn't take her eyes off Sean. She felt so overwhelmed with joy that the one dream she had always held onto was coming true. For the entire ceremony the couple lost contact with their surroundings. They were alone in their own world. It was such a beautiful ceremony; and the atmosphere produced by the couple was electric, leaving everyone awestruck. There wasn't a dry eye in the crowd when it came time to recite their vows.

Sean spoke first, "Emily, you're beautiful. You take my breath away."

He then paused, took a deep breath and continued, "Emily, I remember the first time I saw you. I was looking out the window of my grandma's house. I saw this vision sitting on the slant tree, and you looked illuminated by the sun. I couldn't run out to meet you fast enough. I was so afraid I was imagining you. Then, as I stood at the base of our tree, you turned and asked if you were trespassing; then you invited me up to sit with you. We were just twelve years old, and I've been in love with you every day of my life since then. Several years earlier, I lost my father who had been my best friend. After his death, I felt so alone and lost in the world until that day. You filled a void I was convinced could never be filled. But you did. Em, I came back to life the day I met you.

Then, when we became separated a few years ago, I felt that void again and thought I would never feel the joy you had given me ever again. Do you recall when Grandma told you that you were a miracle? Emily, you are my miracle and I feel like the most fortunate human being on this planet. I will love and cherish you forever and ever. You are my life and my soul. I love you, Emily. I love you so much."

Emily was so choked up by the time it was her turn that it took all her effort to keep from sobbing, but somehow she made it through.

"Sean, you brought life and light into my world the first time I turned around and saw your beautiful face looking up at me from the base of our tree. My life was so empty and here was this wonderful, yet precocious boy who wanted to shake my hand. I can't even begin to tell you what you've done for me from that first moment. You gave me purpose. You gave me a reason to live. Where there was only darkness in my life, you gave me light; and that light has filled my heart and soul with so much hope and courage to become who I've become. I too felt as if the light had gone out in my world when we became separated. Then one day as I walked home, I heard a familiar sound; and as I approached the square, I saw an angel playing a guitar. I thought surely I must be dreaming. But it was really you. The only male I've ever loved in my entire life had come to find me. I love you, Sean Mahoney, with all my being; and I will love you until the end of time."

They were pronounced husband and wife and kissed so tenderly. Then Sean surprised everyone, including Emily. He bent down and kissed her belly, then picked her up and carried her back down the aisle.

When they got to the portion of yard where the reception was being held, Jose was already seated at the mike. His wife Maria accompanied him with vocals. They began with "We Never Danced." Sean whisked Emily to the dance floor, and everyone felt chills as the couple began to glide.

It wasn't until after that dance that Beth told them Melody was there and wanted to interview them. They both looked at each other and laughed. They couldn't believe it.

The first words out of Emily's mouth were, "My god. Melody, you're still just as beautiful as you were that day we met. You were my idol back then, and I've been a big fan of yours ever since. Where are you working now?"

Melody took Emily's hand. "Emily, you have turned out to be an absolutely stunning woman; and, Sean …well, all I can say is 'my, my.'" Then Melody turned to the side. "This is my fiancé, Tony. We would like to do a short interview with both of you. I'm headed up to New York City tomorrow where I will begin co-anchoring for the local CBS affiliate. You know, I have you two to thank for launching my career. And here you are. Fairy tales truly do come true. I must tell you that your vows took my breath away. Somehow I feel there's a story behind both of your vows. Perhaps one day we can talk about that."

"A fairy tale come true" would be the theme of the news story. She interviewed the couple and then had Jose play while the couple danced. Back at the station they edited in some of the old footage. It aired that night locally and on the NY station as well. Little did Melody know, but Tony filmed a surprise ending which the anchors from both stations had the editors throw in at the conclusion of the segment.

When Emily tossed her bouquet, it was Melody who caught it. She and Tony stayed for another half-hour and then excused themselves so they could go get the footage ready for the evening news.

Sarah and Beth were so happy with the entire wedding. Everyone kept talking about how magical everything was that day.

When the couple was ready to leave, Emily thought they were headed back to their house. The next late afternoon they were scheduled to fly out of Boston to Venezuela.

Venezuela possessed so many unique features the couple wanted to experience, including the Andes Mountains and Angel Falls, the largest waterfall in the world. Emily's love for birds was another attraction; some of the world's most beautiful and unique birds live in the rainforests along the Amazon. Before flying out, however, Emily was about to receive yet another surprise.

Peter took Sean off to the side and gave him the key to the cabin. Several weeks prior, Beth told Sean that Peter had been in the process of selling the cabin when she learned of his intentions. She and Bill bought the cabin and the land surrounding it for the couple. It was their wedding gift to them.

"Mom, I don't know what to say."

"Sweetie, there was no way I was going to let that cabin slip away. Your marriage to Emily is a dream come true for me. I've always known you two belonged together, so how could I let go of the cabin where the two of you first discovered that your love was far more than just a childhood crush. And here you are not only marrying Emily, my hero for saving my sweet boy's life; but you're also going to be a daddy in a few months, and I'm going to be a grandmother. I remember the 'boys only' camping and hiking trips you and your dad took. This gives you someplace to take your children so you can teach them about all the wonders of the world and universe. I'm so happy for you and Emily, Sean. My heart overflows for both of you and your future."

Sarah and Zack came over and hugged Emily and Sean as they were leaving. "Emily, sweetie that was the most beautiful wedding I've ever seen in my entire life. Sean, your kissing her belly at the end, then picking her up was like watching a fairy tale. You probably didn't hear all the 'oooos' and 'ahhhs' but everyone was swept away by those gestures. Have a wonderful night and honeymoon, and we'll see you when you get back."

Neither Sean nor Emily realized that Sarah and Zack had furnished the cabin and had it hooked up to electricity and running water for them. Sean assumed it would look as it did years prior. He couldn't wait to surprise Emily.

Jeannie, DD, Lily, Peter, Katie, Paul and Alessa all tied cans to Sean's Land Rover and wrote all over its windows. They were standing at the vehicle with rice and threw it on the couple as they got in and drove away.

It was truly a day in paradise, and more was on the way.

A few minutes into the drive Sean looked at Emily. "Em, you look like a fairy princess today. I swear my heart stopped in my chest when I saw you. It was magical for me. I'm so happy right now."

"Sean, I love you more than life itself. I'm beside myself. Today is the day I have always dreamed of with you, and it was far better than my dream."

"Well, sweetie, it's going to be even better. We're not going back to the house."

She looked totally surprised.

He held up the key. "Do you know what this key opens?"

"I haven't the slightest idea."

"Mom and Bill gave us Uncle Peter's cabin as a wedding present. We're going there for our first night. When you weren't paying attention, I threw all our bags for our honeymoon in the back. We have all tonight and most of tomorrow to be where we first made love."

She was so overwhelmed she couldn't think of anything to say. She just sat quietly and watched as they drove the familiar route. He looked over at her and turned on the radio/CD player which began playing "We Never Danced."

She whispered, "Just like our D-day. Oh, Sean. I feel like that seventeen-year-old girl again. You were so beautiful that day and treated me with such gentleness. I can't believe this is actually happening."

And just like that day, they said no more. They just held hands in anticipation of their beautiful first evening of the rest of their lives.

****

It was dusk when Sean drove down the dirt road next to the lone mailbox. They opened all the windows so they could smell the air. As they drove into the clearing and could see the front of the cabin, Sean stopped the car.

"Oh, Sean, it looks like it did that first time."

As they did so many years prior, they both got out. She waited for him to come around to her side as she stood looking at the cabin, remembering every little detail of that first magical day. Then, he was standing in front of her. He extended his hand which she took. Under his arm was the quilt Martha had given him for Emily that first time.

As they walked to the front door, she felt as if they were walking through an enchanted forest. She soaked in everything and tucked all the details into her heart. She knew he was going to take her to heaven again that night.

When they walked in, it looked mostly the same with some minor changes. The sofa was new, as was the table in the eating area. Over in the corner was a beautiful iron frame bed, and there was electricity and running water with a small bathroom added on to the back side of the cabin. A lamp was sitting on the table next to the bed, and one of Martha's scarves was draped over the lamp. The room was filled with a delightful aroma that was wafting off the scarf.

Emily looked at Sean, "Did your mom do this too?"

"No, Em. I'm pretty sure the interior was your mom. Who else would know about the scarf on the lamp?"

"Oh, Sean. This is amazing. I feel like Snow White."

He chuckled, "Emily, you are far more beautiful than Snow White in your wedding dress."

"Well, you are the Prince Charming I've dreamed of all my life."

They sat on the sofa for a few minutes. There was a bottle of ginger ale and two wine glasses on the wooden eating table. He brought them over and they had a glass together.

"Em, this is to the rest of our lives together. I love you with all my heart, Emily Mahoney. God, how I love you."

"Sean, I loved when you kissed my belly. I couldn't believe it when you did. I think we're going to have a long, truly magical life together. I just love you, Sean Mahoney."

They finished their ginger ale. Then he got up and extended his hand. They walked over to the bed, and he unzipped her dress. She stepped out of it, and he folded it and put it on the chair near the bed. He kissed her face, neck and shoulders as he unhooked her bra. He folded it and put it on the chair. He was kissing her passionately when he reached down and pulled her panties down. She stepped out of them, and he folded them and put them on the chair. She sat on the bed and unzipped his pants and pulled them down along with his briefs to the floor. As he stepped out of them, she reached down, picked them up and folded them then handed them to him so he could lay them on top of her clothes. He unbuttoned the top portion of his shirt while she unbuttoned the bottom portion. He took it off and hung it on the back of the chair.

She stood up and in the dim light they looked at each other as his hand went down to her belly. He loved that she was pregnant with his baby. He loved that she loved him, and she was in heaven that they were there together. They embraced and fell to the bed where they once again danced a lover's waltz as they made exquisite, romantic love. When they were spent, they lay in each other's arms immersed in the heaven they composed together.

Chapter 21

Emily and Sean returned from Venezuela the Sunday after the wedding. The trip allowed them enough time to see the highlights but not enough time to see everything; and when they returned home, they knew they would visit Venezuela at a later date and for a longer period of time. They had fallen in love with the country and its people.

That first Monday back, Sean jumped right back into work while Emily took over managing the house renovation and getting Sean's old room ready for the baby. Sarah was excited about helping Emily with the baby's room.

Although Sean and Emily intuitively knew the gender of their son, they wanted to get a sonogram performed. Both wanted the experience of seeing their little Davie in the womb. That weekend Beth had a small get-together just so the sonogram pictures could be shared.

Beth and Sarah were thrilled to see the developing fetus; and Beth was even more excited when she learned that Sean and Emily were going to name their son David Sean, "Davie" for short.

Emily and Sarah went to work on Davie's room. They painted the baby's room a stimulating bright yellow and, looking at photos Emily had taken while in the Himalayas, she painted the animals she had seen while working there.

On one wall she painted the brown bear, which because of its almost perfectly rounded ears, reminded her of a teddy bear. Right behind the bear she painted the squinty-eyed Tibetan fox. She had heard tales of how these two teamed up for hunts, and she had once photographed a fox following a bear on a hunt for a pika, which looked like a cross between a rabbit and a robust mouse. The bear and fox were painted on one wall, while the pika stuck its head out of its hole on the other wall. She also painted a scene from a trip she had made to Langtang National Park where she had photographed a red panda mother and her two cubs. Emily so loved the Himalayas and it was evident in her mural. Once the mural was finished, the rest of the room was completed rapidly. That's where Sarah took over.

****

Emily expressed a desire that all the furniture be white. Sarah took Emily to a local baby furniture store where she purchased an entire suite to include a crib, bassinet, changing table and dresser. Emily also bought a number of different mobiles to hang from the ceiling. Emily was about to pay for two white rocking chairs, but Sarah insisted that she and Zack would give them those as well.

Every evening until Davie was born, both she and Sean sat in their rocking chairs. Sean played his guitar while Emily read out loud. They were absolutely convinced Davie could hear them because it was the time of day that Davie was the least restless and kicked the least. Sean would often lay his head on Emily's stomach and talk lovingly to Davie, knowing in his heart and mind that Davie knew who he was.

It was a loving nine-month pregnancy, and it drew Sean and Emily even closer to each other.

In January Jeannie had a huge baby shower for Emily. With the invitations she listed a number of suggestions and took Emily to Target so she could list items on their registry. That was a great idea because the gifts worked out perfectly. By the time Davie was born, there were enough clothes, toys and crib attire fitting of the new prince.

****

Davie was born a week early in February, and his birthday couldn't have been more appropriate. He was born on February 14th at 4 a.m.

Although her first months of pregnancy were tough, the birth was quick and easy.

Emily was never a fan of pain so she opted to have an epidural. She wanted to be awake but without the excruciating pain of natural birth. They remained close to Jose and decided early on that she would have the baby at Providence Hospital where she was allowed to give birth in her own private room. Jose was there when Davie was born. He played his guitar and sang during the entire birthing process. Sean was right by Emily, mopping her face and forehead and holding her hand while he helped her breathe. They had both attended several birthing classes offered by the hospital which Emily later said helped tremendously.

When mother and baby came home a few days later, Jeannie was at the house fixing dinner. Uncle DD showed up just as Sean and his tiny family pulled into the driveway. He had worked the day shift. Sean took Davie inside while DD helped Emily. She was still a bit sore.

Jeannie was holding little Davie when Emily and DD came in. "Em, he is as cute as a button. Kinda makes me want a little critter."

She gave him to Emily once she was seated. "So far, he's as good as can be. The nurses said he's one of the most contented babies they've seen in a long time. By the way, thanks for coming over and fixing dinner. This is a real treat."

"We needed an excuse to be here when you got home. I love what you two have done with the house so far. I really like how you knocked down that wall and made it into an eating area. And what a view of the slant tree. I'm dying to see the baby's room. I haven't had a chance to go upstairs."

Emily got up. "Are you at a place you can come up with me? I'm going to put the little guy to bed anyway."

Emily and Jeannie walked upstairs.

Jeannie's eyes got huge. "God, Em, this is beautiful! I love the animals. I've never seen any animals like this before."

Emily smiled as she put Davie in the crib. She whispered, "These are animals I photographed in the Himalayas. They're some of the most interesting animals I've ever seen."

"Well, I love it. And all the mobiles and color. This guy will never get bored."

They walked out. Emily was carrying a baby monitor. "That's the point. Color stimulates baby's minds. I want him to have every chance in the world to be whatever he wants to be."

As they walked back into the kitchen, Sean and DD were talking about the renovation. DD looked at Jeannie. "Did you tell Emily we are buying a house?"

"No." She snickered. "Em, we're buying a house."

Emily laughed as DD rolled his eyes. Emily commented, "Fantastic! Where?"

"It's an older Victorian in Providence. I just finished getting my masters and have put my name in the hat for vice-principal at North Providence. If I get it, I'll get a nice raise."

"That's great, Jeannie. I'll keep my fingers crossed for you."

DD said, "Em, Sean told me you handled the entire renovation. We could sure use some pointers for our house. Although the current owners have done a lot of renovating, Jeannie and I have a few ideas of our own."

"I'd love to help. I was scheduled to go back to Nepal in June, but I've decided to stay here this summer. I don't want Sean to miss any of Davie's first year."

They had a lovely dinner and when they finished, all four did the dishes. As Jeannie and DD were about to leave, Jeannie nudged DD. "John, before we leave, I'd really like for you to see the baby's room. Is that okay, Em?"

"Yes, I can hear him right now. He's awake and I need to feed him in a few minutes anyway."

As Jeannie and John walked out of the kitchen, Emily motioned to Sean to stay in the kitchen. She whispered, "I think Jeannie wants to tweak DD's desire for a family."

She was right. When they walked into the room, John was drawn to the bassinet where he watched little Davie and even stroked his head.

"The room's beautiful, isn't it?" Jeannie turned around to see John stroking Davie's head. "He's sweet, isn't he?"

"Yes, he is. Hmm …what would you think about discussing our having a little one?"

Jeannie didn't say a word; she just walked over to John and kissed him.

Once they were in the car and headed home, John asked, "Jeannie, tell me the truth. Did you bring me up to the baby's room to whet my daddy appetite?"

"Okay, I won't lie. I've been thinking about it for a couple of months, trying to figure out if I was ready."

"Are you ready? Because I've also been thinking about it. I know we've been putting your dad off with intentions of you finishing your masters and our buying a house and, well, we've arrived at that point."

She looked over at John, reached for his hand. "Dad would be thrilled and so would Mom. You'd make such a wonderful father. Let's try."

When they arrived home and walked in the front door, John put his arms around Jeannie and said, "Let's try beginning with tonight."

They didn't make it to the bedroom but made love on the living room floor. They made love every day either before or after John's shift.

Chapter 22

A month later one morning as John and Jeannie were getting ready for work, Jeannie burst into the bathroom as John was shaving. He was completely startled, especially when she took a nosedive to the floor and began throwing up in the toilet.

He bent down next to her. "Are you okay, babe? Was it something you ate? Maybe you should stay home from school today. That's what they have substitute teachers for."

She was throwing up the entire time he was talking. When she finished, she was laughing.

"Jeannie, why are you laughing?"

She grabbed some tissue and blew her nose. "Because," she laughed, "I'm pretty sure I'm pregnant. My period is five days late."

"Oh my god, Jeannie. You really think so?" He looked excited.

"Yes. But just to make sure, I'll pick up a test kit today. We'll do the test tonight; wouldn't that be appropriate because we're supposed to have dinner with Mom and Dad?"

When it was time to leave for work, they kissed and told each other they would be distracted all day waiting to do the test.

****

Jeannie was waiting in the living room when John came through the door at 6:30 p.m. She was clutching the package that held the test.

Jeannie asked, "Are you ready to find out?"

"Let's do it," responded John.

They went into the bathroom and Jeannie peed on the strip. Then after what seemed like a long time, they looked at the strip. It was positive.

"I'm going to be a daddy. Damn, Jeannie, you've made me the happiest man in the world. I never thought I'd be this excited!"

Jeannie threw her arms around DD and kissed him. "Thanks for being my true love. I've been so happy for the last several years and didn't think I could ever feel happier. But I am. I'm going to have your baby, John!"

They were so happy they made love before heading over to Phil and Gladys' house.

When they walked in, Gladys was setting the dining room table. "You two look like two Cheshire cats. What's going on?"

"Where's Dad, Mom?"

"He's in the basement putting a light bulb in the safe room. Why?"

"Because we have something to tell you two."

Just then Phil emerged from the basement as the three walked out into the kitchen.

"Dad, what have you been bugging us about for the last several years?"

Phil looked truly perplexed and shrugged his shoulders. "Well, I don't know. You tell me."

Gladys immediately knew. "You're pregnant, aren't' you?"

John was beaming from ear-to-ear as Jeannie hugged her mom, "Yes. I'm pregnant!"

Phil just sat down. He was stunned. "I haven't mentioned grandchildren for at least a year. I gave up."

Jeannie laughed. "I know, Dad. You've been very patient. But now you're going to be a grandpa!"

Gladys hugged John, "Have you told your parents yet?"

John shook his head. "No. We just found out about an hour ago. Jeannie suspected it this morning when she burst into the bathroom and threw up. I thought she was just sick."

Phil and Jeannie were hugging. "Jeannie, I can't wait! I'm really going to be a grandfather. Finally!" He shook John's hand.

They had a wonderful dinner as they talked about the baby, babies' names and John and Jeannie's new house. When they were finished and the dishes were done, Gladys suggested to John that he call his parents that evening. He did and his mom and dad were thrilled.

On the way home that night, Jeannie called Emily, "Em, you got a minute?"

"Hey, Jeannie. Yea. We're just sitting in Davie's room; I'm feeding him. What's up? Oh my god, Jeannie, that's wonderful. Wait. Let me put you on speaker. Okay, tell me again so Sean can hear you."

"I'm pregnant! We just found out this evening."

Sean said, "That's fantastic, Jeannie and John. Congratulations. Davie, did you hear that? You've got your own personal friend on the way! Have you told your parents yet?"

"Yes. We just came from having dinner with them. They're ecstatic. My dad is thrilled. All he could say was, 'Finally.'"

They all laughed.

****

The next nine months went by in a flash.

John and Jeannie moved into their new home at the end of May and, with Emily's help, immediately went to work on the baby's room. Jeannie followed Emily's lead with the bright yellow walls. She asked Emily if she would paint a mural on the long wall once they discovered the baby's gender.

During her third month, Jeannie had a sonogram. They were having a little girl. John had always been partial to his maternal grandmother's name, Ariel. Jeannie loved it too so she began calling her baby her "little mermaid," and the Disney movie version became the theme for the mural.

Emily had so much fun painting the mural that she told Jeannie she hoped her next baby was a girl. The finished room was beautiful, complete with stars on the ceiling cast by a special night light. Then when it came time to furnish Ariel's room, John insisted that he wanted to have his own rocking chair where he and Jeannie would read every night to Ariel. They both loved that Sean and Emily did that with Davie because Davie seemed to catch onto everything quickly.

****

Davie was crawling by six months and walking by his ninth month. His first steps happened one evening when Jeannie and DD were over for dinner.

Sean bent down to pick him up when Davie stood up and walked away. Of course he fell on the fourth step, but that didn't stop him. He was literally running in another month. He also said his first word by his ninth month.

When Sean asked him if he wanted a cookie, Davie said, "No!" Emily was bent over in the kitchen and came up so quickly she bumped her head on the edge of the highchair. Davie and Sean laughed together. Then Sean taught Davie to give him a high-five, and the two laughed some more while Emily laughed and rubbed her head.

All this excitement with Davie and the anticipation of Jeannie and DD's baby drew the two couples closer together, and they all loved that.

****

Jeannie went into labor during the middle of the night on January 19th. John was working a case when Jeannie called to tell him her water had broken. He immediately sent over an ambulance and caught up with the ambulance in his police vehicle a mile from the hospital. When Jeannie was being wheeled into the delivery room, he was right by her side.

"Pays to be married to a cop" was all Jeannie could think of to say.

She delivered Ariel Marie Bertram at 7:15 a.m. John immediately called Emily right after calling Gladys and his parents. Sean had already left for work, so Gladys picked Emily and Davie up and drove to the hospital. Phil was minutes behind.

By that time, Emily was back to work but on semester break. She had taken a position with her alma mater, Brown. During that semester she and Sean took turns taking Davie to school with them. They weren't yet ready to relinquish Davie to a day care center.

When Jeannie went back to work two months later, Gladys decided that she wanted to take care of both children, which thrilled not only Jeannie and John but Emily and Sean as well.

Jeannie had indeed landed the assistant principal's position at North Providence High School and was gaining a reputation with the students as being tough but fair.

As one male student put it, "She doesn't let us get away with anything."

Jeannie's response was, "That's because I know exactly what you're up to. At your age, I got away with more than my share."

Chapter 23

The next four years were loaded with fun. Davie and Ariel got along extremely well. Although not quite as quick a learner as Davie, Ariel was quicker than average; and Davie taught her a lot, especially how to say "no." They were quite a pair to watch as they grew.

Ariel also had a lot of Jeannie's temperament and tenacity. As a result, she was constantly getting into trouble and often would drag Davie into the fracas. In the end, however, Ariel proved time and time again to be an honorable person because she would always defend Davie when he had nothing to do with whatever problem she had caused.

When Jeannie became upset with Ariel and complained to her parents about Ariel's unruliness, Gladys reminded Jeannie that Ariel was only paying Jeannie back for the trouble Jeannie had caused Gladys. Then Gladys would counsel John that he was just like Phil in that he allowed Ariel to completely manipulate him because he would often step in to save Ariel from Jeannie's anger.

One afternoon after witnessing Ariel's ability to pit Jeannie's anger against John's desire to defend her, Gladys laughed out loud as Jeannie smacked Ariel on the behind and sent her to her room.

"Mom, please don't laugh when I'm trying to discipline Ariel!"

"Oh, Jeannie, I'm laughing because this is a great example of what I continue to tell you. Ariel is constantly testing you. She knows how to make you angry; then she knows how to manipulate you, John, to get her off the hook. I'm laughing now because I see myself in you, Jeannie. You react to Ariel's antics just as I used to. She's very frustrating, isn't she?"

Jeannie was now laughing. "Okay, okay. I remember how I used to test you; and, you're right, Dad always got me off the hook. But that doesn't mean I have to let her get away with it."

John, Phil and Gladys were all laughing at Jeannie's stubborn resolve to be the disciplinarian.

John quit laughing. "Jeannie, I want you to be the disciplinarian because you understand Ariel better than I do. You continue to play bad cop so I get the chance to play good cop. That's something I don't often get to play." He then began laughing again as did Jeannie as she raised her fist to him and scowled through her laughter.

Ariel was sitting on the top step and heard the entire conversation. When they all stopped laughing, she came back down the stairs. She was standing on the bottom step when Jeannie turned and asked what she was doing downstairs when she was told to go up to her room.

Ariel began crying. "Mommy, I'm sorry. I love you and I don't mean to make you mad at me."

How could Jeannie resist her daughter? She went over and hugged her and told her she forgave her and loved her. "Just try a little harder, Ariel. Can you do that?"

"Yes, Mommy. I promise I will try very hard."

This is how the rest of Ariel's upbringing would progress. She would constantly challenge Jeannie, and it would become a tug of war and love between mother and daughter. In the end, Ariel and Jeannie would have a tremendously close, loving relationship.

****

Davie, on the other hand, rarely rebelled. He was as good as gold except that he loved playing practical jokes, especially on his mom. Sean didn't help because he would often encourage Davie so that the practical jokes were jointly concocted, like the Halloween they put a very large, real-looking, hairy spider in Davie's candy bag.

Davie asked Emily if she would reach into his bag and find a Mounds bar for him. She found the Mounds bar, but the spider's legs were wrapped around it. She screamed when she pulled it out and flung it across the room. Sean laughed at this while Davie was laughing so hard he rolled on the floor.

Beginning with the first weekend after Davie's first birthday, Sean and Emily would take Davie for hikes. It was usually Sean who wore the backpack baby carrier while Emily followed behind talking to Davie and pointing out birds and small animals. Davie loved these walks and got excited when he would spot a bird or small animal. He became so familiar with the various birds that he would say their names clearly before either parent could get the name out. He also memorized the sounds birds would make and would say their names before either Emily or Sean saw the actual bird.

In the evening the three often sat on the slant tree. Until Davie was old enough to walk up the tree, Sean would wear a front load carrier so Davie could enjoy the night sky as Sean pointed out all the constellations. This was such a pleasant family event as Sean and Davie would sit and Sean would put his arm around Emily and pull her tightly to both of them.

Davie quickly picked up on the constellations, often pointing them out before Sean could say the names. During these events Sean would tell Davie how his own father, also named Davie, had taught him about the constellations. Emily loved watching Sean and Davie bond, and it made her love for Sean grow even deeper.

Then there was the cabin which the three visited often.

Jeannie, DD and Ariel were frequently invited. In fact, a guest bedroom was built onto the house for Jeannie and DD. Sean also had the corner where his and Emily's bed was located partitioned off for privacy. The two children camped out in the middle of the cabin where a tent would be set up.

Weekends at the cabin became a favorite mini-vacation for both families. It was here one weekend that Davie and Ariel were playing quietly outside that something happened.

****

They were playing in the mud from a rain the evening prior. Davie loved dump trucks, and Ariel loved them too as long as she was playing with Davie. When Davie dug up some worms, Ariel jumped up and screamed. She hated creepy, crawly things; but her fear gave Davie an opportunity to play one of his pranks.

As Ariel was filling the backend of one of the dump trucks with mud, Davie began throwing live worms at Ariel. She told him to quit it, but he continued when one of them went down the back of her shirt. She jumped up screaming as Davie rolled on the ground laughing at her. This made Ariel so angry she picked up a small clump of mud and threw it at Davie, hitting him at the corner of his right eye. Now both children were screaming and crying.

Little did Ariel know but the clump contained a small, sharp rock.

Jeannie was the first one out the door. Davie was crying and rubbing his eye as Ariel stood over Davie with her arms folded. Jeannie immediately assumed Ariel was to blame for the entire incident as she grabbed Ariel's arm, yelled at her and sent her wailing into the cabin. By that time, Sean, Emily and John were outside. Davie continued to scream as he held his eye.

Sean scooped him up and carried him into the kitchen area so he and Emily could get a better look at his eye. Once the cut was cleaned out and examined, it was determined that he needed stitches. All of them went to the emergency room at the Cranston hospital.

Except for an occasional whimper, Ariel was very quiet. She knew she was in a boatload of trouble. John carried her. As he, Jeannie and Ariel waited in the waiting room, he cajoled Ariel to tell him what happened.

She whimpered, "I didn't mean to hurt him, Daddy. He threw worms at me, and they were crawling down my back so I threw some mud at him."

John determined that Ariel was simply reacting and didn't realize that a rock was inside the mud. Jeannie was sitting in the chair next to John and Ariel; and, when she heard this, she immediately felt guilty for assuming Ariel was completely to blame.

"Mommy's sorry, honey."

By this time, however, Ariel's feelings were so wounded that Jeannie had blamed her that she wouldn't look at Jeannie but instead buried her face against John's chest.

What a day!

Davie wound up with three stitches but no damage to his eye, except for the mud which was washed out by the nurse leaving his eye red. A bandage patch was put over the eye and stitches, and Davie was released.

Everyone was quiet on the ride back to the cabin. But once back inside, Jeannie became Ariel's champion as Jeannie asked Davie what happened. "Davie, Ariel is so sorry she cut your eye; but I need to ask you something. Davie, did you throw worms at Ariel?"

Sean and Emily just stepped back, knowing intuitively there was more to the incident than immediately apparent. Plus, when Emily heard the word "worms," she knew immediately that Davie was probably playing one of his pranks.

Sean was about to say something in Davie's defense when Emily grabbed his arm and squeezed, indicating that he should let Davie answer the question.

DD noticed the silent communication between Emily and Sean so he encouraged Davie to answer Jeannie. "Davie, it's okay, but you need to truthfully answer Aunt Jeannie's question. Were you throwing worms at Ariel?"

Davie bowed his head and admitted he was throwing worms at Ariel. She was sitting in the middle of the floor pouting when Davie made his admission. Then something really special happened.

Davie walked over to Ariel, bent down and touched her arm, "Ariel, I'm sorry I threw worms on you. I'm sorry I got you into trouble."

Ariel looked up with tears rolling down her face, "I'm sorry I hurt you, Davie. I didn't know I threw a rock."

He sat down next to Ariel and hugged her as both sets of parents watched this spectacle. Jeannie had her phone in her hand and aimed it at the children and took a photo of this special moment.

When Ariel and Davie were finished hugging, Ariel got up and walked over to Jeannie and touched her hand. "Mommy, are you still mad at me?"

Jeannie showed her the photo, "Baby, how could I be? Mommy loves you very much."

Ariel was laughing joyfully at the picture as Davie jumped up to see the picture as well.

It was a happy ending to what could have become a mess. That evening as the two children ate their dinner picnic-style on a blanket spread on the floor, the four adults sat at the table eating and drinking a glass of wine.

Sean lifted his glass and made a toast, "Here's to the innocence and honesty of our two children. They showed us all that we should keep our big yaps shut before we know the whole story."

Jeannie, knowing he was talking about her and himself for almost jumping to conclusions, exuberantly said, "Here, here!"

Then DD raised his glass, looked at Emily who had hers raised, clinked her glass and said, "Here's to the two good cops who kept their wits about them."

All four adults laughed heartily as they smiled warmly at their two wonderful children sharing their milk and cookies.

Chapter 24

For Davie's fifth birthday, a big weekend was planned. February 14th fell on a Sunday.

On Saturday, John managed to take off from work. The two couples would take Davie and Ariel to Roger Williams Park which wasn't too far from the cabin, so they spent the night at the cabin. Sarah planned a birthday party at her home in Providence for Sunday, and Beth helped decorate the cake.

On Saturday, Sean, Emily, John and Jeannie got up and got the children ready to go to the zoo. Davie and Ariel were ecstatic. They both loved animals.

Jeannie and Emily were cracking up all morning talking about the day Jeannie, a former boyfriend named Phillip, Sean and Emily went to the zoo fifteen years prior. DD was enjoying listening to the story of Jeannie's antics that day because he could clearly imagine them in his mind. He died laughing when Jeannie first told him about Dick the chimp.

According to the story, DD learned that an adult male human, who was eating a vanilla ice cream cone, began taunting the chimp named Dick. The joke was the action Dick took to deal with the male. Dick masturbated in the direction of the harasser, landing his prize on top of the man's ice cream cone.

Jeannie was laughing loudly. "Hey, Em. How long do chimps live? Wouldn't it be hilarious if Dick were still alive?"

The two children were playing in the middle of the floor as they listened to their parents.

Ariel jumped up off the floor. "Mommy, can we see Dick today?"

"I don't know, honey, we'll have to ask where he is."

Then Davie asked Sean, "Daddy, can we get some ice cream when we go see Dick? I want vanilla."

This made all four adults practically fall off their chairs with laughter as the two children looked at each other with expressions that begged the question, "What's so funny?" Then, as if assuming their parents were all nuts, they just went back to playing in the middle of the floor.

The kid's behavior was so hilarious, the four adults just continued to laugh loudly.

By the time they were ready to leave for the park, the temperature outside was unseasonably warm. It was actually in the 70s. So although everyone brought along their winter coats, they dressed the children in light jackets and wore jackets as well.

They had a truly delightful walk around the park. And much to Jeannie's delight, Dick was still alive and as rambunctious as ever. They had to scuttle the children away from the cage that sat in the middle of the monkey house when Dick began to show another stupid human male his revenge for the human's abusive behavior. As they did, Jeannie and Emily were both buckled over with laughter.

In the afternoon they all went down to Roosevelt Lake where they could lease paddleboats. As they waited for two of the boats to become available, they didn't notice that Davie had walked into the water. All of a sudden they heard him yell, "Mommy, Daddy, look!" He was waist deep in the water, and he was holding a fish up in the air. Ariel was standing on the shore clapping with glee.

Panicked, Sean ran into the water and whisked his son up out of the water. Davie still clutched the fish as Sean brought him to the shore where Emily scolded him for going into the water. "Davie, you could have drowned."

They finally settled down, and Davie threw the fish back in the water. That was the end of the paddleboats. Davie was soaked and Sean was wet as well.

On the way out of the park, they did get the kids an ice cream cone each, then went home to get dry clothes.

Later that evening they built a small fire in the clearing out the front door and roasted hot dogs and marshmallows. The kids were having a great time when Jeannie mentioned the fish.

"How on earth was Davie able to catch that fish with his bare hands?"

Emily and Sean just looked at each other and began to laugh.

"What's wrong with you two?" Jeannie asked.

Sean couldn't help himself. "As you know, Davie is named after my dad. Well, guys, my dad used to catch fish with his bare hands. Emily and I are just as stunned as you because I've never been able to do that. It's weird, isn't it?"

Then DD said, "Sean, you're the brain guy. Can that type of

thing be genetic? I've fished all my life, and I've never seen anything like that before."

Then Emily changed the subject, "I don't know if it's genetic, but I don't care. That little stinker is usually so quiet and well-behaved that now I realize we need to watch him like a hawk. He could have drowned today."

Davie heard his mom. He was toasting a marshmallow when he walked over and gave the marshmallow to her. "Mommy, I'm sorry I scared you today. I wasn't going to drown. I just saw the fish swimming in the water and wanted to say 'hi.'"

"Well, Davie, honey. You did scare Mommy. Your daddy nearly drowned when he was a boy, and you just scared me. I love you so much, Davie." She hugged him tightly, all the while marveling in her head at what she had witnessed.

Later that evening when the children were asleep in their sleeping bags and Jeannie and DD had retired, Sean and Emily sat in the rocking chairs on the front porch.

"Em, if we never believed in the vision we had five years ago, I think there shouldn't be any doubt after today."

She was shaking her head in disbelief. "I know. When I was talking to Davie, all I could think of was the story you told me about your dad. But you and I need to keep a level head and realize that he is still just a tiny child. What he did today, going in the water like that, could have resulted in a disaster. God, Sean, I'm amazed, excited, yet scared at the same time."

"You're right, sweetie. I'll have a serious talk with him tomorrow before we go to the party. Okay?"

"Yes. Please do."

He then reached for her hand. "Would you be interested in giving each other our Valentine's cards and then fooling around tonight? Tonight will probably be our only opportunity."

She was delighted as they both tiptoed inside, got their cards and brought them back out to read. As usual, it was obvious that they both took a lot of pains to find just the right cards. When they were finished sharing, Emily said she was going in to check on the children. They kissed.

When she came back out, she had only her bathrobe on. Sean asked if anything was under it, and she coyly answered with a question, "Wouldn't you like to know?"

He then took her hand and laid it on his groin. He was hard as a rock.

She pointed her finger at him as if to admonish him for being so naughty. Then she got up, peeked in the window just to make sure one last time that the children were fast asleep.

"Umm. It's such a pleasant night out here. Unzip your pants. I'm going to sit down."

He smiled and unzipped his pants as she untied her robe. He then scooted forward a little as she turned her back, straddled him and sat down.

He reached around to her breasts and said, "My favorite tits. Umm. You feel so good."

She rocked forward and back, quickening the rhythm when she intuitively knew Sean was about to climax. He came with a moan as he leaned her back and kissed her deeply.

"Oh, Sean, you still make me so horny."

He used a small towel he had just in case to wipe her off, then said, "Sit down on my lap, sweetie. I want to send you to heaven."

She leaned back and rested her head against his neck as he stroked her clitoris. She was licking, kissing and sucking his neck when she came hard. He continued until she came again.

"Emily, I love you like I could never love anyone else."

"Oh, Sean. I'm so happy. I love our family." Then, "What would you think of having another baby?"

"I'd like that, Em. I think Davie would too. Let's try."

They finally went inside and went to bed. They woke about 9 a.m. to the smell of fresh coffee.

When they got up, Jeannie was sitting at the small table; and the two children were playing on the floor.

Sean went over to Davie, scooped him up and said, "Happy birthday, Davie! Are you ready for your big day?"

Emily walked out and was rubbing her eyes. "Where's DD, Jeannie?"

"He ran out to get some donuts for all of us. There's a fresh pot of coffee." She pointed to the coffeepot.

Emily walked over to Sean and Davie as Davie yelled, "Mommy, Mommy, it's my birthday party today. When are we going to

Grandma's? Is Pappy George going to be there?"

Davie loved his Pappy George.

She kissed her son and said, "We're going in a little while, sweetie; and yes, Pappy George will be there. He wouldn't miss your birthday party for the world." Then she kissed Davie again and exclaimed, "Happy birthday, my birthday boy!"

Davie reached for Emily as Sean passed him to her. Then Sean sat down.

Jeannie reached across the table and moved the collar of Sean's bathrobe, "Hmm ... looks like you two had some fun last night."

Sean looked puzzled as Emily, who had put Davie down, came over to look. She started laughing, "Good grief. I didn't realize I did that."

Jeannie just laughed and said, "Way to go, Em!"

Sean, still confused, went into the small bathroom off the kitchen area and looked in the mirror. There on his neck were three humongous hickeys. "Good grief, Em. How am I going to explain these today?"

She was laughing when she said, "Well, I sincerely don't think any of the adults will ask because they all know what they are."

At that moment John walked in with a dozen donuts.

Jeannie looked at John and said, "Hey, Officer Dunkin Donuts, I think you and I went to bed too early last night and missed all the action."

When he came over and put the donuts down on the table, Jeannie pointed to Sean's neck shiners.

All four adults were laughing while the children were begging for donuts.

Just before they left for the party, John gave Davie a small wrapped present, "Hey, little guy, Uncle DD has to go catch bad guys today. I got you a little present for you to wear."

Davie was all excited as he opened the gift. There was a shiny police badge inside. "Does this mean I can catch bad guys too, DD?"

John stood, put the badge on Davie, then stood back and saluted, saying, "You're officially deputized, Officer Davie!" They gave each other a high-five.

****

Davie had a wonderful birthday party. Paul, Alessa and their two children had driven up the day prior, and both Lily and Katie were also there. Lily's husband, Peter, had to work that day, but she announced they were expecting their first child; and Katie was there with her new boyfriend.

Lily was the first person to notice Sean's hickeys. "Looks like you ran into a vampire last night, Sean."

He had a turtleneck sweater on; but when he bent down, they were still very visible. "Yea, a real blood sucker attacked me last night."

Lily laughed, "Good one, Sean. Her name wasn't Emily, was it?"

All the adults were around when Lily was teasing Sean so they all began laughing. Zack just patted him on the back and said, "That's my son-in-law. Way to go, Sean!"

After cake and ice cream, the four children went out to the swing set Zack and Sarah had in their back yard. Beth, Bill and George were sitting at the table when Sean began telling the story of Davie and the fish.

Beth looked very interested. "Sean, I don't know if you remember, but your dad could catch fish with his bare hands."

Sean shook his head. "I know, Mom. I remember. That's the thing that blew me away yesterday. It's very bizarre, isn't it?"

Beth just nodded with a strange look on her face. "It's extremely bizarre."

Prior to the end of the party, George mentioned the fish story, "Sean, I've been meaning to ask you if I could take Davie fishing one day. In fact, why don't you and Davie think about going with me one weekend? Martha and I used to spend some time up on the Deerfield River in Claremont, Massachusetts. I even taught her to fly fish. After that fish story, it sounds like Davie would love to go. What do you say?"

"George, I love that idea! I'd love to learn to fly fish myself. I had a professor back at Berkeley who was an avid fly fisherman. He told me it was the most relaxing experience where he could let his mind wander. In fact, he got some of his best ideas while fishing. Say, Jeannie's husband, John, mentioned he loves to fish. We could make it an all-guy event. You know, some of my best memories with my dad were the boy's-only weekends that he and I would go on. That sounds exciting."

"John. You mean DD?"

"Yea ...John is DD's real name. DD stands for Dunkin Donuts. Being a cop, that's the nickname Emily gave him when Jeannie first met him. It's kind of stuck with him. I think he'd like to go."

George laughed. "I didn't realize DD was a nickname. I like it! Let me look into when we can get a cabin at the lake. I'll give you a couple of dates to include maybe a Friday and a Monday, and you can check with DD to see what might work for him. This should be lots of fun. I loved those trips Martha and I used to take. I haven't been back there since she died. Having you and Davie along would really mean a lot to me."

"Then it's set, George. Just let me know what weekends and we'll all make it work!"

Just before everyone went home that day, Sean and Emily watched Beth as she stared at Davie while he was playing with Paul's son, Walter.

On the way home that evening, Emily looked over at Sean, "I think your mom is beginning to wonder about Davie."

"Yea, I think you're right."

Sean then told her about the conversation with George. She was very excited for them to go. "Oh, Sean, I think that would be wonderful. But you have to promise me that you'll keep your phone handy so you can take pictures. Especially if he catches more fish with his bare hands."

Chapter 25

Emily quit taking the pill the day after Davie's birthday party. She and Sean were getting very excited about growing their family.

The following weekend she and Jeannie had a conversation. It was late Sunday afternoon when Jeannie stopped by just before picking Ariel up from her parents' home.

Sean was out in the back yard with Davie. Davie loved baseball and had gotten a pitcher's mitt for his birthday. Sean used to pitch in Little League; and was having the time of his life teaching Davie. They had a catcher's net set up in the backyard.

Emily was watching the two from the kitchen window when Jeannie knocked on the door.

Emily waved Jeannie to come in. "What 'cha doing over there, Em?"

Emily was smiling from ear-to-ear. "I'm watching my two favorite boys playing baseball."

Jeannie stood next to her. "Sean looks like he's in heaven."

"I think he is. He's such a good dad. What are you doing over in this neck of the woods?"

"I'm headed down to pick up Ariel. She spent the weekend with the grandparents."

Emily offered a cold beverage and the two women sat down.

"John mentioned there might be a boys' weekend coming up. He's all excited about that. Something about fly fishing, which I haven't a clue. I told him I couldn't understand why they wanted to go fish for flies. Of course I was pulling his leg, but he got a kick out of it anyway. We ought to plan a girls' weekend that weekend: you, me and Ariel. Our moms could come too if they wanted to. What d'ya think?"

"Sounds like fun, Jeannie. I'll miss my men, though; but I think it's important that Sean and Davie have time together without me tagging along. I just remember how fond Sean was of those boys-only outings he had with his dad. I'd like Davie to have those memories as well. Say ...I have something to tell you."

"What's that?"

"Sean and I are trying for another child. We made the decision last weekend after Davie's birthday."

Jeannie smirked. "Oh, you mean after your hickey fest?"

Emily blushed and laughed. "Yea. How embarrassing was that? I had no idea I gave him those. He just gets me so hot and bothered I get…well…carried away."

"Kind of a nice thing to say for an old married woman."

They both laughed.

Then Jeannie got her Cheshire cat look. "So, you're trying to get pregnant?"

"Yea. We'll see what happens." Then Emily cocked her head, "You little stinker. You're pregnant, aren't you?"

Jeannie laughed. "Yea, I am. We talked about it over a month ago; and boom, John parked a bun in my oven just like that …presto!" She snapped her fingers.

"That's great, Jeannie! What are you hoping for?"

"Well, I'm not going to play the typical ninny game and say, 'I'll just be happy with a healthy baby.' I'm hoping for a boy this time. One girl for now is more than I can handle. I think John's hoping for a little boy too. He loves watching Sean and Davie. So, we'll see."

"Have you told your parents yet?"

"Yes, and they are beside themselves with excitement. I think they're both hoping for a grandson as well. We told Ariel and she's really excited. She said she wants her own little Davie. It was cute when she said that. How about you? Do you have any preferences?"

"I'd really like a little girl this time. I think it would be fun to buy dresses and the like. Sean is also hoping for a girl. We just told Davie we were going to try and give him a brother or a sister. Guess we should have waited because he asks 'when' every five minutes."

Just then Sean and Davie came in. "Auntie Jeannie!" Davie ran to Jeannie and hugged her hard.

Sean looked exhausted. "This little guy gave me a workout. I think he's a natural-born pitcher, Em."

She opened the fridge and got Sean a bottle of cold beer. "I was watching the two of you before Jeannie arrived. It looked like you were giving each other a workout. Davie, do you want a glass of milk and maybe a few cookies?"

"Yes, Mommy. Can I have Oreos?" Then "Auntie Jeannie,

Mommy and Daddy said I might have a brother or a sister soon. Is DD at work? Where's Ariel?"

Jeannie smiled. "Whew. Slow down, little man. Mommy told me you might be getting a brother or a sister soon. I'm on my way down to pick Ariel up. She's at her grandparents' down the street. Let me see ...was there another question?"

Davie giggled. "Yea ...where's DD?"

Jeannie raised her eyebrows, "Man, Davie. You have a bear trap memory to remember all those questions. DD's catching bad guys today."

Emily put a small glass of milk and three Oreos in front of Davie, sat down and said, "Jeannie's got us beat this time, Sean. She's expecting."

"Wow, Jeannie, that's great. How many months?"

"Just barely a month. Must be something in the water though, because —presto-chango —all I had to do was mention it to John and boom! Well, guys, I better get going. I think Mom and Dad are meeting another couple tonight, and I'm sure they're ready to relinquish my little stinker."

They all hugged and Jeannie was gone.

"Looks like we have our marching orders, Em. Wouldn't it be great if we could keep popping out babies at the same time as Jeannie and John?"

"Yes, but what's with the babies, plural? I think two is plenty. Three at the most."

"You're right. Two to three makes for what I consider to be a perfect family."

They smiled at each other and touched hands. Davie loved watching his parents show that they loved each other. It made him feel very secure and loved.

****

Three months went by, and Emily was beginning to get discouraged. "Sean, I'm wondering if I should ask the doctor for something to help me. It was so easy getting pregnant the first time."

"Sweetie, I think you're trying too hard. Maybe you should go back to meditating as a means of relaxing. I've always heard that trying too hard can become a block. Let's not worry about it …okay? It'll happen when it's supposed to happen. In the meantime, it's been fun having lots of sex; and, besides, I'm happy with our tiny family like it is. Just relax, Em. We have lots of time."

"You're right. I guess after Jeannie told me she was pregnant; I began heightening my expectations. And you're right too about meditating. I should be more aware of when I begin to backtrack with my expectations. This isn't a competition after all."

"Well, that's what you've got me for. As long as you're open to my helping, I won't let you backtrack. In my world you're perfect with all your imperfections. I like my women to remain human. No super humans for me, thank you very much. With that said, let's take Davie to Friendly's for a coffee cabinet and then drive down to Barrington Town Beach and walk along the shore till it starts getting dark."

Davie loved coffee cabinets as much as his mom did. They even stopped at a little shack and picked up a dozen clam cakes (a New England ball-shaped fritter loaded with bits of chopped clams). It was a little too chilly to get out of the car so they sat and ate their clam cakes and drank the cabinets. Davie got into an empty cup sucking contest with his mom. The three had a wonderful evening; and when it was time to go home, Emily hopped in the back seat so she could sit with her little man. He was sound asleep when they pulled into their driveway.

Sean carried Davie into the house and both parents put him into bed. He woke up just before they left and begged for them to read him a story. Sean loved reading to Davie and Emily loved listening to him read so she climbed into bed next to Davie who rested his head against her arm as Sean began reading *Charlie and the Chocolate Factory*.

"These two very old people are the father and mother of Mr. Bucket. Their names are Grandpa Joe and Grandma Josephine. And these are the very old people who are father and mother of Mrs. Bucket. Their names are Grandpa George and Grandma Georgina. This is Mr. Bucket and Mrs. Bucket. Mr. Bucket and Mrs. Bucket have a small boy whose name is Charlie Bucket."

Davie's eyes got very big. "Daddy, Daddy, I have a Grandpa George, don't I? But my name is Davie Mahoney."

Sean looked at Emily who was smiling. "Yes, you do have a wonderful Grandpa George who loves you a whole bunch."

And this is how the evening progressed until Davie was sound asleep and dreaming about his Grandpa George and going to the chocolate factory. Emily had fallen asleep as well.

Sean closed the book, tucked Davie in and put the book under his arm as he kissed Davie's forehead. He was about to pick Emily up when she woke up.

"Shhh ...let's go to bed, sweetie." He kissed Emily so sweetly, picked her up and carried her to their room. "God, how I love you, Emily."

They made tender love that night before falling to sleep.

That same night Emily had a vision during which Martha came to her. When Emily realized she was inside a vision, she began looking around very slowly.

"Em, sweetie, Sean's not here yet. I wanted to talk to you first. He'll be here in a few minutes. Right now I need you to listen."

Emily nodded and told Martha she was so happy to see her. "Oh, Martha, it's just as you said. Davie is the joy of our lives. He's so smart and he loves his daddy so much."

"I know, sweetie. I know. You are both blessed with Davie, and you're about to be blessed even more."

"Am I pregnant?"

"Not just yet, Emily. But it won't be long. That's why I wanted to come talk to you. This will be the last time you see me in a vision."

"But why, Martha? I don't want you to go away. I love when you visit." She looked sad.

Martha laughed lightly. "I'm not leaving, Emily. I'm going to be with you and Sean for a very long time, just in another form."

Emily looked puzzled; then she got a very excited look on her face. "Martha, are you going to become our little girl?"

Martha simply smiled. "Emily, you are going to have two children: twins. But they won't be identical. You're going to have a little girl and a little boy."

"Who is the little boy?"

"You don't know this soul; and, in truth, that doesn't matter. I will tell you that the little boy won't be as easy to raise as Davie is.

Your son is a newer soul, and he is going to require a lot of work and patience."

"But why? I don't understand."

"That's why I'm here to help you prepare mentally and emotionally for your son because he's going to require all the love you can muster. He's only lived one other time. He had a very rough childhood and died at the hands of his parents before he could move to adulthood. He's terrified, but he wants a chance to have a happy home life."

"But I still don't understand. Why am I being given this responsibility? I don't know if I can do this."

"Yes you can, Emily. You are much stronger than you ever dreamed you could be. Look how you raised yourself?

"When you were about to turn twelve, you met Sean and me. Before then, however, you had basically been on your own for several years after Bertie had her stroke. You had so much love inside you that you were able to ignore all the pain your father caused you and grew up to become the beautiful soul you've become. You have a lot of love in your heart, Emily, more than you recognize or give yourself credit for.

"This soul needs a strong teacher who can give him unconditional love. You are such a person and you proved that when your dad died."

"What do you mean 'when my dad died'? I told him I didn't love him."

"Ah, yes, you did. But your actions spoke far louder than your words. Your generosity and more importantly, Emily, your compassion that day was what your father needed. Do you recall that day, Emily?"

"How could I ever forget it? I just wish I could have done more for him. Have you seen him?"

"Yes, he is here and he is extremely sad about how he lived his life and what he did to you and the other children. But he was also very thankful for you and how you helped him transition from that life.

"When he told you what happened to him when he was just a young boy, you listened with compassion in your heart and it was that compassion that shook him to the core. Had you simply professed love for him, he wouldn't have learned the lesson he needed to learn. But you didn't make his end an easy one because you told him the truth. You told him that the way he handled his pain was all wrong. You made him think about his actions for the first time in his existence; and this allowed him to feel true guilt and sorrow, which led him to also experience true love for the first time. He had never experienced any of those emotions until that day.

"Emily, your honesty, truthfulness and compassion were far greater gifts than anything else he had ever encountered in his entire life. It was your honesty, truthfulness and compassion which enabled him to feel the self-forgiveness you told him was far more important than your forgiveness.

"That, Emily, was your gift of love to him and it meant so much more than words could ever have meant.

Because of your actions that day, when Joe decides it's time to try again, I feel very confident he will go back to be with a very loving family; and this time we *all* believe he will be successful. It was your father who suggested that we send this new soul to you.

He knows your courageous words to him when he was dying saved him from having to repeat his errors. He felt absolutely confident that you would be the best possible mother for this child."

Emily began to cry. "Oh, Martha, you don't know how happy that makes me feel. I so wanted my dad to find forgiveness and happiness. Thank you for telling me that."

Martha was smiling. "That's exactly why you have been chosen to become the mother of this fragile soul. He will take a lot of nurturing, patience and, most of all, love, pure love."

"I still don't understand why Sean isn't here listening to this."

"Because this will be a far greater challenge for Sean, and it will be up to you to help him with that. Sean has never known pain like you have, Emily. And now with Davie, he's content with the son he has. Sean has a tremendous capacity for empathy but little capacity for dealing with disappointment. It will be up to you to help form the bond between Sean and his new son. You will need to have enough love and patience for both of you. In the end, love will bond Sean to his new son. You, Davie and your daughter will help that along."

Just then Emily felt something touch her hand. She turned and saw Sean.

"Sean, we're going to get pregnant!"

He then saw Martha. "Grandma! I was wondering when I would see you again. Oh, Grandma, I wish you could see Davie. He's such a happy and good little boy. He's my pride and joy!"

Martha smiled warmly. "I know he is, Seanie. I've been allowed to view you both a few times, and your bond fills my heart with such joy."

Emily couldn't contain her enthusiasm. "Sean, we're going to have twins: a little boy and a girl."

"Is that true, Grandma?"

"Yes, dear, it's true. They will be paternal twins. Your little girl will be easy to raise, but your son will be a challenge. That's why you must promise me that when you feel you are losing patience, you will lean on Emily. She will help guide both of you, and one day you will have a wonderful relationship with him. You will also need to lean on Davie and your new little girl. Do you think you can do that, Sean?"

"Yes, Grandma. I think I can. Emily is the greatest teacher I know for teaching everyone patience and most of all, love. I know that, and I thank my lucky stars every day of my life for her. When will this happen, Grandma?"

"Soon, Sean, soon. I understand you, George and Davie are about to have a huge adventure."

"We're going fishing in a few months. John is coming with us. Did Emily tell you Davie has already caught a fish with his hands?"

"No, she didn't. But a little birdie told me. We have souls who help other souls transition to the human form coming back with stories all the time. I believe Beth is beginning to wonder about Davie."

"Yes, Grandma, she is. She just loves her grandson."

Martha was in the middle of commenting on Beth's intuitiveness when she faded from view.

The following morning, they woke. Emily was already up and getting ready for work. She was in the bathroom when Sean came in. He looked groggy.

"Are you okay, Sean?"

"Yes. I feel a little dizzy, though. Did we have another vision last night? I'm trying to remember, but sometimes it's hard to distinguish them from dreams."

"I think we did. I think I recall Martha telling us we are going to have twins: a boy and girl. Does that sound familiar to you?"

"Yes. It does, a little anyway. Do you think you're pregnant?"

"No, not yet. I just got my damned period. But I'm not going to fret, and tonight I'm going to start meditating again just like you suggested."

She kissed him and told him she was going to get Davie ready for Gladys to pick up. She was about to walk out of the bedroom when Davie came running in the room all excited.

"Wow, little man, what's your hurry?"

"Mommy. Daddy." Sean stuck his head out the bathroom door. "This really nice lady came to see me last night and told me I was going to get a new brother and sister. Am I?"

Sean and Emily just looked at each other in amazement. Sean walked out, sat on the bed and invited both Emily and Davie to sit down on the bed as well.

He put his arm around Davie and said, "Davie, we hope so. It's not going to happen right now, but Mommy and Daddy are working on that. Now what we need you to do is be a good little boy and let Mommy get you dressed so you'll be ready to leave when Aunt Gladys picks you up. Mommy and Daddy need to go to work."

"Okay, Daddy." Davie took Emily's hand, and they walked out of the room. Just before they walked through the door, Emily looked back at Sean who gave her a shrug. Then with her free hand, she gave Sean the thumbs-up for handling that as well as he did.

Later they both agreed the last thing either of them needed was Davie raising the slightest suspicion that he lived in a nut house. Too they were determined that Davie would grow up as normal as possible. Any paranormal thoughts would have to be formed on his own and without their assistance.

Chapter 26

Emily did indeed become pregnant. She missed her period in April; but because she wasn't throwing up, she assumed it was simply late.

On May 17th she bought a pregnancy kit. She picked the kit up on her way home from work after she picked up Davie. She was tempted to do the test immediately but waited until Sean came home. She was preparing dinner when he walked in the door.

He walked over to where Emily was cutting up tomatoes for a salad and was about to kiss her when he saw the kit. "Did you just pick that up?"

"Yes. But I was waiting for you to come home before doing the test. I just put the pot on for spaghetti. Do you want to go do it now?"

"Of course I do. Did you throw up this morning, Em?"

"No. That's why I waited till now to get a kit. I missed my period and assumed I was just late, but now I've missed two periods."

They peeked in on Davie who was watching a Disney movie and went into the bathroom.

Emily looked apprehensive. "You open it. I don't want to get my hopes up."

"Sweetie, even if you're not, it's no big deal. I love you and it will happen. Just have faith."

He opened it and she sat down on the toilet. She didn't look at the strip but handed it back to Sean.

He stood there for a few seconds, then made a face which led her to think it was negative.

"I'm not pregnant, am I?"

She was resigned as she got up and pulled her jeans up. She was buttoning her jeans when he reached around and held the strip in front of her face. It was positive.

"Oh, my god, Sean!"

They hugged excitedly, then composed themselves and went back out to the kitchen where the water was boiling rapidly.

Emily finished making dinner while Sean set the table. He ran outside to the small flower garden Emily had planted near the slant tree and cut a few stems of roses from the rose bush and brought them in. He then got a small vase and put them in it and placed the flowers on the table, grabbed two candlesticks from the buffet and lit the candles.

As Emily put the food on the table, he went to get Davie who was holding his dad's hand when they came back out into the kitchen.

"Mommy, is it my birthday again?"

"No, sweetie, it's not; but Daddy and I have something to tell you. Why don't you sit at the table?"

She finished putting the food on the table, then poured a glass of wine for Sean, milk for Davie and ginger ale for herself and then sat down.

Davie had an expression on his face which basically told his parents to hurry up and tell him.

Sean smiled at Emily as she indicated with a nod for him to do the honors.

"Davie, Mommy and I wanted you to be the first to know. You're going to have a brother or sister right around Christmas.

"I am? When is Christmas? Is it tomorrow?"

Emily was laughing. "No, sweetie, it's not even summer yet. You, Daddy, Grandpa George and DD are going to go fishing; then we need to wait for fall when the leaves will change; then soon after that, it will be Christmas. Do you think you can wait that long, Davie?"

"Maybe." Then he looked really serious. "Can we tell the baby to hurry up so it will come home sooner?"

"Tell you what, Davie. I'm going to the doctor next Tuesday to find out exactly when the baby will come. The following weekend we'll create a calendar and then start marking off the days till the baby arrives. Would you like that?"

"Yes, Mommy. Can I help make the calendar?"

"You sure can."

Both Sean and Emily were laughing so Davie began laughing as well. They had a wonderful dinner and afterward, Sean cleaned up the kitchen as Emily asked Davie to go get her phone so they could call both grandmas. He came running back to the kitchen and was already talking to Sarah.

Once the relatives were informed, Emily called Jeannie. "Oh my god, Em. This is just too good to be true. I love that our kids are going to be born around the same time. Wait a minute; John wants to talk to Sean."

John told Sean that he could get off the first weekend of June, which was one of the weekends George had given them as an option for the fishing trip. Then the men gave the phones back to the women.

"Jeannie, we should plan that women's outing that weekend. Let's talk to our moms. How does that sound?"

"Sounds good, Em! Congratulations! Looks like your hickey fest paid off."

****

The following Tuesday Emily went to the doctor and found out she was indeed two months pregnant. She would have her babies the week just prior to Christmas.

That next weekend Sean bought an inexpensive wooden easel and a big flipchart pad. Sean, Emily and Davie spent the weekend creating a nine-month calendar.

Sean drew the calendars. Emily drew events on the calendars and Davie colored them in. They began with the day Emily confirmed she was two months pregnant. She drew a crib with a mobile hanging over it. For June, Emily drew three figures fishing with a fourth figure catching a fish by hand. Other events she drew were July 4th, Labor Day, her's and Sean's anniversary, Halloween and Thanksgiving. For the week of December 18th – 24th, she drew a baby on the 18th and rattles on the remaining days of that week, explaining to Davie that it could be any one of those days.

Davie became ecstatic when it was time to color in the fishing date. "Daddy, Mommy, that's me catching a fish!"

Sean said, "Davie, we need to be really careful when we go fishing, but do you think you can catch another fish with your hands?"

"If the fish comes next to me, I can," he said with absolute conviction.

Emily snickered. "That should freak out DD!"

****

The men spent the next few months buying rubber boots and fly fishing rods. George had plenty of handmade flies for everyone. He was thrilled about the weekend trip and leased the same cabin he and Martha used to stay in.

The guys built campfires outside the cabin and roasted hotdogs and marshmallows that first night. Davie caught a whole jar full of fireflies. Sean was sending pictures left and right. Jeannie and Ariel had spent the night, since the following day they were going shopping with Sarah and Gladys.

The next morning all four males got up and walked down to the river. George helped Davie put his boots on. While Sean and John put theirs on, George took Davie into the water. They walked out into the middle which put the water midway up to the tops of Davie's hip boots. George stood behind him and showed him how to cast the rod. Davie was a fast learner and was casting like a pro after three tries. Sean just sat on the pebbled bank watching his son with a huge smile on his face. He was clicking away with his camera. He even sent a picture of his happy face which made Emily, Jeannie and Ariel laugh.

John was totally blown away. "God, Sean, Davie continues to amaze me!"

The two men were about to go out into the water to try their hands at casting when Davie dropped his rod, reached down and picked up a huge trout that was swimming around his legs. The three men's mouths dropped.

George, who was standing next to Davie, turned around just as Davie pulled the fish out of the water. "Hold onto that fish, Davie!" he yelled as he picked Davie up and carried both Davie and the fish to the shore.

John took a picture of George carrying Davie out of the water and sent it to Jeannie.

When George put Davie down, Davie dropped the fish into the cooler that was filled with water.

Jeannie, Emily and Ariel were having breakfast at Emily's kitchen table when Jeannie heard the text sound on her phone. "Oh my god, Emily, look at this!"

Jeannie showed Emily the picture with John's text. "Davie just caught this with his bare hands!"

Just as Jeannie was reading the text out loud, Sean sent Emily a text, "Em, Davie did it again. He caught a whooper!" The text included a picture of the fish in the cooler.

"Emily, this is too wild to be a coincidence. I have this strange feeling there's more to the story of Davie than you and Sean are letting on. Spill the beans, please!"

They had about an hour before Sarah and Gladys were picking them up so Emily said, "Let's go in the living room and I promise you, I'll tell you everything."

The two ladies turned on cartoons for Ariel while they went into the living room.

"Jeannie, I don't know if you're going to think Sean and I are crazy people, but here goes."

Jeannie didn't say a word. She just sat there with her mouth hanging down to her chin and her eyes practically bugging out of her head.

"And that's the story about our little Davie, Martha and our mystery babies. Oh, yea, and Martha's message about my father."

The two women sat silent for over five minutes while Jeannie's head spun. Then..." Em, if this were anyone else telling me this wild story, I would call you both bonkers, grab my kid and hightail it out of here. Knowing the two of you, though, and how level-headed you both are, coupled with some of the very bizarre things that I've been privy to and have witnessed, I'm inclined to believe you. Does anyone else know about this?"

"No. One piece of Martha's advice was to allow those who would suspect something bizarre —as you call it, and there's no denying that it is—to come to these conclusions on their own."

"Gosh." Jeannie was now whispering, "I wonder if Ariel has lived before now. I never bought all that mumbo jumbo about heaven and hell, but I have always flirted with the possibility of reincarnation. Hell, I've experienced things and known what to do and wondered how the hell I knew what I knew. John and I have talked about these things before; and, I have to be honest, he's been very suspicious about Davie. He talks about Davie and his abilities

241

all the time. Have you told your mom?"

"Good grief, no. Mom has come a long way, but she's not ready for something as outrageous as this. However, Beth is beginning to recognize things in Davie. We're waiting for that conversation to come around."

"And what will you do when it does?"

"I have no idea. I guess we'll just have to cross that bridge when it's here."

"Gosh, Em, this is some of the most exciting stuff I've heard in a long time. Really opens up all sorts of doors. Do you mind if I tell John?"

"No, but be careful. I sure don't want just anyone knowing about this. We have to protect Davie, but John knows how to keep his mouth shut. We also have to raise Davie just like we would if we didn't know. I don't know if he will ever suspect anything more than what most people know."

Just then they heard a car pull into the driveway. It was Sarah and Gladys. Sarah was driving.

"Mum's the word, girl, not that I was making a pun. I'll go grab Ariel. I'm so excited!"

The women had the best time that day. They met Beth for lunch. She drove down to Providence but had to go back to her office. She and Bill were working on another big case. Then the rest of the day they shopped. Jeannie already knew she was in fact having a little boy so Gladys was going crazy buying clothes. Sarah was so excited about Emily's pregnancy.

They had dinner that evening; then Sarah drove everyone back to Emily's house. Jeannie told Emily she would take her mom home, which she did almost immediately. Gladys was pooped. Sarah told Emily she would stay; but Zack had already texted her whining, as she put it, that he was home alone.

"Mom, I'm just glad you have someone who misses you like Zack does."

"Don't think I'm complaining, Emily, because I'm not. I am so thrilled with my life with Zack that I am glad he is whining. Besides, he's giving me the excuse to hurry home to him. I miss my man."

Emily and Sarah kissed and Sarah left.

Emily was about to go take a hot bath when she saw Jeannie

banging on her back door.

"What's going on? Are you okay? Are your mom and dad okay?"

"Yea, yea and yea to all three questions. Em, you have got to see this. John just sent me a video."

They sat down at the kitchen table, and Jeannie handed Emily her phone. John just videoed Davie playing Sean's guitar.

"Emily, I almost peed my pants on my way up the street. Hang on. I need to use your bathroom."

When she came back out, Emily was on the phone with Sean. Jeannie sat down and Emily put the speaker on.

"Sean, Jeannie is here with me. John sent her a video. She also was asking a lot of questions earlier and, well, I told her everything."

"Well, baby, I'm putting the little guy to bed right now. I think George, John and I are about to have a long conversation. George got me off to the side earlier and asked if Martha had visited me. So I guess it's time to tell John. Jeannie, do you think John can handle this?"

"Yes, I do. John is not even close to being a religious person. He and I have had some pretty strange conversations, especially after Davie's first fish. He's very open to everything."

There was a silence; then Sean spoke, "Okay, Jeannie, there's something we all need to be on the same page with. Davie is still a child. Just like the rest of us, he has no clue about anything beyond the here and now."

Jeannie was way ahead of him. "I understand, Sean. We must behave as if we don't know and just act like we would if we didn't know. Davie needs to grow up naturally without any expectations. Period."

"Thanks, Jeannie. I'll say the same thing to John. We just need to progress through life as if none of this were anything but unusually usual, if that makes sense."

"'Unusually usual.' I like that, Sean. I'll remember for everyone's sake and so will John."

Later that evening Sean, George and John did indeed have the same conversation. Although open-minded, John admitted as he humorously put it, "This is way above my pay grade."

Chapter 27

The next seven months were literally flying by. Davie was becoming more and more excited about what he now knew to be the case. He was going to have both a sister and a brother.

Beth was becoming more and more curious about Davie's familiar personality traits and behavior. However, she was—just as Sean, Emily, Jeannie, John and George were —about to find out that a little boy is still just a little boy regardless of what seemed to be his extraordinary abilities.

Davie was with Ariel one work day in late September. Gladys was watching the two children play in her backyard when she looked out and saw that the children had disappeared. She panicked.

She ran around the immediate vicinity of her house calling the children's names when Ariel came running around the corner screaming.

"What's wrong, Ariel? Where's Davie?"

Ariel was crying, but she had enough wits about her to grab Gladys' hand as they began running.

Davie and Ariel had been playing Superman when Davie climbed up to the top of the rocks —a huge mountain of boulders that had become one of the neighborhood children's favorite places to play—then announced to Ariel that he could fly. Of course he couldn't.

Davie was lying on the ground, and he had a huge gash on his forehead. Gladys was frantically carrying Davie to her car when old man Parker was about to pull into his driveway.

Paul Parker was known to most of the children as the neighborhood drunk. Emily's generation especially dubbed him that; but Paul was now an old man, had dried out more than ten years prior and was trying to live a clean life.

Paul saw Gladys running across her yard when he stopped, lowered his window and called out. "Is everything okay, Gladys?"

"No, Paul. Davie fell off the rocks, and I've got to get him to the hospital as quickly as I can."

"Hop in, I'll get you there. We'll go to the new emergency center just down the road."

Paul jumped out of his car and helped Gladys get into his back seat with Davie.

"Paul, Ariel just ran in the house. I can't leave her here alone."

Just as quick as Gladys said that, Ariel ran out of the house. Paul picked her up and put her in the back seat, secured her seatbelt and hopped back into the driver's side.

"Grandma, is Davie going to die?"

Paul was speeding up the hill when he answered, "No, Ariel. Your little friend is not going to die. We're going to drive to the doctor's office so the doctor can sew him back up. He'll be as good as new. I promise you."

Davie was barely conscious as Gladys frantically talked to him, "Davie, stay awake."

Ariel was holding Davie's hand and crying, "Davie, you're going to be okay. You have a big boo-boo on your head."

Now the three of them were talking. Actually Paul was talking to Gladys. "Don't let him fall asleep, Gladys. We can't risk a concussion." Paul, they would all find out later, had been a field medic in the Army during the initial years of the Vietnam War.

Just then Paul pulled into the parking lot, jumped out of his car and ran around to Gladys' door. He saw no cars were coming or going from the clinic so he instructed Ariel to run into the clinic and tell the nurses. She did that and when she returned, there was a doctor, a male nurse, as well as a female nurse, running out with a stretcher.

The medical personnel lifted Davie onto the stretcher and rushed him inside. Paul, Gladys and Ariel followed.

While sitting in the waiting room, Gladys called Emily.

Emily was not at the university that day. She was on her way back from the Fall River, Massachusetts Nuclear Power Plant, which is one of only a handful of nuclear power plants still operating in the United States.

She had become an important member of a research group of pro-nuclear power scientists from across the country a few years earlier. They were doing extensive research regarding the safety of nuclear energy and its renewability qualities which would be presented to Congress the following year.

Emily was pumping gas when her phone rang. "Gladys, is everything alright?"

"Emily, don't panic. It's going to be okay. Davie got it in his head today that he was Superman and jumped off the rocks. He's got a big gash on his head; but Ariel, Paul Parker and I are sitting here at the new emergency clinic on Pawtucket Avenue."

"Paul Parker?"

"Yes, he was pulling into his driveway when he saw me carrying Davie."

"I'm on my way. What's the address?"

"Hold on." Gladys was about to go to the front desk when she told Paul Emily was asking for the address. He took the phone from Gladys and gave her the directions.

By the time Emily was running into the clinic, Davie was being wheeled out to Paul's car. He had a huge bandage around his head.

Emily bent down and hugged Davie. "Davie, what were you thinking?"

"Mommy, I thought I could fly." Then he frowned in resignation. "Guess I was wrong."

Then Ariel piped up, "Auntie Em, I tried to tell Davie he couldn't fly; but he didn't listen to me."

Just as they wheeled Davie over to the parking lot, Paul said, "Well, I guess my work is done here."

Emily grabbed Paul and hugged him. "You're not done at all. Gladys, Ariel and Davie will ride back with you. We're all going to my house. I'm going to call Sean right now and have him pick up Chinese for all of us. Do you like Chinese food, Paul?"

"Emily, that's not necessary."

"Oh, yes, it is. You have nothing else to do tonight, do you? Besides, it's long overdue that we all get to know the neighborhood hero."

Paul was blushing when Davie took his hand. "Please, Mr. Parker. Please say 'yes.'"

Now both children were holding Paul's hand when he said, "Well, who can resist these two children? Okay. I'll just run by my house and feed my dog, Old Blue, and I'll be back up to have dinner."

"Do you like Mongolian beef, Paul? Or do you have any other preferences?"

"I love Mongolian beef, Emily. It's my favorite."

That evening the house was noisy with lots of people. Phil was there, as were Jeannie and DD. Sean came in around 7 p.m. loaded down with Chinese food. DD ran out to help him carry everything in.

As Sean and DD were walking back in, DD nudged Sean, "This was a wake-up call, wasn't it?"

Sean looked inquisitive as DD smiled. "Guess we all know now that Davie's just a kid."

Around the dinner table where Paul was seated at one end, he began asking questions. "I've been isolated from the entire neighborhood for so long I don't really know anyone."

Sean spoke first, "Well, Paul, that's going to change. Now you have a big, extended family. Is that good for you?"

Paul had a tear running down his check which Ariel reached up and wiped with her napkin, "Don't cry, Uncle Paul."

Her calling him "Uncle Paul" made him cry even more. He was choking on his tears as he stroked Ariel's head. "I'm sorry, Ariel. You're named after the mermaid, aren't you?"

"Well, yes I am. But I'm also named after Daddy's Grandma."

He was now smiling.

"My Karen died nine years ago, and I'm afraid I isolated myself even before that. I actually have a son and a daughter, but neither of them have spoken to me since her death. I have five grandchildren I've never seen. Gladys, you're so fortunate."

At that moment Emily determined that she would do everything she could to change that situation. She looked over at Jeannie, who seemed to be reading her mind as Jeannie bumped Emily's fist. "I'm with ya, sista!"

Jeannie said, "Paul, Emily and I will help you reconnect with your children. Emily has a story to tell them that is far worse than what your kids experienced growing up, and she was able to forgive. Don't worry, by Christmas you'll be reunited with your family."

Paul's voice cracked, "That would be the most wonderful Christmas present I could ever have. I'm eighty-four and I know I'm not going to live a lot longer. I would appreciate any help, Jeannie and Emily." Then he asked with a chuckle. "I noticed Ariel called you Auntie Em and DD ...err, John, what does the DD stand for?"

Everyone except Paul laughed as Davie piped up, "DD is for Dunkin Donuts. He's a policeman, and Mommy named him Officer

Dunkin Donuts before I was born. Jeannie gave Mommy the name Auntie Em after …"

"Wizard of Oz, right, Davie?"

Davie and Ariel were vigorously shaking their heads "yes" as Paul roared laughing, "I'm not glad, but I'm thankful today happened. All of you have been a godsend for me. I've been so lonely that I began giving up on life. Now, with all of you, I have a reason to live and to start feeling hopeful again about my children. Thank you so much for welcoming me into your hearts."

Sean raised his glass. "No, Paul, it's you that we all need to thank. You helped save my little man here."

The two children were giggling as they too raised their glasses.

After dinner, the adults moved to the living room while the children fell asleep watching TV.

They learned that Paul had been in Vietnam for two tours; and when he finally came home, he suffered from PTSD.

"Only back then, no one knew what PTSD was, so I was on my own. I had such a hard time readjusting to a non-combative world that I'm afraid I took to drinking to drown out the memories, nightmares and noise in my head. Of course, that's what drove my kids away in the end. When I buried my Karen, they came to the funeral; and that was the last time I've heard from either of them. It was a hard pill to swallow, but I know that I deserved it."

Emily looked saddened.

"No Paul, you are wrong. It wasn't your fault, and you certainly did not deserve it. What my father did to me also caused me to suffer from PTSD. It's taken me a long time and a lot of healing to put it all in the proper context of my life as a whole. However, in truth, I'll probably always be in a state of healing. Plus, Sean, who is a neuroscientist at Harvard, did his doctoral thesis on PTSD suffered by veterans who came back from Iraq and Afghanistan. So you're in sympathetic company. Don't worry. We are not going to allow your children to miss out on you. I promise you that."

Paul was so grateful. "Emily, I really appreciate everything." Then … "Sean, I would love to have a conversation with you one day soon about the work you did with soldiers."

"We'll do that really soon, Paul. I promise."

Paul was now standing. "Well, folks, it's 9 p.m. and way past this old guy's bedtime. I need to go home and walk Old Blue before turning in. Thank you so much for everything today, and I really look forward to seeing everyone more often."

They all got up as the three women hugged him and the three men shook his hand.

When Paul was gone, DD got up and said, "We need to get our little one to bed. I have the early shift tomorrow."

Phil and Gladys left right behind Jeannie, John and Ariel.

With the house now quiet, Emily and Sean put Davie to bed, then went across the hallway to the babies' room and sat in their rocking chairs. Sean kept his guitar in that room now, so he picked it up and began strumming while Emily read the rest of *Charlie and the Chocolate Factory*. It was one of Davie's favorite books so they felt their new babies, Martha Elizabeth and Dakota George, who was named for both of Martha's husbands, would like the book as well. An hour later they climbed into bed, talked about how fortunate they were and fell asleep in each other's arms.

The following morning Emily woke up as Sean was tiptoeing out of the room. She looked at the clock. It was 4 a.m.

"Where are you going so early, Sean?"

He came over to the bed and sat down.

"I was trying not to wake you, baby. I've got a big day today. Temple Grandin is coming to the University. I think I told you that she's consulting with my group on our autism project."

"I remember. That's exciting, Sean. I want to hear all about it tonight. I think, though, I'm going to go back to sleep. I was giving an exam today, but I think I'll call Heidi and have her administer the exam. I want to stay home with Davie today and make sure he's okay."

"That sounds good, Em. Tell you what. I'll go get Davie and put him in the bed with you. Would you like that?"

"Sean that would be wonderful. Don't forget to eat something on your way to work."

Sean got Davie who was sleeping like a rock and put him next to Emily, then kissed her and left.

Just as Emily was heavily involved with groundbreaking research, Sean was as well. His group was monitoring the brainwave activity of ten autistic children whose parents had heard about their work and fought to get their children into the project. Temple was going to consult with the group about different stimuli in hopes of helping to rewire the children's brainwave patterns. Academically, it was an exciting period for both Emily and Sean.

Chapter 28

On October 16th Jeannie had a repeat performance. It was the middle of the night when her water broke. John was working on a rape/homicide case when Jeannie called him. His partner told him to go to the hospital.

Again he had an ambulance pick up Jeannie. Ariel got to ride in the cab and turn the siren on. John caught up with the ambulance just as it pulled into the emergency entrance of Bradley Hospital in East Providence.

It was another easy delivery, and mother and son were resting quietly by 3 a.m. The nurses wheeled a small cart into Jeannie's room for Ariel, and John went back to work. He'd be back by their sides by the time they woke up.

The week before Christmas, the Mahoney household was chaotic. Emily had two false alarms when her labor pains caused her to think she needed to go to the hospital. Davie was on high alert waiting for his new siblings.

At 10 p.m. on Thursday, December 22nd, Emily's water broke. Sean got her into their new Range Rover and put a sleeping Davie on the back seat, then rushed everyone to Providence Hospital.

Marti was born just before midnight, but Dakota wasn't so eager to meet the world. At 4 a.m. Emily was still in labor, and her epidural was wearing off. The nurses were all abuzz at how this little guy was stubborn and didn't want to come out. Sean asked Emily if she wanted another epidural.

"No, Sean. Something tells me this little fella wants me to feel his pain."

Sean helped Emily breathe, but the pain was excruciating.

Jose walked into her room at about 4:15 a.m. He sat down with his guitar and softly played as he sang to Dakota. Within fifteen minutes the doctors could see Dakota's head. He was delivered at 4:32 a.m., and he was screaming bloody murder.

As the nurses cleaned little Dakota, Emily asked for Marti who was brought to her for feeding.

When the nurse left the room, Jose had a strange smile on his face. "You should have called me in earlier. Your little guy did not want to come out. I sense he was scared of what would happen to him."

Just then the attending nurse walked in with a cleaned-up Dakota who was still crying. However, the minute he was placed in Emily's arms, he stopped, found the nipple and was suckling as he fell fast asleep.

Marti was also fast asleep so Jose picked her up and took her out to the baby ward. He came back in for Dakota, but Emily begged him to let her hold him longer. He nodded with a smile as he motioned for Sean to come sit with him.

Sean was worn out; but Jose sensed something as Sean asked, "Jose, do you believe in reincarnation? I know that's a strange question."

Jose smiled sweetly. "That's not at all a strange question, Sean; and, to answer your question, I absolutely do. Are you familiar with Brian Weiss' book, *Many Lives, Many Masters?*"

"It sounds familiar, but I guess not."

"You need to read that book as well as his other book, *Same Soul, Many Bodies.* Do you suspect your new son to be a reincarnation?"

Sean told him the entire story about Davie, his and Emily's suspicions that Marti is his grandmother's soul and about the vision he and Emily had about their new son.

"That's very interesting and explains why Dakota was so reluctant to be born. He's going to need a lot of love and attention which could cause your other two children to feel slighted. Although, considering what you've told me about them, perhaps not. This actually sounds like a master plan cooked up by those behind the scenes. This is exciting, Sean. Will you keep me informed? I'm really interested in seeing how things progress for your family. I'd love to become an active friend."

"Yes. I promise, Jose. And as far as getting you more involved, I think Em and I would greatly appreciate it. We are babes in the woods, but something tells us we've been given a tremendous job but also a tremendous opportunity. Also something tells me that I'm going to need your shoulder and strength more than Emily will. Given her childhood, she's a natural at this stuff."

Just then, Dakota started to cry; and Emily, who had fallen asleep, suckled him again. She was kissing his head and telling him she loved him. Jose excused himself and Sean went over to his family. He began rubbing Dakota's belly who fell asleep again."

As with Ariel, the nurses had wheeled in a small bed where Davie was sound asleep as he clung to a small stuffed fish his Grandpa George had given him.

Emily and the babies stayed in the hospital one additional day; then they were released on Christmas Eve. Instead of going home, Sean drove them to Beth and Bill's house where they would spend Christmas. Sarah and Zach were already there. Lily, Peter and their baby, as well as Katie, would be over the following day for dinner.

Emily was extremely sore and so exhausted from giving birth to Dakota that she slept until noon on Christmas Eve.

When Sean helped her downstairs where the two babies lay in their bassinets which he had driven home to collect, George was there and was playing a game with Davie.

Christmas Eve night Sean, Emily, Davie and the two babies slept in a downstairs bedroom off the living room where the Christmas tree was. Emily had wrapped all the presents weeks ahead of time, and Sean went home on Christmas Eve to collect all of them. He also put a new blue bicycle with training wheels in the back of the car. Originally Davie was going to sleep in an upstairs bedroom, but Emily insisted they all be together since she didn't want to miss out on watching Davie's face when he saw all the presents that lay under the tree for him. Emily still so loved Christmas; and, as she was learning from her life with Sean, *ALL* things were wonderfully possible.

****

On Christmas Eve, after Davie went to bed, George set up an oval G-scale model train track and placed the Bachmann-Tweetsie R.R. ET&WNC Freight G-Scale train set on the tracks. He loved the Tweetsie, which he had learned years earlier was the passenger train that carried passengers from the Blue Ridge Mountains around Johnson City in Eastern Tennessee to the Westernmost town of Boone, North Carolina. The oval track he set up was just a portion of the tracks he planned to build for Davie in Davie's basement. He had been building and painting buildings for the scene since the summer. Using old photos, he, Davie and Sean would spend hours putting the recreated scenery together for months to come. More than even all the fishing trips, that period of his life would become one of Davie's most treasured memories.

When it came time to open presents, all the adults were up and sitting as they watched Davie and Abbey open their gifts. It was the most fun all the adults had had in a while.

About an hour before dinner, Paul Parker, Jose and his family arrived with the other guests: Zach's son and his new wife Jill, Lily, her family and Katie who brought a new beau she was *very* serious about. They were about to sit down when the doorbell rang.

Emily suspected who it was so she volunteered to answer the door. Minutes later she walked in with two couples and five children. Paul, who was facing the dining room doorway, nearly fell as he pushed his chair back; but Sean caught him.

"Hi, Dad," said Paul Jr.

His daughter Muriel rushed over to him and hugged her dad. As Paul stepped into the hallway with his family, the men hurriedly put together three card tables as the women set the tables. Emily wasn't sure if she and Jeannie had convinced Paul's children, but they were ready just in case.

When Paul and his family finally came back into the dining room, they were seated at their own table only a few feet away from the rest of the group. Paul hugged Emily and cried like a baby as he and his family sat down.

Once seated, Emily took a picture of the new smaller group and sent it to Jeannie who was in the middle of dinner with her family. She jumped up from the table and yelled, "Fucking A!" to which Gladys admonished her and told Ariel she was never to use that word.

"But, Ma, look at this picture!"

They all looked at it as Ariel asked, "Is that Uncle Paul's family?"

Gladys said, "Yes, it is, Ariel. Your mommy and Emily made this happen." Then when Ariel looked away, Gladys looked at Jeannie, gave her a thumbs-up and mouthed, "Fucking A!"

They were all laughing as Jeannie called Emily who gave the phone to Paul so he could express his gratitude.

After dinner and the massive cleanup, Sean, Davie—who got his own guitar for Christmas—and Jose played as Jose and Marie sang Christmas carols while Emily sat in a huge stuffed chair feeding her babies and George sat next to her, stroking Marti's head.

It was the most magical Christmas all those present had ever experienced!

On New Year's Eve everyone gathered at Paul's house which backed up to a huge field. There, they created such a wonderful fireworks display that, when it was time to go to bed, the children were left with brightly-colored sugar plum fairies dancing in their heads.

Chapter 30

The next seven years were happy ones as well as productive years. They were challenging as well.

Marti was walking by her ninth month, as was Jeannie's John. Dakota took a much longer time to catch on to everything. He didn't start walking until he was fourteen months old. He was scared of everything and clung to his mother.

Emily continued to work on the nuclear energy initiative, and the group was making headway. Their Congressional hearing several years earlier had failed to convince enough members of Congress to switch course in favor of renewable nuclear energy.

Congress was still enamored with wind and solar energy, and there were many of them who were still tied to the fossil fuel industry. Emily's group, however, was finally making a case as they demonstrated with evidence that producing the panels for solar energy was proving to be environmentally unfriendly and it just wasn't feasible to litter the land with solar panels or wind farms. Too it became an environmental quandary as more and more bald eagles were being taken out by the huge blades at the wind farms. Other great birds were falling victim as well, but the bald eagle became the poster "child" for the tragedy. There was still much work to do, however; and Dakota's lack of self-confidence helped her think outside the box on how to help him progress faster to free her up to get more involved. So, she went back to listening to her meditation audio as she sat with Dakota at night.

She would sit with him as he fell asleep. However, instead of putting on headphones, she placed a powerful mini-speaker on the nightstand causing the bedroom to be filled with the audio. She had done this religiously every night for six months when she began to notice a difference in his behavior. He was talking more and was becoming more outgoing and inquisitive, and his self-confidence seemed to be growing rapidly.

Sean and Emily were about to have breakfast one Saturday morning when Sean walked into Davie's room and saw Dakota playing with Davie's Legos. He was actually building a rather elaborate building. Sean stood in the doorway watching for a few minutes. He was stunned at what he saw.

When Dakota realized Sean was watching him, he jumped to his feet and ran over to him. "Daddy, Daddy, look what I'm building."

"I see, Dakota. Let's go get Mommy so she can see as well."

By the time Emily came to the room, Davie and Marti were there with Dakota helping him, but it was obvious that he was in charge of the current project. Emily simply stood in the doorway with her mouth opened.

Everyone made a big deal of Dakota's building, and it was obvious that he loved the attention and praise. When Emily and Sean finally sat down to eat, they marveled at what they had just witnessed.

"Sean, I thought I was beginning to detect a change in Dakota. He's becoming less and less clingy and more interested in learning; and I think this has everything to do with the meditation audio!" She was obviously excited.

"Em, now that you mention it, I think I've been noticing a change. Davie even said something the other day. You may be onto something."

She was vigorously nodding her head. "I've got an idea; and damn, Sean, this could become one of your research projects! I'm going to contact Bill Harris tomorrow and ask him if he could work with us on embedding affirmations into the audio. What if we wrote affirmations exclusively for Dakota? And ...what if all four of us—you, Marti, Davie and I—spoke the affirmations? Dakota would be listing to all of us encouraging him and convincing him that he is safe and deeply loved. What do you think? I mean, after all, he's been listening to my affirmations that are embedded in my own personal audio and look what's happening. Can you imagine what could happen if he were listening to all of us praising and encouraging him?"

Sean was visibly excited by this conversation. "God, Em, that's a brilliant idea. What you and I need to do is put a dialogue together regarding how stunted his progress has been, document the progress we're now seeing and then begin documenting his progress once his own audio is produced. Better yet, let's see if you and I can go out to meet with Bill Harris. We need his advice on where to start. He needs to know what level you've been playing with Dakota. He can help us determine if we need to start at the most basic level. What do you think of that idea?"

"You've got a very good point. I've been playing the audio from the more advanced levels of Holosync. We need him to help us decide whether to go back to the beginning. But can you imagine what this could do for other children if you could demonstrate the benefits?"

She did call Bill Harris, and he was ecstatic about the idea. He was coming out east the following week and told her he could make a side trip to meet with them. He mentioned he'd like to personally meet Dakota. He was very interested in doing a joint project with them on a personal level and a business level as well. He saw how such a project could benefit the Centerpointe Institute by creating a program that was relevant to current interests.

They did indeed meet with Bill. In fact, they invited Bill over for dinner where he could meet Dakota and their other two children in the emotionally safe environment of Dakota's own home. Sarah and Zach were also there.

"Hi, Tom, come on in. Zach, Mom and Sean are all in the kitchen area where most of our activity occurs. The kids are in the next room watching a Disney movie and playing with Dakota's Legos. He loves to build things. I think he's going to be an architect one day."

"Thanks, Emily. Oooo …what a lovely home you have. Who's the artist?"

Just then Sean walked into the living room.

Sean's face beamed with pride as he shook Bill's hand, "Why Bill, Emily is the artist. She's awfully good, wouldn't you say?"

"My goodness. She sure is. Emily, we need to talk about commissioning you to do a few paintings for the reception area of the Centerpointe Institute!"

Emily blushed, "I'd love to, Bill. Now let's go out to the kitchen area where I'd be willing to bet Zach is fixing you a drink."

Zach handed Bill a bourbon with a splash of water. "How's my good friend these days?"

Bill and Zach hugged as Bill also greeted Sarah, "Well, Sarah, it's wonderful to see you. How are you getting along?"

"Really well, Bill. My Zach here takes wonderful care of me; and Emily, well what can I say about my wonderful daughter? She's just the best!"

Bill took a sip of his drink, "Emily and Sean, my compliments. You don't hold back, do you? I love Woodford Reserve;" then eyeing the bottle on the shelf, "Double oaked no less. Thank you so much!"

"Our pleasure," they both said as Sean slipped his arm around his lovely wife's waist.

Just then three children emerged from the TV room. Dakota was carrying what looked like a Lego robot. "Mommy, Daddy, look what I made!"

Sean picked up Dakota. "Wow, Dakota, that's a mighty fine robot. Have you named it yet?"

"Yes. It's Davie, my best friend!"

Davie rolled his eyes. "Thanks, Dakota. Now I'm just a robot."

Davie then walked around the kitchen as a clumsy robot would as he bumped into everything, saying over and over again, "That does not compute. That does not compute!"

All the adults broke out in laughter at Davie's antics. Dakota laughed joyously at the attention he was getting.

Introductions were made as Marti looked at Bill, touched his hand and said, "You're the man who's going to help Dakota."

"Well, I don't know, Marti. It looks to me like all of you are already doing a heck of a job in that department."

They had a wonderful dinner and all the adults, Bill included, cleaned up the kitchen before they retired to the living room and a glass of cabernet. Emily and Sean excused themselves while they put their young ones to bed.

When they came back, Bill and Zach were reminiscing about old times. Bill was claiming that Zach was always the one to get him and everyone else into trouble.

Sarah was laughing. "He is a rascal, isn't he, Bill?"

"'Rascal' is putting it mildly, but yes. Everyone Zach's ever met loves the guy."

Sean and Emily grabbed a glass of cabernet and settled into the love seat.

"You have three wonderful children. I can detect a little hesitance in Dakota, but he's really very inquisitive and fun."

Sean smiled. "He's come a long way, Bill. Poor Emily spent over five hours in brutal labor because he just didn't want to come out."

"Well, it wasn't pleasant, but it wasn't brutal either. At least I've had seven years to forget."

Bill then said, "Davie and Marti are wonderful siblings. They seem eager to be supportive. I think embedding all your voices into the audio would be a wonderful experience for Dakota. And even though he has been listening to your more advanced audios, Emily, since this is the first time to embark on such a project, I'd like to play it safe and start at the very beginning. Of course, as you are aware, the first set of audio doesn't normally have any embedded affirmations; but we're going to make an exception and create a set with your affirmations so that Dakota can get the full experience of the love his family has for him from the get-go. I'm very anxious to watch how this all progresses and the impact it has on little Dakota. How does that sound to both of you?"

The entire time both Sean and Emily had been nodding approval at what Bill was suggesting. It was Sean who answered for both he and Emily.

"Coming from a neuroscience area, I think you're right, Bill. It's best to approach this with extreme caution, so starting at the beginning sounds like a smart idea."

"Great! Well, over the next few weeks, why don't you two have Marti and Davie help put together some affirmations? I'll work on my end with the tech people, letting them know what we're going to be doing. I'm going to put my best people on this project. I'll be in touch with you in two weeks if that's enough time, and we'll get this thing going. How does that sound?"

Emily now spoke, "That sounds wonderful, Bill. I think we can get those affirmations locked down in two weeks and be ready to read them. How do you want to do it? Over the phone?"

"No. If you don't mind, I'd like to send a couple of my people out here to do the recording live. I don't want to take any chances on technical interference. We'll figure out where in the meantime."

It was settled. Zach volunteered to check with the psychology department at Brown to see if they had a facility that could be used.

"I know there has to be a facility on campus, Bill, which would be perfect for this endeavor."

Then Sean scratched his head. "And if not, I'm sure we could arrange something with my department."

The rest of the evening was very pleasant as Bill once again admired Emily's paintings, and he and Zach laughed about old times.

Chapter 30

Two weeks later the Mahoney's were set to proceed with their family's audio project. They were scheduled to go to the psych department that Saturday where Zach had arranged for the audio affirmations to be recorded. It was mid-March.

The weekend prior Sean and John planned to take the three boys up to George's favorite fishing spot for the day. The boys left early in the morning while Emily and Marti sat at the kitchen table painting colorful Easter eggs for a neighborhood Easter egg hunt the Sunday following the recording. That afternoon the two females were scheduled to meet up with Jeannie and Ariel to go shopping.

Emily was watching her daughter paint an elaborate pattern on one of the eggs. Marti realized Emily was staring at her.

"Mommy, do you like my Easter egg?"

"Marti, it's beautiful! I do believe you have some artistic talents. I just love the color combination and the big yellow tulip on both sides."

Marti was soaking up the praise, and it was obvious she liked it. Then she put the egg and paint brush down. She had a pensive look on her face.

"What's the matter, sweetie? You look very serious right now."

"I am serious, Mommy. I'm worried about Dakota."

Emily was marveling at how intuitive and mature her little girl sounded at that moment, so she prodded her on as Marti continued to speculate.

"I think Dakota had something very sad happen to him, and he got hurt by it very much."

"What do you think it was, Marti?"

"I don't know, Mommy, but I just know it was bad. Do you think the things we wrote down to say into the machine will help Dakota not be so afraid and hurt?"

"Well, Marti, I'm extremely proud of you for being so concerned and loving toward your brother. I know he loves you a lot too. I also think everything we've prepared, especially what you and Davie have prepared, will help Dakota tremendously. I think we're going to be able to wash away all the hurtful things that you think happened to him."

"I hope so, Mommy. I want him to be happy. He should be happy like me and Davie."

Emily was so taken back by this conversation she couldn't get it out of her head all day.

While shopping, she and Jeannie had a few minutes to talk quietly as the two girls were playing on a jungle gym in the middle of the mall. Emily told Jeannie about the conversation.

Jeannie was listening intently when she cocked her head. "You know, Em that sounds just like something a very young Martha would say. This is so exciting that you know your kids are reincarnations. Keeps me on the edge of my seat. You know, JJ (short for John Jr.) has said some pretty uncanny things every now and then. If I weren't privy to your situation, they would probably fly right by me and never impress me as unusual but now, not so much. Even John has been taken aback a few times. Have you ever heard of regression therapy?"

"Well, it sounds faintly familiar; but tell me, what is it?"

"One of my teachers at the high school brought me a book she wanted her junior class to read. It's called *Same Soul, Many Bodies* by a psychiatrist turned author." Jeannie scrunched her face as she said, "I think …no, I'm sure the author's name is Brian Weiss. I downloaded it to my micro pad after talking to Beth, my teacher. From what Beth told me, regression therapy concentrates on deeply-embedded and even forgotten emotional problems. Some patients even allude to past life experiences. I've read several chapters of Weiss' book and god, Em, it's fascinating!"

"Brian Weiss …you know, now I recall that Jose told Sean about Weiss' books several years ago. I think I recall seeing one of his books on Sean's bookshelf. Hmm …sounds like something I need to read. This knowledge is fascinating but a little frightening at the same time."

****

The Saturday of the recording, Sarah and Zach took Dakota to a Celtics basketball game. They told him it was a special treat for him.

He felt so special he didn't even question that the rest of his family was doing something different.

That allowed Sean and Emily to treat the day as something special for their other two children. They did the recording which turned out to be wonderful. They were so proud of their two children that afterward they took them to their favorite restaurant and then a movie.

By the time everyone got home, they called for a pizza, ate and crashed early. Sarah and Zach stayed for pizza and left immediately after.

The following week Bill Harris called Emily and told her that his audio people were very impressed with the family and their affirmations.

"They were especially impressed with Davie and Marti," he told Emily.

"Bill, you have no idea how proud we are of both Davie and Marti. They put their hearts and souls into this. They are so very supportive of Dakota. Both Sean and I are excited about what this has done for our family and will do for all of us individually. Thanks so very much for all your support and willingness to work on this!"

"You're very welcome, Emily. This is also very exciting for us. We're all looking forward to progress reports. I'll be in touch in about a week. You should receive the audio in about that time frame. Let me know when you receive it."

"I will, Bill. I'll talk to you very soon."

****

And so it began. Marti and Davie were so involved with the entire project that they jointly suggested that every evening they all gather in the TV room, turn off the lights, burn a few candles and sit together and listen with Dakota.

For two years the family moved through the first four levels of Holosync which the Institute called Awakening. Both Sean and Emily marveled at how it was enriching their family unit and helping all three of their children independently.

Dakota's progress was remarkable! His intellectual abilities improved dramatically as the family advanced through the audios.

Additionally, Dakota's self-confidence grew by leaps and bounds.

Moreover, Marti's artistic abilities grew exponentially. Davie's increased abilities were becoming remarkably noticeable as well. He was showing increased signs of compassion and was also demonstrating signs of great intuitiveness. Emily was certain Davie had hidden extrasensory abilities.

Sean kept records of all of this and was publishing the results which were contributing to his reputation within the neuroscience community. He was a featured speaker at most of the conferences around the country, and even European universities were clamoring for him to speak.

****

Davie's extrasensory abilities began emerging when Ariel and JJ's small toy poodle disappeared from their front yard after Jeannie had let him out to use the bathroom. Jeannie and DD had an Invisible Fence around the perimeter of the house so Jeannie knew Bugger —the poodle —didn't run away.

"Someone must have taken him," Jeannie told Emily. She was beside herself, as were DD and their two children.

The weekend after the disappearance, the Mahoney family had dinner with the Bertram family at their home. The children were in the front yard when Davie sat down in the middle of the yard, crossed his legs, closed his eyes and looked like he was in a trance. Ariel became alarmed and ran in to tell her mom something was wrong with Davie.

All the adults ran outside just as Davie was getting up off the ground. Emily and Sean ran over to Davie and asked him what the matter was.

"Mom, Dad, I think I know where Bugger is."

Sean looked stunned, but Emily looked certain that he did.

They all went back in the house and sat around the dining room table. DD was the first to speak.

"Davie, where do you think Bugger is?'

"Uncle DD, there's a man who lives on the next street over who steals dogs and sells them to research laboratories. He still has Bugger, I'm sure of that; but he's going to sell him tomorrow."

"How do you know this?" Jeannie asked.

"I don't know, Aunt Jeannie. I just do."

All four children were staring at Davie with their mouths open when Marti spoke.

"Mom, Davie knows things that no one else does. He found my necklace last week around the slant tree. When I was crying 'cuz I lost it, he put his hand on my head so I would feel better; then he told me to wait a minute because he knew where it was. He went outside and came back with it in his hand."

Sean didn't say a word. He was so blown away by everything that was taking place he was lost for words. Oddly, it was DD who made the next move.

"Davie, if we drove down the street, could you find the house?"

"Yes, Uncle DD. I'm pretty sure I can."

"Okay, well, let's get in the car and drive over to that street. Sean, come with us?"

Sean nodded his head vigorously as the three of them got up from the table.

"Uncle DD," asked Marti. "Are you going to arrest the man?"

"Well, Marti, first I want to find out if we have just cause to search the man's home. Then we'll see. Right now, if Davie is right, I just want to see if we can find Bugger."

As DD, Sean and Davie were walking out of the house, Jeannie told DD to be safe.

"Don't do anything stupid, John. If you have to, call for backup."

"I will, Jeannie. Don't worry, I don't want to blow this. If this guy is doing what Davie is suggesting, I want to be able to throw his ass in jail."

"Well, just be careful!" She kissed John's cheek.

****

There were some very nice homes on the next street over. Many of them were similar to John and Jeannie's home. They were meticulously refurbished Victorian-style homes, so the neighborhood was relatively nice. The street was a long one, though, and the homes further down began to look deteriorated by comparison. At the very end of the street there was an old Victorian-style house that was remarkably run-down. It backed up to an empty lot, and there were several outbuildings in the back of the house. Parked in the front of the house was a ragged-looking pick-up truck.

"That's the house, Uncle DD. He keeps the dogs in those buildings in back."

John didn't drive all the way down the street but parked about 100 yards from the house. He had a pair of binoculars in the glove compartment and asked Sean to pull them out. He looked at the house and then at the pick-up truck.

Suddenly John exclaimed, "I'll be damned!"

Sean asked what the matter was.

John handed the binoculars to Sean.

"Look at the license plate. It's one of those vanity plates."

Sean looked at the plate as he spelled it out.

"DGBGONE!"…then …"Dog be gone! God, DD, that's blatantly outrageous!"

Davie asked, "Aren't you going to go knock on the door, Uncle DD?"

"No, Davie, not just yet. Let me watch a few minutes and think about this. A license plate isn't probable cause."

Then John remembered one of his old friends was currently director of the ASPCA (The American Society for the Prevention of Cruelty to Animals). Both he and Sam Hendricks knew Dan Caldwell. They helped Dan break up a dog fighting ring run by a wealthy individual when Sam and DD were patrol officers several years ago. It was that incident that got Dan promoted to Director of the Providence ASPCA unit. John couldn't remember Dan's phone number, however, so he picked up his phone and called Sam. He remembered Sam and Dan were basketball buddies.

Sure enough, Sam had Dan's number so John called him.

"Dan, this is John Bertram. Don't know if you remember me, but my former partner Sam Hendricks and I helped you break up that fighting ring a few years ago."

"Yes, John, how could I forget? What can I do for you?"

John told him that he was sitting about 100 yards from a house which looked very suspicious. He told Dan what he suspected was going on at the house and about the audacious license plate.

"John, it's funny you should mention this. That house sits at the end of a street in a relatively nice neighborhood, yet that particular house doesn't fit in with most of the other houses, does it?"

"No, it sure doesn't. Listen, Dan, my kids' dog disappeared from our yard several nights ago. We have an Invisible Fence, yet he was gone when my wife went out to bring him in. I caught wind of this guy's activities over here; and, to be honest, I don't know what to do. I don't have a warrant to search the premises and no probable cause to try and secure one. Do you have any suggestions?"

"Tell you what, John. Just sit tight. We've had numerous verbal complaints, and we've been looking for a reason to snoop around that place. We don't need a warrant, just a signed complaint. I'm sending over one of our vans and two of our officers. They'll have you sign the complaint, and then they'll go knock on the door."

This was way beyond anything Sean had ever experienced. Although he felt apprehensive, he also felt excited. John filled him in on the conversation, so the three of them sat there waiting and watching.

About a half-hour later, Jeannie called John. He told her what was going on and assured her that everything was going fine, and they were just going to wait for the two ASPCA officers. She got excited and remarked that it was just like watching one of the shows on the Animal Planet, which made John chuckle.

About fifteen minutes later, a white van pulled up in back of John's vehicle. The two officers got out of the van. John instructed Sean and Davie to stay put. He got out and walked to the back of his car to talk to the two officers who had navy blue nylon jackets on with huge lettering on the back "ASPCA." Davie was very excited because he too watched the Animal Planet channel a lot and knew what ASPCA meant.

"Dad, they're going to save Bugger. Just watch."

Sure enough, John signed the complaint; and the two officers got back in their van and drove up to the front of the house.

One of the officers walked up to the front door and knocked while the second officer went through the side fence and began walking toward one of the outbuildings.

Before either Davie or Sean could say a word, John was on his phone calling for backup as he started his car and raced down the rest of the street. John saw the homeowner come out of a side door brandishing a shotgun.

Before John left his house, he slid his pistol in the back of his jeans. He was out of the car in a matter of seconds as he instructed Sean and Davie to stay put.

John ran over to the house, pointed his pistol at the homeowner and yelled for him to drop the shotgun. The man dropped it and John told him to get down on the ground, put his hands over his head and straddle his legs. John then patted down the man and put handcuffs on him. Just as he did that, two patrol cars pulled up and four officers got out wielding guns.

By this time, Sean and Davie were standing next to John's car watching the event unfold.

Two of the patrol officers had pulled the homeowner up off the ground and were escorting him to their patrol car where they put him in the back seat of one of the cruisers.

The two ASPCA officers were now inside the first outbuilding. They found approximately twenty dogs chained up inside the building and were calling for help from the district office. They then went to the two other buildings and found approximately ten dogs in each building also chained up. John walked over as the two officers were entering the third building. He immediately recognized Bugger. As soon as Bugger spotted John, he began jumping up and down as he yelped with excitement.

Poor Bugger was covered in mud from the wet, muddy floor; and he was shivering from cold and fright. One of the officers cut the chain as John picked Bugger up and carried him out to his car. He handed him to Davie who began hugging Bugger as he began licking Davie's face like it was an ice cream cone. Davie was giggling, and Sean was telling Davie how proud he was of him for saving little Bugger's life.

John went back to talk to the ASPCA officers; but before he did, he talked to the two arresting officers. They left with their prisoner as John told them he'd be right behind them.

As the patrol car pulled away, five more ASPCA vans drove up with two officers in each van. The vans were loaded down with animal crates where the rescued dogs would be put once they were unchained.

John was about to get in his own car when two more vans pulled up. They were from two of the local TV stations. They were news vans. There was also a crowd of neighbors from the street walking down toward the end of the street.

The reporters from the two stations talked to the original ASPCA officers as their camera crews were filming the rescue.

John was about to get into his car in order to drive Sean, Davie and Bugger back to his house when one of the reporters walked over followed by a cameraperson.

The reporter asked John if he could talk to the boy who reported the crime. John gave the reporter his card, told him he needed to follow the patrol car with the prisoner to the station but that he would have Davie's parents give the reporter a call.

John then drove Davie and Sean back to his house where everyone was now outside waiting for them to arrive.

Davie got out of the car first as he carried Bugger. As Sean was about to get out of the car, he saw one of the news vans driving down the street. The reporter and camera crew had followed them home.

John quickly told Jeannie what had happened, then told her he needed to go down to the station to make sure the proper charges were filed against the criminal.

He left just as the reporter and camera crew got out.

The rest of the evening was crazy. Davie was interviewed.

Davie was smart enough to tell the reporter that he had heard from some kids at his school about the dog thief, put two and two together and that was how the thief got caught.

Once the reporter was satisfied with his interview, he and the crew left to go back to the station in order to put their story together for the 6 p.m. news.

The evening news did indeed carry the story, and Davie became a local hero. During the ensuing weeks, all but five dogs were reclaimed. A month later the same reporter did a follow- up story which resulted in the five unclaimed dogs being adopted. Everyone was so proud of Davie and amazed at his abilities.

Ariel, JJ, Marti and Dakota all got the idea that Davie should start his own Pet Private Eye business and said they would help promote it and help with the detective work. The kids put posters up in both of their neighborhoods with Davie's picture on it. He had become recognizable as a result of the news reports on TV and in all the local newspapers.

Within a matter of a few weeks, the kids managed to locate twenty lost dogs and cats. They were having a blast, and the donations they made from the rescues were split five ways and put into savings plans for the kids' future education.

Originally neither Jeannie and DD nor Sean and Emily would accept any reward payments, but the families were so appreciative of their help in finding their lost friends that they began leaving what they called "donations" on Davie's doorstep.

The kids, especially Davie, were developing a reputation for finding family pets. As a result, the news media would now and then pick up a story, calling them "feel good" stories. But all of this excitement and happiness was about to change.

Chapter 31

The publicity also exposed the children to child predators that led to a horrendous incident which happened in early spring three years after the Bugger incident.

Carl Childress, the dognapper, had been charged with multiple offenses, including possession of firearms which, being a convicted felon, he owned illegally, and thirty-two counts of theft of property, as well as thirty-two counts of animal cruelty. The judge who heard the case was an avid animal lover. Thus, once convicted, the judge sentenced him to twenty years at Howard Prison in Cranston, Rhode Island.

Carl had grown up in a cruel and reckless family environment. He was brutally abused by both parents. At age nine he bludgeoned his sleeping father to death, for which he was convicted and sentenced to nine years in the juvenile system. His father had just beaten and drowned Carl's pet baby Beagle he had found abandoned in the woods behind his house. During his years in the system, Carl had become bitter and hostile.

He developed a hatred for children and their spoiled pets, which later inspired him to take up stealing pet dogs and cats that he then sold for purposes of research. He had been kidnapping and selling mostly pet dogs for nearly fifteen years when he was caught.

Use of animals for research purposes had always been a seedy business, and often the respected members of the labs looked the other way when it came to characters like Carl.

During Carl's first year in prison, he buddied up with other prisoners who were suspected of, but not yet convicted of, crimes against children. Most of them were in prison for other crimes.

Carl soon became friends with a particularly nasty character named Ben Claremont whose parole hearing was coming up soon.

Carl and Ben talked about the brats who turned Carl in, and Carl wasn't at all shy about expressing his desire to exact revenge. He wanted to ruin their lives and that of their snooty parents. One parent, Carl often expressed, was the son of a bitch responsible for his incarceration.

Ben empathized with Carl's situation and bitterness. Ben's own hatred for children was becoming stronger by the day. Carl's animosity only fueled Ben's desire to play out his hatred once he was released. He was, after all, a budding serial killer; and his fixation on children made him eager to get busy torturing and killing them.

Prior to Carl's incarceration, he discovered that the brat who turned him in lived halfway down a single street subdivision off Pawtucket Avenue in East Providence. He talked endlessly to Ben about how juicy the pickings were on that one particular street. There were three children in the brat's family, and two more who belonged to the cop. The cop's kids, Carl had learned, spent a good deal of their time, especially after school, at their grandparents' house down the same street. Ben was excited about getting out so he could grab one of these kids.

While in prison, Ben played the system like a pro.

He kept his nose clean and seemed to everyone involved with the decision that he had indeed redeemed himself and was ready for parole. He was released on an early April morning.

His equally nasty, warped younger brother was waiting for him outside the gates.

The brother, Nathan, lived in a dilapidated white house surrounded by a chain-link fence in a lower-class neighborhood in East Providence, a good cover for the two perverts since the neighbors were too busy living their own nightmares to ever notice them, let alone be concerned with what was about to begin taking place there.

The white structure had a large basement in which Nathan had spent the last two years building and installing cage-like rooms. Nathan was a welder by trade. Until his brother was set free, Nathan devoted unlimited hours sitting in the basement listening to heavy metal music, smoking crack cocaine and fantasizing about the prisoners he envisioned he and Ben would incarcerate in their own prison.

The Claremont Prison, as Ben and Nathan began calling it, was set to house ten prisoners; and, with Ben's release, they were excited about filling the prison with spoiled imps.

Nathan had already scoped out three boys, each from different neighborhoods. The three boys lived far enough apart and all three came from lower-class neighborhoods, which Nathan thought was a great way to get started since so little time and expense was paid to recover children of families not thought to be important enough to rescue. The media, after all, had always been attracted to those neighborhoods and families who could afford to make a lot of noise.

During the first few months after Ben's release, he and Nathan did indeed kidnap and imprison six boys. Toward the end of the year, their appetite for cruelty had grown exponentially. They singled out one of the boys who they jointly tortured and murdered, then buried his remains in their backyard.

Also, during that first year, Ben occasionally visited the street where the Mahoney's lived. He sat at the top of the street in a brand-new black Cadillac in the driveway of the now-abandoned McGillicutty place.

Old lady McGillicutty had died nearly fifteen years prior. Her property, on the other hand, languished for those fifteen years in the court system, disputed by siblings. Thus the untrimmed vegetation lent itself as a good place where Ben could sit and watch the kids as they walked to and from the bus stop.

Ben occasionally visited Carl in prison and told him he was biding his time till the opportunity to grab one of them was presented to him. In the meantime, he and his brother filled the prison cell left by the boy they murdered.

Carl was growing impatient as he encouraged Ben to find that opportunity. Thus, Ben began visiting the Mahoney's street more often. His prime opportunity came one Friday afternoon in early November as the children were coming home from school.

Davie and Ariel's bus was the first to unload as he watched the two friends walk with two other neighborhood children past the driveway and down the street. Fifteen minutes later Marti, JJ and Dakota got off their bus.

Ben had his windows open and could hear a girl and a boy arguing as the three walked by. The boy got so angry, he walked over to the curb opposite the driveway and sat down. The girl tried to coax the boy to walk the rest of the way with her; but their arguing became even louder as the girl yelled, "Fine, suit yourself; but I'm telling Mommy what you did when she comes home." She walked away with the other boy as the boy left behind began to cry.

This was Ben's opportunity. Once the other children disappeared over the crest of the hill, he pulled out of the driveway and headed for the stop sign at the end of the street. He quickly assessed the situation. He could see no evidence of any other children or adults around so he backed up and turned around. He stopped his car just in front of where Dakota was sitting and got out of his car.

Ben walked toward the boy who now appeared terrified. Dakota jumped to his feet and began running as he tried to dodge Ben. But Ben was too quick for Dakota. Ben blocked Dakota as he popped his trunk. He then grabbed Dakota and threw him into the trunk, slammed the lid, got back in his car and sped away with his treasure.

Chapter 32

As Marti and JJ walked into Gladys' house, Gladys noticed Dakota wasn't with them.

"Where's Dakota, Marti?"

"He's up the street crying like a little baby. We had a fight."

"What did you fight about?" Gladys asked this as she watched out the side window to see if she could spot Dakota.

"He ripped my brand-new coat before we got on the bus. He was mad that I beat him in a spelling contest today. I told him Mom was going to be mad at him so he sat down on the curb and began crying."

"I'm worried about him, Marti. I don't see him walking down the street."

"Okay, I'll go back up to see where he is."

"No," Gladys said as she called Davie to come downstairs.

Davie and Ariel came bounding down the stairs.

"Davie, stay here with Marti and JJ while I get in my car and go up the street to get Dakota."

Davie began asking Marti what was going on as Gladys grabbed her coat and was out the door.

Fifteen minutes later a frantic Gladys returned home. She was hoping she had missed Dakota and that he was now in the house with the other children.

Once in the house, Gladys became even more panicked and called John.

While she was talking to John, Davie yelled at Marti for leaving Dakota alone. Marti began to cry.

John, now a precinct captain, was on his way to pick up Ariel and JJ when he got Gladys' call. Once he arrived, he had all the children sit at the table in the dining room so he could get all the details.

Marti was still crying and frantically claiming remorse that she got so mad at Dakota and made him cry.

As John was questioning the children, Davie stopped talking, sat very still, then got a very strange look on his face. Later John would relate to Jeannie that, "He looked like he was listening to someone or something. It was really strange, Jeannie."

"What's going on, Davie?" John asked.

Davie came back to the moment, looked directly at John and answered, "Uncle DD, I just remembered seeing a black car sitting in the McGillicutty's driveway. I've seen that car a few times sitting in that same place."

"Davie, did you notice what kind of a car it was?"

Davie was thinking very hard. "I'm pretty sure it's a new car."

Then Davie drew the emblem on a sheet of paper, from which John determined it to be a Cadillac. Davie described the car which sounded like the new Cadillac Sedona which had just come on the market that year. John asked Davie if he could remember the numbers on the license plate, but Davie said he couldn't because of all the brush that had grown up in the driveway.

John wasted no time. He rushed back to work. As he did he had the station begin doing a search for all 2026 black Cadillac Sedona's sold in the Providence/East Providence area in the last several months.

By the time Emily, Sean and Jeannie arrived at Gladys' house, Marti was so distraught Gladys was beginning to worry about her. She was shivering and choking on her tears. She also threw up several times.

Emily immediately put Marti in a warm bath to calm her down. Emily was a wreck herself as she did her best to stay calm for Marti.

Around eight p.m. John called the house and talked to Sean. He told him that he believed the Cadillac had been involved in a couple of other abductions in some less affluent neighborhoods. He asked Sean to load Emily and their two other children in their car and drive down to the station. The FBI had been called in, and several agents were on their way to the station.

Sean was desperately trying to keep his own cool as he drove the car down Pawtucket Avenue. He was about to cross the Washington Street Bridge when Davie, who was sitting in the front passenger seat, yelled.

"Dad, turn left here."

Sean jumped from fright at the alarm in Davie's voice, but by now, neither he nor Emily questioned Davie's intuition, so he swung the car hard and took the left turn. Emily, who was in the back seat comforting a now-sleeping Marti, was on the phone with John telling him where they were when Davie began barking orders, "Turn right here. Turn left there."

They soon pulled down this one street and Davie yelled, "Stop!"

Sean screeched the breaks as he stopped the car. A car behind them nearly rammed into them, but the driver swung around them, yelling and cursing out his window.

Davie pointed to a rundown white house sitting on the corner lot, just ahead on the right. Sean pulled over to the curb and sat. He turned the lights off as they sat there.

Emily told John where they were as John had one of his people punching in the street number. The house belonged to a Nathan Claremont. The name sounded familiar to John so he had a team member run the name. The search honed in on the name Ben Claremont who had recently been released from the same prison Carl Childress had been sent to.

John instructed Emily to stay put in the car. "Lock the doors, Emily."

Emily relayed John's message to Sean, who immediately locked the doors. Soon they could hear sirens screeching as they got closer to where the Mahoney family vehicle sat.

The police cars pulled up to the white house. John was in one of the unmarked cars. He and several other police officers got out of their cars and were about to walk up to the front of the house when someone in the house began shooting.

The shooting continued for several minutes, then stopped. John got on the bullhorn and yelled for Ben and his brother to come out of the house with their hands in the air. More shots were exchanged; however, after several minutes, Ben opened the front door and waved a white cloth. He was commanded to throw out his gun, which he did. Then he was commanded to come out walking backward and with his hands on his head. As soon as he was on the front porch, John yelled for Nathan to come out as well; but Ben yelled back that Nathan wasn't home.

"Nathan's not here. I'm by myself!" They would learn later that Nathan had left the house approximately fifteen minutes earlier to go get beer and cigarettes.

Ben continued to stand on the porch with his back to the police and his hands on his head when John commanded him to lie spread-eagled on the porch with his hands above his head. For a split second it appeared as if Ben was complying with the command; however, at the last second, he made the fatal decision that he would never be returned to prison.

Ben whipped around and pointed a gun he had hidden in his pants. Before he could get off a shot, however, the officers opened fire. Ben went down. John yelled to the officers to stop shooting. He then went up to where Ben was lying in a huge pool of blood as John kicked his pistol off the stoop, then bent down holding his pistol ready to shoot. Ben had a bullet hole in his forehead. The blood was flowing out the huge exit wound in the back of his skull. He was dead. John called the all clear as several officers entered the house, guns drawn as a precaution.

By this time a crowd from the neighborhood was gathered close by. Sean and Davie were walking toward the crowd and house when Davie tugged on Sean's jacket sleeve. They both stopped as Davie pointed to the back side of the house. They could see the door of the basement bulkhead was slightly opened, and it looked as if a male figure was popping his head out.

Sean commanded Davie, "Hurry, Davie, go tell one of the officers."

"What are you going to do, Dad?"

"Just hurry, Davie!" As Davie began running, Sean yelled, "Hurry, son!"

Sean ran over to what looked like a separate garage just yards from the bulkhead door.

As Sean arrived at the street side of the house, he saw the new black Cadillac parked in the driveway. He assumed it was the car Davie had described. He grabbed a 2x4 board that was leaning up against a tree and crouched down in back of the car. Meanwhile, Nathan thought he had a clear run to Ben's car so he took off running. He ran around to the driver's side of the car as he fumbled in his pants pocket for the keys. He was about to climb into the car when Sean jumped out from behind the car, raised the 2x4 and walloped Nathan right smack in the back of the head. THOCK! Nathan went down as Sean lifted the 2x4 again ready to strike once more. He lowered the board as he saw Davie and two officers running toward them. It appeared that Nathan was out cold. However, before the three got close enough, Nathan began stirring and was trying to get up.

Sean felt pure rage as he realized Nathan was coming to. Sean was now standing over Nathan as he turned over to see Sean towering above him. Nathan grabbed Sean's leg and this enraged Sean even more. For the moment Sean blocked out that the officers were coming to his rescue. Instead, he focused completely on Nathan. Sean wanted to kill this man who he imagined had done serious harm to his little Dakota. Then in this moment of fury, Sean thought he saw Emily's father's face looking up at him.

As Davie and the two officers were just feet away from the two men, Sean raised the board and pointed the board down directly aimed at Nathan's skull. To both Davie and the officers, the manner in which Sean was holding the 2x4 led them to believe Sean was about to drive the board into Nathan's skull. A desperate Davie screamed, "Dad, stop!"

Sean looked up. He had a look on his face Davie had never seen before. However, the officers recognized that look as they pointed their pistols at Sean and both simultaneously yelled, "Stop!"

Sean was still clutching the 2x4 above Nathan's head when Emily and Marti ran toward the scene. Marti was screaming, "No, Daddy, no!"

Now John was with the group. He stepped out so Sean could see him and yelled, "Sean, he's not worth it. Drop the board or these officers will be forced to shoot you, and I won't be able to help you."

Fortunately, it was John's words and his command of those words that shook Sean back to reality. He no longer saw Emily's dad. Instead, he saw only Nathan. He felt a surge of emotions as he dropped the board and fell to his knees. By then, the cops had put their guns away and were restraining Nathan.

John walked over to Sean and helped him up. "Let's go get your son, Sean."

A stunned and shaken Sean got up, and together he and John walked over to the open bulkhead door and disappeared. Davie and Marti were clutching Emily's shaking hands as she wept.

"It's okay, Mom." Davie, who was now as tall as his mom, put his arm around Emily as she buried her head against his. Marti was crying as well. They held hands waiting for Sean and Dakota to emerge from the basement.

A few minutes later Davie called, "Look, Mom. Look, Marti!"

Sean had Dakota in his arms as he climbed the last step and began crossing the back yard to his family.

Davie, Emily and Marti hurriedly walked over to Sean and Dakota. As the family stood in the back yard clutching each other and crying, John emerged from the basement and walked over to them.

"Sean, Emily, why don't you all go on home? We've got this now."

Full of remorse, Sean looked at John. "Aren't you going to arrest me?"

John somewhat chuckled, "No, Sean, I'm not. There's no crime for thinking about killing someone. Go on home. Take your family and go home. I need to stay here until we wrap this up. We'll need to have you all come down to the station tomorrow, however, so we can talk to Dakota."

As the Mahoney family arrived at their car, Emily quietly said, "Sean, get in the car with the kids. I'm going to drive us home."

He was so shaken that he complied without protest.

Emily climbed behind the wheel and looked over at Sean, who had Dakota on his lap as he hugged him. Marti reached over the seat, touched Dakota's shoulder and cried, telling him, "Dakota, I'm so sorry I got mad at you earlier."

Remarkably, Dakota was very calm. In fact, they would all later discover that he had been calm throughout the whole ordeal. He looked at Marti and said, "I know, Marti. I'm sorry I ripped your coat and made you mad at me."

On their way home, Dakota told his family he was scared, but he knew Davie would find him and that everything would be okay. Later the six remaining boys told the same story.

They said that Dakota was the bravest of all of them, and he kept them hopeful. The oldest boy told the police that it was Dakota who yelled for all the boys to lie on the floor when the shooting began.

When the Mahoney family arrived home, Davie got out and helped Dakota out of the car. He held his hand as Emily helped her dazed husband into the house. They all collapsed in the TV room.

Several minutes had passed when Emily asked Davie and Marti to take Dakota up so they could all get ready for bed. "We'll be up in a few minutes to tuck you all in. I need to sit here with your dad right now."

Davie took the lead and encouraged Marti and Dakota to go up with him. The three disappeared around the corner.

Emily now sat on a stool in front of Sean. "Sean, honey, are you okay? Can I get something for you to drink?"

Sean leaned forward and put his head in his hands as he rested his elbows on his knees. There was a long silence when Emily finally put her hand on his. "Sean, it's okay. It's all over."

He looked up and tears welled in his eyes. "I don't know what happened to me back there. I think I was going to kill that man. I've *never* felt anything like that in my life!" He appeared absolutely exhausted and distraught.

"It's okay, Sean. You didn't and that's what's important. If I were the one with the board in my hands, I don't know what I would have done. That man and his brother intended to hurt our son."

Sean finally sat back against the chair and breathed a long, labored breath. "I saw him lying on the ground. Then, I don't know, Em, I thought I saw your father staring back up at me. Between what I know your dad used to do to you and what I suspected this guy had done or was going to do to Dakota, I just lost it. I know I scared all of you, but I scared myself as well. I'm just glad John was there. I heard sense in John's voice, and it brought me back to myself."

Sean was now shaking as Emily sat on the arm of the chair and consoled him. He lay his head in her lap. She gently stoked his head.

About fifteen minutes later, Davie came down and told them the other children were in their beds.

Sean looked up and as both he and Emily got up to follow Davie back upstairs, Davie said, "I'll be in my room, Mom and Dad." Then he paused, looked back over his shoulder and said in a sweet voice, "I love you, Dad."

Sean was softly crying when he and Emily walked into Dakota's room. As Emily turned on the light, Dakota sat up. Sean sat down and hugged his little boy. Then Emily sat on the other side of Dakota and stroked his head. Dakota was now the one consoling his father.

Through tears, Sean whispered, "Dakota, we were so scared we lost you."

Dakota felt overwhelmed with love for Sean as he hugged him hard. "I wasn't scared, Dad. I just knew Davie would figure out where I was, and you and Mom would come get me. It's okay, Dad, honest. I'm okay. I promise."

Emily, who was now hugging Dakota, spoke, "Oh baby, your dad and I are so proud of your bravery. We love you with all our hearts and are so happy you're now here in your own bed and we're sitting next to you. Go to sleep now, baby."

The three sat holding each other for several minutes. Then Sean kissed Dakota once more and told him how much he loved him. "We're going to go see your sister now."

"Okay, Dad. Tell her again how sorry I am for making her mad at me."

They left the room but left the door cracked so it wasn't pitch-dark for Dakota.

When they opened Marti's room, she turned over and began crying again.

Both parents sat down and held her. "Everything's okay now, Marti," said Sean. "Everyone's safe and sound."

Then Emily said, "Honey, we're so proud of you for loving your brothers so much. You're the best sister either of them could ask for."

Both her parents' soft words soothed Marti, who was now smiling and drifting off to sleep. They both kissed her forehead, turned off the light and left her room, leaving her door cracked as well. They both wanted the hall light to help both children feel safe.

Next they walked into Davie's room. He was in his pajamas and sitting on the side of his bed.

As Sean and Emily entered his room, Davie looked at his dad and said, "Dad, thanks for believing me tonight. I want you to know too that you're my hero. I was scared of what you would do to that man; but if you hadn't of hit him first, he may have gotten away."

Sean sat down and again looked remorseful. "Thanks, Davie, I don't feel like much of a hero because I wanted to kill that man."

"Well, you didn't, Dad; and that's what's important. You'll always be my hero."

Then Sean smiled as he looked at Davie. "Davie, you're *our* hero! If it weren't for you, we may never have seen our little Dakota again. There are so many stories like this that end that way; but because of you and your gift, Dakota is asleep in the other room." Then Sean leaned over and stoked Davie's face, "Davie, I'm learning that when you get a certain tone in your voice that I need to just do exactly what you tell me to do. I don't know how you do this, son; but your mom and I are so proud of you and so very happy you're our son. We both love you with all our hearts."

Emily hugged her oldest boy. "You are a hero, Davie. We love you so much and are so fortunate you're our son."

With the three children now safe and sound in their own beds, Emily and Sean went to their own bedroom, sat on the bed, held each other and cried.

Chapter 33

The following morning Davie woke around 5 a.m. He had a dream in which an older lady visited him. He felt groggy but couldn't remember the dream. He then thought about the previous day's events and how distraught his dad had seemed the night prior. He decided to get up and also wake Marti and Dakota. He wanted to prepare breakfast and serve his parents in bed.

He first went to Marti's room. She was wide awake. She told Davie about a dream she had just had; but, like him, she couldn't remember the details. She got really excited when Davie suggested his breakfast idea.

"Let's go get Dakota. I know he would want to help," exclaimed an excited Marti.

The two children entered Dakota's room. He was still sound asleep. When he woke and turned over, Marti and Davie were sitting on his bed.

"God, guys," he said as he rubbed his eyes. "I was just dreaming about this really nice lady."

Marti and Davie told Dakota about their breakfast plans. He became very excited, "I think that's what the lady was telling me."

"What did she tell you?" asked Marti.

"She said we needed to do something special for Mom and Dad to show them how much we appreciate them."

Marti looked like she was remembering something when she said, "You know what? I think she was Mom's grandmother. She looked like the lady in the photo Mom has on her dresser!"

Both Davie and Dakota looked pensive as Dakota excitedly said, "You know, I think it was Mom's grandma! How did you know, Marti?"

Davie and Marti both spoke simultaneously, "'Cuz that was the lady in my dream."

All three looked at each other with bewildered expressions. "Is that even possible?" asked Marti.

"I don't know," answered Davie. "But let's go fix Mom and Dad breakfast. We can tell them about our dream when they're awake."

All three children tiptoed down the stairs. Davie went to Sean and Emily's bedroom and closed the door. He didn't want to wake them till it was time to serve them. When he walked into the kitchen, Marti had the frying pan on the stove, and the coffeepot was dripping the coffee Emily put in it the previous morning.

As the three participated in preparing breakfast, Davie described for Dakota the bravery and actions of Sean when he hit Nathan on the back of the head with a board. "He helped save you and the other boys last night. That guy Nathan was about to get away."

"Wow," said Dakota. "I didn't know Dad was a hero too. He just kept telling me I was a hero."

As Davie was frying several pieces of bacon, he asked Dakota to go get a few flowers for a vase. Dakota ran out the door with a pair of scissors.

Marti was sitting at the table. "Davie, I'm going to draw a couple of pictures for Mom and Dad. Okay?" She assembled two trays with collapsible feet and dressed them up with red-and-white checkered napkins.

"The trays look nice, Marti. Thanks! Yea, draw a couple of heroes to look like Mom and Dad. I think they'd like that."

Soon the breakfast was finished and two plates, each holding bacon and eggs and raisin wheat toast, were sitting on the trays. Dakota was filling two separate small vases with water. He had placed a few chrysanthemums in each vase. Marti showed both brothers her picture.

"Wow," said Dakota. "Mom and Dad will really love this!"

Marti drew two action figures. One, the male, had a blue and yellow leotard with a flowing red cape. In the middle of the man's chest was a Superman-like emblem, only this one had a SD in the middle for Super Dad. The female looked like Wonder Woman with angel wings.

Both Dakota and Davie were admiring the drawings when Davie asked, "What's with the angel wings, Marti?"

"The lady told me that we needed to tell Mom how much we appreciate all the love and kindness she teaches us. I don't know ...I kind of like the wings."

"We do too!" said Davie as he patted Marti on the head.

"Let's go wake up Mom and Dad. Err ...our heroes!" said an excited Dakota.

When the children opened the bedroom door, Emily was sitting up in the bed. Sean was already in the bathroom shaving. He heard all the commotion, opened the door and stuck his head out.

"Sean, look what our wonderful children did for us!" exclaimed Emily. "Come out and eat your breakfast."

Sean wiped his face and walked out to see his children who were now sitting on the floor next to the bed. "This is wonderful, kids!"

Dakota, Davie and Marti were smiling with glee at this special moment when Davie said, "Marti, give them your picture."

She jumped up and handed Sean the picture she drew.

"Look, Em!"

Emily was so proud of her kids at that moment that she couldn't help getting teary-eyed.

"Children, this is so special. We love the three of you so very much!" Then she laughed at the image of herself. "You know; your dad once gave me a Wonder Woman doll for Christmas. All three of you children were so brave yesterday. It fills my heart that we have such a wonderful family."

"Dad," said Dakota. "Davie told me what you did last night. You helped to save me."

Sean looked a little embarrassed. "Well, Dakota. I think it was really your big brother and DD who actually saved you; but I did keep that nasty brother from escaping, didn't I?"

The rest of the early morning was filled with the children feeling so proud of themselves and thankful for their superhero parents.

Around 9 a.m. they all heard a commotion outside their house, and Davie ran to the living room to see what was going on. He ran back into the bedroom.

"There's a bunch of reporters out there!" said an excited Davie.

Emily and Sean looked alarmed. They didn't want to expose Dakota to these vultures, so Sean found his phone and called DD. Just as Sean was talking to DD, Emily's phone rang. It was Melody Rogers.

She and her station had caught wind of the story so she called to see if she could do an exclusive on the entire family. Knowing Melody would practice complete discretion, Emily told Melody that she wanted to first talk to her family. Melody was very accommodating as she told Emily she would wait for her to call her back.

In the meantime, John arrived in an unmarked car followed by several squad cars. John got out, went to the front stoop and told the media they needed to leave because they were trespassing on private property. As he did this, a patrolman and a policewoman physically moved the media people off the lawn, then established a perimeter using yellow police tape. For the next several days, officers were posted in front of the Mahoney house. John was determined to protect his friends from the feeding frenzy. In the meantime, the family did visit the police station so Dakota could be questioned about the incident. The prosecuting attorney was present. She asked Dakota if he felt confident enough to testify at Nathan's trial when the time came. Dakota told her he was. In the meantime, and from interviewing the other boys, the murdered boy's body had been recovered. The boy's body had been buried in a vegetable garden Nathan planted each year. One of the local newspapers ran a story with the title, "Murdered Twelve-year-old Meant as Fertilizer for the Claremont's Vegetable Garden." The story described the grisly details of the murder and what was intended for the other boys they were keeping prisoner.

****

The following day Emily and Sean had a family pow-wow. They told the children about Melody's request. By now, Dakota knew what the other children were saying about his bravery.

"Mom, Dad. I don't know if I was brave or not. It was pretty scary down there. The other boys told me about the one boy who had disappeared, and there was another boy who was convinced he was going to be next. I just sat on the floor in my cell and did what I've seen Davie do. I was very silent and went into my head. That's where I felt the safest because I was able to feel all of you around me."

Then Davie spoke up.

"Dakota, that *was* a very brave thing to do and you *are* a hero because all the other boys followed your lead and you helped them feel safe. I honestly think I heard you talking to me and telling me you were okay. I think that's how I knew where you were. This sounds stupid, but it was the same way I felt when we were all looking for Bugger. Somehow I could feel and see you just like I felt and saw Bugger."

Marti then said, "That's not stupid, Davie. Dakota and I are just so happy you're our big brother because you help us feel safe." She was hugging Dakota while she said this.

Then Emily spoke, "Davie, Marti and Dakota are very right. You have a talent that not many people have, and we're all very lucky that you do. Your dad and I, however, are concerned that if this gets out, the media will make a circus out of it and it will put you and the rest of us back in danger."

Sean continued, "This is what your mom and I would like to do with the permission of the three of you. We'd like to invite Melody to do an interview. We don't mind letting Melody know about the meditation because, Dakota, that contributed a great deal to your bravery and confidence that we'd find you. However, we want to completely avoid completely talking about Davie's special talents.

"Also, kids, we think it's time for you all to give up the pet detective work because it might cause another creep to take an interest in you. We want to do this right. We can't protect you from the media completely; but, if we cooperate with Melody, we know she'll do a good job letting the public know how special our three children are regarding all of your bravery and support for one another without exposing anything else.

"Now, why don't you three think all of this over and let your mom and I know what you've decided tomorrow? In the meantime, I don't know about you, but I'm starving. We haven't eaten since early this morning and it's now 2 p.m. What do you say?"

Davie looked out the front window and saw that only the patrol car with a policeman and a policewoman were out front now.

"Can we call for a pizza?"

Dakota and Marti seconded this call so the Mahoney family called for pizza and also had one dropped off for the two patrol officers out front.

The rest of that day and evening was calm as the family members enjoyed one another. They watched a couple of movies and played Monopoly till it was time for the children to go to bed.

****

The next day was a Sunday so they all hopped in the car and headed over to Beth and Bill's home where the relatives and family friends were gathered for a wonderful celebration and tribute to the three children. Everyone was there, including Jose and his family, Jeannie and her immediate family and even Paul Parker and his children and grandchildren.

Later that evening after everyone except the Mahoney family had left, Beth asked Emily and Sean if she could talk to them. Beth asked earlier if they would all stay the night and it was agreed. So once the children were in bed, Beth, Bill, Emily and Sean sat around the kitchen table. George had stayed behind. He was also sitting at the table. Emily and Sean already had an inkling what was going to be discussed, and they were right in their assumption.

It was obvious that Beth felt completely awkward about asking the questions she wanted to ask, so at first the discussion involved the kidnapping incident and the fact that it was Davie who helped save Dakota and the other boys.

Bill just sat with his mouth shut the entire time. It appeared to both Sean and Emily that he wasn't entirely comfortable with the discussion but was being a supportive husband.

About a half-hour into the discussion, the room became silent. Bill was the first to talk, but what he had to say had nothing to do with the intended topic. Instead, he took the opportunity to ask if anyone wanted anything to drink.

"I'm going to get a glass of wine. Would anyone else like me to bring them one?"

Beth waved a "no" to Bill, and George said he had had enough to drink for one day. On the other hand, both Emily and Sean said they would like a glass. Then as they squeezed each other's hand under the table, they also both simultaneously thought to themselves that a little alcohol might make this conversation more bearable.

While Bill was gone, Beth wiggled in her chair, looked off into the distance, then blurted out her question, "Do any of you think reincarnation is possible? I mean, Sean and Emily, I realize that both of you are scientists and, well, you probably think my question is completely bonkers; and, George, I'm sorry to sound a little crazy right now, but ...I can't help thinking that Davie is just too much like your dad, Sean. Now maybe that's genetics at work, but ..." She fell silent, then she almost whispered, "I just don't think so."

As she whispered those words, Bill came back into the room

with the three glasses and handed one each to Emily and Sean.

Bill felt the awkwardness in the atmosphere so he simply sat down, moved his chair back away from the table and began sipping his wine.

Sean took a sip of his wine, put the glass down, pushed it to the side, folded his hands in front of him on the table top and looked thoughtful. Emily knew Sean was about to say something. The folded hands on the table top indicated that she was off the hook as the first to speak to Beth's comments.

"Mom, I'm going to tell you what Emily and I know. We've both individually and jointly experienced phenomena that would seem for many people unreal and even lunatic in nature.

You're right, Mom, we are both scientists. However, as a neuroscientist, I am learning that things I would have thought impossible in the past are actually possible. So I guess that's helped me to be open-minded to unusual phenomena. And, Mom, I am, after all, the person who came back from a coma, picked up a guitar and began playing."

Beth breathed heavily. Emily could see Beth's body melt from the tension she felt prior to Sean's words.

"Mom, Emily is a different type of scientist; but you know, Mom, that Emily has lived a very unusual life and has overcome a lot. I know you also are aware of her meditation which has not only helped her overcome so much, but it's helped little Dakota as well. It's also the very thing that has helped Davie develop his unusual talents and Marti her artistic talents which are becoming more and more sophisticated by the day. All of this results largely from the family meditation we've been doing over the last two years. So, yes, I am going to tell you what Emily and I know and have experienced. When I'm finished, you can believe us or not. It's up to you."

He continued to talk about the many dreams he'd had where he would wake up feeling as if his father had visited him. He told her about the many visitations Emily had had from her grandmother, Bertie and from Martha. He then told her all that had happened to both Emily and him during the trip he took to Katmandu. He then took a deep breath.

"Mom, during those three weeks a lot of very strange things happened."

Sean was now again holding Emily's hand under the table.

"I want to show you something, Mom."

He looked at Emily. She intuitively knew what he was going to do so she relaxed her hand as he raised both their hands. Emily's left hand was now raised so Beth could see the engagement and wedding rings.

"Mom, I did not have these rings with me when I went to Nepal. In fact, I don't remember if Grandma ever showed them to me. The first time I saw them was during a visitation when Grandma came to me, told me I had been totally lazy about my plans to marry Angela and that I needed to give Emily her engagement ring before I left for home."

Beth was sitting in her chair with her mouth opened.

"Grandma gave these to me during that visitation. In fact, it was right after Emily told me she was pregnant and I reached for her face to assure her I was good with the pregnancy that the rings fell from my hand to the bed. Mom, it was also during that visitation that Grandma told me that Dad and I would soon be reunited."

Sean finished by telling Beth that both he and Emily had a joint visitation from Martha and that she had basically told them that their baby would be the reincarnation of Davie.

At this point Beth had tears rolling down her cheeks. Bill leaned over to Beth and whispered something in her ear, then excused himself and went to bed.

Both Sean and Emily looked a little stunned.

When Bill was out of the room, Beth spoke.

"It's okay. Bill has been having a very difficult time grasping all of this. I'm not certain, but I think he may feel a little threatened. It's something we're working on. It'll be alright."

She was about to say something else when the four heard a sound coming from the hallway. Davie had come down the stairs to use the bathroom. He walked through the kitchen.

He was half-asleep when he saw that his grandma was crying.

"Are you okay, Grandma?"

"Oh, Davie, yes. I'm fine."

He walked over to her, bent over and hugged her. "I love you Grandma. You're my favorite grandma." He then paused and looked at Emily. "Sorry, Mom. I love your mom too, but I just have a special place for Dad's mom."

Beth hugged Davie tightly. "Davie, sweetie, I love you too. Go on back to bed. Everything is good."

"Night, Mom and Dad. Night, Grandma and Grandpa."

"Goodnight, Davie."

Davie chuckled as he left the room, "Sleep tight, don't let the bed bugs bite." Then he grabbed his behind and laughed. "I think one just bit me."

Sean, Emily, George and Beth all laughed.

"Just like your dad. What a ham!" Beth then paused and looking relieved, "Oh, my god, you two. I've been so nervous about talking to you about all of this. But I just couldn't stop thinking about all the personality traits and now his very special talents that it all just seemed too coincidental to be accidental."

Then Beth cocked her head and said, "Hmm …and what about Marti? There's a reason you named her Martha Elizabeth, isn't there? I just so often see glimpses of your grandma in her. She is, isn't she?"

George spoke for the first time. "Yep, she's my Martha alright."

"This is some crazy stuff, but I feel so much better now. It'll take some getting used to, but I do feel like a huge weight has been lifted from my shoulders."

Emily looked empathetic and asked, "Beth, are you sure everything will be alright with Bill?"

"Yes, sweetie, it will. It's just going to take a little time for him to adjust to what he heard tonight. He knows how much I love him. I'm going to just make sure I reinforce that with him. That's all. Besides, what this knowledge does for me is make life feel so much more hopeful. You know, the older I get, the more I think about being mortal; and, well, this knowledge is very comforting."

The four adults talked a little while longer; then Beth said she was getting very tired and needed to retire. They all hugged each other and said goodnight.

When Emily and Sean were alone in the bedroom, they discussed the conversation. They were both concerned for Bill and Beth's relationship. However, at breakfast the following morning that concern dissipated when Beth came out to the kitchen where Bill was making coffee. She walked up to the back of Bill, who turned around and gave her a very passionate kiss. They were both grinning from ear-to-ear.

Chapter 34

Later that day as the Mahoney's drove back home, they talked about Melody Rogers.

It was Dakota who said, "Mom, Dad, Davie, Marti and I have discussed Melody Rogers; and we feel okay with her doing the interview."

Sean looked at the children through the rearview mirror. "Are you sure, kids?"

All three vigorously nodded their heads.

"Then it's settled. Em, when we get home, why don't you call Melody and schedule her visit?"

****

Melody came to the house the following weekend. Her husband, Tony Russo, accompanied her and did the recording. When Tony came through the door, Emily noticed a wedding band on his finger.

"Oh, my," pointing to his band. "When did that happen?"

Tony smiled. "I had been after Melody for several years to tie the knot. When she caught your bouquet at your wedding, she told me it had to be a sign. We were married a few months later."

"Well, a belated congratulations is in order!"

Melody did the interview and was very careful not to ask any questions other than about the actual abduction. She concentrated mostly on Dakota and what the other boys were saying about his bravery. She also did a segment with the family regarding the meditation and the role it played in the entire incident helping Dakota to stay calm, focused and positive. It turned out to be a real feel-good interview ending with her comments regarding how remarkable Dakota's parents and siblings were. Her exclusive interview managed to keep the rest of the media at bay as the family went back to everyday living.

The children disbanded the pet detective service; however, there were still those families that contacted the family to help them find their beloved furry family members. As a result, and with the help of

DD, the family decided to allow Davie to find the occasional pet, informing the client families that they would be thoroughly investigated by the police department in order to protect the children from additional dire incidents.

And so it went.

****

The Mahoney children adjusted to a normal existence as they matured into young adults. Sean went back to concentrating on his discipline which eventually led to him becoming engrossed in a project which involved the development of electrodes embedded into micro-chips.

The first micro-chips were implanted into volunteers who began showing early signs of Alzheimer's disease.

The chips were implanted in the area of the brain where the limbic system is housed within the temporal lobe.

The electrodes sent subtle electric shocks to the hippocampus and amygdala, which are responsible for memory and emotional reactions, thus allowing patients to stave off the progression of the disease. The success of the progress led to implanting chips in patients with advanced Alzheimer's.

Many of the patients were able to heal themselves completely.

Still working with the Centerpointe Institute, Sean's group discovered that even more patients were able to heal themselves when meditation with embedded messages were used on a daily basis. The work he and his colleagues were doing was remarkable and well-publicized. As a result, it led to tremendous government funding that would help further the research.

Sean's group thought they were on the path toward helping to cure other ailments, including cancer. When Sean finally retired at age seventy-four, he was not only a world-renowned neuroscientist, but he was also extremely wealthy, much of which came from speaking engagements and from the institute he founded in his early sixties.

Emily was also well-known in the field of environmental science. Her work with renewable nuclear energy finally convinced the federal government to embrace nuclear energy to turn around the global warming that had become alarming by the year 2030. During the prior decade, scientists succinctly determined and demonstrated that the earth *was indeed* headed toward the next major extinction event. The impending catastrophic event was largely due to the accumulation in the atmosphere of carbon dioxide emissions as well as the lethal production and emission of methane gas.

Methane, a colorless/odorless gas is lethal to humans and other living organisms. Methane in its gas form is an asphyxiate which, in high concentrations, has the ability to displace the very oxygen needed for breathing. The overabundance of this gas in the atmosphere was *largely* caused by the waste of animals raised then slaughtered by the food-based animal industry. By 2030 even evangelicals, who for decades had resisted the notion of global warming, were on board and voting for candidates who promised to make global warming a top priority.

Too, as a whole, the U.S. population was becoming increasingly aware of the extreme danger of a high methane gas concentration in the atmosphere. This concentration led to a strong and joint Vegetarian/Vegan-Based lobby group effort to sway the Federal Government to push forward a pro-vegetarian/pro-vegan diet based project similar to the fitness based one of the John F. Kennedy era. The Mahoney family had transitioned to vegetarianism many years prior. The project had become a popular effort begun and pushed by the Junior Congresswoman from Illinois, Malia Ann Obama.

Following in her mother's and father's footsteps she was a hugh champion for a healthy planet and had recently become a member of the United States House Committee on Science, Space and Technology which was chaired by the Congresswoman from New York State, Chelsea Clinton.

By the time Emily officially retired at age seventy-four, the air in the U.S. rivaled the clean air in France, which was an early leader in the nuclear energy field. Too, with the financial help of the U.S., China was well on its way to clean air as well as establishing a democratic government. A silent revolution had been underway in that country for several decades.

By 2048, nuclear energy made up 60% of the U.S. energy resources. Also, the U.S. was a leading nation in the World Organization for a Healthy Pale-Blue Dot (WOHPBD), named in honor of Carl Sagan, who many believed to be the father of the clean air movement which had begun more than a half-century earlier. As one of its functions, the WOHPBD helped other countries, including many struggling third-world nations, acquire nuclear energy.

Emily's group won the Nobel Peace Prize in 2039.

By the time both Emily and Sean celebrated their fortieth wedding anniversary in 2051, all three children were grown, married and themselves parents.

Davie, encouraged by his uncle DD, earned his bachelor's degree in Criminology. Davie then went on to receive both his master's and a doctorate of criminal justice. Once he earned his doctorate, he applied to and was accepted into the FBI.

He became an invaluable member of the Behavioral Analysis Unit at the FBI headquarters in Washington, D.C. where he lived with his wife, Briana, a University of Maryland English Literature professor and their four children, two boys and two girls.

Marti went on to the University of Rhode Island School of Art, where she earned her master's, then later her PhD. Five years after she received her doctorate, she became curator of the Corcoran Museum of Art in Washington, D.C. and later married a fellow artist, Christopher Henry, who owned an art gallery in the D.C. area.

Marti visited her parents often, driving the eight hours with her family of five, which included two girls and a boy.

Dakota followed in his dad's footsteps. He became a neuroscientist and, until his Dad's retirement, was heavily-involved in many of the research projects Sean worked on. He was also married which resulted from a strangely wonderful coincidence.

Dakota met and married the daughter of Charles and Angela Caballero.

Angela's former name was Hawthorne, the same Angela Hawthorne who had been engaged to Sean when Jeannie reminded him of his promise to find Emily.

Angela spent several years at the University of California at Berkeley in the neuroscience department.

Charles Caballero was the young man who jumped at the opportunity to become reacquainted with Angela after she and Sean broke off their engagement.

Charles was a neurosurgeon when Angela was asked to join the

Harvard faculty. Charles came from an old-world Spanish family that owned vineyards in California's Sonoma Valley. His parents helped him set up a practice in the Boston area where Charles eventually founded the Massachusetts Neurological Alliance.

****

When Angela came to Harvard for an interview, it was at first very awkward for both her and Sean who, as a member of the faculty, interviewed Angela. Of course, it was a no-brainer for Sean who had kept up with Angela academically. He was well-aware of her remarkable qualifications in the field.

The interview took place on a Monday afternoon.

Sean told Emily that morning that he was nervous as hell about it.

Emily reminded him what Martha had told them during one of her visitations. She told them that Angela would one day thank Sean because she would come to realize after the breakup that she was madly in love with Charles.

At three p.m. Sean heard a knock on his office door.

His hands felt sweaty from the tension. He had been wiping his hands with a bandana he kept in one of his drawers.

When he heard the knock, he grabbed the bandana and vigorously wiped his hands, shoved the bandana back into the drawer, got up and went to the door.

Angela looked at Sean, smiled and instead of shaking his hand, she hugged him.

"It's so good to see you again, Sean. I've kept up with your work over the years, and I'm so excited that I may have the opportunity to work with you once more."

Now smiling, Sean said, "Angela, I've kept up with your work as well. Come on in. It's so good to see you."

They had a wonderful conversation. She was the leading candidate. Sean promised he would do everything he could to have the position awarded to her.

When the interview process was finished, Sean, his colleagues and Angela went to dinner at the original Legal Seafood restaurant.

While the group was waiting for their table in the lounge area,

Sean excused himself, went out to the sidewalk and called Emily.

"So how did it go, Sean?"

"Baby, my hands were sweating and I think that damned bandana was wringing wet when she finally knocked on my door. But when I opened it, she actually hugged me. She's doing well and is extremely happy. She made a point of telling me that she was thrilled at catching our wedding news report Melody did."

"That's wonderful. I told you there was nothing to worry about; but I'm sure if the tables were turned, I would have felt every bit as nervous. So did she get the position?"

"I'm pretty sure she did. I'll know absolutely in the morning after a faculty meeting."

"Well, when she and her family move here, we need to have them over for dinner."

"I'll mention that to her before she leaves. Thanks for being so supportive, sweetie. Now I better get back before I'm missed. I should be home around eleven p.m. And, Em, if you're up to it at that time, why don't you slip into that naughty red bra and panties I love so much? I want to devour my little Irish Colleen."

"I'm waiting with a wet pussy, Seanie!"

"I love when you talk dirty to me. See you soon, baby."

Chapter 35

Angela was indeed awarded the Harvard position. She and her family moved to the Boston area in 2040; and one Sunday, a month later, Angela, Charles and their youngest daughter, Trish, had dinner at the Mahoney's. Dakota, who was still working on his doctorate while living at home, was there as well.

Emily was standing at the kitchen island when the three walked in through the side door. Sean had gone out to meet them when he heard their car pull into the driveway. Dakota was sitting at the kitchen table watching a program on the small counter screen and eating an apple.

When Trish walked in, Dakota dropped the apple on the table. Emily immediately noted Dakota's captivation with this young, beautiful woman.

Introductions and drinks were made. They all sat around the veranda at a large farm-style table. Dakota sat across from Trish, and he couldn't take his eyes off her.

It was obvious that she was also smitten. For the first hour she stayed in a perpetual flushed state, titillated, yet embarrassed, by Dakota's stares.

Soon the room became silent when Trish pointed toward the huge glass window and asked about the curious tree which she had spotted on their way in. That was Dakota's opportunity.

"We call it the slant tree, and it has a wonderful history. Would you like to go out and see it? It's slanted so that you can actually walk up the trunk."

They were about to go out the door when Emily noticed Trish's shoes.

"Trish, what size shoe do you wear?"

She looked perplexed, "Eight, why?"

Emily kicked off her slip-on, rubber-soled tennis shoes. "Because you'll slide right back down the tree with those shoes on. Here's mine. They're rubber-soled. I also wear a size eight."

"Wow, thanks, Emily, but what are you going to do?"

"Not to worry. I have another pair in the hallway."

Sean was in and out of the hall carrying Emily's other pair of rubber-soled shoes. He put them down on the floor next to Emily who lovingly stroked his face as she quickly slid them on.

Angela watched this interaction, noting how Sean and Emily seem to be intricately intertwined. She commented to herself how everything had worked out just the way it should have. They were happy and she and Charles were as well.

Once outside, Dakota led Trish to the slant tree. He began climbing, but she remained at the base. When he turned around, he could see she wasn't totally sure of climbing so he walked back down and extended his hand.

"Come on. Take my hand. It's really safe and it's wonderful up here. You'll see."

She blushed again as she took Dakota's hand which sent a rush up his spine.

This is the one was Dakota's mental reaction to that rush.

When the two walked up to the first big limb that jutted straight up to the sky, they sat down.

"You were right. It is wonderful up here. Tell me about the tree."

Dakota was only too eager to tell her the entire story.

He began with the story that his great-grandfather told his dad.

"Supposedly there was a hurricane that came through the area. The high winds knocked the tree over and nearly uprooted it. Yet the tree was never removed so it remained as you see it today and just continued to grow. This is where Mom and Dad first met forty-four years ago. My great-grandmother lived in this house. Dad spent a lot of time here."

"Who owns the land?"

"Mom and Dad do now. Grandma Martha bought two acres from Bay View Academy after Mom and Dad went off to college. She called this 'sacred land' and wanted to keep it in the family. Mom and Dad planted the rose bushes."

"Tell me more about when your parents met."

He did. Pointing across the street, he told her the entire story about where Emily lived with her family.

"Mom had been sexually abused by her father."

Trish looked horrified.

"It's okay. Mom is one of the strongest human beings I think I've ever met in my entire life. She overcame all of that and even took back her control from her father when she was about thirteen years old. Dad and Mom have been in love all these years."

"What do you mean 'she took back her control from her father'?"

"The way Mom tells the story, it was Dad, Grandma Martha and Mom's best girlfriend, Jeannie who gave Mom the will and determination to defy her father. She stabbed him in the hand one day when she was sure he was going to take the abuse to the next level. He was going to rape her, but she found a pencil and stabbed his hand, declaring her freedom.

"Gosh, Dakota, that's one of the saddest stories I've ever heard, yet it's also one of the most remarkable. I'm working on my doctorate in clinical psychology with a specialty in child psychology. I want to set up my own practice. I've actually thought about concentrating on abused children. Do you think your mom would ever be open to talking to me more about her experiences? I mean I don't want to pry or bring up old wounds, but her story is inspirational. You love your mom a lot, don't you?"

"Yes, Mom is a very special person in my world, not just because she's my mom, but because she's been the main character in helping me overcome my own self-doubts. Dad's been my inspiration as well. In fact, I guess you could say that I'm following in his footsteps. I'm also working on a doctorate in neuroscience. I'm very fortunate to have both Mom and Dad as my parents. And wait until you meet my brother and sister! Do you have siblings?"

"Yes, I have two brothers who are older than me."

Trish heard a dog barking, looked down at the base of the tree and saw the cutest little three-legged dog she'd ever seen.

"Is that your dog?"

"Yes, that's Munchkin."

"What happened to his right back leg?"

"Munchkin's a girl. She lost it one night when I was walking her. I was supposed to have her on a leash, but I let her off for a few seconds when she saw one of my friends and ran across the street. One of the teenage kids from down the street was racing his car up the hill, didn't see Munchkin and ran over her leg."

"Good grief, Dakota, you're full of odd stories," she laughed delightfully. "How old is Munchkin?"

"She's three. She actually belongs to Mom, who named her for the little munchkins in the Wizard of Oz. Oh, and one day you'll get the connection because Mom's best friend Jeannie, I mentioned a little while ago, nicknamed Mom 'Auntie Em.'"

They were both laughing when Emily stuck her head out the door and called them to dinner.

Dakota helped Trish climb down the tree. They were still holding hands when they walked in. To both sets of parents, they looked perfectly natural and at home with each other.

Later that evening and just before Trish and her parents left, Dakota asked Trish if he could see her again.

"I'd be disappointed if you didn't. How about next Saturday night?"

They exchanged phone numbers and had a wonderful first date that following Saturday.

****

Shortly after the family left, Emily and Dakota sat at the kitchen table talking about Trish. He was totally smitten with her and sensed she felt the same or soon would.

"What did you two talk about out there? You were out there for two hours before I called you in."

"Everything, it seems. I told her the story about the tree and about how you and Dad met. She's working on her doctorate in clinical psychology with a specialty in child psychology. She plans to have her own practice and has considered specializing in abused children. She was captivated when I told her your story. I hope you don't mind, Mom. She may ask you to talk with her about it. I told her what an inspiration you've always been for me."

Emily was blushing when Sean walked into the room and sat down with them.

"That went well, don't you think, Em?" He put his hand on Emily's and squeezed it.

Dakota loved watching the affection exchanged between his mom and dad.

"Yes it did. I like Angela and she and Charles seem lovely together."

"Dakota, you spent a lot of time with Trish. What's up with that?"

"Dad, this may sound premature, but I think Trish is the girl I've been waiting for."

"Well, if she's even half of what your mom is for me, I'd say, 'Run, don't walk!'"

During the conversation Emily admitted to Dakota that she had an uncanny feeling she was familiar with Trish.

By this time in the history of the Mahoney family, everything was discussed openly and truthfully. All three siblings fully accepted and believed in reincarnation.

"Who do you think Trish is, Mom?"

"I don't know, honey. Maybe it's just my imagination, but I feel a strange connection to her at a primeval level. I'm looking forward to getting to know her better."

Just prior to climbing into bed, Sean asked Emily about her comment. Again she repeated that she may be imagining, then sat quietly and said, "No. I'm not imagining. I know I have a connection to her. She's a very sweet girl, don't you think, Sean? And I've never seen Dakota so taken with a female before. It was fun watching him as well as the two of them. She seemed to remain crimson all evening. I wouldn't be surprised at all if we are planning a wedding soon."

"Never a dull moment in this family, is there? Now let's get under the covers and do some exploring. What do you think?"

Emily giggled, wiggled out of her jeans, pulled off her top, climbed into bed, covered her head and waited for her fellow explorer to join her. They both giggled for the next hour as they explored all the nooks, crannies, crevasses and formations they could find.

Chapter 36

Dakota and Trish dated for the next year. Six months after their first date, they moved in together. They were both only months away from receiving their doctorates so they announced their engagement and intentions to wed during an Easter dinner at Trish's parents' home.

Later while sitting in a backyard covered atrium, Angela commented to Sean, "Now I understand why we were supposed to get to know each other all those years ago. This is such a happy day for me. I just love your Dakota. He's such a gentleman and treats my Trish like a queen."

Sean settled into one of the colorful Adirondack chairs nodded and smiled. "Angela, we're fortunate as well. Trish is a beautiful woman. Dakota deserves the best and it seems he's now gotten the best."

Both Emily and Charles were sitting with Sean and Angela during this conversation. They caught each other's eye and smiled approvingly.

Charles couldn't help himself. "All is well with the world. All is well."

****

The wedding was in October and it was a beautiful one. Trish chose her favorite fall colors for her bridesmaids; and the huge wedding cake had beautiful orange, yellow and red leaves painted on it.

The couple followed in Dakota's parents' footsteps when he and Trish decided to spend two weeks in Venezuela. Trish had never been, but Dakota had been numerous times. It had become one of his family's favorite vacation destinations. Trish fell in love with the country, its people, scenery and animals especially.

In fact, the first thing she did when they got back and settled into their new home, was look for and found a beautiful Sun Conure parrot that she and Dakota named Zwayla. While in Venezuela they flew over to Brazil for a float down the Amazon. It was there they saw the beautiful bright yellow birds with orange cheeks sitting on the branches of trees along the Amazon.

Dakota and Trish bought a house in Norwood, Massachusetts, which was not quite halfway between Cambridge where Trish's parents lived and East Providence where Dakota's parents lived. They found a beautiful small white Cape Cod structure surrounded by a quaint white picket fence in a neighborhood that wasn't too far from the BC which stood for the Big Connect.

The Big Connect was the name for the underground tube railway system that shuttled people in and out of the Boston area at breakneck speeds, cutting down hours of traffic jams and allowing commuters the ability to live virtually anywhere in the Providence/Boston area and work anywhere as well.

Dakota now had his doctorate and, with the help of his powerful father, was able to land a position as an assistant professor at Harvard.

He commuted every day from Norwood to downtown Boston. In the meantime, Trish had indeed hung up her own shingle in Norwood; and, encouraged by Emily, began working with abused children. Trish especially wanted to specialize in sexual abuse which would eventually lead her to include adult former victims as well.

Massachusetts and Rhode Island were bastions of the Catholic Church. Despite the reign of two popular Popes who advocated for the end of sexual abuse, it was still a problem. Politics seemed to stall and stand in the way of establishing sanctions and severe punishment for known pedophiles. However, when the media would get hold of those cases which found their way into the courtrooms, those priests were dealt with handily. Yet, because of the cloud of shame that victims lived under, most of the abuse went unreported or unattended.

Priests were still transferred from one parish to another, while lay perpetrators remained protected by the blind eyes of relatives who would rather acquiesce to the tribe mentality than protect the youngest members of their clans. All the while, those secretive practices only added tremendous burdens to the victims as they grew from once-innocent children into adulthood. Thus, Trish always had plenty of victims to fill her hours of operations. Too, once she began seeing adults, her volume of clients doubled. In addition to private sessions, many of the adults were eager to join her group therapy and psychoanalysis sessions.

Since psychoanalysis understands the impact of the subconscious mind as it influences irrational behavior stemming from subconscious damage caused by childhood trauma, Trish strongly encouraged her patients to meditate regularly to Holosync.

She was a busy lady; yet she wanted desperately to become a mom.

****

Trish was an advocate of psychoanalysis. When a new patient expressed an interest in the therapy, Trish was very clear about what it entailed.

"My approach to psychoanalysis therapy is designed to treat your past trauma by investigating the interaction of your conscious mind and your unconscious one. The objective is to uncover, and more importantly, to help *you* to release repressed fears and conflicts that stem from your molestation."

With Emily's blessing, she would reference her mother-in-law's trauma and how, over the years, Emily was able to put her trauma in perspective so that it no longer negatively influenced her life. She would explain that the therapy involved the use of the meditation audio program, Holosync. The patient needed to understand this for the therapy to work.

"I'm fortunate to have access to the program at a great discount which I will pass on to you. However, if you want this therapy to work, you must be willing to commit to meditating on a daily basis using the audio program. Without that commitment, I cannot promise that this therapy will work."

Once the patient would commit to the therapy and the purchase of the Holosync audio program, Trish would further explain.

Using a plastic brain model, she described the function of its different sections. She then elaborated on how the unconscious mind interacts with the conscious one causing dysfunctional behavior. She found that a complete understanding of the physical brain and how each section interacted with each other was important. It would help her patients understand the process of the therapy thus influencing them to commit firmly to that process.

"Similar to rape, molestation creates obvious trauma. Also, and more importantly, molestation causes deep-seated memories and fear. The part of your brain that houses these memories lacks any sense of time. Thus, that part of your brain perceives the danger still exists. Consequently, your fear influences behavior thus causing dysfunctional behavior, which in turn causes unhappiness up to and including depression. During our sessions, we will discuss your molestation as it has affected your life emotionally. We will explore your fears and behaviors that you perceive as dysfunctional; those that cause you to have unrealistic expectations as well as those that cause you problems with relationships for example. Then, once you begin to meditate, we'll discuss the results. For instance, do you find yourself crying uncontrollably without knowing why?"

Trish would tell each patient that, if he or she was religious about coming to the therapy sessions and meditating, "I am confident that dramatic changes will take place."

News of Trish's reputation was spreading. She was a busy lady, yet she wanted desperately to become a mom.

****

One warm evening, while the full moon was high in the sky, Emily and Sean climbed the slant tree and sat side by side snuggling and kissing. That night, she told Sean she had something to tell him.

"Sean, I have this uncanny feeling that Trish is the rebirth of my father's soul. I know that sounds crazy, but it's just a feeling I've had for a very long time."

"Why on earth would you think that? She's a wonderful person."

"I know she is. But do you remember what I told you a long time ago? During one of Martha's visitations, she told me that my father was sorry for the way he had lived his life and the crimes against children he committed. She told me that my last discussion with him was the catalyst that allowed him to see how horrible a person he had been and that he also learned the meaning of both love and remorse for the first time in his existence."

Sean was sitting next to her listening.

"Em, I know I don't need to say this; but I'm going to anyway, so forgive me. I hope you don't intend on telling anyone else this."

"Of course I don't. I've thought about how that would make a person feel, no matter who it was. I've often thought of what lessons I was meant to learn in this life. I've wondered if I became the victim of abuse because I had abused in a previous life. I can't stand the thought of that being possible so, no, I would never tell anyone other than you. But I'm telling you because I have to tell someone. If she is my dad, I'm so very proud of who his soul has become. She's done and continues to do such wonderful work for children and adults who have suffered as I suffered. She simply makes me proud of our Dakota too that he was attracted to such a generous soul. I'm just so happy she's in my life."

They sat silent for several minutes; then Sean looked at her and said, "There's something else, isn't there?"

Emily was silent for several more minutes before she spoke.

"Yes, there is. I should know by now that you know me so well you'd never let me not tell you everything."

"Well, tell me, sweetie. Tell me the rest." He said this as he turned to her and kissed her hard.

"A few years before Marti and Dakota were born, my grandmother came to me one night. She told me she had talked to my dad a number of times. She told me that he had stayed in the other world longer than most souls because he wanted to make absolutely certain that he learned everything he needed to learn before he came back. She then told me that the last time she saw him, he told her he was ready to come back and that he would return as a female. Because of me, he wanted to know what it was like to be a female. Then she told me that his name would become Trish. I had forgotten about this visitation until I had a conversation with Trish last week."

Emily adjusted herself on the tree, then continued, "As she and I discussed a case of a young girl whose story sounded very similar to the one Dakota told her about me, she turned to me, held my hand and said, "Emily, I'm so sorry for what your father did to you. I've learned so much from these victims that I just had no idea what their suffering was like until I began doing this work." She then told me she was so thankful for me for encouraging her because I helped her by making the introduction to Centerpoint. Then, and this was the uncanny part of that conversation, she turned to me, hugged me and told me she was so proud of me and also so happy for me that I had found the happiness I sought and that I had produced one of the most wonderful families she'd ever met."

"Em, that doesn't sound strange. It sounds like she's grown very fond of you and grateful for everything you've done for yourself and for her and her work."

"I know. It doesn't sound strange. In fact, it sounds like a simple conversation, but you would have had to have been there. It was the way she said it and the way she held my hand. It was during that conversation that I totally recalled my grandma's visitation and that she told me the female's name would be Trish.

"It's been something that I've yearned for. I've longed to know that my dad was happy and that he would never have to suffer again but would instead come back to find the true meaning of love which she's found with Dakota. It's almost as if their coming together was meant to happen. She's given him purpose and the total adult love he missed out on in his previous life; and he's rewarded her with absolute and total admiration and love. It's just such a wonderful end to a story."

When Emily and Sean had this conversation, Trish was pregnant with her third child. She and Dakota knew they were having a little boy this time around and had just finished preparing the room for their son when Emily had another visitation. This time it was her mom who visited her.

****

Sarah had died a few years earlier, five years after Zach passed. Several months after Zach's passing, she told Emily that she was so grateful for how her life had turned out. She and Zach remained totally in love and dedicated to each other their entire time together. She missed her man and knew she would follow not long after. It was a conversation Emily had difficulty having with her mom. She didn't want to lose her so soon. She wanted her to be around forever, but she knew that wasn't possible and also knew that her mom would go on to live many more lives.

The one thing that so comforted Emily was knowing that her mom had found tremendous happiness after Joe died. It helped Emily to know too, that the next life and all those thereafter would no doubt be joyful ones for her mom's soul.

When Sarah came to Emily, she was thrilled and excited to tell Emily the great news. She and Zach had spent all their moments in the other world together. Zach had just recently gone back and was born to a family who lived in the Boston area. He was sent back this time as a female. Sarah was excited because she knew she was coming back as a male, would once again be reunited with Emily and that she would grow up in the same area where she and Zach had lived. Before Zach's rebirth, he promised Sarah that he would find her so they could do it all over again, only this time for a much longer period.

"Sweetie, you and I are going to be together again. I'm going to be your grandson. Isn't that just so wonderful?"

"Yes it is, Mom. I've missed you terribly. Have you seen Dad at all?"

"No, sweetie. He went back a long time ago, way before I passed over. My mom and dad are here. They decided to stay. In fact, they spend most of their time helping other souls transition back to human form. Mom's going to help me transition. I know I'm not supposed to tell you this, but I think Joe went back as a female and is doing work as a counselor who helps victims of sexual abuse."

"Seriously, Mom? Did Grandma tell you that?"

"No, it was actually my dad. Dad's still such a devil. I've had so much fun with him. He makes all the other permanent souls look tame."

"Mom, did Grandpa tell you what Dad's new name is?"

"Well, I know he did his best not to tell me. He knew Mom would be ticked off at him, but he whispered her name to me. He told me her name was Trish, which is short for Patricia."

"Mom, that's the name of your new mother! She's a counselor who works with abused children. She's a wonderful person, Mom, and a wonderful mother. You have two older twin sisters and they adore their mom. I hope you don't mind me telling you that, but I know you won't even remember once you transition."

"Oh, honey, even if I did remember, I would be happy. I've had such a wonderful experience here, and knowing how your dad turned out has been part of that wonderful experience. I know he did a lot of bad things, but I also knew him when he was a young man before he started doing those things. He was a good man at heart. I'm glad you told me that. Kind of makes things even more exciting, even if I never remember. I have to go, sweetie. I hear Dad calling me. It's nearly time for Mom to help me transition."

"Bye, Mom. I love you and I'm so excited I'm going to get to see you again soon."

Emily fell into a very deep sleep; and when she woke the next morning, she had a tough time waking up. But it was a Saturday so she took her time getting up. She didn't get out of bed until nearly 11 a.m. which was very unusual for her. In fact, Sean came in as she got up and asked her if she was okay.

"I was beginning to worry about you, Em. I don't remember you ever sleeping that late, especially since we went to bed at 10."

She was smiling when she said, "Let's go downstairs. I'm starving. I have some things to tell you."

Sean prepared breakfast for Emily. She sat at the kitchen table drinking a cup of coffee, staring out at the slant tree and twirling her hair with one finger. She was lost in thought.

He put a plate stacked with strawberry shortcake pancakes, dressed with slices of fresh strawberries and topped with a whipped strawberry based sauce on the table in front of her. He then poured himself his third cup of coffee for the morning and sat down across from her.

She was still lost in thought when he waved his hand in front of her, "Earth to Emily. This is Houston calling."

She looked at him and laughed at his silliness then said, "Oh, sorry, I was just recalling my mom's visitation last night."

She began eating and told him everything.

"Wow, Em. You were right about your feelings. I don't know why I ever doubted you. I should know better by now. So Sarah is going to be our little grandson?"

"Yes," she answered excitedly. "And even more exciting, although neither of us will be around to witness this, but Zach is now a baby girl somewhere in the Boston area. He promised Mom that when he grows up, he'll come find her so they can have a longer life together. Isn't that just wonderful? Kind of reminds me of when you came looking for me.

"Oh, Sean, when you and I finally die, I hope we get to do this all over again. I've had the most wonderful life imaginable. You have made me the happiest woman on this planet and, my god, our sweet children have just completed my happiness."

He leaned over and kissed her. "Em, I can't imagine living any life without you. I promise you with all my heart that we will be together again. We are soul mates, Em; and I think once soul mates find one another, they always find each other. Don't you?"

"Yes, I do; but I want to come back and marry you again. I don't want to come back as your daughter or parent. I want you as my lover, and I hope I come back as a female because I love being a female; and besides, you make a wonderful male."

He was blushing. "Em, I know you just got up, but look." He moved his chair out from behind the table, and she could see he had a magnificent boner.

She giggled, walked over, took his hand and said, "Let's lie down. You can still make me feel horny, Sean. I love you so much."

Once in the bedroom, they both undressed and climbed under the covers.

Emily sweetly kissed Sean and smiled, "You first this time!"

He smiled as she lifted the covers and, using K-Y Jelly, began stroking his penis. She was watching his face as he closed his eyes.

When he was about to come, he opened them and begged, "Kiss me!"

She put her tongue in his mouth as he moaned and devoured her tongue. As he shuddered, she opened her eyes and watched his face. She loved giving him exquisite pleasure.

Soon, he too opened his eyes and lovingly whispered, "Now your turn."

She adjusted her body and spread her legs as he grinned then climbed under the covers and, with his tongue traveled down her still perfect body to her sweet button. With his right hand, he reached up and fondled her breasts.

Several minutes passed when she began to moan. Once spent, he climbed back out, leaned on his elbow and proudly smiled. He then told her he would always find her because he belonged to her and no one else.

Chapter 37

On November 3rd, 2045, Emily answered her phone. It was Dakota and he sounded excited.

"Mom, you're the grandmother of a 7-pound 13-ounce baby boy!"

"Oh, Dakota, that's wonderful. How's Trish doing? When are she and little Dakota coming home?"

"Trish is great! She was a trooper during the entire birth. They're coming home this afternoon. Listen, Angela and Charles are having a get-together this weekend to celebrate our little one."

"Well, you know we'll be there. I'll give Angela a call to see if there's anything she needs us to bring. Congratulations, sweetie. Give my love to Trish?"

"I will, Mom. Love you. See you this weekend."

Emily immediately called Sean who was working from home that day. She could hear chattering in the background.

She gave him the wonderful news, then asked him what all the chattering was.

He laughed, "It's Henry. He's unhappy because I'm upstairs and he's downstairs. I'm about to take a short break. I'm going to bring him upstairs and put him on the perch."

****

Henry was an African grey parrot Emily had gotten Sean for their thirtieth wedding anniversary. She bought Henry the day she and Sean went to pick up a Sun Conure for her anniversary present.

Both Emily and Sean had fallen in love with Trish's Conure, Zwayla. They had talked about getting a parrot for years but never seemed to get around to doing it. So when Sean asked Emily what she wanted for their anniversary, she immediately said, "A Sun Conure."

While at the pet store, Sean became captivated by a fifteen-year-old male African Grey, named Henry, who was talking up a storm. Henry had recently been dumped off by the young man who owned him.

A friend had given Henry to the young man; but when the man discovered that there was a lot of responsibility involved with caring for another creature, he put Henry and his cage in a spare bedroom and basically never again interacted with him except to feed him and change his water.

Of course, poor Henry desperately needed to socialize and was becoming depressed and frustrated. The man made the decision to get rid of the "damned bird" when Henry bit him as he changed his water.

Henry, the female store owner explained to Sean, had been totally quiet ever since he had been dropped off two weeks earlier. She was trying to bring him back to a healthy appearance since all the stress had taken a toll on Henry's appearance. Out of loneliness and depression, Henry had plucked most of the feathers he could reach. He was in sad shape. In an effort to help Henry find his forever home, she showed Sean another African Grey in the store.

"This is how Henry once looked and, with a lot of love, will look again. I just hope I can find a good home for poor Henry. He obviously wants companionship desperately. This is the first time he's spoken since he was dropped off."

Sean stayed with Henry as Emily talked to the owner about a Sun Conure. He was completely taken by Henry.

Emily watched the interaction. She was close by as the owner discussed Henry's situation with Sean. It was all Emily needed to convince her that Henry was meant to go home with them. So, she secretly negotiated with the owner to purchase Henry and his cage for half the price the woman was charging. The owner was happy to place Henry with Emily and Sean who she knew would give Henry everything and more.

Sean was completely blown away when it came time to leave the store.

After loading the first bird cage into their vehicle, he was about to shut the back door when the woman rolled the other cage out, followed by Emily with the Sun Conure in one box and Henry in a second larger box. He asked both the owner and Emily what was going on.

"Happy anniversary, Sean. You and Henry are about to embark on a wonderful adventure together."

The two were inseparable. Except for those times when Sean was at work in Boston or sleeping, Henry was perched right up on his shoulder or on the roll-about perch he kept in his home office.

Occasionally, Henry even went to work with Sean. Sean would carry him in a small animal carry case as he traveled via the Big Connect into Boston. Henry loved riding the Big Connect and, much to the joy of other riders, would talk the entire trip in and from Boston. The folks at the Brain Power Institute which Sean had founded the year prior loved it when Henry would visit. He talked up a storm and seemed to pick up a lot of his own brain power while at the facility as the staff interacted with him.

In the meantime, Emily was totally in love with her beautiful yellow bird she named Petey.

Petey was a typical Sun Conure. He would speak a few simple words, but, in general didn't talk much at all. He was, however, a crafty manipulator. He learned quickly how to get his way as he often slept with Emily, Sean and their little Munchkin. Petey would sleep up beside Emily's head as he nestled into her hair. Sean took many pictures of the spectacle. He even captured a shot of Petey chasing Munchkin off the bed one day; but it was only a game. It was obvious to everyone that Petey and Munchkin loved one another. In fact, Sean also took numerous photos of Petey hitching a ride on Munchkin's back. Petey would often take naps next to Munchkin's head as she lay on the sofa.

****

Saturday rolled around quickly as Emily and Sean got ready to meet their new grandson. Angela had asked Emily to bring dessert. Thus, Emily baked Dakota's favorite cake, tomato soup with butter cream icing and with the words "Welcome to the World Dakota Jr." written in blue.

They arrived just as Trish was coming down the stairs holding her little bundle. He was such a beautiful baby, and his hair was flame red, which surprised everyone. When Trish handed little Kota —short for Dakota —off to Sean, he began to cry. However, when Sean passed him to Emily, Kota became very quiet and content. Trish remarked that Emily was the first one that Kota didn't protest being handed off to. So far, he wanted to be in his mom's arms and no one else's. Even Dakota Sr. hadn't been able to hold his son long before he began crying.

"That's weird, Mom. I'm envious," was what Dakota Sr. said as he kissed his mom's cheek.

"Maybe it's the red hair," was Emily's response.

Later in the day, Davie, Marti and their families arrived, as did Trish's two older brothers, Charles Jr., who brought his family and Peter who was single. Angela had also invited Jeannie and DD who arrived last. Ariel and JJ were with them.

Having just received his bachelor's degree in Criminology from URI, JJ was currently attending the police academy. He wanted to follow in his dad's footsteps which proved to be very big shoes since DD was now the Providence, Rhode Island Chief of Police.

Ariel was currently living in the San Francisco area, was yet to find her forever partner; but, was a successful pilot for Big Bear Airlines based out of San Francisco. She swapped schedules with another pilot so she could come home for a visit.

When the four entered, Jeannie made her usual grand entrance. When she spotted Emily with little Kota, she whisked over calling, "Auntie Em, Auntie Em." It was the first time Angela had had the opportunity to meet Jeannie; but as she watched, she laughed the entire time.

Angela immediately loved Jeannie's big personality. At dinner they were all captivated with the stories DD and Davie told them about some of the arrests they had individually made. Angela asked Davie how he came to join the FBI.

Davie pulled out a small badge from his pocket and told her that it was his Uncle DD who influenced him when he gave him the badge for his fifth birthday. DD just sat back beaming with pride from the flattery. He beamed even more when he announced that John Jr. would graduate at the top of his class. JJ simply blushed.

Then everyone turned their attention to Davie. They had already heard about Davie's unique abilities so Trish begged him to tell the stories about Bugger and then about Dakota.

Davie was a little embarrassed so everyone else enthusiastically helped him tell the stories.

While all this chatter was taking place, Angela and Jeannie both realized that Peter and Ariel were nowhere to be found. The two women looked at each other as if they could read each other's minds, got up and went looking for the two. When they walked into the kitchen, they went to the back window and saw the two sitting under a shade tree on two Adirondack chairs. They were talking up a storm and laughing.

"Hmm …wouldn't it be wonderful if Ariel has finally found her forever man!" was what Jeannie said.

"It would be wonderful. Peter has been so lonely for a long time. He was married for four years, but she left him two years ago for another man. They look like they're having a great time, don't they?"

By then, everyone else was in the kitchen stretching their necks trying to get a glimpse of the two. It was Trish who went out holding little Kota. Her premise was to ask the couple if she could bring anything out to them. Trish loved her brother Peter. She was, after all, his baby sister.

Both Ariel and Peter answered that a glass of wine and slice of cake would be wonderful so Trish gave Ariel Kota and went back in to get the goods.

"That was a sneaky ploy, Trish," said Jeannie. "Let's hope it works. I so want Ariel to find someone who can make her happy."

"Well, to be honest, Jeannie, I never thought of it in that vein, but, yea, maybe it will give both Ariel and Peter a little push. That would be great. Ariel seems so full of life which is exactly what my Peter needs."

It wasn't the baby but a simple element called body chemistry that sparked a wonderful romance between Peter and Ariel.

When she flew back to San Francisco later that week, she immediately put in for a shot at the Boston flights. As it turned out, the person she swapped with was looking for a change, so he was thrilled to encourage the airlines to swap Ariel's Tampa route with his Boston. Ariel flew into Boston once every week, which led to a whirlwind romance with Peter who was a radiologist at New England Baptist Hospital.

Soon after they began seeing each other, Peter put in for a vacation and returned with Ariel to the San Francisco Bay area. It was a thrill for him to fly on the plane Ariel was piloting. She, of course, embarrassed him when she announced that her very handsome boyfriend was sitting in first class. The plane exploded with applause as it did again when they landed.

The plane flew through several strong storms with a lot of

317

turbulence which made for a very scary ride.

That evening Peter called home and bragged about how Ariel handled the flight, getting all the passengers safely to the ground and gate.

It didn't take long for the couple to tie the knot.

****

After flying back and forth seeing each other on a weekly basis for six months, the couple decided it was time to make it permanent. Ariel loved living in San Francisco but told Peter she would gladly put in for a transfer. He insisted, however, that he would be the one to relocate.

"Besides, I'm ready for a change, and winters without snow and ice would be a wonderful change."

When he began looking, he found an opening at UCSF's radiology department for the University of California's Moffit Hospital. It was perfect. Once he was hired, the couple found a beautiful renovated Victorian house on Steiner Street just east of Alamo Square. It was one of the row house areas San Francisco was famous for.

They were both making plenty of money and decided to get just what they wanted. Their house really stood out with its soft pastel aquamarine color, a bay window and an ornate arched entrance.

The couple also begged both parents to let them get married in Alamo Square, and that's where their wedding was held.

They spoke their vows in front of one of the many gazebos that dot the park. The reception was held at the Steinhart Hotel where Emily and Sean had spent their Christmas during their freshman year of college.

It was a beautiful wedding and everyone was there.

Later the couple flew out for a two-week honeymoon in Hawaii on the island of Oahu soaking in the sun and enjoying the lush green of the island.

****

When everyone arrived in San Francisco, neither Emily nor Sean were aware that their three children had pitched in to put them up at the Steinhart in the same room in which they had spent that Christmas break.

When the Mahoney's gathered at the San Francisco airport, Davie had reserved a van to escort his mom and dad, along with his family, to a less expensive hotel not too far from where the wedding was to be held. Instead, however, Emily noticed that they seemed to be headed in the other direction.

When she asked where they were going, Davie responded, "Just enjoy the ride, Mom. You'll see soon enough."

She and Sean were totally taken off-guard when they realized they were sitting in front of the Steinhart. Waiting at the entrance were all their children and their families. Jeannie, DD and JJ were there as well.

It was Jeannie who gave the kids the idea to put their parents up in the Steinhart. She even managed to get the room number from Emily, who hadn't realized why Jeannie was asking for it.

Once they were in the room, Marti went over to the bed and exclaimed, "Mom, look, there's a box here with your name on it. What do you think it is?"

Emily had no idea so she opened it immediately and found a naughty red teddy inside. She was blushing from ear-to-ear while all her family were clapping their hands, and Jeannie was asking if there were going to be another hickey fest that night to which Sean gave his promise to do his absolute best to make sure there was.

It was an incredible stay for Emily and Sean, giving them the delight of recapturing some of the best memories of their youth and the opportunity to give each other such pleasure that would carry them forward in time.

****

The following day and during the rehearsal dinner, Jeannie made a huge deal about a humongous hickey on the back of Emily's neck which she tried her best to hide with her long red hair. Everyone had a wonderful time teasing Emily and Sean who secretly were loving every minute as a testament to their undying love for one another.

Chapter 38

At seventy-four both Sean and Emily decided it was time to kick back and enjoy life. They both retired.

The kids held a huge retirement party for them, and everyone was there. Many of both Sean's and Emily's past and present colleagues attended. Their now good friend, Bill Harris, even made a special trip out for the get-together. Bill later told them he wouldn't miss the party for the world.

"You both have done so much for me and the Institute." Both Emily and Sean responded that he, the institute and Holosync had done a ton of good for them personally and for Sean's career as well.

During the roasting, Emily and Sean were asked how they planned on spending retirement.

They looked at each other, smiled, kissed and said, "Staying home a lot. A little bit of travel but not much. It's too stressful. Mostly we just want to enjoy our home, spend a lot of evenings on the slant tree, love our animals and hope to have frequent visits from all our children and grandchildren."

They were granted *all* their wishes.

At least one full weekend every other month, the house was filled with laughter and love.

****

DD had retired fifteen years earlier, and Jeannie retired soon after him. They had never had the chance to do much traveling so they spent a lot of time and money doing that. They also downsized on their house.

Jeannie's parents had both died years earlier, leaving them the house she had grown up in. The couple moved into it. When they weren't traveling, they spent a lot of their time with Emily and Sean.

All four adults were experiencing a lot of the usual aches and pains of growing older, but they were all fairly healthy and remained very active. They spent lots of weekends at the cabin building bonfires and telling stories as they reminisced about all the happy times they had spent together over the years.

Those years in retirement were wonderful for the four adults, but life has a tendency to end way too soon and when no one is looking.

****

DD was the first to die. He was six years older than the other three; and although in excellent health, he had something happen that no one expected. He suffered a ruptured aneurysm one night while he and Jeannie were spending a quiet evening at home.

He was walking from the living room to the kitchen to refill his and Jeannie's wine glasses when Jeannie heard a thud and glass shattering.

She ran to see if DD was okay, but it was too late. The aneurysm, which was located in his brain, had burst. He was gone.

"I didn't even get to say goodbye" was all Jeannie kept saying for months. She was traumatized.

Emily and Sean did all they could for their friend as they invited her into their home where she stayed for three months before deciding it was time to go back to her own.

Jeannie never seemed to recover from the loss of DD. Although she always put on her happy face, Emily knew Jeannie was depressed as she let her health deteriorate.

At age eighty, Jeannie came down with the flu. Emily spent all her time with Jeannie nursing her back to health.

Jeannie nearly died, but it was stubbornness that kept her alive. When she recovered, she vowed, and stuck to that vow, to take better care of herself.

By that time, Jeannie was a great-grandmother. Stephie, one of JJ's granddaughters, came to live with her while Stephie attended URI.

Dakota Sr. was now CEO of Brain Power, and the institute was doing some incredible work. They were on the verge of developing a micro-chip that would help cure cancer when, at age eighty-six, Emily was diagnosed with cancer. Like all other illnesses of the elderly, it came on fast and unexpected. She was given twelve months to live.

As was everyone, Sean was shattered. In an effort to perfect the chip, Dakota added more funding and hours to the project. However, he soon realized it wasn't going to happen.

"Mom, I'm so sorry. I've tried so hard to get the chip ready, but we keep running into problems."

"Honey, that's okay. I know you've done all you can. Some things are just not meant to happen. Everything will be fine. I've had a magnificent life, and I know I will the next time around as well."

"Mom, there is something we can do. We've been working on a skull cap with electrodes that are capable of relieving pain. It's in the experimental stages; but, if you're willing to be a guinea-pig, it might help you so you don't have to take medications with all sorts of side effects."

Sean and Dakota had talked about this; and Sean was now helping the group hurry along the cap.

"Sign me up, Dakota. I don't mind being sick, but I want to be lucid during this whole ordeal. I want to be able to fully enjoy every minute I have left."

Within a month Emily was fitted with the cap, which Sean insisted should be red.

With Jeannie present, the family had a small celebration one Saturday as they sat Emily in a chair in the middle of the living room, put a small red velvet footstool under her feet and crowned her Queen Emily as they all bowed to her highness. It was so much fun; it momentarily made light of what was taking place.

Within another month her doctors reported that although the cancer was still alive and well, the electrodes seemed to be slowing it down. Even better, she was pain-free while also medication-free. In addition, she was meditating every day, sometimes twice each day; and that seemed to help slow down the cancer even more.

Emily lived another two years. But by her eighty-eighth birthday, it was evident that she didn't have much longer to live.

It was Davie who confirmed that he could sense his mom was on her way out after her birthday celebration.

At first, he was reluctant to tell anyone, but Emily insisted that he and she let everyone know.

"Honey, this is too much of a burden for you to carry. I want to have everyone here when the time comes. I don't want any surprises for anyone, nor do I want guilty consciences."

All her children came home every weekend for two months.

They came home for their mom and for their dad too.

Sean wasn't taking any of it well. He seemed totally lost and even withdrawn when they would visit. They were worried about their dad, especially once their mom was gone.

During the two months before Emily's departure, she had a remarkable discussion with Trish.

Trish had come over with her three grandchildren one evening while Dakota worked late. She made dinner for the couple; and after dinner, Sean played a board game with the three kids. Trish went in to sit with Emily who was spending a great deal of time in bed.

They talked about the work Trish had dedicated her life to. Emily felt something uncanny about that evening. She couldn't explain the feeling, but she felt unusually close to Trish; and Trish felt the same.

At one point Emily took Trish's hand and told her how very proud she was of her. She told her the profession she chose gave Emily a sense that something she had said a long time ago inspired Trish. Emily also told Trish how grateful she was to Trish for having given Dakota such a wonderfully loving life.

During their discussion Trish asked Emily a poignant question.

"Emily, you don't have to answer this if you don't want to. I'll understand, but I'm just curious. During all these years, have you ever felt forgiveness for what your father did to you?"

Emily looked off into space as she considered the question. Then she answered as honestly as she possibly could.

"Trish, having something as terrible as molestation happen to me has given me the ability to think outside the box, and not only that, but the gift of recognizing there actually are no boxes. It's given me the freedom to create my life as I live it. For example, when things go bad, I know they're temporary; therefore, I don't get bogged down in them. They don't control me. My resilience to bounce back assures that. I'm able to laugh at myself and things that happen to me. As a result, I've pondered your question on many occasions, and I believe with all my heart that I have forgiven him. That forgiveness, however, was never a conscious decision. Instead, it happened as a result of my realization that what I endured at my father's hands was nothing more than a temporary situation which caused me temporary discomfort and sadness. My focus has *always been* happiness. In the end, I've been able to let go of anger, sadness and desires for revenge, as well as negative emotions like hatred. Those are all too time-consuming and are blocks to happiness. So, yes, I believe I forgave Dad a long time ago."

Trish had an uncanny look of relief and even contentment on her face as they talked a while longer. Soon it was obvious that Emily needed to sleep.

Just before Emily drifted off, she said, "Trish, tell Dakota I love him with all my heart and that I just know I'll see him again soon."

Later that night while Dakota and Trish got ready for bed, she told Dakota about the discussion.

"Dakota, I don't know why, but that conversation and the words your mom spoke to me touched me at such a deep level. For a moment, I felt connected to her like I've never felt connected to another human being. Your mom is a very special person. I'm so very happy you and I found each other because without you, I would never have gotten to know your mom. I've come to understand your deep love of her."

****

Emily died on February 15th. She lived one more Valentine's Day just so she and Sean could give each other one last card.

The week before, she had asked Marti, who had taken time off to spend with her mom and dad, if she would go to the Hallmark store and buy up all the most wonderful cards they had for husbands.

Marti brought ten cards home, and Emily read each of them as she found the one card she wanted to give her love.

That evening Dakota carried his frail mother outside and walked her up the slant tree to where Sean was waiting with a blanket.

It was a full moon that evening which seemed to be nature's way of celebrating this special couple.

As Emily was placed in a sitting position on the tree, Sean wrapped the blanket around her and kissed her.

"I love you, Em. I've loved you all my life, and I will love you until there is no more time, and I promise you I will find you if I have to travel to the edges of the universe to do that."

Emily silently wept as she laid her head on his shoulder.

Sean opened up the card he bought for her and pulled out a

flashlight so he could read it to her. He lightly laughed as he flipped the switch on the flashlight.

"A Boy Scout is always prepared."

Although she was extremely weak, Emily giggled and whispered, "God, I'm going to miss you, Seanie!"

The front of the card was white with silver hearts and a huge red rose in the middle. It read, "I'll always love you."

He opened it and read the printed words on the left side which were surrounded by the same silver hearts.

"The best love is a lifelong love that sweetens the joys, softens the hurts and strengthens two hearts as it grows."

He then shined the flashlight on the right side and read the words.

"I marvel at the many changes life has brought our way and how our love has strengthened us and grown with every day ... I'm certain that we share a love that comes to very few. And in the days and *lives* to come, I'll still be loving you. Happy Valentine's Day."

He handed Emily the card, and she caressed it as she saw that Sean had crossed out the printed word "years" and scribbled "lives" above it.

As their eyes met, a tear escaped from the corner of Sean's eye. Then, he read his own written words. Those words were simple yet sweet. "I love you SO much, Em! Your Seanie."

Emily was crying tears of love, joy and sadness as well. She so loved her Sean and felt his pain.

She pulled out her card from under the blanket and, as Sean shined the light, she read.

"To my husband ...MY FOREVER VALENTINE. I love you more than ever."

She then opened the card and read the printed words to the left.

"In sharing everything together through the years, I've found that I've grown more in love with you. The smile I fell in love with ...your kind and thoughtful ways ...your loving, warm embrace ...these have become more beautiful and more meaningful to me each year."

Then she read the words to the right.

"I love you more than you could ever know. Happy Valentine's Day, My Love."

Last she read her own written words.

"The cover says it all, Seanie: 'I love you more than ever.' I will miss you, my love. Most of all I will miss our sex. I know that sounds strange; but Sean, if it had not been for you, I would never have known the absolute beauty and pleasure of a tender sexual relationship. You have given me the most exquisite loving pleasure a woman could ever know. My heart flew out of my body the first time I saw you, and my heart quivers every time I see your sweet face and feel your tender touch. I will wait for you for as long as it takes because I know that when we are both reborn, you will find me and I will be waiting. I love you forever and ever. Em"

It was Sean who was now crying like a baby as he held Emily with one arm and waved the flashlight with the other signaling Dakota to come get her.

That night Marti called Davie. He wasn't planning to come home until that weekend, but Marti told him she thought he needed to come home the next day.

"Davie, I don't think Mom's going to make it through the rest of this week."

He was on the first plane out the next morning and arrived at the house around 10 a.m.

At noon, Emily asked Sean to bring everyone in.

"It's time, Sean."

He was sobbing when he called his children in. He then went over to the bed and climbed in next to Emily, who was extremely weak but still lucid.

Marti and Dakota sat on the opposite side of Emily. Dakota had his head leaned against his mom while Marti held her hand. Davie sat next to his dad. He wanted to be there when his mom passed to give Sean support. He held his mom's hand, kissed it and began stroking it.

The only words Emily said were, "I love you all with every ounce of my heart and soul, and I'm so proud of each of you. You've made motherhood such a great joy. Take care of your dad. He's going to need all of you now."

She then leaned her head against Sean's face and whispered, "I love you, Sean. I love you so much."

She took her last breath and slipped away.

Davie was holding his dad as Sean cried the most excruciating moan any of them had ever heard.

They all sobbed, not only for their loss but also for their father whose pain they felt at the core of their souls.

An hour later Marti whispered, "I'm going to go call everyone."

Davie got up and asked his dad to come out with them.

Sean pled, "No, Davie. Please. I just want to stay with her a little bit longer."

He kissed his dad and motioned to Dakota that they should leave.

Dakota got up, walked over to his father, bent down and kissed his head.

Sean looked up, touched Dakota's face and smiled. "Your mom loved you so much, Dakota."

Crying like a baby, Dakota left the room as he leaned on Davie. He was, after all his mom's sweet baby boy.

The first person Marti called was Jeannie. They only talked for a few seconds as Jeannie pulled on a coat and was out the door. She knocked on the back door five minutes later.

Marti then called Abbey, as well as her own husband and each of her kids. Jeannie helped make some of the phone calls. By the time everyone was informed, it was seven p.m. Sean was still sitting with Emily. He had fallen asleep.

When he woke, Marti was sitting on the bed. She told him the funeral home was there for Emily.

"Dad, I hope you don't mind; but when I called everyone, I told them we'd have Mom's memorial here two Sundays from now. I thought that would give everyone enough time to arrange to be here."

"That's fine, Marti. Thanks for handling that. I'm just not up to any of it. I think I'll just go to bed if you don't mind."

"Of course, Dad."

Sean left the room and went up to his old room, lay on the bed and cried himself to sleep.

****

Usually when souls pass over, they don't contact anyone of the still-living for a while; but Emily knew the state Sean was in and, as in her human form, she thought of him first and of herself second.

327

She came to him in his sleep and told him that it was truly wonderful on the other side. Her grandmother and grandfather were there to greet her. DD was there as well. But she was concerned for Sean, so she wanted to come back just for a few minutes to console him.

She then cocked her head and said, "Shhh …listen, Sean."

Sean concentrated, then heard a faint melody which became ever louder. It was Neil Young's voice singing "We Never Danced."

"He's here too, Sean. He's going back soon, but he wanted to sing to us one more time."

Emily extended her hand as Sean took it. As they clasped hands, Sean realized Emily appeared exactly as she had the day of their wedding. She was beautiful, and the sight of her took his breath away. They glided to the song, but now the words meant more than they had ever meant in the past ..."Where the couples glide in the ever more. Floating through the clouds..."

Then the music began to fade, and they stopped gliding.

She was sitting next to him, stroking his head. She now appeared as she had just prior to being diagnosed. For those few moments, Sean felt Emily with him as she always had been. He loved her so completely and she loved him the same.

"It won't be too long till we're reunited, Sean. But you need to promise me that you won't mope. The kids need you right now. They are hurting as well. They need you to be alive. Can you promise me you won't close yourself off from them?"

He promised. She believed him, then kissed his lips and told him she'd be waiting.

When he woke the following morning, he could smell something sweet. He rolled over to see that the same scarf his grandma had put over the top of the nightstand lamp years earlier was once again draped over the lamp. The sweet smell was the scent wafting from the heat of the lamp which had been left on all night. He knew in his heart that Emily had laid it over the lamp, so he picked the scarf up, held it to his face, breathed it in and put it in his shirt pocket where it could be close to his heart. He then saw her locket lying on the stand just next to the lamp with a note, "Give this to Marti for safe keeping." He could feel Emily's presence, yet his heart ached.

He went down the stairs where Jeannie and all his children were sitting. The air in the room was thick.

Jeannie got up when she saw Sean. She walked over to him, put her arm around him and helped him to the table. As he sat down, she stroked his head.

It was obvious that all three of his children had been crying, but it was also obvious that Dakota was the hardest hit. He asked Dakota to come sit next to him as he pulled an empty chair close.

Dakota sat down and leaned his head against his father's chest and began crying. His cry was full of pain as Sean stroked Dakota's back.

"Your mom loved you so much, Dakota. You were truly her baby."

Then Sean paused for a moment.

"Your mom came to see me this morning."

Dakota stopped crying, looked up and asked, "Did she really?"

"Yes, dear, she did."

He pulled out the scarf and told them she had draped it over the lamp just like his grandmother had done so many years ago on the last night before he and Emily were separated by miles and years when they both entered college.

Sean then turned to Marti and opened his hand as he clutched the locket and note.

"Marti, this was left on the nightstand for you."

Marti took the locket and read the note. She was crying, but her tears didn't seem as if they were full of pain. Instead, they were tears of hope.

"Daddy, is Mommy happy?" she asked.

"Marti, she told me it was beautiful on the other side. She was there with her grandma and grandpa."

Then he looked at Jeannie and told her that DD was there as well.

Jeannie looked stunned as tears rolled down her cheeks.

Davie then asked, "What else did she say, Dad?"

"Sweetheart, she told me it wouldn't be long before I see her again; but she made me promise that I wouldn't mope. I think I'm going to need all of you to help me with that. Except for those early years when we were separated, your mom and I haven't been separated for more than a day or two. I'm going to have a hard time being alone without her."

Jeannie spoke up, "Sean, I'm just down the street. I'm lonely without my John. I'd love to be able to help keep you company. Maybe you can help me learn how to meditate. I have yet to see John again, and I think it's my own mind that prevents that from happening."

"Jeannie, I think it would be good for us to keep each other company; and, yes, I will try to help you break through."

They all sat at the table for several more hours talking about Emily, the wife, mother and best friend, when they heard a knock at the door. It was Abbey and her husband. They were each carrying a deli tray.

Davie got up and let them in. "Hi, Abbey. Hi, Tom."

"Hi, Davie," Abbey said as she gave the tray to him, then went over to Sean and hugged him.

"I'm so sorry, Sean. I know how hard this is for you to have lost your best friend."

"I know you do, Abbey. Thanks for coming over and bringing us something to eat. I don't think any of us have eaten since early yesterday."

Chapter 38

On the second Sunday after Emily passed, it was the third of March. The red and yellow tulips Emily had planted years ago had multiplied and were carpeting the two acres that surrounded the slant tree. The air was crisp but not cold, and the sun was high in the sky.

Some of the older grandchildren were sitting on the slant tree. Davie and Dakota had brought out a few Adirondack chairs as well as a few patio chairs for some of the adults to sit on.

Marti helped her dad over to the red Adirondack chair. Before he sat down, he stopped at the slant tree and put his hand on the slash marks he and Emily had carved into the tree as they counted down the days to their glorious D-Day. He bowed his head as if in meditation as he traced the gashes. One of the grandkids heard him whisper, "I love you, Emily."

Later, a second grandchild swore she could hear someone else whisper, "I love you too, Sean." When a few of the other children teased her, Dakota, who had been standing next to his father said, "I heard it too, Karen. I heard it too."

That afternoon was a lovely one. Everyone talked a little about Emily and what she had meant to them. Everyone cried, but not out of pain. Instead, the tears came from gratefulness that they had been granted the special gift of having known her.

"She was and always will be one of the greatest human beings I will ever know," Trish said.

Sean didn't speak that day. He couldn't. He was lost in thought about his most wonderful Emily.

When it came time to spread her ashes, Sean's hands were shaking. It was Jeannie who steadied his hands with hers. And so together they spread Emily's ashes over all the tulips.

Several days later, the house was empty, and Sean was left to fend for himself. He remembered his vow to Emily that he wouldn't mope, so he put Henry on his shoulder, put Petey in a small carry cage and went out to the red Adirondack chair that was still sitting near the slant tree. Spring came early that year and it was unseasonably warm.

From that day on, he never again climbed the tree. It just didn't seem right to climb it without his Em. However, he often sat in the Adirondack chair and greeted the tree as he would also often fall asleep among the tulips and then among the rose bushes as they came into full bloom.

Little Petey didn't live more than six months after Emily passed. His little heart broke when she died, and he was never as cheery as he had been when she was around. Somehow Sean knew that he left to go be with her. He wondered if animals came back as well.

Sean had Petey cremated and asked his children to spread Petey's ashes with his own ashes when his time came.

Two years went by and Jeannie did as she promised. She visited Sean almost daily, often cooking dinner and watching a movie with him. His children and their families visited often as well. They all came to the house for Thanksgiving and Christmas, filling the house with love and joy just as Emily would have wanted.

On one particular Christmas Eve, one of the great-grandchildren, Erin, had gotten up to get a glass of water. She became excited when she saw a glow around the slant tree. She climbed on a stool so she could get a better look. She almost fell off the stool when she saw a young girl with long red hair sitting low toward the base of the tree.

She jumped off the stool and ran to wake the others. They all came to the window and saw the same figure sitting on the tree. Sean was the last person to enter the bathroom; but when he did, everyone moved to the side so he could look directly out the window. As he did, he sobbed and whispered, "Emily." Sean could have sworn he saw her holding a shiny object which, when he looked closer, appeared to be a Swiss army knife. The moon was full that night as well, and the blade of the knife shimmered in the glow of the moon.

Then as suddenly as the little girl appeared, she disappeared.

The children remained excited and begged Sean to tell them the story of the shiny Swiss Army knife. So he sat on his bed as all the children sat on either the bed or the floor and told them about his first Christmas Eve with Emily. He described how she had given him a Swiss army knife because she knew he had lost the one his father had given to him a few months before he died. He then told them about his Grandma Martha's gold chain and heart-shaped locket with his picture inside, which he gave to Emily as her first Christmas present that night as the full moon shed its light down on them and they sat at the base of the slant tree.

It was this kind of moment that filled the Mahoney family with love and admiration for one another. There were so many wonderful memories and stories to share, and now there was a genuine magic which made the Christmas season feel even more enchanted. None of them would ever forget that Christmas Eve, the night they saw their grandma and their grandfather told them a wonderful story...a fairytale that was *real*!

The following Christmas season, everyone would realize just how special that previous Christmas Eve had been. It was, after all, their last Christmas Eve with their father, grandfather and great-grandfather.

****

Sean was ninety-one when Valentine's Day came around one last time. He wanted to be alone that night. So he spent it with Henry on his shoulder, a glass of red wine and the box full of Valentine, birthday and anniversary cards he and Emily had given each other over the years. He needed to read all of the cards she had given him.

He drank at least four glasses of wine as he read each of the cards out loud to Henry. There were cards on his lap and strewn on the floor when Sean fell asleep.

That's where Jeannie found him the following morning, still sitting in the chair with the now empty wine glass nestled between his legs and Emily's cards on his lap and on the floor. He was holding one card in his hand that had slid down beside him on the cushion of the chair.

Sean died that night. In the middle of Sean's lap lay a small gray body. It was Henry. He was forty-four.

Sean's memorial was held two Sundays later. Both his, Henry's and Petey's ashes were scattered in the same area Emily's had been spread. Their family, as well as Jeannie's family, said goodbye once again to their mother, grandmother, great-grandmother and friend as they also said goodbye to their father, grandfather, great-grandfather and friend.

At this memorial, however, there were few tears of sadness shed.

Instead, the tears were those of joy because they all now knew that Sean had finally been reunited with the love of his life.

****

That evening Davie had an uncanny sense that they should all stay down on the enclosed veranda and keep a vigil as they watched out the window. He encouraged Jeannie to stay with them. Once again the moon was full, and it washed its light over the shadow of the slant tree.

It was approximately two minutes after midnight when someone yelled for everyone to look. They all stood at the window as each saw the same image. They saw a little red-headed girl, the same one they had seen a few years earlier; but on this occasion, there was a little dark-haired boy sitting next to her. This time, however, the two were sitting high on the slant tree, and the moon's light framed their bodies as they sat with their heads leaning against one another.

One of the children opened the back door, ran back in and told everyone to come to the door. They all did. In fact, they walked out into the yard so they could see the children and what they saw was no more amazing than what they heard. They heard the two children talking and laughing.

Jeannie was standing off to the side. She had her hand over her mouth when Davie turned to see what she was gasping at. There in the dim light just on the other side of the tree stood a figure. He realized it was John as a young man. The figure had a blue police uniform on. Davie moved close to Jeannie and put his arm around her.

She whispered, "It's John. He's telling me what a perfect life he had with me and that he is waiting for me."

"It's wonderful, isn't it, Jeannie?"

John's figure was the first to fade away as Jeannie and Davie turned their attention back to Sean and Emily.

"Oh, yes, and Sean and Emily look just as I remember them all those years ago. It is wonderful. Thank you for encouraging me to stay."

Then just before the two smaller figures vanished, they all heard, "I love you forever, Emily," …and…"I promise with all my heart, Sean, I love you too."

The following week a little boy was born to a loving couple in Cranston, Rhode Island. Three months later a little girl with red hair was born to a loving couple in Hingham, Massachusetts. The little girl's mom's name was Shannon. Dakota's daughter, Shannon, lived with her husband in Hingham, Massachusetts.

And so the cycle began anew for Sean and Emily as they danced in the evermore.

We Never Danced
Written by Neil Young

Between heaven and earth
There's a ballroom floor
Where the couples glide
In the evermore.

Floating through the clouds
Dancing in the rain
Eyes that see no lies
Hearts that feel no pain.

Hope it's not too late
We were more than friends
I can hardly wait
'Til we meet again.

If you don't really know
Where you want to go
It makes no difference
Which road you take.

Hope it's not too late
We were more than friends
I can hardly wait
'Til we meet again.
We never danced
We never danced

We never danced
The night away.

We never danced
We never danced
We never danced
The night away.